Three Little Things

by
Patti Stockdale

Janis,
Please enjoy!
Patti
Stockdale
4/28/2020

SMITTEN
HISTORICAL ROMANCE
LIGHTHOUSE PUBLISHING OF THE CAROLINAS

THREE LITTLE THINGS BY PATTI STOCKDALE
Smitten Historical Romance is an imprint of LPCBooks
a division of Iron Stream Media
100 Missionary Ridge, Birmingham, AL 35242

ISBN: 978-1-64526-065-3
Copyright © 2020 by Patti Stockdale
Cover design by Hannah Mae Linder
Interior design by Karthick Srinivasan

Available in print from your local bookstore, online, or from the publisher at:
ShopLPC.com

For more information on this book and the author visit: https://pattistockdale.com/

Brought to you by the creative team at LPCBooks:
Eddie Jones, Pegg Thomas, Shonda Savage, Steve Mathisen, Jenny Leo, &
Kelly Scott

Library of Congress Cataloging-in-Publication Data
Stockdale, Patti
Three Little Things / Patti Stockdale 1st ed.

Printed in the United States of America

Praise for *Three Little Things*

Three things I loved about this book:
1. I fell in love with Arno and Hattie
2. The sayings and songs of WWI: I found myself singing "Over Here, Over There" and I want to join a knitting brigade!
3. The promise of more books by Patti Stockdale. I want more!

~Debbie Macomber
New York Times #1 Best-Selling Author of *Window on the Bay*

Charming and moving, *Three Little Things* tells a sweet story of two wounded souls. Hattie and Arno are appealing characters, and their personal growth and their building romance will draw you in. The novel also sheds light on women's roles on the Home Front in WWI and the persecution of German-Americans, something rarely discussed. With touches of both humor and depth, this story is a keeper!

~Sarah Sundin
Bestselling and Award-Winning Author of *The Land Beneath Us*

A beautiful story, beautifully told. Patti Stockdale's debut marks her as an author to watch!

~Roseanna M. White
Bestselling Author of *The Number of Love*

Three Little Things is a beautiful, sweet war-time romance. The letters will melt your heart.

~Kimberley Woodhouse
Best-selling and award-winning author of *The Golden Bride*

Patti Stockdale's debut novel *Three Little Things* pulls readers from one chapter to the next until they turn the final page. With compelling characters, historical charm, and a finely-honed plot, this historical romance earns my highest recommendation. I eagerly await more compelling fiction from Patti Stockdale

~**Shelly Beach**
Author and Speaker
Christy, Selah, Reader's Favorite, and Golden Scroll Award Winner

Patti Stockdale brings the beauty and sacrifice of the World War I era vibrantly to life with her debut novel. Brimming with longing, courage, and romance, *Three Little Things* will whisk you away and leave you yearning for more. A truly stunning debut!

~**Tara Johnson**
Author of *Where Dandelions Bloom*

Patti Stockdale was inspired by her grandparent's WWI love letters. The result is her debut novel *Three Little Things*. Stockdale's powerful attention to detail reflects hours of research depicting the reality of life during WWI. It chronicles the lives of Iowans Arno Kreger and Hattie Waltz and how they kept connected by letter writing. Stockdale's deft storytelling effortlessly weaves from the letters to the action showing how war affects not only those headed overseas, but also the ones left behind. *Three Little Things* is a definite "must-read."

~**Mary Jedlicka Humston**
Coauthor of *Mary & Me: A Lasting Link Through Ink*

Acknowledgments

This experience humbles me. Over the years, hundreds of people have touched my writing life at conferences, in classes, through books, and friendships. I'd love to thank each one by name, but that's impossible. Still, I need to recognize a few.

Steve Stockdale, my husband and biggest blessing—Since I was sixteen, you've held my hand and my heart. Our love story is my favorite one.

Pegg Thomas, my Smitten editor—You took a chance on me, taught me to talk and think like a real man, and polished *Three Little Things* until it twinkled like Arno's blue eyes.

Kelli Whitney, my beautiful and brilliant daughter—Your wit and insights helped shape the plot, characters, and me.

Blake Stockdale, my beautiful and brilliant son—Your humor and history-loving heart added joy, depth, and authenticity to the pages.

Shannon Stockdale, my amazing daughter-in-law—You snapped the background photo of the letters on the cover and the stack tied with the ribbon on the backside. Like you, they're amazing.

Grace Elliott, my precious mom—You trusted me with your parents' cherished love letters. What a difference that made in my writing world.

Terry Wallace, my instructor and mentor—I'm the writer I am today because you believed in me, championed me, and nurtured me beyond the written page.

Alice Crider, my author coach and friend—This experience is sweeter with you by my side. I know you'll catch me if I stumble.

Peggy Westphalen, Susan Stockdale, Cindy Moore, Carolyn Farlow, Lori Bushman, Rebecca Hope, and the original Story

Spinners (Amanda Cox, Crystal Caudill, KyLee Woodley, Kelly Goshorn, Angela Couch, Lucy Nel, and Tammy Kirby) —At some point on this journey, you offered a key critique or a helpful hand.

My heroes, the WW I soldiers—Your sacrifices humble me beyond words.

God, my Light—Day by day, I'll keep building my life upon Your love.

Dedication _1917_

To Mom and Dad, who taught me to love three big things:
God, others, and books.   _cute!_
And to Grandma and Grandpa,
the beautiful inspiration for *Three Little Things*.

CHAPTER ONE

September 15, 1917—Split Falls, Iowa

Not once in eighteen years had Hattie Waltz considered praying for a plague. But if a swarm of locusts intervened, she'd not complain. That's how much she hated the idea of singing in public. A train whistle blared, and she jumped, her button-top boots clearing the platform.

"Don't fret." Daddy locked both hands onto her shoulders, his voice full of confidence. His straw hat rode low, and he wore his good coveralls, not his old pair with the patched crotch.

"Do you remember the last time I sang in public?" Hattie had tried to replace the ugly memory with a pretty substitute. But no such luck.

"You had a touch of influenza. We all did. That's in the past. You sing like your mama, and she had the most beautiful voice in the world. Sing for her."

Hattie gulped the brisk Iowa air deep into her lungs.

"If your Mama were here, she'd say, 'Never let fear swallow your talent.' Ain't that right, Button?"

"I suppose." She'd do anything for Mama, even if it meant one scary step toward conquering her stage fright. Still, she stalled. "I don't suppose you'll swap places with me."

"Nobody wants to hear my caterwauling." Daddy's warm chuckle eased her nerves, at least a little. "I brought along this peach crate. We want folks to see your pretty face."

At five-foot-nothing in her church shoes, Hattie tended to blend into the mix. Daddy helped her climb onto the wobbly perch, and she held her breath until the instrumental cue. Her stomach gurgled and her mouth watered, a telltale sign she was about to—

Then a miracle happened.

She sang to the dozens of spectators, recognizing half their faces.

A three-piece band, heavy on the bass drum, boomed "My Country' Tis of Thee," almost overpowering her lyrics. A few poignant words must have crept through the din to pluck at fragile heartstrings. Ladies scavenged through pocketbooks and overcoat sleeves for hankies.

Months ago, President Wilson had declared war, luring men to boot camps across the country. In less than an hour, they'd bid ten locals goodbye, all scheduled to depart on the eleven o'clock train.

A stage-shaking gust caught Hattie's skirt, rippling the garment sideways. She wiggled her hips to rearrange the material back into place which only inched the hem higher. Torn between bending to adjust her clothing or pretending not to notice her dilemma, she fumbled the lyrics. A slow burn started in her neck and crept to her cheeks.

Coal smoke and valve oil dusted the air as the final chorus soared. Mayor Carmichael had handed out miniature flags, and a dozen folks waved theirs in the feisty breeze. She fiddled with hers.

A second squall almost knocked her off the crate, driving her skirt even higher. To divert the audience's attention, she shot her arm high, swooping her flag left and then right. Her ploy worked, and soon a sea of patriotic symbols shot toward the heavens, banding together in a rhythmic sway.

After a quick eye drop for an apparel check, Hattie froze. A pearl button had popped off her shirtwaist, exposing a less-than-Sunday-best corset. She clutched the front of her dress, tugging the garment closed and toward her heart. Likewise, men across the platform tossed back shoulders and slung hands over their loyal hearts.

Nobody appeared to notice her dilemma except Arno Kreger. Tall and proud, he raised one eyebrow. She broke their eye contact, hefting her chin. *Ignore him. He doesn't matter anymore.*

Off to his right, a handsome stranger, measuring no higher than Arno's shoulder, offered a dazzling smile. She returned his grin, curving her lips upward around the lyrics. Based on his fancy three-piece suit and paisley tie, the man didn't plant corn or milk cows for a living.

The minute the song ended, she hopped off the crate, snagged her overcoat from the platform, and secured the buttons. Applause thundered. She grinned in appreciation, accepting the compliments while inching from the spotlight.

"Same as always, you done me proud." Daddy patted her arm then left to buy feed at the grain elevator.

She searched for her fellow Knitting Brigade member—Lena Kreger. A hand cupped her shoulder, and she wheeled around to stand nose-to-chest with a human wall. Arno.

"I have to say your singing voice has improved over the years. I especially appreciated how—" Midsentence, his cousin tugged on his pantleg. Garbed in a corduroy overcoat and smart hat, she held one hand behind her back. "Molly! How's my favorite four-year-old?" Arno asked.

"I'm five."

"Impossible."

That's when the tickling started. A fit of giggles and squirms followed.

Hattie laughed, too, picturing Arno as the sweet little boy who'd snared her heart long ago, not the firebrand she barely knew these days. Last week, he'd crashed his daddy's tractor after a night on the town, and she'd not spotted him at church services in a month, not that she was the congregation's attendance tracker.

Molly's mother raised a hand in acknowledgment and continued her conversation with a trio of women nearby. Hattie waved back.

"I made you something." With a bounce to her tiptoes, Molly presented a crumpled paper heart.

"For me?" Arno crouched to the child's eye level.

"It's to help you remember me while you're gone."

"I could never forget about you, Molly," His words carried a tender tone, while his big hand cupped her little cheek.

More than anything, Hattie longed to ask—*What about me?* Instead, she pursed her lips to hold the worry inside where it belonged.

He dropped one knee in the grass to fish something from his pocket. When Arno opened his fist, a brass compass rested in his palm.

"I know what that is. Father has one." Sunshine glinted off the metallic rim. Little fingers reached for the gleamy object. "He says it helps him find his way."

"My *opa* gave me that compass way back when. Now, I'm giving it to you."

"Thank you. I'll love it forever." Molly's arms circled Arno's neck before she squealed and raced to her mother's side.

The sweet exchange hooked Hattie's heart, opening it wider. "You're her hero."

"Don't say that." He stood, sadness turning his eyes to pale blue. "I'm not even close."

Those four little words kicked at Hattie's gut. According to his sister, he blamed himself for their brother's death and hadn't found a big enough brush to sweep away his guilt. "Sure, you are," she whispered.

A wry smile twisted his lips. The combination of a sun-kissed complexion, corn silk-colored hair, and spellbinding eyes often turned women's heads and hearts alike. Hattie wasn't an exception. "Before our interruption," Arno nodded toward Molly, "I was about to pay you a compliment."

"Really?" She crossed her arms and narrowed her eyes. They'd barely spoken in two years, and now he wanted to offer praise?

His right brow arched high. "I particularly appreciated how you sang and, at the same time, fought to control your skirt and hide the gape in your blouse."

Had he been as sweet as a strawberry dipped in sugar two minutes ago, or had she imagined his entire conversation with his cousin? "How inconsiderate of you to mention my mishap."

"Perhaps, perhaps." He nodded as he spoke. "But who would give his little cousin a favorite possession—a gentleman or a cad?"

Hattie opened her mouth but decided not to tumble down a path littered with awkward insults. "Lena told me you're anxious to leave for boot camp."

"My sister yaps too much."

"Only sometimes."

"I'm itching to go and ..."

Hattie missed the end of his sentence, too fixated on Arno's nearness. Clean-shaven and muscular from long hours of fieldwork, his shoulders stretched twice as far as hers. A new scar marred his skin between his bottom lip and chin cleft.

Arno leaned forward. Raised eyebrows, blond and wispy, prodding her response to whatever she'd just missed.

She pumped her brain for an intelligent reply, staring past him at cornstalks, flapping beyond the railroad tracks on a hill. "You don't say."

"Besides, nobody's keeping me home any longer." He slipped a hand into his trouser pocket, rocking back on his heels.

"I heard that news as well." Lena had detailed the demise of Arno's courtship, centering on the other party's flirting—coupled with Arno's jealousy—a head-butting combination. How long until he found a new girl to take Priscilla's place? Or would the pair soon patch up their differences? *Either way, it's not my concern.*

"Of course, you did." His smile reached his eyes, still as potent as ever. "According to Lena, you two are passing out socks this morning."

They'd tucked a proverb into the footwear for each departing soldier. What were the odds Arno would bother to read the message in his? Poor at best.

His teasing grin quickened her heart, and she placed her hand against her chest to quiet the thumping. "I reckon I should go … find your sister … dole out those socks." When would she see him again? What if he died in France or some other faraway place? From his brow to his chin, she captured his image in her mind before extending her hand for a farewell shake.

"I reckon so." His palm connected with hers.

Same as always, tiny arrows stabbed from the point of contact straight to her heart. Current and past noise ceased. Peppermint candy laced his breath. Same … as … always.

Then his eyes strayed to her lips, triggering prickles across her spine. Would he kiss her? Would she let him? Against her better judgment, the answer was yes. She'd waited and waited for this moment, always in the background.

"When I look at you, I still see a little imp, the tomboy who shadowed my steps." Like always, he made one thing spring-water clear—he'd never reciprocated her schoolgirl crush.

"I know." She whipped around, blinked back tears, and then stomped away from Mr. Temptation. Over the years, Arno would dangle a smile or a sweet glance before reeling her in like the white sucker fish in Catfish Creek that they'd caught as children. But no more.

The same gentleman she'd eyed from the stage blocked her path, squinting in the wind and sunshine. "Your voice rivals the songbirds." He spoke with a drawl thicker than hotcakes drenched in maple syrup, delicious but mushy. "I wager those same birds are green with envy."

Although over-the-top, this man knew how to issue a proper compliment, unlike someone else. "Highly unlikely, but thank you nonetheless."

He chuckled and lowered a brown suitcase to the ground. "I never argue with ladies, but I'm fairly certain I'm correct."

"I'd hate to label a stranger a fibber, but …" She spread her arms wide. For someone who rarely garnered male attention, she stood knee-deep in a puddle of flirtation. Perhaps not everyone considered her an "impish tomboy." Were those Arno's exact words moments ago? She glanced back but couldn't find him in the crowd.

"I'm Barrett Jordane, born and raised in Louisiana. I lived there up until a year ago." A captivating shade of light brown eyes, bordering on gold, invited her to forge a friendship. "There. Now we're no longer strangers."

"And I'm Hattie Waltz, same as the dance."

"Ahh, a pretty name for a pretty girl."

cute! analogy

Why did some men scatter absurd compliments like chicken feed? Then again, some girls gulped them up like silly birds. Not her.

Barrett shifted his weight from foot to foot. "I realize we only met a couple of sentences ago, but may I ask a personal question, Hattie?"

Strangers and personal inquiries rarely mixed. Against her better judgment, she nodded.

"Do you have a brother or a beau boarding today's train?"

"Only friends." The label fit some departing soldiers better than others. She lumped all the men into the same category, more than acquaintances but not a single I-can't-live-without-him relationship in the bunch.

"Splendid."

Was it splendid her loved ones hadn't received orders to report for duty, or because she wasn't attached to a departing soldier? More importantly, why analyze every word he spoke? No wonder she'd never had a beau to call her own.

Barrett motioned toward the black locomotive, stately in the sunshine, where passengers flocked around the entrance. The fresh recruits wore civilian clothes, their uniforms waiting at camp. Daniel Hook, a departing soldier, leaned from an open train window. Two fellows on the ground boosted a female high to kiss the military man's lips.

Hattie squinted. Was the woman Priscilla Snodgrass, Arno's

old flame? A rousing cheer followed.

"I've heard Split Falls is best known for crops and livestock, but I'd like to add pretty girls, present company with her blushing cheeks included."

Holy smokes. She should walk away, not stand and lap up his sweet talk, particularly when delivered with a husky drawl.

"How long you wager until the army whips us greenhorns into crackerjack soldiers? A month? Two?"

"Let's hope nobody changes overly much." Hattie wrote a mental note to pray for only positive adjustments, especially for Arno.

On tiptoes, she peered right and then left, stretching to locate Lena, her fellow Knitting Brigade member. "I'm on a mission myself, handing out socks to the soldiers. If you like, there are extras, but they're with my friend. Shall we find her?"

"After you."

Together, they veered right. There stood Lena armed with a bushel basket.

"I've been on the lookout for you. Your song ended a while ago. I'm happy to see you survived your ordeal." With a sassy grin lighting her face, Lena eyed Barrett from Panama hat to two-toned shoe tip. "Who's your handsome friend, Hattie?"

It was one thing to think the man resembled a Sears, Roebuck and Company clothing model, another to blurt the fact.

Barrett tossed his head backward and howled. "Aren't you sugary sweet?"

"Am I, Hattie?"

"Like a beehive." In a flurry, she rushed the introductions, freed a pair of wool socks from the basket, and passed Barrett the footwear.

"I apologize for my forwardness, but will you write me while I'm at boot camp?"

Before Hattie could utter a word, Lena intervened. "Look over there." She motioned toward a scuffle alongside a row of mismatched evergreens. <u>Two men wrestled in the grass</u> as gawkers hurried toward the skirmish. "I'm guessing somebody should put a stop to that."

"Are you implying me?" Barrett removed his hat to drag his hand through cropped black hair.

"I wouldn't dream of it." Lena's laughter rang loud and bold, same as church bells.

"I know what to do with a couple of crackpots. Ladies, if you'll excuse me." After winking at Hattie, Barrett bowed and then beelined toward the interruption.

"He's cute, but I don't know, fussy. However, his accent is divine." Lena propped a hand on her hip while the soldier darted toward the action.

"Perhaps bowing is customary in the South."

"I think not."

Hattie rolled her eyes and cocked her arm before loading and cradling a half-dozen socks. They'd knitted far more footwear than necessary over the last three weeks, but Lena had insisted. "Let's go warm some tootsies."

"And find you an adorable suitor—I mean soldier—to write to. Someone more to your liking than Mr. Fussy Pants."

Two seconds ago, Lena had implied Barrett rivaled the best of the beautiful. "I like him fine." Perhaps Hattie would write the man the second she returned home, and the following day, and the one after that.

"Nah, you don't."

She sighed, weary of Lena's know-it-all opinions. "<u>Why don't we concentrate on our task, handing out socks? That</u>'s all."

Lena fiddled with her lemony-yellow hat with a rolled brim until Hattie lent a hand to tilt it to a picture-perfect angle. Then the girls separated to deliver their stockpiled footwear.

Nervous laughter blended with enthusiastic shouts and chatter, drowning the more intimate conversations teemed with goodbyes. Hattie suspected most of the exiting <u>men considered boot camp an</u>

adventure. Plenty had yapped about plans to whoop the Kaiser's backside in no time. She prayed the boasts twisted into reality.

Arno milled alongside his family, but his eyes trailed Hattie until Lena snaked her arm around his waist. After a sniffle, Mother sopped tears with a handkerchief.

"Mind yourself." Max Kreger stuffed his hand into his trouser pocket, emphasizing the no-need-for-a-handshake message. His other hand clutched a whittled cane.

"Yes, sir."

"You're a Kreger. It's time you wore the name with pride."

Father, wounded while rescuing a family trapped in a burning house, had earned admiration for his bravery and a carved walking stick for his damaged leg. Although he touted worthy advice, it presented a predicament—how to fight a German enemy and, at the same time, bear a German name.

"I'll try my best." Someday he'd make his father proud or, probably, die in the effort.

Father mumbled something unintelligible.

Arno caught two words—*not enough*. He gritted his teeth. The minute the war ended, he'd buy a few acres of his own to farm, get out from under Father's thumb.

Sunshine lit the tears on Mother's face. She nudged her husband aside. "I'll pray for you morning and night, son. I already lost one boy. I can't abide losing another."

Oliver's earnest face appeared before Arno blinked his kid brother aside and embraced the woman who'd loved him first and without conditions. She smelled like a lilac bush, and he tugged her close, whispering words to fade her worries. "I promise to return."

"It's not your say-so." She hiccupped, and he tightened his grip.

They swayed, rocking to a silent rhythm before a final whispered goodbye. Arno held her at arm's length and offered a reassuring smile, but it flickered and failed.

"Let the boy go, Gen." Father's firm voice drew glances from bystanders.

Arno cringed.

With a final pat to his sleeve, Mother stepped aside and laced her fingers.

Lena, never burdened by public opinion, stretched to kiss him on both cheeks. "That's how they do it in Europe. Don't be a dolt while you're over there." She tugged his ear toward her mouth. "Behave yourself." No doubt, he'd miss her most of all.

With his trunk snug on his shoulder, Arno maneuvered through the crowd. A short line of soldiers lingered near the train's entrance. Searching for his buddy Karl, he swung right and almost rammed Hattie, who sidestepped to avoid the collision.

"Close call," she said as her bright smile wilted.

"You need to watch your step." Why was it so fun to tease her? In many ways, she reminded him of the china doll still propped on Lena's pinewood chest of drawers—brown eyes, cocoa brown hair that curled, and ivory skin. Although both pretty enough, the doll and Hattie, only one had stolen his heart long ago.

But he'd never tell her. He couldn't.

"I believe you almost trampled me."

He grinned, nodding toward her armful of socks. "Gonna pass me a pair or horde the entire batch?"

"Of course, we knitted these for you." She raised her armful. "Not only you—all the soldiers. The proverb inside is a good one."

"Aren't they all good?" His grin grew, pulling him back to an easier time when friendships were only one-layer deep. He reached for her gift and caught the fresh scent of soap as if she'd scrubbed her skin minutes ago.

Her eyes darted from the train to Arno. "Isn't it time to board? You don't want to start your army life in trouble."

A muscle pulsated in his cheek, drumming to the cadence of Hattie's lecture. "How sweet of you to worry about my welfare. Wait a minute, do you still like me?"

Her face flamed, but she raised her chin, pinning him to the ground with her stare. "For Lena's sake, you better come back in one piece."

When he crossed his heart with a fingertip, her smile reappeared. For years, that simple childhood action had guaranteed they'd never break each other's promises. In his eyes, that crossing of the heart carried the same weight today. *Do you want me to come back too?*

Another man approached, the same fellow who'd bent Hattie's ear minutes before. "Is this man disturbing you?" The citified stranger wrinkled his forehead.

"Barrett, this is Arno, Lena's brother. Arno, Barrett." Although she spoke to the intruder, her eyes remained fixed on Arno. "We're saying goodbye."

The two men shook hands. Barrett's palm was as soft as pudding, not callused like most men who worked to put food on the table.

"Now, that makes perfect sense. You claimed you didn't have a beau." With a hearty slap, Barrett thumped Arno's back. "You know how the mind jumps to conclusions." He turned to Hattie. "You never answered my question. Will you write to me?"

She flashed a not-so-tomboyish smile and rested her hand on the man's showy jacket sleeve. "It would be my pleasure."

"Kreger." Barrett touched his hat brim with two fingers before luring Hattie away.

The train's whistle blared, signaling the end of his old life and the beginning of something fresh. Still, Arno remained rooted, watching the departing couple until the crowd swallowed them.

Over the years, he'd looked at Hattie from a slew of angles. But never this one.

CHAPTER TWO

Ten days after Hattie sang at the train station, she huddled next to a bonfire at the base of her sloped yard. Lena and her beau, Wilhelm Mueller, arrived late. Giggles sounded before the flames illuminated their faces.

"It's about time you two showed." Hattie sidestepped an onslaught of pungent smoke before joining the duo. Clustered in groups of twos and threes, the Waltz's guests circled the crackling blaze. Bandit, her family's black-and-white border collie, barked and raced from guest to guest.

"Someone spent an extra-long time primping." Wilhelm, the local heartthrob and longtime family friend, nodded toward Lena in an exaggerated manner. An olive-green newsboy cap topped his head. A few honey-colored curls peeked from beneath.

The army had rejected Wilhelm's services due to a faulty ticker, stemming from a childhood case of rheumatic fever. According to him, the ailment amounted to nothing more than a hill of beans. Hattie prayed he spoke the truth.

"And doesn't he look adorable?" When Lena laughed, her beau gripped her middle and tickled until she escaped, racing for the shadows. Riotous laughter soon followed. Everybody suspected an engagement. Hattie anticipated an imminent announcement, but what did a romantic novice like her know?

The autumn air nipped the night, stirring thoughts of hot cocoa and downy comforters. A lengthy silence brewed while folks stared at the hypnotic blaze. Daddy elbowed her arm, coaxing her into singing a few ditties while he puffed on a harmonica. Before long, everybody raised their voices for a hearty rendition of "Hail! Hail!

The Gang's All Here."

Afterward, she slipped away to check on Hawk, her seven-year-old brother, who'd left earlier for a cup of cider and never returned. Moonlight lit a path of swishy leaves, and halfway to the house, Lena came up alongside her. "I have two things to tell you." Her friend bounced on her toes, either eager to deliver the news or a visit to the privy was in order.

"Where's Wilhelm?"

"With your big brother, but let's focus on my announcements. Guess what?"

"Wilhelm proposed."

"Don't be ridiculous." Lena ran both hands through disheveled hair, plucking a dried leaf from the back of her head. "What I need to tell you has nothing to do with Wilhelm or me. It's about last night's Knitting Brigade meeting."

"Old news." Hattie resumed her stroll toward her hilltop home, where an electric light glared from each window.

"What you don't know is this." Lena swung Hattie around by the elbow to stand face to face. "The Brigade needs a new leader. Meridee Moss is stepping down, and I nominated you."

"What were you thinking?" Hattie gasped and then covered her mouth. The prospect sounded scarier than singing before strangers with her apparel topsy-turvy. After a piercing glare, she continued up the hill, Lena on her heels. "I can't possibly manage such a responsibility. In case it's slipped your mind, I dropped out of school when Mama died. Did you hear me?" She stopped to shout at the moon. "I was e-le-ven!" The last syllable echoed across the hills.

"However, you've since read a thousand and one library books on every subject under the heavens, including philosophy and arithmetic." Lena latched onto Hattie's arm, leading her up the porch steps. "I'll fasten myself to your side the entire time. We'll do it together."

"Why didn't you volunteer yourself?" Hattie wrestled her arm free and, for the umpteenth time, wished for the impossible—Lena to stop fussing with her life.

"Those ladies would never appoint me. I'm too … I don't know … unpredictable. All those biddies on the county level snub me." A crease sprang between Lena's brows. "They probably think I'd make a mockery of the entire Brigade, all the way from the national level to us locals. I wouldn't, but I'd likely spice it up. Trust me, the committee can stand a pinch of seasoning."

Hattie raised her hand. "Let me get this straight. At this point, I'm only nominated, not elected, which means there's a strong possibility another candidate will fill the position, correct?"

"Nope, they chose you last night, a unanimous decision."

With an *oomph*, Hattie collapsed onto the porch swing.

"Want to hear my other piece of news?" Lena wedged her rear onto the same paint-chipped seat.

"No, thank you." What was the proper protocol to remove oneself from a committee appointment and, at the same time, hush a best friend's mouth?

"Arno mailed me a letter, says he's more than fine."

Over the last ten days, Hattie had trained herself to picture Barrett's handsome face whenever Arno's mug trespassed through her thoughts. "Good for him. I pray for all the local boys each night by name."

"Oh, me too. Sometimes twice a night."

"Sure, you do." Thick skepticism laced her reply.

"Arno sent you a letter too, stuck it inside my envelope. I didn't read it."

Hattie balled her necklace into her fist. Other than baths and bedtime, she wore Mama's pearls nearly nonstop. The soothing touch calmed her pulse.

In two shakes of a cat's tail, Lena yanked the evidence from the pocket of her fox-collared overcoat before dangling the envelope within Hattie's reach.

Should she peek into Arno's new life? Glean his thoughts?

But why fiddle with fire? The boy reeked of trouble. She knew it, Daddy believed it with his whole heart, and Lena was biased.

"What's wrong?"

"Why would he write me out of the blue?"

"I'm holding your answer." Lena ran her fingers through her long blond hair, the same shade as Arno's.

Hattie pushed her shoe against the porch's floorboards to set the swing in motion. "I never told you what happened on my sixteenth birthday at your aunt and uncle's barn dance. You suffered in bed with a nasty cold."

"I beg to differ. I was on the brink of pneumonia."

"And I was on the brink of a huge mistake." Hattie sighed, uncertain how much information to divulge. "I waited alone on a tree stump for Daddy to haul me home, plucking flower petals from a daisy patch. A decent full moon hung overhead."

"That's specific." Lena started to braid three strands of hair, Arno's letter in her lap.

"It's why I remember everything so clearly. I heard rustling and peered over my shoulder. Here comes Arno, minus a dancing partner. He plops into the grass near my feet. For the first time in years, we talked like friends. Our conversation hopped from fishing to the price of corn to hair ribbons." Hattie glanced sideways at Lena. "According to him, they're silly."

"Go on."

"We debated who'd win a footrace, him or me, and when I reached for another flower, he propped a finger under my chin and tucked a daisy behind my ear. Our faces were inches apart." Hattie closed her eyes. Sometimes, in the privacy of her bedroom, she relived that night, embellishing the details by adding bigger smiles, richer laughter, and the wittiest verbal exchanges known to man or woman.

With the swing in a backward motion, Lena jammed her feet against the floor, halting the sway. Hattie slid down the incline until her black boots stopped her.

"And neither of you thought to tell me this afore now."

Hattie merely shrugged and returned to the porch rail before hitching her hip against it. "Although neither Arno nor I realized it at the time, Daddy stood a breath away in the barn's shadows. He ordered me to climb into the cart. A minute or two later, he followed suit, and off we rode toward home. After that, Arno bounced back to ignoring me, at least for the most part."

"True or false—you no longer hold tender feelings for my brother?"

Hattie's childhood case of puppy love had eventually blossomed into a bigger breed of some sort. But never once had Arno encouraged her feelings. Instead, he'd ignored her the last few years, choosing to roughneck across the county.

She deserved more, something better—wagonloads better. Someday, she'd find a man who loved her as much as she loved him, and he wasn't Arno Kreger. "I'm over your brother."

With a shove, Lena resumed the swing's back and forth rhythm. "Then what's the harm in reading his note?"

"Le-na, where are you?" Wilhelm's husky voice traveled in the dark, rising from the far side of the house near the orchard.

Lena placed a fingertip against her lips before transferring Arno's envelope to the flat railing within Hattie's reach. "Sometimes, risks lead to happiness. You can't tell me a part of you isn't excited to learn what he wrote."

"Did you hear a single word of the story I told you one minute ago?"

"In my opinion, you need a dose of excitement in your life, and perhaps reading Arno's missive is the first step."

After an exasperated sigh, Hattie crossed her arms. "You do know it's rude to imply I'm a dullard, don't you?"

"Le-na. Come out, come out, wherever you are."

"First, I'm not insulting you." Lena wagged her finger. "I merely want you to consider new experiences. Second, it's time to scare the dickens out of Wilhelm." Without waiting for a reply,

Lena tiptoed into the dark.

Alone on the porch, Hattie returned to the swing. If a person favored books over dances and horseback riding to primping, those preferences failed to pigeonhole. Or did they? More importantly, it didn't pitch anyone into a category labeled boring. Or did it?

The loamy aroma of soil and dried leaves hung in the air. Without looking at it, Hattie retrieved the envelope and stuffed it into her overcoat pocket. The last thing she wanted was for Daddy to find it.

Inside the house, after a thorough walkthrough to extinguish lights, Hattie returned to the parlor, where Hawk had burrowed under a blanket on the horsehair sofa. She smiled, relieved to find him where he belonged. She tugged the afghan off his head and met the unblinking stare of Betty Lou, the snuggly housecat. Hattie gasped.

"Meow."

After a pat on the cat's head, she tucked the blanket around Hawk's shoulders and dropped a kiss on his cheek.

Rather than returning to the bonfire, she joined her brother on the end of the sofa, borrowing a corner of the blanket to cover her calves. The lamp's glow streamed, perfect for reading. She reached for her well-worn copy of *Sense and Sensibility* on the nearby secretary. Barrett's one and only letter served as her bookmark, and she tugged the stationery from the envelope.

September 20, 1917

Dear Hattie,

It sure was sweet meeting you. You are very pretty, and your voice is a dream. Most fellas are jealous of my good fortune and not just because I have a gal who writes me letters. Plenty of the higher-ranking officers show me favor too.

We're all falling into line. Most of us are quick learners, but I'd say plenty miss their mamas. There's no room for that nonsense in the army.

Last night for supper, we had green beans and corned beef. Breakfast was biscuits and gravy, which tasted worse than paper. We ate grits in the South. They are delicious. Have you tasted grits?

I best shove off now. I'll write again sometime soon.

Sincerely,
Private Barrett Jordane

Unfortunately, his letter failed to improve with a second reading, and the word *boring* sprang into Hattie's mind. With a gulp, she slid a finger under the flap of Arno's envelope.

September 19, 1917

Hattie,

I reckon you're surprised to read this, that is, if you even opened it. I'm ranking the odds at fifty-fifty. On the one hand, you're curious by nature. On the other, you're stubborn.

She slapped the slip of paper onto the sofa's arm, grumbling over Arno's assessment. Any woman with half a brain would toss the letter on the bonfire without reading another word. The cuckoo clock squawked ten times, prompting another peek at Arno's correspondence. A minute later, she nabbed the bothersome thing.

Since we haven't conversed much over the past couple of years, you're probably wondering how I might make such a brassy statement. Even though we've strayed apart, I know you well. There's no denying that truth. Besides, Lena and I talk, not that she gossips about you.

True to my promise, I not only read the proverb in the sock, I also memorized it. Are you impressed?

I'm returning the favor and handpicked one for you. "Her ways are ways of pleasantness, and all her paths are peace." It certainly fits you more than me. If you write me back, I'll send

19

you another.

I've bumped into your pen pal, Barrett Jordane, a time or two. He's a real—

"You're mighty absorbed in something or another." Daddy leaned a lazy shoulder against the doorframe. A toothpick played on his lips, a constant companion.

Hattie's pulse fluttered, same as the ivory stationery floating to the floor. The letter had cinched her attention in a vise, making it impossible to hear squeaky floorboards. With what she hoped resembled nonchalance, she reached for the fallen missive before burying it deep within the folds of her skirt. She hunted for a distraction. "Has the fire burned down? Do you need my help? Have all our guests departed?"

Daddy motioned toward her lap. "Is that letter from the fella you met at the train station?"

Never was the number of times she'd lied to her father. For a second, she weighed whether or not to now. "It's … not."

Every now and again, Daddy battled the blues, and she hesitated to pile more worries onto his hefty stack. While he rubbed at his whiskers, she waited.

"No? Who then?"

She sighed, wishing to say any name other than the one about to spill from her lips. "It's from Arno." His last name wasn't required. Except for the Arno River located in Italy, which she'd read about a week prior in a geography book, she and Daddy only knew one Arno, a man saddled with the last name of Kreger.

"That's odd. I thought we decided to forget about that boy."

"I did, I mean, I am. Arno mailed me a proverb from camp. It's rather sweet, I think."

Daddy crossed the room and sank into a faded armchair near the sofa. A smoky scent curled around their heads. He leaned forward, bracing his elbows on his knees and his chin on gathered knuckles. "Arno Kreger has a reputation as a hooligan. Every time

I turn around, I hear he's linked to one scrape or another. Maybe the army will straighten him out, maybe not. You're playing with fire, little girl."

She wasn't a little girl, but Daddy rarely remembered. "Speaking of fire, should we join our guests?"

"I'm gonna tote this one to bed." He nodded toward Hawk. "You go. I want to chew on your news a tad longer." The tone attached to his words brooked no argument.

Daddy's eagle eyes captured hers until she fled. By the time her boots hit the lane, she'd opened into a full-fledged sprint, stopping a few feet from the thinning bonfire. Only Jeb, her big brother, crouched near the dying flames.

"If it isn't my long-lost sister. Where you been?"

"I was reading." Part of her longed to finish Arno's letter. The other half, the sensible portion, screamed *Don't be a fool. Why let him hurt you again?* Hattie tossed the stationery onto the sizzling pile, watching the corners turn orange and curl. "And now I'm burning."

Side-by-side, the siblings squatted to watch Arno's words disintegrate. The wind whisked charred leaves, and she coughed, backing away from the sting.

"That must have been one quintessentially disagreeable letter." Jeb poked at the cinders with a red-ended stick that resembled a lit cigarette.

"Since when do you use words like quintessentially?"

"It means a sterling example." With a round face and a heavy sprinkling of freckles, Jeb resembled an adolescent more than a twenty-one-year-old man. His shirt sleeves were rolled up to his elbows despite the dropping temperature.

"Answer my question."

About the time Hattie thought the silence might petrify, Jeb shrugged and prodded the cinders, stirring up the smoldering patch. "Ever since I asked Sadie Parker on a date."

"I need more details than that, especially when it's concerning

Miss Parker."

"I paid a call, and she slammed her front door on me." Jeb studied the ground, unwilling to meet her eyes. "That's not entirely true. First, she told me to go home and read a book, and then her door banged shut."

At fourteen, Jeb's formal education had ground to a halt, not because Mama passed but to help Daddy on the farm. Later that same year, he accidentally shot himself in the hand while messing with a firearm, suffering nerve and tendon damage. The affliction rarely limited him, only piled on more toughness, more fearlessness. He longed to serve his country, but his country had refused his earnest offer.

Some might claim Jeb lacked polish. Although true enough, he was loyal, caring, and far too good for the likes of snotty Miss Parker. "If you ask me, she has awful taste. Ever notice how much face powder she wears?"

"The thing is, I don't mind improving myself."

Most days, it felt like she and Jeb lagged behind their peers in one area or another. Was it because they'd dropped early from school or for another reason, one she'd failed to pinpoint?

"Thanks to Sadie, I've decided to learn one new word each day, starting with quintessential. I like it."

"It's a good word." Although Hattie smiled at Jeb, a single tear dampened her cheek. Whether she cried for herself or her brother, she wasn't sure—probably half and half. Her stomach churned with something akin to regret as Arno's letter turned to soot.

CHAPTER THREE

October 6, 1917—Camp Dodge, Iowa

Amidst the thick cigarette smoke, Arno rearranged the playing cards in his hand, tossed coins into the pot, and fought a smile. A trio of queens stared back at him. But faster than spit, another soldier's full house beat his three of a kind.

"Welcome home." In the back portion of the Y.M.C.A. after a long day of drilling, Frankie Jesberger raked a greedy arm across a tabletop, drawing a heap of winnings against his chest. He stacked his coins in straight rows like a regiment during inspection.

Ten minutes had skipped away since Arno's introduction to the art of poker. The following lesson centered on losing every dime in a novice's pocket. Without question, Mother and Father opposed gambling. They'd made their choice. He'd make his.

It didn't take a genius to discover squandering money rarely paid off.

After the game, most everyone shuffled toward the other end of the building to view a moving picture. He slouched at the abandoned table, folding a sheet of stationery into accordion pleats.

Karl, his hometown pal since grammar school and a self-taught artist, had captured Arno's likeness on the paper, including the disappointed frown when he'd lost his gambling money. He wasn't jealous of his friend's talent, far from it. But he wouldn't mind a bit if Karl chose another mug for his doodle practice.

With time to waste until guard duty, a short snooze enticed, but oversleeping did not. He borrowed a guitar from the corner of the room, then ducked outside. Night had settled into camp. Leaning against the wall, he braced one foot, raising his knee to set the guitar on. He plucked the chords to "Buffalo Gals." The familiar tune drew his thoughts home.

Did Hattie ever sing that song? Did she ever think of him? A shake of his head failed to fling her image from his thoughts. *She's not the girl for me.*

Hopefully, she wasn't the gal for Barrett Jordane either.

Arno pushed away from the wall and kicked at a dirt clod, telling himself to forget about Hattie for one excellent reason. Dating led to courtship, and nine times out of ten, courtship developed into marriage. Next thing you know, a baby —the last thing Arno wanted. Even if he changed his mind on that, Chester Waltz wasn't about to grant permission to step out with his daughter, not in a dozen leap years.

He sighed.

The distance between home and Camp Dodge measured a whisker shy of one hundred miles. Since arriving, Arno had already received a half-dozen letters from six different gals, including Priscilla despite their breakup. Like victory gardens and bond drives, most citizens wrote encouraging letters to members of the armed forces. Newspapers and community leaders rallied for every American to focus attention on service.

The air stilled, and Arno peeled his damp collar from his neck, wishing for a better breeze. He leaned against the wall and strummed a few more chords, then paused when a soldier stepped from the shadows, sucking on a dwindling cigarette.

"Why'd ya stop?" Cigarette smoke curled into the evening, while box-elder bugs romped in the electric light overhead.

"You play?" Arno asked, rubbing a guitar string between his thumb and finger.

"Nah, can't hold a tune in a bucket."

"Your name's Hyland. Isn't it?" At first glance, the man appeared taller than six-foot, same as Arno. Stocky too. A broad-brimmed campaign hat sat squarely on the man's head, and a scar, shaped like a question mark, zigzagged from left temple to cheek.

"Clyde Walter, but I go by CW. Only my ma calls me Clyde." His chest swelled with another draw on the cigarette. "And you?"

"Arno Kreger. Pleased to meet you." Arno extended his hand, but CW scoffed.

"Kreger sounds German to me."

Careful not to mar the instrument, Arno rested the guitar against the wall, straightened his posture, and spread his legs to distribute weight in equal proportions. German blood surged through his veins, no use denying it. Ever since stepping foot in camp, he'd expected a confrontation. Still, his pulse quickened. "What's your point?"

CW flicked his cigarette aside as the Y.M.C.A. door swung open, delivering a flash of bright light. Out strolled Karl.

Arno sent his pal a slow smile.

"I wondered what happened to you, Kreger. We saw that same picture show back in Split Falls." He jerked his thumb at the Y., then paused. "Am I interrupting?"

"Clyde, here, questions my loyalty to our country."

"Say it ain't so." Karl grinned as if he'd never heard a more amusing tale.

"By the sounds of it, he doesn't fancy my name, considers it too German."

Under his breath, CW cursed and folded both arms across his tank-like chest. "Ain't true. Them's your words, not mine."

"Then he's gonna hate mine with a passion." Karl stretched his neck toward CW. "Lud-wig. L-U-D-W-I-G."

"You're a mighty fine speller, my friend." Arno clamped a hand on Karl's sweaty shoulder.

"*Danke.*"

Arno cringed at Karl's word choice before eyeballing Hyland, but the man's stony face masked inner thoughts. Nobody with a brain uttered German these days, especially around camp.

"You fellas have me pegged all wrong." CW wore a thin-lipped smile. "I even married a German-American girl once. Of course, we're not together no more but not on account of her being a foreigner." CW lit a second cigarette.

Arno studied the night sky, thick with stars and milky-white streaks. He should walk away, ignore the lousy bigot. But, cripes, the man had sullied his name. At the same time, any hope to advance through the military ranks meant a clean record. The army had preached that message too many times to count.

Karl slapped Arno's back. "Just so there's no future misunderstanding, my buddy and I are one hundred percent American, born and reared here. We enlisted to defend our homeland, same as you, I reckon."

"And," Arno draped an arm over Karl's shoulders, "since the army finds us fit, I suggest you back off."

CW clapped, clamping his cigarette between his teeth. "Nice speech."

"Thanks, it was off the cuff." Arno retrieved the guitar and opened the Y.'s backdoor.

"Wait a minute, fellas." CW spread his arms wide. "I think we ought to start over. We're fighting on the same side, ain't that right?" He offered both men a cigarette, which they refused.

Arno let the door swing shut before returning the guitar to the ground. Then he eyed the man, suspicious of his quick change of heart.

CW and Karl leaned against the building, discussing camp life and hometowns. CW hailed from Burlington on the banks of the Mississippi. "Either of you think we'll get furloughs home soon?" Karl asked.

Arno shrugged. Yesterday's newspaper had predicted a swift victory over the Germans since America had jumped onboard. Today's edition opined a decade-long brawl.

"Can't be soon enough," CW answered. Next, the conversation veered toward families.

"Don't mean to pry, but I'm a snoopy son of a buck." Karl picked up a pebble and tossed it down the road. "Whatever happened with your wife?"

In no apparent hurry, CW cracked his hairy knuckles, one at a time. "I used to tell her she was the prettiest gal west of the Mississippi, and then she always said to me, 'What about the rest of the country?'"

Arno smiled, picturing the playful scene. His mother and father teased like that, at least they had before Oliver died.

"Then one night, I caught her laughing and sitting too close to the neighbor man on the porch. First, I laid him out flat, then she skedaddled. Nary packed a thing."

"Huh," Karl said.

"Never got around to divorcing her, but I ain't seen her in close to a year now. Ninety percent of all women are unfaithful. They can't help it. No offense if you two is married."

What an idiot. Since arriving in camp, Arno had met all sorts— good, bad, mean, and in-between. CW lived on the bottom of the barrel.

"In due time," Karl said.

Arno bent and tied his bootlace. "How do you make a living over in Burlington? Farmer, right?"

"Why you suppose that?" CW tipped his head to the right and kicked Arno's shoulder, knocking him sideways into the dirt. "Because farmers are uneducated? Hicks?"

Arno scrambled to his feet.

Before he lunged, Karl locked both arms around Arno's middle. "Simmer down," he whispered.

He closed his eyes and breathed deeply. How long since his last fight? Six months? Longer? Could he avoid a tussle until overseas duty? Probably not. Hyland asked for trouble. Arno itched to answer.

"You said it, we're on the same side here, Hyland." Karl dipped his head toward the soldier. "Afore long, we'll all be knee-deep in France, so there's no reason to jump the gun at camp. I'm a farmer. Arno's one too. Proud of it."

With the intensity of a fire-and-brimstone-preacher, Hyland focused on Arno. "Nobody disrespects me and gets away with it, especially a German." He slammed his fist into his open palm, then stalked away.

Drawn by the ruckus, a few curious soldiers gathered near the corner of the building, close enough to catch the action firsthand but far enough to avoid a wild punch.

"Hyland belongs in a loony bin," a chubby soldier said, followed by murmured agreements by his buddies.

"Sounds 'bout right." Karl retrieved Arno's cap from the dirt and shook it off. "Show's over for tonight, fellas."

The spectators scattered, more than likely disappointed the quarrel ended without a punch.

Arno leaned a shoulder against the cool wall while crickets chirped. "All I've ever wanted to do is farm, buy a few acres of my own. Hyland makes it sound like it's the worst job in the world."

"Since when do you care what he or anyone else thinks? Don't let the man get your goat."

Arno grunted before collecting the guitar and opening the Y.'s backdoor. He returned the instrument to its rightful home. Finally, his pulse plunked along at its normal pace. "Are you ready for the barracks?"

Karl grinned. "I'm as ready as a rabbit in heat."

"That's vivid."

"Thank you."

The pair hit the street. Except for missing home, camp met expectations with three square meals and a decent bed. Their sleeping quarters, lined with iron cots and straw-filled ticks for mattresses, occupied the second floor of the looming structure ahead. A fair-sized kitchen, a long rectangular mess hall, several storerooms, and officers' quarters occupied the lower level.

In the night's quiet, some soldier with a pitch-perfect bass voice belted a familiar tune.

"I wonder who's kissing her now,
Wonder who's teaching her how,
Wonder who's looking into her eyes,
Breathing sighs, telling lies ..."

<u>Who kissed Hattie now?</u> <u>Arno never had</u>, but that didn't mean he'd not imagined it a time or two. Any red-blooded male would likely foster the same hope. "You have no idea how much I hate that song."

"Aww ... it's my favorite." Karl sang, butchering the lyrics. They plowed up the steep staircase to the second floor.

"Will you stop already?" Arno shoved Karl's arm, prompting his buddy to howl even louder.

"Shut up," someone hollered, pitching a pillow in Karl's direction. "Some of us are trying to sleep."

"What's the time?" Arno scooped the missile from the floor and fired it back. The barracks reeked of body odor.

"Aren't you on guard duty tonight?" Karl yanked a pocket watch from his trousers.

"Yep."

"Then you're almost late."

With a groan, he bolted toward the exit for the armory. The last bunk on the right at the entrance to the staircase belonged to Hyland who lay spread-eagle across his cot.

"Hey, Kreger."

Arno paused long enough to peer over his shoulder.

"<u>You'll</u> want to watch <u>your backside tonight</u>. It's plenty dark out there. Never know what hides in the shadows."

"I'm not afraid of the dark. Never have been. I can't think of a single thing that scares me."

Hyland's gritty laughter trailed Arno down the staircase. A few steps before the exit door, he came face to face with Barrett Jordane. Smugness smeared the man's mug, same as every other time they'd crossed paths at camp.

"Move." What did Hattie see in this two-bit weasel who refused to budge? "Don't test me tonight."

Jordane offered a mock two-fingered salute. "Tomorrow then. Name the place and time, Private Kreger."

CHAPTER FOUR

"Ladies, I'm waiting!" Meridee Moss, the outgoing Knitting Brigade chairperson and committee originator, leaned forward at the Split Falls Savings and Loan. Her too-tight navy suit, with a sparkly elephant brooch clamping her décolletage, gaped at each buttonhole.

The boxy room buzzed, ladies ignoring the question on the table. The committee had already hashed over a range of topics, Brigade and non-Brigade related, stretching from the price of yarn to Meridee's shoe size, a ten. Stale air swirled, mixing with nauseating perfumes.

Hattie tiptoed to a nearby window and propped it open with a wedged stick, prompting cool October air to gush inward, upending loose paper and hairstyles.

In ten steps, Meridee banged the window shut. "It's late, and my nerves are frayed. Do we, or do we not, have a volunteer?" The woman's eyes, dark as two clumps of Iowa dirt, pierced Hattie's. "Fine, then I'll appoint a delegate."

Hattie scooted back to her chair. On a scale of one to ten, her desire to step into Meridee's sizeable shoes registered at negative three. Official duties as the incoming leader hadn't yet commenced, not for another few weeks. She fussed with some papers on the table, praying she appeared busy.

"We'll go," Lena said, grinning until dimples drilled into her cheeks. "Hattie and me. We're both ready for an adventure, and this trip fits the bill."

Hattie rolled her eyes.

"Need I remind you, this is a business venture, not folly."

Meridee shoved droopy spectacles up the bridge of her hawk-like nose.

"I understand." Lena bumped her knee against Hattie's, harder than she'd probably intended. "All work, no folly."

"Count me in, as well." Garbed in a turquoise dress with an iridescent sheen, accordion pleats across the bodice, and layers of beads roped around her neck, Priscilla Snodgrass challenged Meridee for the most-overdressed-for-a-routine-committee-meeting prize.

Oh, bother. Of all the women around the table, why this traveling companion? Hattie rubbed a pearl over her bottom lip.

"Very well then," Meridee clapped. "Say, Hattie, why don't I drop by your house one night next week with the meeting details? Does Tuesday suit, say about suppertime?"

"That'll be fine." *Poor Daddy.*

Meridee's deceased husband, a well-to-do banker, had left behind three grown sons and an alleged fortune. Why the lonely woman targeted Daddy for a potential husband remained a mystery to everyone in town, especially him. For the last six months, the widow had pursued her prey the same way she spearheaded meetings—with gusto, a complicated agenda, and high expectations.

Daddy kept a low profile around town these days.

Within minutes, the older committee members, including Meridee, waltzed from the room amidst a flutter of skirts and gossip. Hattie gathered her belongings.

Priscilla stood in the doorway. "Correct me if I'm wrong, but we do intend to stop at Camp Dodge, while we're in Des Moines, or am I totally off the mark?"

"Why?" Lena leaned forward and drummed her thumb against the tabletop. "Do you hope to see Arno or someone else?"

Hattie squinted at the two women before her. Was a boot camp visit part of the upcoming agenda? And was Priscilla still attracted to Lena's brother? Not that it mattered.

"I'm always interested in the well-being of our soldiers,

especially the locals."

Hattie fiddled with her pearls, weighing Priscilla's wishy-washy response. Was the woman purposefully vague to cover up her true feelings or simply unaware of her heart's desire? Other than physical beauty, Arno and Priscilla—who'd courted for close to a year—differed in every imaginable way.

"I just thought of something." Lena swiveled to face Hattie. "If we do find time to visit Camp Dodge, perhaps you can meet up with Barrett. Obviously, you like him more than I first suspected."

"Who?" Priscilla asked.

"He's a fella I met the day the boys left for boot camp," Hattie said. Perhaps they could squeeze in a short visit to Camp Dodge, after all.

"Tell me more." Priscilla's eyes narrowed.

Hattie shot Lena a glance. It was never wise to divulge too much information to Priscilla because it often backfired. Still, why not boast a bit? "Yes, and now we exchange letters."

"It just so happens I met him that day too." Priscilla twisted a gaudy opal ring around and around on her finger. "If I recall correctly," she curved her hand alongside her mouth in a confidential manner, "he's handsome."

Nobody argued the woman's point, so Priscilla continued. "Let me get this straight. You met Barrett," she pointed at Hattie, "and then you offered to write him letters. My, my, my, that's forward of you. But I'm impressed, you little minx."

"Actually," Lena crossed her arms, "Barrett begged Hattie to write to him."

"I wouldn't say *begged*." Hattie aimed to keep the facts straight, even though Lena's version packed a more impressive punch.

"Good for you, that's all I have to say." Priscilla buttoned her overcoat. "I look forward to our adventure. We can overnight at my aunt and uncle's home. Their property sits a hop, skip, and a jump from Camp Dodge. Goodnight, ladies." Heels clacked in the corridor before a door banged shut.

"Thanks for nothing." Hattie brushed past Lena to reach the exit.

"How was I to know she'd bounce onto the bandwagon?"

"Ugh!" Hattie led the way to Daddy's Buick.

"Sorry to push you into the meeting and the trip."

"I know I'm the proper person to attend, but if I have to go, I'd rather not bunk at Priscilla's relations. Won't that be awkward, staying with strangers, especially her family?" Guilt over her pettiness gnawed.

"She's not your cup of tea, is she?"

"I'll put it this way—I drink mine straight, and she's like three lumps of sugar." But Priscilla's sweetness was superficial, at best.

"You both held a sweet spot for Arno once upon a time."

Why she and Priscilla had gravitated toward the same man was a head-scratcher, a mystery for the ages. Or, at least, for this minute in time. "The most important part of your sentence is the ending."

"If you two were china patterns, she'd be a hodgepodge of colorful swirls, and you'd be a simple white with a golden rim."

Hattie rolled her eyes.

"And if you were dogs, she'd be a—"

"For the love of all that is good and decent," Hattie forced a loud sigh, "I'm begging you to stop with the comparisons."

"Duly noted, but there's one more thing I need to say."

Hattie let her shoulders sag. "Let's hear it."

Lena bounced onto the tips of her pointy Mary Janes with a squeal. "We're going to Des Moines!"

"Get into the auto, or I'll leave you behind." Of course, she'd never follow-through, but the idea tempted her now and again.

Two nights later, Hattie lowered a piping hot bowl of chicken and dumplings onto the table. The meat juices perfumed the kitchen. "Dinner is served."

"Smells just like Mama's." Jeb slid into his chair, same as Daddy,

Hawk, and Wilhelm—a frequent guest during corn-picking season.

"Thank you for the high praise." Hattie smiled at her brother.

"Are you going to the dance tomorrow night, or do you need more time to ruminate over your answer?" With his sleeve, Jeb brushed grime from his chin.

"Ruminate?" Daddy asked. "That's a fifty-cent word."

Hattie gathered the side dishes and hunted for a fresh topic. "Who thinks we'll finish corn picking soon?"

Jeb predicted ten days, and Daddy surmised a couple of weeks, while Hattie examined the fine cuts on her hands from the corn leaves.

"Everything smells delicious, especially the pecan pie." Wilhelm's deep voice broke into the corn discussion. "Thanks for the invitation."

"It's plain and simple." Daddy rested his toothpick onto the lip of his plate. "You work our fields, you eat our supper."

Hattie carried a bowl of turnips in one hand and boiled potatoes in the other. She made space for the vegetables on the table and then wriggled her way to a chair squashed between the rectangular table and the kitchen wall. "I cooked plenty. You can take a plate home for your pa, Will."

If her night proceeded as planned, they'd polish off the meal lickety-split, she'd breeze through cleanup, and soon tuck Hawk into bed. Other than Sundays and a few stolen hours here and there, they'd toiled in the fields for a string of days, hurrying with the harvest, which meant everyone needed a good night's sleep.

Daddy blessed the meal, followed by the clink of cutlery.

"Will you help me with my spelling list after supper, Hattie?" Hawk speared a potato and then proceeded to eat it like a candied apple.

She released a ragged sigh. The boy needed an updated etiquette lesson. "I suppose."

"Can you help me finish my arithmetic too? It's subtraction. Yuck!"

"Close your mouth while you eat." Halfway through her reprimand, Hattie realized she'd committed the same sin and gulped her mouthful.

"Aye, aye, captain." The boy saluted with his fork, pitching the tuber onto the floor. He scrambled to retrieve it.

"When you're done helping Hawk, I'd like you to take a gander at my ledger." Daddy scratched his scalp with the handle of his fork. "For some doggone reason, my figures don't line up. I've checked 'em three times."

When Jeb raised his spoon in the air, Hattie eyed him with suspicion. "My gray shirt is missing a button. Can you fix it?"

She rolled her eyes. "What about you, Wilhelm? Do you have a special request? There's a vacant half hour between eleven-thirty and midnight."

"I do."

She dropped her chin to her chest.

"Why don't you come with us tomorrow night? Lena is."

Daddy plunked both elbows onto the table and eyed his daughter.

"There's little time for dancing these days." She stabbed the bitter turnip on her plate. "I'll travel to Des Moines soon. Between now and then, there's corn picking and cleaning. My stack of mending is sky-high."

Should she stop rambling or plow forward? "I plan to cut a new pattern for a dress tomorrow night. I'm not about to present myself at the state Brigade meeting looking like a ragamuffin. I have no time for dances."

"Nor the inclination, I wager." Jeb shoved back his chair and crossed his ankles. "If you're not careful, little sister, you'll wind up an old maid."

"There are worse things. I'd read a million books."

"I'm gonna be an old maid too." Hawk licked the length of his knife.

Hattie tugged it from his hand. Everyone chuckled, especially

Jeb.

"Time will tell." Daddy finished his bite and wagged his fork toward his youngest. "And, son, they call unmarried men bachelors."

With deliberate movements, Hawk stared at each male at the table in turn. "I'll be jiggered. We're four bachelors."

Laughter spilled.

Daddy peered over his spectacles at Hattie. "I don't recall the last time you attended one of them dances in town."

"It was the night good old Delwyn Nordeen paid a call over a year ago. Ain't that right, Hattie?" Jeb considered not teasing his sister a sin. A popular topic—her dreary dating life, not that he had room to boast.

Although she'd grown accustomed to his taunts, she still bristled around the edges. Forced to choose the most horrific night of her life, she'd rank the Delwyn date second worst, Mama's death the first. She'd sown the perfect dress out of a sheeny, striped fabric of blue and gold. A lace collar and cuffs had completed the frock. She'd stroked her hair one hundred times before twisting the tresses into a stylish chignon. The final touch—a black felt hat with a tasteful purple wildflower pinned to the brim. Too bad her escort dimmed in comparison.

Lena's cousin had arrived with gravy stains on his shirt and a horse he expected Hattie to ride. In her Sunday best. Daddy had hitched the mangy animal to their cart instead. The young farmer had yapped nonstop about hogs for the entire drive. All in all, that had been the shiniest part of the evening.

"Why haven't you gone again?" Wilhelm sliced his meat with a fork. "Did he stomp on your toes?"

"Delwyn dumped me for Priscilla two minutes after arriving. The worst part of the evening occurred later. A band member, someone who'd once heard me sing at a church social, convinced me to join him on stage."

"Oh, that's right." Jeb elbowed Wilhelm. "You were up north at a funeral, I think. Tell him what happened next, Hattie."

"I already felt nauseated." She nibbled her bottom lip. The incident still conjured nightmares. "Other than church and family-type functions, it was my singing debut. My nerves raised a ruckus. I knew the tune, but the lyrics disappeared from my brain. The band started from scratch, but this time instead of freezing, I retched."

"I'm sorry," Wilhelm whispered.

Jeb laughed, slapping the table.

Daddy popped his toothpick between his lips. "Delwyn was just one rotten apple. There's still ripe ones for the picking, Button."

Perhaps she had one in Barrett. His letters had perked up over the last few editions. "I don't mean to contradict you, Daddy, but most eligible fellows have either left for boot camp or soon will."

While the men discussed upcoming departures, four locals at last count, Hattie and Hawk devoured pie.

"If everyone's done eating," Hattie rose and collected the serving platter from the table, "I'll start on the dishes. There's a busy agenda on my plate tonight." By the time she set the crockery on the sideboard, everyone had escaped to the parlor, except for Wilhelm.

"Go join the menfolk." She tried to shoo him from the kitchen with her hands, but he refused to budge, planting his feet on the rag rug.

"I'm sorry I pried. If recalling and telling your story stirred hurtful memories, that wasn't my intention."

"It's fine. I probably ought to feel shame for airing those sad stories in your presence, but I don't. You're like a third brother." Will possessed a special knack for making her feel better about herself. He reserved judgments, even when someone deserved a negative ruling.

His hazel gaze studied her until she collected a stack of dirty plates. His stare failed to stir an ounce of self-consciousness. They knew each other too well for even a fraction of discomfort.

"I have to say, I certainly don't see you as a sister."

What? She turned away, struggling to make sense of his

comment. Perhaps it stemmed from being an only child, lacking firsthand knowledge of siblings. Maybe she'd misheard his words.

Either way, she'd probably not sleep a wink. She peeked over her shoulder at one of her oldest friends. The raggedy bracelet she'd braided together out of foxtail weeds during their afternoon break still circled his wrist. He'd begged for the trinket.

"Delwyn Nordeen is a jerk. Only a fool would pick Priscilla Snodgrass over you."

A strange sensation gurgled in the pit of Hattie's stomach.

"All women deserve to feel special, particularly you, Hattie."

What in tarnation did he mean by that? Heat climbed her neck, and she fled up the staircase whispering, "He's being nice. He's being Will. He loves Lena."

CHAPTER FIVE

The morning state Brigade meeting coincided with visitor's day at Camp Dodge, which meant Arno waited in the Y.W.C.A. Hostess House for his special guest. Soldier after soldier greeted sweethearts and families amidst pumped handshakes and lingering embraces. But still no Lena.

After a quick scan of the oblong room, Arno zeroed in on Jordane. The man gnawed a fingernail and cased the door's entrance. He halfway stood as if his guest had finally burst through the entry, but then he plopped onto his chair. Did he wait for a family member or a friend?

Or Hattie?

Lena's tardiness was typical and forgivable. Even if his little sister rattled on nonstop for the entire afternoon, he'd gladly take it. How long until a furlough back to Split Falls?

He circled the crowd to reach the room's far side where coffee and spice cake, slapped with vanilla icing, waited. The blended scents drew his thoughts homeward, a regular occurrence.

He glanced at the doorway before he reached the cake. Lena, flanked by Priscilla Snodgrass and Hattie Waltz, strode into the room. Leave it to his sister to not mention two key components regarding today's call.

He shoved his hands deep into his trouser pockets as he walked toward them. Hattie wore a dress that fit her as snug as a new coat of paint. He stopped when her eyes met his. She was even prettier than at the train station.

Lena flung herself against him, clucking how she'd missed her big brother. Priscilla followed Lena's lead and nuzzled close in a familiar fashion. The woman's overpowering perfume made his eyes water.

Jordane had already herded Hattie away, the man's hand clamped to her elbow. They crossed the room where they sat and smiled at one another. Arno couldn't look away until Lena tugged him toward a quiet corner, where they snagged three chairs.

"Look at all these men." Her eyes roved like a hound dog in a smokehouse. "Personally, I'm uninterested, of course, but aren't the fellas spiffed up nicely, Priscilla? I love the dapper uniforms."

"Uh-huh." Nobody spoke to him until Priscilla said, "Is the army treating you fine?" while studying the room's occupants.

"More than fine." If he reported the mess hall only served porcupine and skunk for breakfast, dinner, and supper, the preoccupied women probably wouldn't blink.

"Good, good." Priscilla patted his sleeve. "Look at Hattie's fella. He's a dreamboat."

Arno grumbled and craned his neck for a better view. Hattie's dark head teetered too close to the Louisianan's. "Thought they were just pen pals."

"Oh, Arno." Priscilla laughed. "You've not changed a speck. You're still as naïve as ever."

He wasn't green, not even a light pear color. But Priscilla liked to toss verbal darts, aiming for vitals. She wore a skimpy dress and a sly grin, pointing at a soldier to her right, then her left. Although she carried a soft side, she hid the evidence six days a week. He bristled, crossing his arms, citing one more reason they'd canceled their courtship.

Karl arrived carrying two glasses of lemonade. "Ladies, may I entice you with a beverage and a tour of the facilities?"

"Yes, please." Priscilla hopped to her feet. "Can we see the living quarters?" She winked at Lena who laughed.

"Are you coming, Arno?" Lena raised her brows. "We've barely spoken two words, and I have loads to tell you."

"Nah. I've seen the joint. You're not shoving off for hours, go kick your heels."

Lena latched onto Karl's bicep, and the threesome swept away, giggles straggling behind.

He should have tagged along and spent every possible minute beside his sister, but Priscilla's *naïve* comment stuck in his craw. The last thing he wanted was more criticisms pointed in his direction. But why sit here? Arno shoved to his feet. *Choice of words* — Navy not army [handwritten marginal notes: "?", "Navy not army"]

Hattie sat alone between him and the door. Minus a hat, sunbeams streaked her brown hair. She gaped at her surroundings until her eyes cut to him, stopping him. He arched one eyebrow, and her lips tipped a smidge upward. That smile held enough promise to start Arno walking again. When he reached her table, he flipped a chair around to straddle it. "You're a surprise."

"I thought Lena wrote and told you we'd pay a visit after our meeting." Skepticism crinkled her straight nose.

"She mentioned *her* upcoming arrival, not yours and Priscilla's—a pleasant surprise."

Hattie nodded. "It's refreshing how you and Priscilla get on so well since ending your courtship. I think it's admirable. I truly do."

Why bother to correct her? "Where's Jordane?"

"Duty called him aside, something to do with meeting an officer of high standing. He expects to return, but who knows when?" She raised her palms upward.

Typical of Jordane to ditch a gal to wiggle his way into the brass's good graces. Hattie's open smile sent his heart tripping. If he didn't pull himself together, he'd give away all of his secrets.

Loneliness nagged even the strongest soldiers, making everyone hungry for conversation with a female, if only for an afternoon. To leave Hattie risked a random soldier snaring her. He couldn't let that happen.

"Since you and I are outdoors people, why don't we stroll the grounds until your friend returns?" Arno nodded toward the door. "I can point out the more interesting sites, such as the library."

Hattie scrambled to her feet. "You don't suppose we dare

venture inside, do you?"

"If the door's unlocked, sure."

They roamed for an hour, Arno pointing out the writing room, mess hall, base hospital, and drilling ground. She applauded with gusto when the infantry band played. In the library, she ran a finger along book spines, tugging a few volumes off the shelves to leaf through pages.

Back outside, she relayed details of her first train ride and the awe of seeing the big city of Des Moines firsthand. Her overnight stay at Priscilla's relations hadn't played out as expected. The cousin and her spouse had locked onto an argument for half the night. Hattie counted the experience an adventure, albeit a noisy one.

In a swoosh of words, she detailed the morning's Brigade meeting, emphasizing her nervous excitement and resolve to chair the Butler County committee. According to her, she'd either succeed or perish while attempting her hometown best.

Hattie gasped, halting her spiel and steps.

"What's wrong?"

"I've talked your ear off, and I'm sorry." With her fingertip, she tapped a pearl on her necklace. "Will you please tell me the million and one new things about your life since arriving at boot camp?"

Her earnest expression cranked up his pulse. Twice in one afternoon. "There's not much to tell. But answer me this—am I the world's best tour guide?"

She mirrored his stance—one hand on her waist and a tilt of her head. "First, you tell me this—who makes more outrageous statements—you or your sister?"

"It's not even a competition. Lena is borderline ridiculous, and I'm," he waved a hand in the air, searching for the perfect words, "witty."

"And vain."

"Only on Saturdays." They laughed together, continuing their tour in an easygoing companionship.

Hattie's cheeks flushed pink from either the chill or the laughter, likely both. Angled toward the sunlight, wisps of brown hair had escaped her stylish hat and now floated with the breeze. She smiled at the horizon.

His breath hitched. Mother had once dubbed Hattie a cutie pie. Back then, he'd admired her scrappiness more than anything else. But then she leapfrogged from a rough-and-tumble tomboy into a five-foot … heartstopper.

Annoyingly, the other soldiers noticed Hattie too. No matter where they'd walked, men stole glances. Some grabbed a second look, and others flung wide grins, but she appeared oblivious. Vanity wasn't part of her nature.

While she scanned the grounds, she twirled a squatty hat on her finger until the headpiece sailed into the dirt. They both bent, with Arno retrieving it first.

"Where're the flowers?" He brushed it off.

Hattie gaped at him.

"What? Did I miss a speck?"

"No, I'm surprised you noticed I tend to adorn my hat with fresh flowers."

"My guess is everybody notices. It's your calling card, same as how everybody knows Lena speaks her mind, and Priscilla bathes in perfume. Hattie Waltz wears flowers."

"I'll be jiggered."

"I know plenty about you." He raised a finger. "For one, you prefer to ride bareback and not with a saddle. Also," another finger joined the first one, "you prefer ice skating to sledding."

She picked up a maple leaf and then twirled the stem, stretching the silence. "Much to your surprise, Mr. Smarty, there's plenty you don't know about me, at least not anymore."

"I suppose you're right. But it's funny, the things a person recalls. Once upon a time, you liked to kneel in your pasture, braiding flower stems for hours. What were you, five or six?" Only Catfish Creek and a fence line separated Kreger land from Waltz property, and it felt like yesterday when he'd watched her do that.

Hattie blinked, her beautiful brown eyes almost doubled in size.

What if he kissed her? Would she run? Slap him? Or return the favor?

"Hattie." Jordane approached with a clipped tone, hooded eyes, and stern face to deliver a loud and clear message—*I'm jealous*. He dropped a possessive hand onto Hattie's shoulder, tucking her under his arm and against his side. "Thanks for looking after my gal, Kreger."

Arno fought the urge to shove Jordane's offending hand into the next county. "Your gal?" he asked.

Nobody spoke until Hattie wiggled free, distancing herself from both men by a couple of steps. Hands on her hips, she squared her shoulders. "Although I'm apt to shock the pair of you, I don't require looking after, haven't for some time now."

She'd knocked Barrett down three or four pegs with that. The girl possessed more moxie than a dozen other women combined. Satisfaction widened Arno's grin.

Still, Jordane left with the girl, steering her back toward the Y. But not before she tossed Arno a heart-thumping smile.

His stomach leaped like a feisty trout in a sleepy stream, and it took a minute to collect his wits. The couple disappeared around the corner of the post office. Twice Arno had lagged like a dimwit, watching Barrett lead Hattie away. If he had any say in the matter, there wouldn't be a third.

But why moon over the one woman whose pa hated him? Arno rubbed at his tight neck muscles. Of all the women in the world to snag his attention, why her? She was practically small enough to fit into his hip pocket or a saddle bag. He'd wager his next paycheck that Hattie was the type who dreamt of happily ever after. He, on the other hand, preferred happy-for-now. Regardless, he charged after the pair.

Janis moxie

CHAPTER SIX

Instead of paying attention to the soldier at her side, Hattie replayed her conversations with Arno in her head, especially the part centered on picking wildflowers in the pasture. He'd watched her way back when. Arno Kreger had studied her from afar.

She caught snippets of Barrett's speech. Disappointment she'd not waited for him and elation over an anticipated promotion at the next round of formal appointments. Little else.

"Someday, I'll make captain, and—" Barrett cleared his throat. Coffee lingered on his breath. "I think it's important I told you how I feel. Don't you agree?"

Hmm … should she admit her mind had tiptoed elsewhere or pretend she'd clung to his words? "Yes, we ought to share our concerns."

He flashed her two rows of straight, beautiful teeth.

She sighed, grateful she'd chosen the make-believe route.

They strolled down a wide street brimming with soldiers, guests, and conversations. A stray black kitten trotted alongside Hattie's leather pumps with shiny buckles, and she paused to pet and cuddle the bundle of fur.

"Thank you, Hattie. I was beside myself when I returned to the Y. I figured some fella had lured you away but not Arno Kreger, of all people."

What did he mean by *of all people*? After a final squeeze, she lowered the kitty onto a grassy patch.

"I wondered if you fancied him." Barrett laughed, but it wasn't a totally pleasant sound. "Kreger is the absolute last person I want chasing my girl. He's prone to fistfights, a real roughneck if I've ever seen one."

Barrett's tone rankled with a jealous thread. She hadn't seen this side of his character, the opposite of endearing. But, and it was a big but, if he spoke the truth about Arno's unruly behavior at camp—uh-oh. That meant Arno remained foolhardy and immature, two crummy qualities in a potential suitor, not that he entertained becoming her beau.

"I don't want to talk about Arno Kreger." Barrett rested his head against hers.

"Nor do I, but I believe you're jumping to conclusions. There wasn't any chasing involved." And for a good reason—Arno would have caught her lickety-split. The realization blindsided, skipping Hattie's thoughts back to her conversation with the boy from home.

"You know what I mean, sweeping you away."

Hattie fought a groan. "Arno noticed me sitting alone and asked if I wanted to see the library. You may not know this about me, but I'm partial to books."

"He knows these sorts of details?" Barrett balled his hands and parked them at his waist.

"You've forgotten he and I grew up together, and his sister is my dearest friend. We're neighbors."

Barrett looked as if he'd swigged a pint of cod liver oil. "I don't like it."

Their conversation bordered on ridiculous. Who Hattie bumped into back in Split Falls, or anywhere else, wasn't Barrett's concern. "It's not worth getting your nose out of joint."

"A minute ago, you encouraged me to share my concerns. Now, you act like it's wrong to not trust Kreger."

Why hadn't she admitted the truth when Barrett caught her daydreaming? Lies had a way of biting a person in the backside. Anyway, that's what Daddy always said.

They trekked to the Y.M.C.A. Hostess House in silence, with Hattie measuring the two men against one another. Arno, soft-spoken unless provoked, towered a foot above her and sported fair skin and hair, burly shoulders, and a pair of riveting blue eyes capable of swallowing hers in a single glance.

Barrett measured an average height and weight, with olive skin tones and raven-black hair—a winning combination. His eyes, equally captivating, held a similar draw.

The biggest difference between the two soldiers hinged on Barrett's desire for Hattie's company, at least for longer than an afternoon.

They paused while others exited the Y. "You know I'm not truly your gal, Barrett, don't you? We're yards from such an announcement."

Courtship introduced an engagement, a serious step. Hattie would never move in that direction without the hope of an eventual marriage proposal. Was it Barrett's face she pictured at her future breakfast table each morning and in her bedchamber each night? Not yet.

"I've meant to talk to you about that. I'm ready to advance to the next step, turn our friendship into courtship." His face, hopeful and eager, charmed. Still, they'd only known each other for a matter of weeks.

The Y.'s door flung wide and out ambled Priscilla painted in fresh lip stain and swinging her beaded pocketbook. "Where have you been, Hattie, sneaking off with your beau? *Tsk, tsk, tsk.* Hello, Barrett. It's lovely to see you again." Priscilla's checkered dress showcased the perfect ratio of curves to angles.

"We've met?" Barrett raised a brow to Hattie.

Deep inside, she smiled, delighted. A frosting-like grin and a flirtatious figure had failed to dent Barrett's memory. Rather than announcing the soldier wasn't her man, she entwined her fingers with his. "We went for a stroll." Satisfied she'd one-upped the woman, her grin stretched.

"How lovely." Priscilla peered over Hattie's shoulder and waved big and bold. "Arno, over here. Join us, won't you?"

Hattie unlaced her hand from Barrett's while her traitorous heart exploded against her ribcage. She gulped a deep breath and whispered silent pledges. *I deserve a two-sided relationship with someone who sees me as a woman, not a spunky kid. I deserve new adventures, and courting Barrett falls smack dab into a category labeled exciting.*

Despite her self-encouragement, jitters shortened her breath. She forced a smile toward Priscilla. "If you care to join us, Barrett and I intend to visit the refreshment table. If not, I'll locate you shortly."

Arno arrived with a self-assured stride, chest out and arms swinging.

"It's a pleasure to see you doing well at camp." Hattie's words sounded stiff and formal as if a stranger had blurted them. She willed herself to focus on Arno's shirtfront, but—same old, same old—her eyes disobeyed and zeroed in on his beaming smile.

"According to my calculations, it's your turn to mail me a proverb." Arno chipped at Hattie's newfound determination. His eyes tempted with a capital *T*, drawing her deep into his stare.

"I didn't realize you two corresponded," Priscilla raised her pitch. "Did you, Barrett, or am I the only one in the dark?"

Hattie dragged her gaze from Arno.

Priscilla tapped her toe like a ruler-wielding schoolmarm waiting for the correct answer.

"I demand an explanation," Barrett said.

Indignation rumbled in Hattie's belly, darted upward, and then tumbled from her mouth. "You won't get one, but here are three little things I will say. First, I write a boatload of soldiers, as do Priscilla, Lena, and most every other female our age. We view it as our civic duty to raise your spirits."

Barrett drew a step backward at her outburst and narrowed his eyes.

She cared little and continued her spiel. "Second, lest you forget, you and I are friends, Barrett. At this point, that's all I desire. And third," she wheeled around, pointing her finger at Arno, who wore a superior grin, "if you want a proverb, I suggest you track one down yourself."

With a flick of her head, she spun around and caught Priscilla's wink. Shoulders back, she marched into the Y., clinging to her pearls with both hands, focused on finding Lena and leaving Camp Dodge forever. She passed the refreshment table, catching a whiff of apples and cinnamon. A beautiful autumn centerpiece held court.

Lena, circled by a ring of soldiers, basked in the room's noisiest corner. After several futile attempts, Hattie finally captured her friend's eye and then pointed to the doorway. She mouthed *Let's go home*.

While Lena dawdled, Hattie fiddled with a tortoiseshell button on the front of her dress. Finally, her friend extracted herself from her admirers who begged her not to leave. "We can't go yet," Lena said, nearly breathless with twinkly eyes. "I've barely spoken to Arno, and this," she tilted her head toward the animated soldiers, "is rather fun."

"If you want to talk to your brother, do it. Don't waste your time with these fellas." Hattie motioned toward the men and rolled her eyes.

"Words hurt, lady," a soldier hollered as his friends laughed.

Hattie drew a labored breath. Why hadn't she lowered her voice? During the last few minutes, her day had slithered down a disappointing hole, one requiring more than a ladder to free herself.

A second soldier, leaning backward on the hind legs of his chair, pouted. "Say now, we have feelings too." And then he pretended to cry. Howl, really.

The lump wedged in Hattie's throat refused to budge. She'd pay a buck for someone to get her out of her current mess. She looked around but couldn't find any takers, not even Lena who'd cupped a hand over her mouth as if suppressing a fit of giggles. "I'm so, so sorry. I never meant to offend."

"Too late," a fellow, diminutive and freckly, yanked a handkerchief from his pocket to sop at artificial tears. "How you gonna make it up to us, lady?"

"Gentlemen," Lena raised her voice, "this is your lucky day. Before you stands the one and only Hattie Waltz, singer extraordinaire. An admirer once claimed her voice rivaled the songbirds—from a robin to a meadowlark."

A half-dozen enthusiastic faces grinned with encouragement.

Hattie squirmed. *No, no, no!* But the sooner she complied and gained the overblown need for forgiveness for her thoughtless words, the sooner she'd ditch the Y.'s Hostess House.

"If Hattie agrees to sing you a ditty, do you promise to let bygones be bygones and welcome my friend into your good graces?" Lena, reveling in her heyday, glowed.

A swarm of agreements followed, and then one man rose. "Miss, if you know the words to "Danny Boy," I'd be eternally indebted. Even the chorus alone would comfort my homesick Irish heart."

She'd never see these soldiers again. If she made a fool of herself, at least it wasn't in Split Falls. She clenched her trembling hands together and emptied her thoughts before tugging the touching lyrics from her memory.

> *"Oh, Danny boy, the pipes, the pipes are calling.*
> *From glen to glen, and down the mountainside.*
> *The summer's gone, and all the flowers are dying.*
> *'Tis you; 'tis you must go, and I must abide.*
> *Oh, Danny boy, oh Danny boy, I love you so."*

After a hushed silence, a swell of applause stormed. The soldiers gushed forward with praise, jostling her toward a nearby doorway. Did it lead outside the grounds? Hemmed in by the suffocating attention, she gulped for breaths. What if she fainted? Not that she ever had.

She spotted Lena tied to Arno in conversation and Priscilla alongside Barrett. With the hope nobody noticed, she ducked into the afternoon air—crisp and quiet—and sucked in the sunshine before hurrying away from the chaos.

Hours ago, the three women had agreed to meet at the facility's entrance gate if they separated during the day. With thirty minutes to spare, Hattie scurried toward the designated location, savoring the solitude. Soon, they'd collect their suitcases from Priscilla's relatives and head home.

Across the street stood rows of unpicked corn as rigid as soldiers. A low flock of geese honked overhead. Camp Dodge wasn't what she'd expected. It was clean and tidy, despite more men underfoot than she'd met in a lifetime. Plus, the rules appeared different than back home, with silent salutes and nods, even the lingo sounded foreign at times. In the library, the scent of masculinity had overpowered the familiar aroma of old books.

Hattie leaned her back against the chilly bark of an elm tree. She missed why Lena longed for adventure. But that wasn't completely true. Parts of the two-day jaunt had exceeded her expectations. Even Arno's attentiveness had turned her head, although not for long. Or did she mean not for long enough?

A squirrel scampered across a dangly branch, bobbing the overhead limb. Hattie moved to a safer tree. She slumped to the ground. How many times had she told herself to forget Arno? He'd never once proven himself worthy of her time and attention, not to mention love. And now a handsome man with a warm drawl appeared more than smitten. But a big, brawny roadblock obstructed their path to happiness.

Hattie sighed, raising her face to the sky. Barrett carried chinks in his armor too. He'd certainly displayed his shortcomings today.

Eyes closed, she repeatedly bumped the back of her head against the tree trunk but not hard enough to hurt.

Seconds later, she gasped, ramming her shoulders against the unmovable elm.

Arno squatted before her, grasping a bouquet, strangely similar to the flowers gracing the tables in the hostess house. His grin tightened her stomach muscles. "I realize they're not wildflowers, but they're the best I can do on short notice."

She inhaled the glorious posies, sweet and perfumed by God. "Thank you. They're beautiful. Did you pick them yourself?"

"I chose them for you."

She refused to smile at his thievery, but it wasn't easy. His heart-melting grin perked up her pulse. "Can you give me an honest answer?"

"I'll try my best."

"Are fisticuffs in your past or part of your present too?"

Minutes of silence blared the answer.

CHAPTER SEVEN

"Forward, march," boomed a drill sergeant.

Arno, along with the rest of Company E, advanced toward the rifle range, a lengthy jaunt from the barracks. A flock of ducks quacked their farewells overhead. The temptation to point his gun at the unsuspecting fowl nagged, conjuring visions of a roasted duck dinner with all the trimmings.

Low-flung clouds delivered a chill. It was anything but a typical autumn day. He wasn't in the field picking corn or squirrel hunting in the timber. He was surrounded by acquaintances and strangers, except for Karl, and miles and miles from the comforts of home.

Camp life had fallen into a predictable pattern of endless drilling. He'd only missed one target during rifle practice, meaning the odds of securing a spot on the sharpshooter squad had spiked over the last few weeks. With any luck, he'd snare a position after today's showing. Would that finally impress Father? Maybe.

Unlike some of the other soldiers, Arno had wielded a gun for years. The first time Father propped a small-gauge shotgun, minus the ammunition, into Arno's hands coincided with day one of grammar school. In time, they'd hunted together, tracking everything from foxes to bucks, honing their art with each shot. At least, they had before Oliver's death.

At the rifle range, Arno stood three men deep behind CW Hyland. The soldier still whispered "German-lover" whenever their paths crossed and nobody else stood within earshot. Arno suspected the bigot would continue the trend, an excellent reason to avoid the man.

He studied the competition at the one-hundred-yard mark.

The first soldier missed two targets, the second man three, and then CW nailed all five shots like a deadeye. His gun spoke again at the two-hundred and five-hundred targets, reverberating across the grassy acre.

"Beat that." CW strutted past, shooting bullets from his eyes instead of his rifle. A boastful grin accompanied the arrogant remark.

Arno ignored him and pictured drilling the bullseye. When his turn arrived, he clicked the trigger and fired, nailing the mark each time until his final attempt when someone sneezed. The bullet careened haywire.

"You choked." CW's voice, hushed and deadly, pierced when Arno filed past to reach the end of the line for another attempt.

The rain started as a whisper, pitter-pattering on his campaign hat, with the wide brim sheltering his face. Soon, a downpour pelted the ground, stirring up a fresh, earthy fragrance.

Without sparing CW a second glance, Arno stewed in silence, more due to his failed marksmanship than the man's taunt. Still, *you choked* defined his performance. If a mere sneeze interrupted his concentration, how would he manage a hundred whizzing bullets on the battlefield?

Later that afternoon, on the tail end of a half-day leave, Arno and Karl occupied a corner booth at a Des Moines diner on Dodge's outskirts. The day's specials featured a draft, scant leg room, and high-backed seats. Grease and freshly ground coffee blended with smoke and onions to clutter the air. A cloudy sky hovered beyond a smudged window.

The joint crawled with soldiers. Karl stabbed a bite of his second piece of pie with a bent fork. His idea of a three-course meal was apple pie, cherry pie, and coconut cream, heavy on the filling. "Is Hattie Waltz courting Barrett Jordane?"

Arno choked on his sip of coffee and knocked over his cup,

leaving a mess on his uniform and across the tabletop. The two sopped the brown liquid stream until their napkins dripped.

"Best wash your shirt before the next inspection." Karl cupped a hand around his ear. "What do I hear?" He stared into the distance over Arno's shoulder as if listening for a voice. "Yep, it's the sergeant, chewing you out again."

A waitress paused by their table, sporting a lopsided uniform cap and dark shadows under her eyes. A portion of the day's menu clung to her apron. "Besides more napkins, what else can I get you, boys?" She flashed a sassy smile while tugging a couple of cloths from her apron pocket.

Karl wriggled his eyebrows. "What are my choices?"

From nearby, a brusque voice grumbled like a thunderstorm. "What's a man gotta do for service around this joint?"

The waitress ignored the bark and reached for a squatty menu stationed between the wall and a vase of shriveled flowers. "If you want choices, I suggest you read this."

Karl drummed fingers against his chin. "How about warming my coffee, unless you'd rather warm me?"

"Not tonight, soldier. I've got bigger fish to fry." She splashed thick coffee into their cups before plodding toward her next customer.

Arno held his laughter. "I think she implied you're a minnow."

"It's called the art of flirtation," Karl said around a mouthful of pie. "I was practicing, sharpening my skills."

"How flattering."

"Shut up."

Arno raised his hands in surrender.

"Hattie ever write you back?"

"Not yet."

"It's been weeks."

"Why don't you skip to your point." Until a couple of days ago, Arno had expected to hear from Hattie. Then he'd overheard Jordane tell someone she still wrote him twice a week. Since then, his hope had dried up and peeled away.

Karl spread his new napkin on the tabletop, folded it in half, then quarters, until it failed to obey his design and flopped open. "She's a looker, ain't she? And that voice of hers. Mercy."

During Hattie's visit to boot camp, he'd have bet the last dollar in his pocket she fancied him. Obviously, he didn't know her after all.

"Jordane carries her photograph around, shows it to purt near everyone," Karl said.

"Good for him."

"What about his recent promotion?"

"He earned it." Arno disliked Jordane more with each passing day. Why had Hattie chosen the Louisianan over him? Was he envious of Jordane's military advancement? Without question, but not the soldier's method of achieving success.

"Meaning he's a bootlicker?"

Arno's acquaintanceship with Jordane amounted to diddly squat, but he knew a back-scratcher when he saw one. Jordane had once squealed when a fellow soldier broke curfew. More than once, the man had trailed after the upper brass like a mangy mutt, and he'd overheard Jordane say, *I'll do whatever it takes to get ahead.*

Hattie deserved better, same as the army.

"He and Hyland are pals now." Karl shoved his cup aside. "You won't believe what I heard this morning."

On any given day, a hundred rumors whirled throughout camp, everything from the night's film title to who caught the dickens for insubordination. Giant-sized holes riddled most tales, yet a slim few held kernels of truth.

Arno shrugged.

"I met this new arrival from Burlington. Nice guy. He knows Hyland from back home."

"Lucky him." Arno tapped his spoon on the rim of his cup.

"Nope. This fella told me Hyland once spent a lengthy stint in the hoosegow."

"For what?" The possibilities were endless.

"Assault."

Arno set down the spoon. That night Hyland had boasted about beating the neighbor man, the one who'd paid an inopportune call, had that led to his arrest?

"Two nights ago, he flipped over a table at the Y. and threatened a soldier with a broken bottle."

"You saw it?" Although Karl tended to exaggerate, especially with a dull story, Arno leaned toward believing his buddy this time.

"I did. CW raised the fuss. He'd lost a chunk of money at cards. I do that all the time—lose money, not threaten people. Someone should have hauled him out by his ear if you ask me."

Arno dug into his pocket, tossed a few coins onto the table. "Let's beat it back to camp. I need to study for our next exam. I'm on KP duty tonight."

"You used to be a barrel of laughs, Kreger. What happened?"

Arno retrieved his hat before turning toward the narrow aisle, nearly slamming into CW's chest.

"Why was you two dragging my name through the dirt?" CW swayed as he blinked blurry eyes at Arno. Alcohol clung to the man's breath, something stronger than rhubarb wine. "I heard you. Sound like a pair of hoity-toity church ladies."

"Why don't you tell us about your jail time then," Karl said, curling his fingers into fists. "Give it to us straight from the horse's mouth."

"Is that what you want, me to give it to you?" CW braced one hand on the back of a chair and then inched his chunky face closer to Karl's. "You picking a fight with me, little man?"

Although Karl barely reached Arno and CW's shoulders, that hadn't ever stopped him from swinging a fist at an insult. Arno shoved Karl back. "He's not worth the trouble."

"And you, Kreger, you can't shoot worth naught. You're not as smart as you think you is neither." CW bumped his hip against the table and teetered.

Arno drew in a calming breath before facing his foe. "Did we lie, Clyde?"

CW cursed, dropping into Karl's vacated chair. "Don't call me that." The soldier hiccupped and then propped an elbow on the tabletop before cradling his head in his hand. His eyes closed.

"Let's get out of here." Arno led Karl toward the exit.

"Wait, mister," a female hollered.

Arno and Karl turned. Hyland charged after them.

"You've not yet settled your bill, fella, and you're not leaving until you do." The waitress raised her voice loud enough to turn a roomful of heads and then parked herself in front of CW, blocking his path.

"What a nincompoop," Karl said, shaking his head on the way out the door.

Before camp, Arno had set a goal to avoid fistfights no matter the circumstance, but with Hyland and Jordane stoking his ire most days, how long until fists flew?

Back at the barracks, Arno shuffled toward his cot. On the middle of his bed sat an envelope. The return address belonged to Hattie Waltz. Pulse racing, he tore it open.

November 6, 1917

Dear Arno,

Ever since we last spoke, I've thought about our parting words. You claim you've changed, and I asked you to prove it. Words are flimsy but actions strong. Ten days have passed since I visited Camp Dodge, and I've received zero correspondence from you. In my estimation, that's no action.

Something else about our last conversation also troubles me. Twice now, you've mentioned how well you know me. Other than talks at the train station and boot camp, we've not spoken in two years. We truly knew each other once, but that doesn't mean we know each other anymore.

Although it's probably foolish to dredge old news, I had a crush on you for years based on a kindness you showed me back in grammar school. Then, on my sixteenth birthday, we almost kissed. Deny the claim all you want, we both know it's true.

Instead of that almost-a-kiss spurring me toward a deeper infatuation, it opened my eyes. I'm not that love-struck little girl any longer, and you're not that sweet boy who stole my heart. We've changed.

To prove my point, here are three little things I wager you don't know about me.

I consider my singing ability a gift I don't deserve or appreciate. Although it's a pleasure to excel at something, I sometimes feel like a puppet on a string. To sing in public scares me to death. It's disappointing to feel so ungrateful, but it's the truth.

Although Mama died during childbirth, I want a houseful of children one day but not necessarily tomorrow.

I'm not courting Barrett. One day, I may, but for now, we're merely acquainting ourselves.

I'm unsure why I feel obliged to share three little things, but I do. I've prattled on for far too long, and it's time to wrangle Hawk into bed.

As always,
Hattie

P.S. Here's a proverb to ponder: "Even a child is known by his doings, whether his work be pure and whether it be right."

Arno stared at a page teeming with words he thought he'd never read from a woman he truly didn't know. Not yet.

CHAPTER EIGHT

Hattie snuggled in the middle of her fluffy bed, a quilt tucked between her chest and chin. Her toes tingled from the cold. Arno's unopened letter rested on her nightstand atop a stack of novels.

Jeb had dumped the mail on the kitchen table in the early afternoon, snatched a handful of oatmeal raisin cookies, and then left to tinker on the Buick's motor. After rolling out a pan of biscuits, Hattie'd divvied the mail into piles—rubbish, personal, and business. When her fingers brushed Arno's ivory envelope, she froze.

The postmark read Little Rock, Arkansas, but Lena had already recited that detail a day prior. Although tempted to rip it open, she buried the precious letter under her bed pillow for a private read later.

Preoccupied with the waiting epistle, she'd carried out one chore after the next in a distracted state—dusting the mantel with her skirt hem and pouring sugar instead of flour into her biscuit bowl. When dusk dropped, she plated the pot roast, rushed supper, scrubbed the dishes, and hurried Hawk's bath before the iron cook stove. Then she excused herself for a night of reading upstairs, failing to mention the nature of her reading material.

After a king-sized gulp, she picked it up and drew a letter opener underneath the flap.

November 20, 1917

Dear Hattie,
No doubt you noticed the Arkansas postmark, but that's probably old news, knowing Lena. We passed through a dozen

or so nothing towns along the route. The minute you blink, they disappear. Plenty of folks turned out to greet us between home and camp.

Most of the soldiers here hail from Ohio, Alabama, and, naturally, Arkansas. Overall, we hitch together well but found ourselves in an awful chewing match yesterday at dinner over which is the best state. Based on noise levels, I'd say it's us. Everyone claims life at Pike is a chore, but we're hardy stock, and I'm guessing we'll survive.

Your letter surprised me. You'd left the impression you'd never write. When I told you my trouble-seeking days remain in the past, you doubted it. The way I see it, it'll take time to determine which of us is correct.

You've always struck me as brave. After reading your three personal disclosures, I see that hasn't changed. Without question, your voice is a gift. Don't feel guilty for not wishing to perform on cue. That sounds downright annoying.

Encouraged by your lead, here are three little things you don't know about me:

Ever since Oliver died, I don't think I'd make a good father.

One of my favorite memories is singing with him, especially with Pa on the fiddle.

The news you and Barrett aren't an item, at least not yet, fills me with hope. I'm uncertain what I'm hoping for when it comes to you and me. What do you want? Did you note how I didn't presume to know the answer?

Time to peel spuds, so goodbye for now.

As always,
Arno

P.S. The following proverb reminds me of you. "Train up a child in the way he should go: and when he is old, he will not depart from it." I'm not calling you old. I'm calling you wise enough to chair the Brigade.

With a wide-open grin, she tossed her blanket over her head, savoring Arno's thoughtful words, sinking into the warmth of her covers. But then she remembered another important tidbit from the letter—the part dealing with fatherhood.

Before she could reread the letter, her bedroom door banged open, minus a knock or a *may I enter?*

Hattie yanked the blankets from her face to expose Jeb's lazy grin. "What do you think you're doing? Don't you know it's common courtesy to announce yourself before charging into a female's bedchamber?"

"And don't you know it's polite to sit with your family after supper?"

"Oh, bother." The sooner she determined his motive, the sooner she'd return to Arno's epistle. "Did you want something?"

He flopped onto the foot of her four-poster bed, smelling all woodsy like an evergreen forest. "Did you enjoy Arno's letter?"

The siblings stared at one another until Hattie cringed, remembering who'd collected the mail, at least it hadn't been Daddy. "It's private and personal."

"Tell me more."

"And it's nobody's business other than my own." A branch scratched the windowpane, delivering an unsettling chill up Hattie's spine.

"Uh-huh." Jeb's nods arrived one after the next. "Keep talking because everything you've said is tantamount to a hill of beans."

"Tantamount," Hattie said under her breath while shoving against her brother's bulk with both hands. "Go read your dictionary. I thought you had a date with Priscilla tonight? Or was it with Sadie Parker?"

He grunted. "Sadie won't give me the time of day. Plus, she's back with Karl Harms. Funny thing with Priscilla—she caught an awful bug and canceled on me last minute."

A sucker for the prettiest gals, they never loved Jeb back. An unexpected thought slammed against Hattie's brain, or perhaps her heart, the similarity between her romantic history and her brother's. Stricken by the comparison, she shuddered.

"You know, I don't see you and Priscilla as a match made in heaven." On this particular topic, talking to the floorboards beat staring at Jeb's scruffy face. "Although you're ornerier than sin sometimes, you deserve a kind woman, not a barracuda."

With one hand on his gut, Jeb laughed, rolling onto his side. "Next time my path crosses Priscilla's, I'll be sure and mention your little nickname."

"Please don't, she's my friend." Hattie slouched, weary of finding fault in others.

"I've thought loads worse of people, but let's get back to you and Kreger. You-know-who won't approve."

For the love of Pete, why couldn't Jeb drop the topic? "It's Hawk's bedtime."

"Fine, we can finish this conversation at breakfast."

"Don't you dare mention Arno's name in front of Daddy." She snapped to her feet.

Jeb sat upright, squeaking the coiled bedsprings. "If a tasty meal kept my mouth busy, I might remain silent."

"I'll make you flapjacks."

"You can do better than that." He ran a hand over his stomach.

"And fried eggs."

"What else?"

How much work was his silence going to cost her? "Flapjacks with walnuts dripping in warmed syrup, fried eggs and potatoes, bacon, bluegill, and that's it. Did you know blackmail is illegal in Iowa?"

"It's still effective."

"You're gonna work me to the bone."

With his fist clenched, Jeb drew his hand against his breastbone. "That's the price you pay for love."

"Get out." She shouted the two words in a less-than-ladylike manner.

⌒∽⌒

The next night, Hattie hosted her first county Brigade meeting in the comfort of her parlor. After a day of dusting and polishing, she welcomed twelve women now roosted on the room's worn furniture, including a piano bench and four kitchen chairs. A toasty fire sizzled in the hearth, holding drafts at bay.

With the coffee poured and cherry pie served, Hattie dried her slick palms on a napkin and stood. Should she open with a speech, a thank you, or jump straight into the agenda and pray she didn't fall face first at everyone's feet?

"Hello."

A chorus of voices repeated her greeting. Within five minutes, a lively discussion ballooned, touching on the critical need to raise more funds for the soldiers, a point driven home at the state meeting.

"What if we held a knitting bee?" Meridee asked, sweeping crumbs from her ivory bodice to the floor.

A dozen remarks followed, all in favor of the potential fundraising event.

"I know," Lena rose, gesturing with her hands, "we'll charge an entry fee of fifty cents and offer prizes for the best scarves, socks, and hats."

Priscilla tossed in her suggestions. "We'll need to find unbiased judges and perhaps hold the event over two or three days." She clapped. "We'll offer speed rounds. I don't care to brag, but I am the world's fastest knitter."

And the messiest. Hattie bridled her tongue.

"It's a lovely idea for spring, but let's also plan a more elaborate function for summer or fall," Meridee added. "Let's not be hasty. What are your fundraising ideas, Hattie?"

"My ideas?" She looped her necklace around her finger.

❧ 65 ❧

"There's, umm … I'd rather hear everyone else's suggestions first." A headache hammered. Nobody had warned her to prepare proposals.

"Tell us more about your plans for the event next summer, Meridee," Lena spoke with her hand in front of her mouth to hide her chewing.

"This is off the top of my head, but perhaps a weekend celebration with a list of entertainers, speeches from dignitaries, that sort of thing." A handful of ladies nodded.

"And it can coincide with the opening of the new veterans' wing at the hospital." Priscilla's mother, a more refined version of her daughter, sipped tea from a pink-rimmed cup. The silver buttons on her smart suit jacket matched the color of her stylish hair. "I hear it's to open late summer, if not before."

Fresh suggestions collided, shooting from every direction. Hattie slumped in her seat, while dread crawled like a prowling spider. The room hummed with outlandish plans such as inviting the President of the United States or, as a runner-up candidate, the First Lady. It all sounded fine and dandy, but not from the vantage point of chairlady, the one responsible for the shindig's success or morale-splitting failure.

Meridee toyed with her colorful brooch. "Let's not forget Hattie is in charge. Go ahead, dear, tell us your plan, don't leave out the details."

On the edge of her chair and nerves, Hattie's leg bounced until she pressed against the riotous limb with both hands. She had a sneaky suspicion if she failed to suggest a proper proposal, someone, probably Priscilla, would chuck her into a snow bank.

"Thank you for asking." She cleared her throat. "What are your thoughts on a … a tea party, where people bid on auction items we each donate." Hattie grinned, relieved to recommend one spur-of-the-moment idea.

"They've held similar events in Waterloo, all a bust." Priscilla covered a yawn with her arm. "From what I hear, the Blackhawk

Brigade barely broke even. Let's hear your other suggestions, your best suggestions."

She squirmed. What else? What else? "How about a cakewalk?"

"In my experience, they're not worth the trouble," Meridee said. "We'd probably clear five, ten bucks tops. We didn't mean to put you on the spot tonight, Hattie, so why don't you think about the possibilities and ready a list for next month's meeting?"

Hawk was flailing both arms above his head from the kitchen doorway. Hattie excused herself, delighted for an excuse to flee the parlor. "What do you think you're doing?" She shoved her brother deeper into the room, next to the cook stove.

"Daddy wants to go upstairs, but he's afraid the widow will catch him when he sneaks past."

"Good grief. Where is he now?"

"On the porch."

Hattie marched through the kitchen, which still reeked of burnt potatoes, and then flung open the frosty door. A frigid draft scurried inside but not her pa. He hunched on the stoop, blowing warm breaths on his cupped hands.

"It's freezing out here." A draft shot up her skirt.

"That's why I'm hankering to come inside."

"You're acting ridiculous and gonna catch a death of a cold."

Daddy cowered on the stoop like a naughty puppy. "But—

"Hattie, we're waiting on you." Meridee's voice and steps drew near.

Daddy plastered his back against the wall next to the door. Was that fear in his eyes?

Meridee slung the door wide before sticking her nose into the sub-zero air. "Are you hiding from me, Chester?" The big-boned female towered, waiting with the patience of a rainbow, prepared to hang on for the storm's aftermath.

Daddy hemmed and hawed.

Unwilling to stay and watch, Hattie returned to the meeting. She approved two future events, organized subcommittees to oversee details, and retained veto power for every critical decision. With Lena at her side, she'd muddle through the specifics and, hopefully, make money in the process. If not, she'd never again enter polite society and die a hermit's death.

Within minutes, the guests wiggled into their overcoats and hurried to depart before daylight waned. Jeb offered Priscilla and her mother a lift since Meridee, their ride home, announced her plans to delay her departure. While Jeb readied the sleigh, the women lingered near the parlor window.

"I'm glad I'm not in your shoes, Miss Chairlady." Priscilla made a show of tugging on her imported kid gloves.

Hattie collected dirty china scattered around the room, nesting the hand-painted teacups together. "Hard work never hurt anyone." When had she turned into a sage old grandmother? Or Daddy, for that matter?

"True, but if you mess this up ..." Priscilla ran a finger across her pale throat from left to right, a gesture favored by Hawk and every other eight-year-old boy.

"Goodness, you're theatrical." Priscilla's mother wrung her hands, her favorite fidget. "Hattie, don't fret. You'll be more than fine."

Jeb clomped into the room, dripping snow onto the floorboards while the Snodgrass women tossed out farewells. Before following them out the door, he winked at his sister. "See you later, barracuda." His eyes grew wide. "Now, I've put you in a conundrum."

Over and over, Hattie bumped her forehead against the upright piano. Would Jeb tell Priscilla about the unflattering nickname, or did he merely want Hattie to think he'd stoop to that level?

"I hate to point out the obvious," Lena said, "but your brother is one odd duck. Barracuda?"

"Never mind. It's a long, tedious tale."

"I think Priscilla ought to consider joining vaudeville. They pay excellent money for her brand of theatrics." Lena grinned, reaching for another slice of pie from a platter resting on the ottoman.

"Of course, I won't die if I flub these Brigade duties, but I'm pretty sure little pieces of me will wilt. And who are we kidding? I'll never dream up worthy ideas, the type to raise buckets of money for the soldiers."

"Now who's melodramatic?"

Over-the-top laughter spilled from the kitchen. At first, it only belonged to the widow, but then Daddy joined in. Hattie and Lena shot looks at one another.

Hawk skipped into the room and then paused before the hearth to warm his hands and his backside.

"What's so funny?" Hattie motioned toward the kitchen.

"Widow Moss asked Daddy when he's likely to drop by for supper, and then Daddy said *when you-know-what freezes over*."

Hattie gasped. "He did not say that."

"Word for word. Then, after nobody said nothing for several seconds, the widow goes, *Then I'll expect you Thursday, Friday at the latest*. That's when they busted out laughing."

With a drawn-out sigh, Hattie plopped onto the sofa, almost squashing the cat.

CHAPTER NINE

"Is that a sock under your bed, Private Kreger?" The sergeant, whip-thin and homely as a cow pie, crammed his face next to Arno's on a bleak, sunless morning during inspection. The man's breath reeked of black licorice.

"I'm not sure, sir." Arno stood statue-like, except for the rise and fall of his chest.

"Check again, soldier."

On his hands and knees, Arno retrieved the errant footwear and snapped back into position. He stared straight ahead at the far wall, the sock in his fist.

"Is it yours?"

"I don't believe so, sir."

"Who put it there? God?"

"He's good with miracles, sir." Arno knew better than to rankle the officer, yet that insight failed to stop him.

Someone chuckled.

"If I'm not mistaken, you consider Kreger a comic," the sergeant said matter-of-factly. "Good for you, Private Iverson. Enjoy the double calisthenics with Kreger."

Arno groaned silently. Two days straight of double jumping-jacks, push-ups, and sit-ups had whittled into his letter-writing time. Since Hattie's first letter, she'd continued to write twice a week. He owed her a letter and, come plagues or poison, aimed to complete the task before lights out. But first, he needed to end the sock game.

Arno had checked and then double-checked before this morning's inspection—nothing. Either the sergeant had planted the garment when he bent to eyeball the floor, or someone else had dropped the goods. <u>Probably Hyland</u>, but how? He knew why—the man hated him.

<u>Father's advice to not kindle trouble</u> and serve as an exemplary soldier haunted Arno most days. In only a matter of months, he'd already failed his old man, same as always. Although his pa hadn't ever lent voice to the words, <u>everyone knew he blamed his eldest for his youngest son's demise.</u>

Sad! *·*

The sergeant cleared his throat. "I better not find anything under your bed a third time, Private Kreger. Do you catch my meaning?"

"Loud and clear, sir." Arno would end the footwear charade one way or another.

❦

Thick clouds pitched the warm December night into inky darkness. The moon broke through now and again. Although a busy wind muffled most sounds, <u>the footsteps of a buck rustled beneath the tree where Arno waited.</u>

The patch of woods resembled back home, a place he'd spent long hours fishing and hunting. How many times had he, Karl, and Oliver fought with stick rifles until Mother clanged the dinner bell and they'd tossed aside their homespun weapons for knives and forks?

Arno listened for another crunch. Two soldiers, one slim and the other hulking, drew near—trench guards. He inched down the branch, careful not to snap the limb.

"If you ask me, this amounts to nothing more than hide and seek, and I don't play young'uns games," the first man said. "That is unless I'm calling the shots."

Hyland, the fool, lit a cigarette, announcing his whereabouts and making this training exercise that much easier for Arno.

"Except nobody's seeking." That was Ted Killion, one of Hyland's sidekicks. "I'm bored with this child's play. If they plan to attack, what's taking so long?"

"They're a bunch of chicken livers. You see the men pegged to play the enemy? Not one in the bunch I care to soldier alongside, especially Kreger."

Killion laughed at the jab. "Reckon he's figured out how a sock sneaks under his cot before inspections?"

"*Hoo hoo hoooooo!*" The predetermined owl signal, eerie and convincing, sounded from nearby.

Killion crouched, drawing his rifle to his shoulder before swinging the firearm right, then left. "You hear that?"

"Be deaf not to. It's either a hoot owl or a dang good copycat."

"Let's go." The twosome retreated at a fast pace.

Arno dropped silently from the tree and tracked the men. The captain's firm order was to remain hidden until a stone's throw from the trench. Killion peered over his shoulder, and Arno ducked deeper into the shadows.

"*Hoo hoo hoooooo!*" sounded closer. Time to storm the trench.

Arno crept forward until he rammed his rifle barrel between Killion's shoulder blades. "Move, and I'll shoot. You're my prisoners."

When CW dipped a shoulder to turn around, Arno smacked the blunt end of his rifle into the man's fleshy backside. "Got a hearing problem?"

Captain McKenzie's voice sliced the night's stillness. "Looks like easy pickings, Kreger." The man's reputation as fair and just had earned the captain favor around camp.

Arno continued to jam his rifle tip into Hyland's uniform. "Yes, sir. What should I do with the pair?"

"Run them into the trench. We'll see how the rest of the fellas fared."

Arno marched his prisoners into the opponent's headquarters at rifle point. The clouds parted, and stars shone through.

With everyone accounted for, the captain paced, hands clenched behind his back. The opposing side had failed to capture a single member of Arno's sharpshooter squad. McKenzie paused before Hyland and Killion. "What do you two numbskulls have to say for yourselves?"

"We came up short today, sir." Killion's voice wasn't much more than a whisper.

"And you?" The captain redirected his stare to Hyland.

"Kreger cheated, sir."

"How so?"

Hyland licked his fat lips. "Not sure how, sir, but I wager the German-lover cheated one way or another."

Before the captain replied, Karl stepped forward. "Permission to speak, sir."

"If it's relevant."

"Killion knows a thing or two about cheating, 'cause he hides socks under Kreger's bed before inspections. Seems to me, the big difference is Arno caught his prisoners fair and square. Killion does his deed in a more underhanded, sneaky manner."

His buddy's unflinching support tightened Arno's chest.

"Nobody asked you." CW's words and glare were sharper than strong cheese.

"Does Private Ludwig speak the truth, Private Killion?" Captain McKenzie cocked his head.

"Yes, sir."

The captain paused, nodded, and then dismissed the winning team back to their camp. The other soldiers offered Arno a mix of good-natured ribbing and compliments before each man climbed into a two-person pup tent. Instead of sleeping, Arno replayed the night's events in his mind.

How long until a new method of torment arrived from the conspiring duo, Killion and Hyland? It was anyone's guess. But he knew one thing for certain, whatever the pair plotted, he'd take the punishment like a man—like a soldier.

Cold stiffened the grass by morning. Arno and the others lounged around a campfire for a breakfast of hardtack. They'd earned a peaceful reprieve. Without orders for a specific time to return boots to camp, everyone soaked in the day's lazy sunshine and temporary freedom.

Arno tugged Hattie's latest letter from his pack and meandered to the edge of a rocky brook. The swift current gulped, and he swept the bank for a skipping stone without success. A dry, flat rock served as a chair to reread Hattie's latest letter.

November 28, 1917

Dear Arno,

Thank you for the reassuring proverb. Before chairing my first Brigade meeting, I repeated it a couple of times. It helped calm my nerves. Overall, the assembly went well, and now we're busy knitting mountains of socks, scarves, and sweaters. We intend to hold two to three larger events next year, all with a goal to raise a bushel of money for the soldiers. If you think I'm equally apprehensive and excited about my duties, you're right on the nose.

Out of the blue, the pastor stopped by for supper last night. I feel sorry for the bachelor, and I'm unsure if he's more lonely or hungry. I'd fix him up with Meridee Moss, but I do believe Daddy is softening toward the woman.

My favorite part of our letter exchange is the three little things. On that note, here's a few more.

Barrett now knows you and I exchange letters, and he threw a minor conniption fit. For the past five days, I've received two letters per day from the man. I'm curious if he's said anything to you about this. According to his last note, he's working to arrange a furlough to visit me.

Like you, one of my favorite memories includes Oliver. He and I sang together in Sunday school class, always at the top of our lungs. Naturally, the teacher ordered us outside to hush and repent. One time, you strolled past and asked why we sat in the rain. Then you led us in a spirited rendition of "Row, Row, Row Your Boat." Do you remember? Soaked to the bone, we howled until our parents ended our fun.

Daddy dislikes the idea of you and me corresponding, which complicates everything. I'm not inclined to go behind his back, not to mention the bigger no-no—a commandment addressing fathers and honor. However, if you've truly changed—quit your unruly ways—why won't he offer you a second chance?

I'm unsure how furloughs work. Are they scheduled for a precise time, or do they arrive willy-nilly? More importantly, is there a chance you'll receive one soon? In case you're wondering, I hope so.

As always,
Hattie

Arno scooped a handful of rocks and dirt from the bank before hurling his fistful toward the creek. If Jordane had truly weaseled a furlough back to Iowa, Arno intended to as well. Since he'd never before missed a Christmas, why start now?

He returned to the tent and gathered his belongings for the three-mile hike to Pike. Frankie Jesberger puffed on an old harmonica. A few sang ditties, others hummed along. A bluebird twittered in tune. The easy pace and camaraderie added a welcomed spring to Arno's steps.

Outside their quarters, Karl greeted the returnees with a broad grin. "Aren't you a merry band?"

"When'd you and your teammates get back?" Frankie asked, readjusting the supply load he toted.

"Hours ago, you slackers."

Arno laughed. Most shuffled off to store the tent equipment or disappear into the barracks. Only Karl and Arno remained outside.

"How long have you known about Killion?" Arno asked.

"I caught him red-handed … him and Hyland. They whispered about their little trick last night. Idiots."

"Yep."

"Killion received orders to report to the captain when we arrived back at camp." Karl lowered his voice. "You ought to have seen his face." With a forlorn expression—saggy eyes, mouth, and shoulders—he imitated the man's look.

"Not surprised." Arno flung open his barrack's door, holding it wide for Karl to enter.

"What do you figure he's catching Hades for—being captured by the enemy or badgering you during inspections? Either way, you're to blame."

The two clomped up the stairs, raising a racket on the wooden steps. "I'd say he deserves whatever the captain dishes out."

When Arno passed CW's bunk, the man sprung to his feet and then shadowed him down the corridor. "I got a bone to pick with you two."

The room grew quiet as a country road, with several soldiers turning their attention toward the shouting.

Tired of the man's lip, Arno whipped around and bumped his chest against CW's. "Pick away."

He had one split second to regret opening his mouth before he ducked, avoiding a right cross.

CHAPTER TEN

December 13, 1917, Split Falls

Bundled from head to foot, Hattie traipsed to the mailbox through a foot of snow. Powdery drifts slowed her steps. Between the woolen scarf wrapped around her face and a downy cap riding low, only her eyes met with winter's icy sting.

The wind howled like a pair of coyotes signaling one another. The first cried long and loud, and the other whispered soft wails. A whiff of manure from the stockyard clashed with the landscape's pristine beauty.

They'd not received mail in days. Nonetheless, only two envelopes waited in the box, both originating from Little Rock.

Back inside, she filled a cup with steamy tea and sat in her sewing chair. Its hand-embroidered cushion had flattened over the years. Frayed threads interrupted the floral design. Still, it served its purpose. Betty Lou nuzzled onto her lap, purring low and loud. The scent of fresh yeasty bread circled the cozy room.

She turned over the envelopes. Arno's penmanship bordered on illegible while Barrett's was award-worthy. The two men, different as yes and no, expected two dissimilar things. Barrett desired courtship and Arno …

What Arno wanted from her was anyone's guess.

December 7, 1917

Dearest Hattie,

I hope you're fine with me calling you dearest because that's what you've become, the most precious person in my life. It's your face I picture every evening before bed. Your photograph is smudged and tattered. I fall asleep with it under my pillow every night.

Hattie gripped Mama's old pearls. Tears stung. If Barrett uttered the truth, and she leaned toward believing him, his tender words opened her heart wider. Not since Mama had anyone delivered such a touching tribute on her behalf. Daddy and the boys loved her, but Barrett's sentiments filled an unnamed void.

Before returning to his letter, she stole a glance at Arno's envelope poised on the windowsill, waiting for a fair shake.

I continue to work hard around camp, wanting to prove myself and earn the higher officers' respect. Now that I'm a corporal, I'm rubbing shoulders with Captain McKenzie more. I hope to one day match his temperament, conduct, and respect from all circles.

Arno Kreger continues to drum up trouble for himself with fisticuffs and such behavior. I hope he's not turning your head.

She fanned her face with the stationery. It wasn't true, was it?

I've earned a Christmas furlough. If all goes as planned, I'll be on the December twenty-third train set to arrive in Split Falls at noon. I'll make lodging arrangements at the hotel in town. My parents moved back to Louisiana. Iowa is too cold for their blood.

Although I'm sure you're busy with the holidays, I sincerely hope you'll carve out some time for me. I'd love for you to meet me at the train station. I don't expect to horn in on your family's functions. Of course, I won't refuse any offers.

Previously, you rejected the idea of courting. Any chance you've reconsidered? As much as I want to know your answer, don't respond by letter—save your reply until we're face to face. A yes sounds sweeter in person.

Soon, I'll ask you the most important question of your life.
In the meantime, ready yourself!

Fondly,
Barrett

Emotions tangled into a hundred different knots. Ill-equipped to unjumble even the simplest ones, Hattie stewed over the more personal nature of Barrett's letter. Over time, his epistles had improved, with a smidge less attention focused solely on himself. No doubt, his army world ranked more exciting than her run-of-the-mill life, but he rarely inquired about her opinions or day-to-day happenings.

With each rock of the creaky chair, Hattie grew more and more convinced the key to gauging her compatibility with Barrett hinged on side-by-side time. And Christmas, brimming with holiday parties and cozy hearthside conversations, offered the perfect setting to either weed out nonsense or plant a foundation. She'd be able to determine if Barrett possessed lifelong potential or failed to reach that high mark.

One-sided relationships never prospered. Hattie's firsthand knowledge ranked her an expert on the topic. Betty Lou stretched, hopped to the floor, and abandoned the kitchen. On the edge of her chair, Hattie drew a settling breath before opening letter number two.

December 7, 1917

Dear Hattie,

How's the weather in Iowa? Winter blew into Camp Pike with a sleet storm. Thanks for the socks you knitted. Overall, it's warmer in Arkansas, but this cold snap means business.

Hope all is well with the Brigade. Did you settle on a January fundraiser? Here's my idea—a kissing booth. No doubt, you'd raise a heap of money! Hattie, are you blushing?

Once again, she fanned her face with the letter. Maybe Arno knew her better than she suspected.

> *The army pays us for the odd jobs we perform around camp. I'm now an experienced window washer, potato peeler, payroll worker, and camp guard, plus a dozen other titles. Too bad they don't pay us for letter writing. We'd all be millionaires.*
>
> *Ready for some good news? I'm coming home on a Christmas furlough December twenty-third on the noon train. If you aren't too busy then, perhaps you'll pencil me in for ice skating at the creek.*
>
> *You have no idea how I enjoy our three little things, or two big and one little, every combination. My latest revelations follow.*
>
> *My favorite food is Mother's cinnamon coffee cake, enough said.*
>
> *I like your laugh. Sometimes you snort, and other times, not a single sound squeaks out. Only your shoulders quake. I'm grinning at the memory.*
>
> *There's a good chance I'll regret writing this, but I'm unable to stop thinking about you. I've tried to talk myself out of falling for you, but I'm afraid it's a lost cause. I certainly hope you're not offended by my admission. If so, I apologize.*
>
> *I'm counting the days until I'm home again. Are you eager for the same?*
>
>

As always,
Arno
>

Silent snowflakes swirled against the window, gracefully dancing with one partner, then the next. Warm tears dribbled, smearing Arno's signature. How many nights had she dreamt about this moment, the day he finally returned her affection? In a secret corner of her mind, she'd always hoped their honest and open letter exchange might morph into more than a disguised flirtation.

Then a disturbing thought dawned, and she grabbed Arno's epistle to reread his third confession. *I've tried to talk myself out of falling for you.* What? His behavior resembled Mr. Fitzwilliam Darcy's in *Pride and Prejudice,* the character's most unbecoming trait.

What if Arno hurt her again? And what if he and Barrett arrived on the same train and found her waiting on the platform? Who would she choose?

Hattie slumped at the piano that evening, drumming one finger on an ivory key. Dried cedar snapping in the fireplace swept a sweet, woodsy scent throughout the house. Her thoughts traveled to Little Rock.

"Either play a song or hush the heck up." Jeb peered over the top of a *Wallace's Farmer* newspaper. "It's disconcerting."

"You're the one who is disconcerting." Hattie swirled around on the piano seat. "I have a dilemma. I'm working out the problem in my head."

"It sounds to me like you're working it out on the daggum piano. If you bang that key any harder, you're apt to ruin it."

When a ruckus boomed from the kitchen, they both rose to investigate.

"Come quick," Hawk hollered. "It's the widow. She's trying to bust inside."

"For land's sake, don't be rude." Hattie darted forward with Jeb on her heels. "It's freezing outside."

"But Daddy told me not to let her in the house ever again." Hawk wedged his back against the door with determination flashing in his eyes.

In a steady rhythm, Meridee hammered on the other side of the door.

Jeb scooped up their brother and tossed the boy over his

shoulder like a sack of feed.

"I'm gonna tell," Hawk shouted as Jeb toted him off.

After a deep breath, Hattie ushered their guest into the kitchen. "I'm so sorry for the misunderstanding. Do come in." Maybe the woman would accept her apology and white lie. "Hawk was confused a moment ago."

"Misunderstanding, my foot." Meridee shrugged off fuzzy mittens, a matching hat, and a woolen overcoat before unfastening snow-caked boots. Dressed in a two-piece white sweater dress featuring a clunky sailor collar, the widow handed over her wet garments. "I don't blame Hawk. I blame your father."

Hattie hung Meridee's things on a coat rack in the corner. "Can I fetch you something warm to drink?"

"If it's not too much trouble, I wouldn't refuse a cup of tea with sugar." The woman patted her disheveled hair, black with silvery patches. "I turned stir-crazy back home and talked myself into a sleigh ride."

"I'm glad you stopped by."

"The sun still shone when I left. I made a couple of stops. Next thing you know, I'm hunting for the entrance to your lane." Meridee leaned forward, lowering her voice, "Is your father about?"

Hattie caught a whiff of talcum powder. "He's upstairs, but I can fetch him if you like."

"Land sakes, no. Don't bother. I want to talk to you."

With cherry cheeks and steamed-over spectacles, Meridee settled at the table while Hattie prepared the tea. They chatted about the doings in town before switching topics to the Brigade.

"Of all the fundraising ideas suggested at the last meeting, I'm delighted we went with yours," Meridee said. "How do you feel about the box social?"

The word *petrified* was an apt description, but why sound an alarm? Why confirm that Hattie lacked the know-how to oversee the upcoming responsibility? "The indoor venue makes me a tad nervous. In the past, we've always held picnic socials in the park."

"The town is bubbling over it. Everyone's excited about the opera house site. Who doesn't look forward to a big social event during the middle of winter? Now, how can I help?"

Since the first day Hattie accepted the gavel, Meridee had provided the perfect combination of motivation and reassurance and never in a condescending tone. "For the most part, I'm ready, but I appreciate your offer. I couldn't pull this off without you and Lena."

"Fiddlesticks. It's my pleasure, and not because I've taken a shine to your father, either."

Hattie poured streams of boiling water from the squatty teapot into matching cups, dished up two plates of leftover apple crisp, and carried the treats to the kitchen table.

Wide bangled bracelets clanged as Meridee cupped both hands around her cup and blew on the brew. "To put it mildly, Chester is testing my patience."

"He's been known to do that now and again." Hattie sat, curling a leg beneath her.

"He pretends he's not interested in me, but I know better. He's lonely, and I reckon he likes me in spite of himself."

Hattie blinked, lumping Daddy into the same category as Arno and Mr. Darcy, men who'd developed feelings for a woman despite their better judgments. "Daddy said you two had a lovely supper a few weeks back."

"It's true. I didn't burn a thing. Perhaps I overcooked the vegetables, but Chester ate his beets without complaint." The woman's weighty sigh shook her shoulders. "But I think he's scared."

"Of what?"

"I'm merely speculating, but perhaps he's afraid of abandoning your mama."

Hattie lowered her cup onto its matching saucer. Without exception, Mama had desired the best for her family. If that meant a second marriage for Daddy, she'd probably hop on the bandwagon.

"It's been over <u>seven years since she passed.</u>"

"Those who grieve don't carry around a calendar, dear. Plus, I wager Chester fears I'll interrupt his life."

Hattie nodded.

"Even though he grapples with these emotions, I refuse to let him push me aside without a fight. It's not like I'm expecting him to marry me tomorrow." Meridee retied the bow on her sailor collar. "<u>Next month suits fine.</u>"

Hattie almost choked on her sip of tea. "Next month?"

"It's a simple joke, dear. Call me foolish, but I still want to grow old, or older, alongside someone I love. I don't need a pal." She squeezed Hattie's hand. "I miss being in love, the special jokes only you and he share, playing footsie under the table."

"And holding hands."

"And snuggling before a fire in the hearth."

Hattie gulped, drawing her chair closer to Meridee's. "I'm facing a few romance issues of my own. I've wished I could talk with Mama. Daddy once called her the world's best listener."

"Heaven knows I'm not your sainted mother, but if you wish to bend my ear, <u>I'm a decent listener too.</u>"

About the time Hattie decided to remain mum, she blurted her predicament. "I'm writing two soldiers—I've known Mr. A. all my life and first met Mr. B. in September." She clutched her necklace in a tight fist. "From what I gauge, Mr. B. truly cares about me, and I believe Mr. A. is leaning that direction too."

"Interesting." A single nod accompanied the one-word response.

"Herein lies the problem, <u>they're both coming to Split Falls on a Christmas furlough, and both expect my company.</u>"

"Even more interesting."

"I think you mean terrifying." Hattie had compiled a mental list of potentially disastrous scenarios featuring her, Arno, and Barrett—each one more humiliating than the next. She hadn't a clue how to entertain two soldiers at the same time.

With one elbow propped on the table, Meridee studied Hattie over the rim of her cup. "Let's cut to the chase. Mr. A. is the Kreger boy, the one you've carried a torch for all your life, correct?"

Hattie squirmed. "If I'm not mistaken, he finally likes me. But I'm concerned I've merely piqued his interest. On the other hand, there's another gentleman who genuinely cares about me."

"But how do you feel about him?"

She had asked herself that same question, at least, a dozen times. "I don't know him well enough to make that determination, which means the Christmas furlough is an opportunity to deepen our friendship."

"Or shove him out of the running." After a sympathetic smile, Meridee patted Hattie's forearm.

"Perhaps."

"But if Arno is truly falling for you, you may ruin your chances with him by spending time with the other soldier. And your father despises Arno, another wrinkle to iron." Meridee nodded with enthusiasm. "You're in a quandary alright."

"I haven't the foggiest idea why Daddy dislikes Arno so much. Back in the day, Arno picked plenty of fights, but he's matured since then." Best not to mention Barrett's warning that Arno's rebellious theme continued at camp.

"From my experience, the best way to find out why a person dislikes someone is to ask, but are you prepared to hear your father's answer?"

Footsteps thumped on the stairs, and Hattie placed a warning finger against her lips before Daddy swept into the room. His glances roamed between his daughter and the widow. If he was surprised by Meridee's presence, he didn't show it.

"You got a question for me, Button?" Daddy replaced his stale toothpick with a fresher version from a canister next to the cook stove.

Meridee nodded her encouragement. "Go ahead, dear. Here's your chance."

After a fortifying breath, Hattie plunged forward. "Why-why do you … hate … asparagus?" She groaned inside and kicked herself for not raising the proper question, the one that truly mattered.

Daddy gripped the back of a kitchen chair and shuffled his toothpick to the side of his mouth. "I guess I'm not much for green vegetables. You either like 'em, or you don't. It's like you and peas."

"I see." Hattie tapped at a pearl.

"That's it?" Daddy asked. "That's your big question?"

Hattie screwed up her courage for attempt number two. "There is one other thing I'm curious about." She gulped. "Why do you hate Arno Kreger?"

In the room's unsettling quiet, only the kitchen clock ticked until Daddy cleared his throat. "Hate is an ugly word."

With an upward tilt of her chin, she stared into her father's eyes, same brown shade as hers. "I couldn't agree more."

CHAPTER ELEVEN

A bone-chilling wind stroked Arno's neck. He turned up his overcoat collar, then stuffed his hands inside his pockets. Temperatures, lingering between raw and frigid, had formed a thin glaze that crunched beneath their boots. "It feels cold enough to snow."

"And I feel mad enough to spit smoke." Karl hunched his shoulders against the chill. "For the life of me, I can't believe some of the fellas who've made corporal. If you ask me, those who slide the best, skate in."

"They're slippery suckers." The two shared a commiserating smile. Another round of promotions and another failure for Arno, Karl too.

Between the icy air and a rumored measles quarantine, not many roamed the quiet side street between the Y.M.C.A. and the barracks. The hearse had crawled down the road twice last night. A troubling sign the illness was spreading. Arno had suffered the ailment as a boy.

"Why don't they base promotions on what we've learned?" Arno shivered.

He'd memorized his drill manual—bayonet maneuvers, hand grenade detail, trench warfare, first aid, military courtesy, and everything in-between but still no promotion. With each passing day, he hoped for the recognition, if for no other reason than to write Father with the update.

"I hate it when a corporal barks an order for something he could easily do himself." Karl coughed, stopping until the hacking ended. "All you can say is 'Yes, sir' and then snap to it."

Arno couldn't agree more, but the army played by its own rules and the sooner he and Karl accepted the new way of life, the easier the transition. At least, that's what Arno told himself. "What job did you pull for tonight?"

"I'll put it this way," Karl bumped a shoulder against Arno's and whispered, "if I peel one more spud, I may go AWOL."

He laughed at Karl's often-repeated joke. "I'm not standing guard until midnight, but I'll watch for fence hoppers."

"Nah, it's too cold tonight. I'll wait until it warms up a little."

Sleet pinged against the barrack's tin roof as they entered. The busy room droned. A ring of men hung close to an arm-wrestling match in the dormitory's far corner. Others dealt cards in groups of four or lounged on cots, sleeping or reading. Someone picked at a banjo.

Alongside Karl's bunk, Arno released a low whistle, admiring the mail scattered across the bed. "Nice haul."

"Ain't it though!"

Arno reached his bed and found two letters—one from Hattie and the other from Father. He shed his outer garments before sitting near the heat register. He nudged the chair closer to the warmth and then ripped open Hattie's envelope.

A snapshot fluttered onto his lap. Perched in the lowest crook of an apple tree, she mugged for the camera, sporting a familiar dress and a sweet smile. A ribbon tied back her hair, with a few wispy curls twisting in a breeze.

Emotion clogged his thoughts until he flipped over her likeness to regain composure. How had a simple photograph unnerved him? With a deep breath, he unfolded the sheet of stationery.

December 17, 1917

Dear Arno,
Your family must be thrilled about your upcoming furlough home. No doubt, Christmas wouldn't be the same without you.

The photograph is an old one, but I thought you might like it just the same.

The Brigade is progressing nicely. We're holding a special function at the opera house in January. While the kissing booth idea held merit, we've chosen a box social instead. The gals expect me to sing during the program, making it my first performance on the venue's stage. Of course, I'm nervous, but I fully intend to persevere. I wish you could attend and bid on my basket. If so, I'd prepare your favorite dishes.

Hope all is well in Little Rock, and they're not working you too awfully hard. Most days, you'll find me nuzzled somewhere with a book in my lap. Mind you, I'm not neglecting my chores, but everything slows down during the winter months. You know how that works.

I'm thrilled to learn you love our three exchanges, whether they be little, medium-sized, or large admissions. This time, mine are doozies.

Regarding your upcoming furlough, I'm eager to see you. However, Barrett also intends to visit Split Falls during the same period. That complicates matters, doesn't it?

One giant stumbling block between you and me is Daddy. Recently, I asked him why. He hemmed and hawed and then recited your history of fighting. Although news to me, he also partially blames you for Jeb's gun accident. What exactly occurred back then, or should I ask my brother? It's a mystery, at least from where I'm sitting. Daddy alluded to a third reason but chose to keep the particulars a secret. No doubt, it stems from the family feud between your father and mine. Why is that whole business secretive?

Finally, thanks to Meridee Moss's strong negotiation tactics, Daddy agreed to allow our continued letter exchanges, but he has a stipulation. Every month we write one another, I'm required to date a boy from back home. It's his opinion that I'll find somebody new and lose interest in you. The entire notion is absurd, but I'll pay the price if it means we're allowed to grow our friendship.

Sorry to report this development. If you decide it's too much of a bother, I'll be disappointed but understand. But if you still want to meet during your furlough, I'd like that. I'm ready to skate circles around you.

As always,
Hattie

Arno crumpled the letter while digesting the news. Was she worth the trouble of more suitors and a meddling father? He felt a tug toward yes. But he had no business pursuing her when he couldn't offer her a future, at least not the type that included a house full of noisy children.

Arno returned to his footlocker, kicking the corner, not once or twice but until his toe throbbed. His day stunk like skunk family reunion, and he'd not yet opened Father's envelope.

Shouts from the arm-wrestling fans snared his attention until Karl dumped an armful of goodies onto Arno's bed.

"This is your take. I'm splitting my mail fifty-fifty with you."

"It's my lucky day, isn't it?" Although Arno appreciated the windfall, he couldn't shake Hattie's troubling message about dating more men, plenty of more men.

An orange, taffy, picked nuts, sugar cookies, peppermint candy, a necktie, and a *Popular Mechanics* magazine sprawled across his cot. "There's also a foxy photograph from Sadie Parker, but I'm not about to rip her picture down the middle." Karl laughed, but his guffaw soon switched to a drawn-out series of coughs.

"Gonna make it, buddy, or should I fetch the medic?"

"I can't lick this lousy cough. Otherwise, I'm more than fine." Karl drew a handkerchief across his mouth. "What did you get in the mail? I'm ready for my fair share." When Karl cupped his hands, Arno forked over Hattie's balled letter. "What's this?"

Arno grunted. "Mail from Hattie."

"No, thank you." Karl tossed the crinkled stationery over his shoulder. "What else you got, anything smelling like food and tasting like your ma's cooking?"

"Father wrote for the first time. I haven't read it yet."

With a sigh, Karl flopped onto the edge of Arno's bed, brushing aside his handouts. His raised eyebrows said more than a dozen words.

Arno sucked in a deep lungful of air. "Hattie's pa forbids her from writing me unless she dates a series of local men."

With a hand on his belly, Karl howled, driving home Arno's theory—Chester's plan was crazy. "Thinking she'll fall for someone better. No offense."

"None taken. Plus, Jordane is headed to Split Falls on furlough, the same time as us."

The shouting escalated across the room. Arno tossed Father's unopened envelope onto his bed. "Ready to blow off steam?"

"Not in the least, but I'm willing to root for my best pal." He stood and stretched. "My way is less work."

CW held court at the arm-wrestling table. Arno and Karl, along with the rest of the audience, watched three challengers lose in rapid succession.

Karl raised a brow, and Arno nodded in agreement. CW possessed the strength of two average-sized men or perhaps three scrawny ones. But was he starting to tire? A film covered the soldier's flushed skin, glinting in the electric light. The space stank of sweat.

"Come on, you poor suckers," CW hollered loud enough to wake those who napped. "Who's next?" For a minute, nobody accepted the bait.

Without fanfare, Arno claimed the empty seat, situated his right elbow on the small round table, and then clasped CW's clammy hand.

CW threw back his head and howled. "You made my day, German boy. Every donkey thinks itself worthy of standing with the king's horses."

"That's mighty philosophical." Arno eyed his opponent, picturing the man's disappointed face after his upcoming loss. "Which critter are you?"

"We're about to find out."

Another soldier, a mediator, grasped the competitors' hands, ensuring neither started with an unfair advantage. "On your mark, get set, go!"

Although Arno failed to match CW's size, he rivaled the soldier's stamina and strength. Neither offered an inch. Sweat formed, and he fought the urge to wipe it away. If he won, he'd silence the poor excuse of a soldier once and for all. Time ticked, yet Arno's power flourished. Slowly, like a calf's first cautious step, Arno inched CW's hand toward a victory.

"Had … enough?" CW's stale breath swept Arno's face.

The thought of slamming his foe's meaty fist against the wooden table kept Arno going. Then he would label himself the king's horse, making CW the—

"Listen to this." Someone hollered with a tone of urgency.

Although interest piqued, Arno concentrated on his task, growing in importance with each drop of sweat. The way CW's hand shook, Arno's hope to pocket a win inched closer, tasting as sweet as a butterscotch candy.

"The army just issued a quarantine," the message-bearer said. "It's official. All leaves are off until further notice." *oh no!*

The packed room whirred with the shattering news.

Hattie. Without seeing her in person, he'd never gain a proper footing to court the girl. But was that his true objective—courtship with Hattie Waltz? For a brief moment, he squeezed his eyes shut. Her pa would never allow it.

The second Arno's grip lessened, CW slammed it against the table.

"You loser, Kreger!" After a fist smack against his chest, CW jumped to his feet, jarring the table. "Who's next?"

Nobody answered. Karl doubled over and hacked for a long spell.

"Go to the medic." With a shove against the table, Arno rose, and pushed his way through the knotted soldiers, hurrying toward his bunk.

"It's better than your chore," Karl said, a few steps behind.

Arno swiveled around, arching a brow. He'd pulled guard duty, but his shift didn't start for hours. "What?"

"Breaking Hattie's heart."

Did he hold that influence over the girl? Not likely. "Perhaps they'll call off the quarantine in a day or two, and we'll still make it home for Christmas."

Frankie strolled past. "Don't count on it. I heard the shutdown is to last a week or longer. Hope we don't cry if Santy Claus fails to track us down in Arkansas."

Arno lacked a reply and continued to his cot, while reality settled into his pores. His new destination—Disappointment Street, not Split Falls. With a sigh, he opened Father's envelope.

December 14, 1917

Arno,

Your Uncle Ethan died from pneumonia. They buried him today. We didn't make the trek to Philadelphia.

Your ma says you'll be home on furlough by Christmas. She'll like that.

We've not received word about an officer appointment. Seems you ain't trying hard enough.

Father

P.S. We made good money on the corn this year.

Flat on his back, Arno searched for the last time he and Father saw eye-to-eye on anything of importance. Two years ago? Three? No, a week before Oliver died. They'd built a cedar jewelry box for Mother's birthday.

With nimble hands and a yard of patience, Father had demonstrated how to etch curlicues with a sharp tool pressed against the box. Then, he supervised while his sons added final touches to perfect the gift. Mother gushed over her present the next morning before generous servings of birthday cake and vanilla ice cream for breakfast.

His uncle's death wasn't a complete surprise. Cancer had wormed into the man's body six months prior. Still, the news darkened Arno's mood even more.

Minus children of their own, he and Aunt Charity had spoiled their nieces and nephews with expensive porcelain dolls and bicycles. Until Father had mailed a reminder to his in-laws that too much coddling spoiled youngsters. Goodbye, fancy gifts.

Arno dumped everything littering his cot into his footlocker except for the peppermints. He buried those in his trouser pocket. Before lowering the lid, he spied the corner of the book where he'd hidden his cousin Molly's paper heart for safekeeping. He pulled it free.

Perhaps he'd write the girl tomorrow. His thoughts were too jumbled today. Had she kept track of *Opa*'s compass?

Grandfather, the salt-of-the-earth type, had lived with them for years, passing away the same cold winter as Oliver. With a story for every occasion, he'd taught his grandsons how to whittle, tie fishing lures, and cheat at checkers, which they promised never to confess. He called Arno *scout* and Oliver *champ*, perfect nicknames.

Two of the people Arno loved most in the world had died within months of one another. An ache gnawed daily. Would it ever taper off to nothing more than a memory? Not with his luck.

On a whim, he folded Molly's gift. The army could issue a quarantine, alter his trip-home plans. But it couldn't take away the little piece of home he tucked into his pocket.

Somewhere on the other side off the room, a soldier sang loud and clear.

Patti Stockdale

"Deck the halls with boughs of holly
Fa la la la la, this stinks real bad."

CHAPTER TWELVE

Today was the day Hattie's life would change forever.

Daddy paused the team for a slow-moving family to cross the street. Unable to sit still one minute longer, she hopped from the sleigh. "Bye, Daddy."

"I'll fetch you in two hours. You be sure you're ready."

She nodded, tugging down the sleeves of her overcoat to better cover her bare wrists. "I will, and thank you."

His head cocked to the side. "For the ride?"

"For not lecturing me. Gotta go. Bye." For the entire jaunt to town to meet the train, she'd expected a full-blown lecture on why she mustn't pitch her hopes and dreams on a soldier, particularly Arno Kreger. Daddy didn't know what to think of Barrett, but that was about to change. She added a skip to her steps.

Daddy hadn't mentioned their absurd arrangement either, the one where she accepted dates from random local bachelors. Hattie paused in the middle of the snowy street. What if no suitors called, forcing her to make the first advance? She brushed aside the cringe-worthy thought and hurried toward the depot, sidestepping the icy patches. The crisp air smelled like Christmas, piney and promising.

Over the last few days, she'd mulled over her predicament—two men arriving and one woman waiting—and then decided to wing it. She'd written both men a letter explaining the scenario. Her goal was to eliminate surprises and awkward moments. But the odds weren't in her favor.

By the time she reached the train station, the morning's snowflakes had sputtered to a near stop. A busy wreath garnished with shiny red bells and golden bows decorated the stout door. Ice-covered windows prevented passersby a peek inside.

A few townsfolk congregated near the tracks to greet the travelers. Hattie stretched on her toes, searching for Arno's family. Where were they? Lena had specifically stated she'd not miss Arno's arrival. Whether that meant the excitement of having her brother home again, or Hattie's upcoming juggling act was anyone's guess.

The wooden platform shuddered. Ladies waved hankies, men smacked each other's backs, and Hattie smiled—bigger and broader than she'd grinned in months. The train rumbled into the station. Brakes squealed, and a black burst of smoke belched high into the air. She clutched Mama's pearls in one hand and steadied herself on the wooden ledge with the other. Those waiting rushed forward.

The doors finally burst open, and passengers spilled forth. A woman near Hattie introduced a newborn to his fresh-faced pa, possibly a soldier although he wore civilian clothes. The threesome's tears mingled. Hattie's eyes watered too.

A hulking soldier emerged and clutched a honey-haired lass bundled in a chinchilla overcoat. He lifted the speechless woman and spun her in a full circle, and then, inch by inch, eased her down until their lips met.

Heat rushed from Hattie's neck to her face.

Similar reunions played out right and left until the last passengers alighted from the train. The jubilant cheers dimmed, and the welcome parties and guests of honor dispersed. Hattie twirled in a circle. No Arno and no Barrett. Where were they? She stared at her mittened palms as if they held the answers.

She hurried into the bustling depot and then waited in a line to inquire about the missing soldiers. Every few minutes, she glanced at the pendulum clock by the window. Her turn finally arrived, and a clerk broke the heart-crushing news—neither man was on the passenger list. He even showed Hattie the evidence. After mumbling thanks, she plodded outside. How long until Daddy returned?

She settled on a cold wrought iron bench tucked against the

depot's brick wall. Where was Arno's family? A frigid wind slapped at her bare skin, and she longed for her muff and wool overcoat, a warmer but less flattering number than the one she wore.

After tugging her feet onto the bench and draping her dress over her legs, Hattie rested her forehead against shivering kneecaps. She didn't care what anybody said—absence failed to turn the heart fonder. In reality, the muscle grew confused. Lately, the only time her life touched Arno's or Barrett's was courtesy of the United States Post Office.

"What a day." Lena claimed a seat beside Hattie.

"He's not here."

"I'm sorry I'm late, but you'll never believe what happened minutes before breakfast."

"Did you hear me?" Hattie gulped the chilly air to calm her thoughts and faced Lena. "Arno didn't show."

"I know, sweetheart. We received a telegram. There's a quarantine due to a measles outbreak. No furloughs for the time being." 1917

Little by little, Hattie's shoulders deflated. "Why didn't you telephone?"

"I nearly did. Instead, I lit the kitchen drapery on fire." Lena wore a sheepish grin and shrugged. "What can I say? I'm prone to accidents."

Hattie laughed. It felt good to chuckle instead of pity herself.

"Havoc broke out the next minute, and by the time I rang your place, Jeb answered, calling my telephone voice mellifluous. I'm sorry, but he's behaving mighty strange lately. And then he said you'd already scurried off to town. I intended to race here straightaway because I knew you'd be fretting, but Father demanded I clean my mess first."

Hattie rested her head on Lena's shoulder. "Looks like we're both having a rotten day."

"It's merely one in a string of awful days for me."

"Why?" She squeezed her friend's arm. Lena rarely complained.

When she did, an excellent reason always accompanied the grumble.

"I'll tell you my woes, but first let's drown our sorrows in cinnamon and sugar."

It wasn't the worst idea Hattie had heard all day. "If you can find the treats on short notice, I'll happily devour one or two."

"Cousin Lottie bakes every Saturday, and sweet rolls are her favorite. Come on."

They crossed the now-deserted road. "How'd the fire start?" Hattie held her collar closed with one hand and her feathery headpiece in place with the other. Too bad she'd chosen beauty over a warm, substantial bonnet.

"You know how I tend to fling my arms while I speak?"

"You've hit me more than once." They laughed, bumping shoulders.

"I detailed my lengthy list of Christmas tasks to Mother, baking and gift purchasing, those sorts of things. Only I did so with a red-hot fireplace poker in my hand. For future reference, that's not wise."

"I should think not."

They both giggled. "No true damage occurred, only a pair of sooty drapes, a discolored wall, and a black dent on the floorboards."

"That's all?"

Lena raised a red mitten. "And a lengthy lecture from Father."

"I'm sorry." The girls stepped around snowdrifts to reach the shop across the street.

Tucked in the town's cradle, the Split Falls Mercantile—Lottie's to the locals—was a longstanding establishment with a white picket fence around it. Black shutters boasting ornate curlicues bordered each window. Evergreen and giant poinsettias poked against the panes. From gingham fabric to the newest chewing gum, Lottie's carried the finest merchandise in the county.

A lively bell tinkled when they opened the door. A sprig of mistletoe hung head-skimmingly low, making it impossible for patrons to miss the greenery tied with a plush red bow. The pleasant scent of gingerbread welcomed guests.

Lottie greeted them with a wave of her fleshy arm before returning her attention to a slump-shouldered man at the counter. "Excellent purchase. Can I help you with anything else?"

"How about a cinnamon roll or two?" Lena interrupted, raising her voice.

Lottie punched a key on the cash register, dinging open the drawer and accepting her customer's payment. "There's a pan upstairs on the kitchen table. Help yourselves to some hot cocoa too. It should still be warm."

The customer at the counter peered over his shoulder. "Hello, ladies."

"No." Hattie dropped her pocketbook, spilling loose coins onto the slushy floorboards.

"Didn't mean to startle you." Delwyn approached, his grin growing with each step. He swept aside his shaggy bangs with his sleeve.

Trembling, Hattie stooped for her wayward pennies, wiping each one clean with her mitten before pocketing them. *Just my luck. No Arno. No Barrett. Just Delwyn.* Before standing, she stole a peek at the dangly mistletoe. Why did business owners torture their customers with the Christmas greenery? *Ugh.* She stood.

Delwyn blocked the path to the staircase. He reminded her of a reedy cattail plant, the type to tip in a big wind. According to Lena, he'd failed his military physical due to flat feet. They matched his flat personality.

"It's been too long, Hattie." He shot his cousin a glance. "Lena."

"Delwyn." Frost lined Lena's tone.

The man's dingy-blue eyes flashed to Hattie. "Just the other day, I was thinkin' on you and that lovely voice of yours. How about you and me take in a picture show, say next week?"

Daddy's unreasonable stipulation jabbed at Hattie like a red-headed woodpecker. But Delwyn Nordeen? "Thank you, but no."

"You know," Lena looped her arm through Hattie's, "my friend here has a beau. Two, in fact."

"Care to make it three?" Delwyn flashed a trio of wiggly fingers.

Bile swirled Hattie's stomach, but she fought it down.

"If you recollect the last time you paid her a call, you treated her rather shabbily." Lena's voice dipped toward sub-zero temperatures.

Thank you, Hattie mouthed her gratitude.

Delwyn ran his thumb and index finger down the sides of his open mouth until they met in the middle of his bottom lip. "But I wasn't expecting to bump into Priscilla Snodgrass. She's a … a stunner."

"What does that make me?" Hattie cringed. Why had she asked such an idiotic question if she feared the answer?

Delwyn backtracked and stammered. "Yo-you're fetching in your own right, but Priscilla is more … more on the order of one in a million, and you're more of a—"

"Stop." Hattie interrupted with a raised hand. "Please, I'm begging you not to say another word." Since the floorboards failed to open up and swallow her, she grabbed Lena's hand, shoved past Delwyn, and dashed toward the staircase.

"I like your hat," he shouted. "I'm partial to feathers."

She added a punch to her steps, tugging Lena along. "If your cousin and I never cross paths again, I'll count that a blessing."

"Amen."

Lottie's welcoming kitchen reflected its mistress, cheery and messy. Brightly striped turquoise and cream chintz drapes framed windows, and dirty dishes littered the basin. Dust covered most surfaces, and stacks of sheet music and magazines littered the floor. A crackly fire blazed in the hearth, toasting the room.

"True or false," Lena said with a straight face. "Delwyn is kissable." She dipped a ladle into a warm pot of cocoa, filled two cups, and passed one to Hattie.

How could Lena even ask that? "Ick."

"I'm funning with you." Dressed in a deep pink frock with

black velvet cuffs and a wide patent leather belt, Lena drew her name on the frosty windowpane before taking a seat at the kitchen table.

"Other than trying to burn down your house, what else ruined your week?" Hattie chose a chair across from her friend.

"Wilhelm asked me to marry him, and I … I said, 'no thank you.'"

Hot, sweet-smelling chocolate lodged in Hattie's throat until she forced a swallow. "Say that again, only slower."

"You heard me perfectly fine."

Hattie's heart sank like the paper boats they once floated down Catfish Creek. Lena and Wilhelm—a perfect match based on kindness, values, amiable personalities and, although it ranked low on the priority list, gorgeousness. They belonged together, same as Saturdays and baths, butter and sweetcorn, thread and needles. Everyone agreed except the misguided woman across the table.

"It took me less time to say no than it's taking you to respond. Go ahead. Tell me I'm about to make the biggest mistake of my life." Lena popped a piece of roll into her mouth and chewed.

After the world stopped tilting, Hattie gawked at her dearest friend. "I thought you loved him." She wanted happiness for Lena and longed to sweep the woman into a bone-crunching embrace to congratulate her on upcoming nuptials instead of dissecting the end of a beautiful and endearing courtship.

"I do love him, but I'm not ready to marry the man." Lena folded her hands in her lap like a docile wife. "I suppose you think someone else will snatch him before I reconsider my decision."

"True." How many local women between the ages of sixteen and twenty-six had practiced, at least once, writing Mrs. Wilhelm Mueller on a sheet of stationery?

Lena struggled to shove loose hair into her messy bun before giving up and allowing it to tumble. "Perhaps he'll never give me a second chance, that is, if I decide I even want one."

"Are you happy with your decision?"

Lena grasped Hattie's sticky hands. "I'm not like you. I don't need, or want, a thousand and one wildflowers tossed on my feet by the man I love. And I've never dreamt about a romantic wedding on the back lawn surrounded by family and friends." She squeezed Hattie's fingers for emphasis. "Perhaps I'll become a mother one day, but I'm not yearning for that. In other words, the answer to your question is yes."

How was it possible that neither Lena nor Arno longed to start a family? For Hattie, motherhood was stamped on her heart, a natural progression. It wasn't a question of *if I have children* but *when I have children*. Would she ever change Arno's mind on the matter? And what about Barrett's opinion on parenthood?

"My dreams take me overseas to work with the Red Cross or someplace like New York City to march with the suffragettes." Lena shoved the plate of cinnamon rolls across the table toward Hattie. "I want to eat food other than meat and potatoes, trace the Liberty Bell with my fingertip, and meet people who don't drive tractors or wear coveralls. Is that too much to ask?"

Hattie shrugged, pretending not to care.

"If I'm ever going to live such a life," Lena raised her chin, "I'd best start."

Please don't leave me was what she wanted to say. Instead, she forced her voice not to wobble. "Perhaps I'll tag along?"

"You'd hate it. And, I'm not going anywhere tomorrow or the next day. If I lose Wilhelm in the process, that's a risk I'm willing to take. I think the whole reason he proposed last night sprung from fear. One minute I detailed my plans, and the next he proposed."

"Why not explore the world together, side-by-side?" That scenario made the most sense to Hattie.

"That's another sticking point." Lena ran her fingertip around the rim of her cup. "He's not apt to leave Iowa nor his pa, and I'm determined to accomplish this next step on my own."

Their hometown lacked perfection, but it measured close. Everyone Hattie loved possessed a Split Falls address. Why wasn't that enough for Lena? She dug deep to find the proper response from one good friend to another. "Your happiness is important to me. You know that, correct?"

"Thank you." Lena's eyes turned glassy, but no tears fell.

"If that includes gallivanting, so be it. However, I insist you mail me a postcard from every destination you visit. Then I'll experience your adventures too."

Lena pounced from her chair, raced around the table to tug Hattie to her feet, and hugged with brute-like strength.

"Stop, that's too tight." She groaned, regretting her second cinnamon roll.

With a laugh, Lena tightened her embrace before freeing her friend. "You never know—maybe I'll remain in Split Falls forever, marry Wilhelm, and eke out a dozen babies."

Hattie laughed, picturing Lena and herself nine-months pregnant, waddling side-by-side and chattering nonstop. "You paint a glamorous picture."

"Seriously, I don't want to settle for a consolation prize, and Wilhelm deserves more than Mr. Runner-up. His merits far exceed his detriments."

"What exactly do you consider his detriments?" Hattie cocked a brow, eager to hear the list.

"He loves me."

"Now I'm truly confused."

Lena threw her hands wide, and Hattie grasped her hot chocolate to safeguard it. "His marriage proposal ruined everything. He's sad, and I feel guilty. We both deserve happiness."

Hattie forced a sympathetic smile and hoped it appeared genuine. "Once upon a time, life was simpler."

"But not nearly as exciting."

"In my opinion, excitement is overrated."

After a chuckle, Lena shook her head, tumbling her hair. "That's definitely not true."

"Your pa is here to fetch you, Hattie." Lottie's sing-songy voice climbed the staircase.

"I'll be down in a minute."

"Already?" Lena snared Hattie's wrist. "See if you can stay longer."

The sooner she left, the sooner she'd drown her sorrows in a gallon of milk. But if she remained in town, could she change Lena's mind? "Let's ask."

They hurried downstairs.

Later that evening, Hattie discovered an empty cookie jar, a trail of crumbs, and two notes on the kitchen table.

> *Hattie,*
>
> *Spoke with Lena this forenoon on the telephone. She said they'd received a telegram from the army. There's a measles quarantine, so your soldiers aren't coming into town on today's train. I reckon you know that by now.*
>
> *I'll be home late. At Priscilla's.*
>
> *Your brother,*
Jeb
>
> *P.S. Don't eat all the cookies. You do that when you're sad. Oh, that's right, I finished them on your behalf. Aren't I gallant?*

Gallant? At Priscilla's home? After retrieving the hidden tin of snickerdoodles in the back-corner cupboard, Hattie collected the second note and wandered into the empty parlor to lounge on the sofa.

> *Button,*
>
> *Hope supper in town with Lena cheered you up. I assume you thanked Lottie for carting you home.*
>
> *Hawk and I are tuckered and decided to hit the hay early.*

We ate supper at Meridee's. She served a dish called spaghetti and meatballs. I prefer the usual fare at our place. She's miserable with a cold and didn't mind that Hawk and I pulled out early.

I bumped into the pastor at the hardware store. He commented on the fine roasted goose you cooked, and how he appreciated your efforts. He asked my permission to pay you a call next Friday. He's hankering to take you somewhere special, a restaurant.

In light of our recent arrangement, I told him yes. I think it's for your own good.

If you decide to seek revenge, please don't burn the eggs and bacon at breakfast. Feel free to scorch the green beans at lunch.

Lovingly,
Daddy

Hattie tipped sideways onto the sofa, curling into a ball. "Not Pastor Neymeyer."

SAP!

CHAPTER THIRTEEN

Arno fidgeted in a plush seat at the Split Falls Opera House between Karl and Wilhelm, waiting for the Brigade's box social to begin. With a goal to raise funds, the concept was simple and straightforward. A woman prepared a meal for two, stuck the food in a showy basket, and men bid on the dinner. Then bingo. The winner dined with the preparer.

The risk was not knowing which woman created which supper. The possible reward was a blue-ribbon-worthy meal, a little conversation, and perhaps something more ... like a kiss. Arno's goal was to win the bid for Hattie's basket. Even if it brimmed with nothing more than sauerkraut, he'd devour it with a grin and ask for a second helping. And he despised sauerkraut.

The recently remodeled stone opera house ranked as the fanciest building in town atop a hotel, a hardware store, and a restaurant. He hadn't stepped foot inside the joint until today. The room shouted first-class money and taste. Attendees streamed into the building, raising a racket.

"I'm ready to settle down, and Lena wants," Wilhelm scrunched his shoulders, "something more."

Karl peered around Arno to face Will. "Sorry, buddy, I'm siding with Lena on this one. I'm not ready for a life sentence to only one woman." He slugged Arno's arm. "What about you, Kreger?"

Courtship, maybe. Marriage lingered somewhere down a long and dusty road. "You fellas bidding tonight?"

"Yeah," Karl said while Wilhelm remained silent.

"I suppose you're gonna go for Hattie's hamper." With more force than necessary, Karl elbowed Arno's ribs.

"Huh?" Wilhelm's voice raised an octave. "When did this all happen?"

"It's a new development." Arno shot a glance at Karl before searching for Hattie.

At the far corner of the stage in front of a black curtain, she popped into view. Arno scrambled to his feet and swung an arm high, hoping to draw her attention. She returned the wave, swinging her arm above her head before beckoning him.

Due to his three-hour late train arrival, they'd not yet spoken. Without a word to his seatmates, Arno shoved toward the aisle and almost rammed Jordane.

"Get out of my way. Hattie needs to speak with me." Barrett hurled a snarl and a scathing glance before resuming his mission to reach the girl.

Arno grunted. Despite a glut of new arrivals on the stairs, he reached the base of the stage just behind Jordane.

"It's wonderful to see you both," Hattie said.

She wore a green dress. That's about all he noticed, except for her full lips and smile. He couldn't miss those two features. He thrust his thumb in Jordane's direction. "This is a tad uncomfortable."

She hid a nervous laugh behind her fingers.

"Easy to remedy. Shove off, Kreger." Barrett squished Hattie into an embrace, her arms stuck against her body.

"There, there." Her voice muffled by the man's shirtfront, the suffocating hug lingered.

Once it ended, and unsure whether to follow Barrett's example or not, Arno shifted his feet.

While he second-guessed his next move, Hattie stepped into his arms. "Welcome home."

Eyes closed, he savored her softness and lemon-scented hair tied up all fancy.

"I saw your wave," Barrett interrupted. "Is there something you needed? You look beautiful, by the way."

Barrett's words hit like a fist to Arno's gut. Why hadn't he complimented her looks? If he said something now, he'd sound like a lousy mimic.

Hattie blushed and clutched her pearls. "I thought I'd give you a small clue, so you'll know which box to bid on in a few minutes."

Did he look half as dumbfounded as he felt? "You're telling us both?"

She cupped a hand over her chuckle. "I can see how this might sound ridiculous, yet I believe it's only fair." Hattie ran her palms down the sides of her dress. "Except what I'm about to do is the opposite of fair. It's cheating."

"I'm intrigued," Barrett said.

Cheating and *Hattie* were two words Arno couldn't pair together. Part of him objected to the cat-and-mouse game, but he either played along or forfeited the girl. To Jordane. He'd rather eat a live snake.

"I wrote a special poem for the occasion. I'm fairly certain Meridee will read my verse aloud when my basket hits the auction block."

"Excellent move, Hattie." Barrett was apparently delighted to have gained an advantage. "Thank you for the tip, and may the best man win."

"I intend to." Arno crossed his arms.

Jordane squished Hattie in another bone-crunching hug. "Until we meet again at supper." After an over-the-top bow, he strolled away.

"I suppose if I called him pompous, you'd label me jealous."

Hattie shrugged but smiled.

"In that case, I'll button my lip." Alone with the woman who'd monopolized his thoughts for weeks, Arno searched for a witty conversation starter, abandoning one option after the next. He wasted precious time.

She fiddled with her necklace, avoiding his eyes.

Then Meridee peeked around a corner of the thick drapery, snagging their attention. "It's <u>time to start</u>, dear. Hello there, Arno.

I hope you enjoy your evening back home."

"Thank you, ma'am. I'm trying my best."

"One minute." Hattie addressed Meridee before turning her attention to Arno. She studied his face, her eyes roaming every inch. Twice, she opened her mouth before shutting it again.

The silence stretched between them until the orchestra tuned up.

Arno spoke over the racket, "Let's hope you raise lots of money with the basket auction." With his fingertips, he brushed her velvety shoulder as if wiping away a speck of dust. But her dress was spotless. He only wanted to touch her again.

"I hope you have deep pockets."

"Deep enough, I think. Are you nervous?"

"I'm shaking like a twig in a twister."

"You'll shine." One at a time, he reached for her icy-cold hands, hoping to transfer his warmth and confidence. "When you sing tonight, sing to me, nobody else. Can you do that?"

She tilted her head. "What if I stumble?"

"I'll catch you."

On her tiptoes, she kissed his cheek and then rested her forehead against his chest. "Thank you," she whispered. Far too soon, she scooted behind the curtain.

The kiss scorched his skin like a cattle brand. He touched his face to savor it. A cymbal crashed to the floor, jerking him into motion. On the way to his chair, he checked his money clip. Eighteen dollars was far more cash than necessary to buy a hamper brimming with food. But he refused to lose to Jordane, not when time with Hattie rode on the win.

The orchestra conductor raised his hands followed by a sweeping instrumental performance. Upon the crescendo, the draperies swung wide. Latticed shelves featured rows of decorated picnic baskets, boxes, and hampers of varying shapes, sizes, and colors.

Applause bellowed when Hattie stepped onto the stage.

She smiled, searched the audience, and then nodded toward the conductor.

You're okay, Hattie. You can do this.

> "*... Meet me tonight in dreamland,*
> *Under the silv'ry moon.*
> *Meet me tonight in dreamland,*
> *Where love's sweet roses bloom ...*"

Her rich voice rallied the hairs on Arno's arms to stand at attention. If she was nervous, he couldn't tell. Her lyrics delivered a jolt, and he leaned forward.

> "*... Come with the love light gleaming*
> *In your dear eyes of blue.*
> *Meet me in dreamland,*
> *Sweet, dreamy dreamland,*
> *There let my dreams come true.*"

The song ended, and someone yelled, "Why wait for dream time? What's wrong with right now?" Laughter and exuberant applause mixed.

Arno jumped to his feet, hunting for the ardent admirer. Delwyn Nordeen? His first cousin grinned from the front row of the far-right side where a handful of out-of-towners stretched to slap the man's back.

When the noise ebbed, Hattie raised a hand in the air. "On that note, it's nearly time to open the bidding. Thank you for your kind applause and for braving the winter weather. Hopefully, more snow holds off until we're tucked nice and tight into our warm beds tonight."

One by one, Hattie introduced her fellow Brigade members who waved and smiled on cue. Next, she invited Meridee and Pete, the local auctioneer, to join her front and center on the wide stage.

After a quick embrace with Meridee, she scurried to join the other Brigade members stretched in a line behind the mismatched boxes.

"Who is ready to raise funds for our servicemen?" Applause rang. Meridee tented a hand above her eyes to peer at the audience. "If I'm not mistaken, a few soldiers joined us tonight. Will you please stand while we show our heartfelt appreciation?"

Amidst a wave of handclapping, the soldiers stood. The ovation lasted a while. Those in nearby seats pumped Arno's hand and offered encouragements. The same scenario played out around the room before everyone returned to their seats.

"Here's how it's going to work, folks." Meridee strolled past the prize lineup with a raised hand as if a dinner platter rested upon her palm. "We'll auction off these lovely picnic baskets, and you'll spend all your hard-earned cash for the right to enjoy supper with a beautiful woman."

An overwhelming percent of the crowd cheered, but a few scattered naysayers commented, including one raised voice, "You'll have to pry the cash out of my cold, dead hands."

"My pleasure, sir." Meridee paced the length of the stage. "If you notice, some baskets feature ribbons and other notions, but the best part of each hamper is the contents." She leaned forward, her ample backside to the audience as she sniffed the contents before swinging around to face the onlookers. "Mm ... mmm. Can you smell the fried chicken? Pickled cherries? Tangy potato salad? Gooey chocolate cake?"

Hoots and hollers filled the room, raising such a commotion that two Brigade members covered their ears.

"I'll give you two bucks, right now, for Priscilla Snodgrass's basket," someone shouted down front.

The audience chuckled while Priscilla beamed, bending into a sweeping curtsey.

"What if she can't cook worth a lick?" Meridee asked, propping a hand on her wide waist.

"Who cares," the voice replied, stirring more merriment. "My offer stands."

"I appreciate your gusto, mister, but that's not how the Brigade's box social operates. Nobody knows whose box is whose. Isn't that correct, ladies?"

The women nodded except for Hattie. She merely smiled.

"And, gals, when the bidding starts, you're to maintain a straight face. Let's practice." It appeared the women had rehearsed their schtick. No smiles softened the stone-faced bunch, much to the spectators' giddy delight.

Meridee lifted the first basket and set it on a stand beside her. She raised the wooden flap to peer inside. "My, my, my. This particular meal smells like a chunk of heaven broke away and dropped smack dab into the heart of Split Falls. Who'll start the bidding at five cents?"

Hands flew high.

"Watch and learn, boys," Arno whispered, drawing his wallet from his trouser pocket. "I'm about to win tonight's grand prize."

"We'll just see about that," Karl said, with a good-natured grin. Arno chuckled. "I'm not worried, not in the least, not about you two numskulls." He flicked his hand to include both of his buddies. "It's the other red-blooded men in the audience who want to dash my plans."

"Hush up," a lady in the row behind the trio tapped Arno's shoulder.

He apologized. When he turned to smirk at Wilhelm, his pal was slouched in his seat, refusing eye contact. Arno scratched his jaw. Besides a broken heart, what pestered Will? Before he could ask, Karl nudged his shoulder.

"Who in the Sam Hill just paid ten bucks for a basket? What a muttonhead."

CHAPTER FOURTEEN

Only two lonely picnic baskets lingered on the shelf, Hattie's brown wicker contraption and a mystery box decorated in red, white, and blue. Hers flaunted buttermilk chicken, three-bean salad, a quart-sized Mason jar of cinnamon applesauce, a blackberry pie with a crisscross crust … and her hopes and dreams.

Who would win her basket, her heart? Was Arno the right man for Hattie or merely the man she knew best?

The event steamrolled toward a monumental success. The Brigade had raised more money than Hattie had dared to predict, and the commemorative tablecloths hadn't yet hit the auction block, nor the night's dance with a five-cent entrance fee. But Hattie continued to stew.

"What will our next prize fetch?" Meridee approached the sparse shelf, rubbing her hands together.

Please, pick mine and put me out of my misery.

"We're down to two tasty hampers, ladies and gentlemen. Which one first?" Shouts bombarded the stage, yet Meridee stalled, drawing out the drama. She selected Hattie's contribution, swung toward the audience, and then stopped mid-motion before returning the hefty basket to the shelf.

A groan inched up Hattie's throat.

"No, I think it's time to bid on this patriotic number." With a broad grin, Meridee carted the colorful box to the top of the wooden podium. "Isn't it gorgeous, and what's this? It appears the preparer attached a poem."

Hattie's jaw dropped but only for a second before resuming her best nonchalant pose. Only Lena knew about the poetry. Nobody in the female lineup twitched. Was it coincidental? Had someone overheard the poetry plan and copied it?

Meridee patted her skirt pocket before freeing a pair of spectacles. She perused the verse. "Looks like a play on a Mother Goose poem."

"Roses are red, violets are blue,
Pick my basket, and I'll sup with you."

"Aww … that's sweet." Meridee drew her hand against her breastbone. "Let's start at ten cents for the extra effort."

The bidding soared to seventeen dollars, a ridiculous amount, with three bidders competing for the prize. Blinded by the stage lights, Hattie couldn't see the actual bidders. Surely two were Arno and Barrett, but who was the mystery bidder?

Like flour through a sifter, the temptation to warn the boys trickled at first, but then it piled into a substantial mound. She toyed with the idea to shake her head. Instead, common sense ruled. She'd cheated, and the unfolding scenario was her punishment.

"Going, going … gone." The auctioneer slammed his gavel against the wooden podium with a resounding thud. "Sold for eighteen dollars on the nose to … to … is that you, Arno Kreger?"

"Yes, sir." Pride filled his voice. Congratulations rallied from all corners of the room.

Hattie winced and sucked in a raspy sigh, while Priscilla squealed in an over-the-top fashion.

"How delightful, Arno. We're much obliged for your generosity." Once the room quieted again, Meridee then retrieved the lone auction basket. What do we have here? Don't tell me it's another poem. My, my, my."

"To share a meal with you
Is sweeter than the plumpest strawberry,
The flakiest lemon tart, or the smoothest drop of honey.

> *It's a stretch of time we'll never get back or forget.*
> *My hands prepared the feast,*
> *But my heart sprinkled the seasoning."*

Hattie's poetry netted exuberant applause and fetched eleven dollars and fifty-five cents for the basket, the second most expensive prize of the night. The auctioneer announced Barrett had edged out Delwyn for the pleasure of her company, a mammoth blessing.

Meridee proceeded with the commemorative tablecloth sale and then invited the attendees to the upcoming dance. A chorus of appreciative "oohs" followed. She instructed the stagehand to dim the lights before inviting the successful bidders to make payment and claim their respective prizes.

Karl, sporting a jaunty smile and a crisp army uniform, hit the stage first. Even though not classically handsome, his happy-go-lucky demeanor and witty sense of humor ranked him a favorite among the local gals.

"Ladies, Prince Charming has arrived." After strutting a few steps, he doubled over with laughter, cupping his trouser knees with both hands, cranking his neck to face the ladies. "I can't pull off that title, can I?"

Lena looped her basket handle over one wrist and captured Karl's arm with the other. "All you need is a little more practice." Good-natured laughter trailed behind the duo, departing the stage.

With hands raised and palms heavenward, Jeb next approached the lineup of females. "Ladies, I'm ready for my clandestine supper."

Meridee giggled like a schoolgirl before collecting her basket. Red-faced, Jeb paid the woman her due before the pair beelined for Daddy, lounging in the front row. Hattie's heart ached for her brother, caught between Meridee and Daddy for the rest of the evening.

Transactions continued until only two women remained on the opposite ends of the stage. From the wing closest to Hattie, Arno ambled forward while Priscilla fussed with a decoration on her hamper. After a dozen steps, Hattie and the handsome soldier stood face to face. She inhaled his peppermint breath.

"I'm sorry," he whispered. "At first, I thought Priscilla's hamper belonged to you, and then I started to second-guess because the poem didn't shout *Hattie*. But I noticed both Jordane and Delwyn bidding, so I figured I better follow suit." A beautiful smile accompanied his shrug. "Will you save me a dance?"

"Yes, please." She gave his callused hand a quick squeeze. "That's a heavy sum you donated to the Brigade. Thank you."

"Oh, Arno." Priscilla strutted forward in a poufy dress more fit for dancing than dining. "You must have sensed this box belonged to me." She hugged the dinner container against her chest as if toting rubies and diamonds, not a second-rate meal.

"To be honest, I didn't."

Guilt oozed down Hattie's spine. Why had she cheated?

"And thank you for spending the most money this evening, Arno, making me the belle of the ball." Priscilla ran a tapered fingernail down the length of his sleeve. "Where's your fella, Hattie? Stand you up, did he?"

"Nonsense." Barrett's shoes clapped against the stage floor. "You folks run a mighty high-priced box social. I had to dash back to the hotel for extra funds." He slung an arm over Hattie's shoulders, tugging her close. "I hope the contents of this basket taste as good as it smells."

"No promises." She forced a laugh that resembled a squawk.

The two men eyed one another like hungry cats over a saucer of milk until Priscilla wrapped a possessive arm around Arno's waist. "Mercy, I'm famished. Shall we find us a quiet corner, Arno?" She arched a sparse brow.

Although he shot Hattie a close-mouthed smile, he headed for the dark backstage corridors with his former sweetheart. Priscilla's giggles continued even after the pair disappeared.

"Where to?" Barrett's grin, wide and sparkly, lit his face. His eyes appeared darker than she'd remembered, intense but warm.

"What if we sit on the edge of the stage and dangle our feet into the orchestra pit? We'll pretend it's a beautiful summer day, and a peaceful little pond lies below."

"It's not exactly private, but you paint a pretty picture." He led the way. With a flip of his wrist, he floated the basket's tablecloth onto the stage before the pair unpacked the rest side-by-side.

Hattie issued herself silent little reminders. *Concentrate on Barrett. Determine if he's marriage-worthy. Don't think about dancing with Arno.*

Their conversation flowed like the natural spring at Catfish Creek, refreshing and unending. He praised her cooking, laughed at her trite jokes, and poked fun at his few missteps at camp. Between bites, he bragged on her food, calling her the best cook in the United States. Then, he raised the stakes to the entire world.

"If you dance half as beautifully as you cook, this may be the best night of my life."

Hattie bumped her shoulder against his in a playful way. "You should know I'm not immune to your flattery."

"I certainly hope not."

The weighty words fluttered her heart and thoughts. *Is this it? Is this the night of my long-awaited first kiss?*

Barrett cupped her cheeks. His hands were smooth. His breath smelled like fried chicken. His smoky eyes studied her face, settling on her lips before inching forward, every coherent thought escaped.

Someone cleared his throat far too loud and far too close.

Air whooshed from Hattie's lungs, and she turned toward the intruder.

"Hope I'm not interrupting." Sarcasm oozed from Arno like a strawberry jam sandwich.

"Liar." Barrett drew backward with a snarl, his hand still latched onto Hattie's shoulder.

Nobody spoke until Arno dropped to a crouch before flicking a crumb with his thumb and forefinger. "I'm shoving off but first wanted to remind you about our dance, Hattie."

Barrett flinched as if Arno had swung a punch. "She's going with me. Why don't you go find your own date?"

"Worried it only takes one dance to woo her away?"

"Please stop," Hattie yelled louder than she'd intended. "I'm a grown woman, someone capable of deciding who I want for dance partners."

"Excellent point." Arno's teasing blue eyes stole her breath, held it hostage.

Supper with Barrett had exceeded expectations. But if she refused Arno, she'd always wonder *what if*.

What if one dance truly made a difference?

CHAPTER FIFTEEN

From the sideline, Hattie studied Jeb. He resembled a besotted sheep, trailing Priscilla onto the packed dance floor. The woman twinkled under the electric lights, garbed in a silver taffeta dress cinched at the waist. Even her hair glittered. If Hattie's vocabulary resembled her brother's, she'd call the sparkly sight a phenomenon.

Hattie scanned the dancehall again. Where was Arno? Had he changed his mind, chucked the entire notion for a better offer? What if he'd only asked her for a dance to lure Barrett into an argument or a shoving match like schoolboys on a playground?

Jeb and his partner swooped past. How had Priscilla captivated him and most every other male between the ages of eighteen and eighty? As the pair danced, an obvious and troubling clue surfaced—you couldn't slide a sheet of paper betwixt the twosome.

Slumped in a chair, she sighed. How long until someone cooed into her ear on the dance floor? Ever the gentleman, Barrett had dashed across the street to fetch her sweater from the opera house.

"I'd label tonight a colossal success." Lena slung an arm over the back of her seat and swiveled toward her friend. "I always knew you'd be a shiny star."

"I was a bundle of nerves until I opened my mouth. Then everything miraculously fell into place." That wasn't exactly true. The auction had unspooled far differently than she'd hoped.

Shivers puckered Hattie's skin. Where was Barrett with her sweater? Her frock featured a skirt that spun like a top when given half a chance, a lacy collar, and short poufy sleeves. Her eyes trained on the swirling bodies, she tapped a toe to the lively beat. Although dancing ranked low on her list of favorites, she might change her mind after one waltz with Mr. Temptation. But would he show?

The Blue Notes, poised on a paltry corner stage, drew a huge following. While the band's repertoire featured mostly old favorites, they'd added a handful of snappy new tunes. Their current song featured a jolly beat and almost yanked Hattie onto the dance floor without a partner.

"How was supper with Karl?"

"He's a hair shy of Prince Charming. Do you think Priscilla copied your poem idea to trick Arno into purchasing her meal? My guess is she heard us talking about it earlier today. She's a shifty one, isn't she?"

"It serves me right for sneaking the news to the boys beforehand. If anyone acted deceitfully this evening, it was me."

Karl swayed past with Sadie Parker, his off-again, on-again sweetheart. Jeb waltzed nearby. Whom did Priscilla want more— Jeb, Arno, or both? "I promised your brother one dance."

Lena tapped her knee against Hattie's and rubbed her hands together. "Say now, I was about to leave this little foray, but your last sentence changed my mind."

Across the room, Wilhelm rested a shoulder against the brick wall as if it might tumble to the ground without him. A half-dozen rowdy out-of-towners, those who'd raised an uproar at the auction with catcalls and wolf whistles, loitered near an open window.

"He looks lonely tonight." Lena frowned at her old beau. "I miss not having a permanent dance partner."

"You know there's a way to fix your dilemma." Hattie nodded toward Will, wishing, once again, the two would kiss and patch up their differences.

When Jeb and Priscilla swept past one more time, Hattie gripped Lena's wrist. "God forbid, but what if Priscilla becomes my sister-in-law one day?"

"Or mine?"

The dire thought almost strangled Hattie, and she drew a deep breath. Then Arno came strolling along the dance floor's rim. A stylish double-breasted trench coat, reaching well past his knees, covered his army uniform. He carried a cap in one hand and a navy scarf in the other.

Somewhere, a glass shattered against the floor. Arno twisted toward the racket, catching Hattie's eye. His slow grin exploded fireworks inside her. An imaginary rope hung between them. He grasped one end while she, hand over hand, drew him forward until he stood inches from her dancing shoes. The whole time, his eyes never left her face.

"You're beautiful."

Lights and music blurred together as Hattie gripped the sides of her chair. Had he truly blurted the compliment, or had she imagined it? "What?" The single syllable barely squeaked past the peach pit-sized lump in her throat.

Lena leaned closer, wearing a pleased-as-punch smile. "He thinks you're the prettiest thing this side of heaven."

Hattie placed both hands on her knees to stop the trembles.

"I wanted to tell you earlier, but ... I'm a dimwit." His grin rivaled late springtime—warm, gorgeous, and promising, minus the occasional downpour.

"Thank you."

"Where's Jordane?" Button by button, Arno unfastened his overcoat before draping it across an empty chair and tossing his other outerwear on top.

"I left my sweater across the street." She pointed with her thumb. "He's fetching it."

"How chivalrous."

"Indeed." Lena grinned as if she'd won a stack of blue ribbons at the Butler County Fair.

"Since your date is currently AWOL, how about a dance, Miss Waltz?"

When she stood, his eyes traveled from the hem of her skirt to the green ribbon twined through her hair. "You still don't reach my chin, but you're definitely all grown up."

On cue, a blush heated her face. She no longer needed her thick sweater. With Arno's two hands gripping hers, he drew her toward the dance floor.

"Behave yourselves," Lena hollered.

Arno rolled his eyes. By the time he and Hattie reached the middle of the room, the smooth tones of "I Love You Truly"—perfect for a romantic, slow-tempo dance—floated through the air. Despite their height variance, Arno's embrace remained natural and right. They glided and swayed to the rhythm.

"I thought you'd escort Priscilla to the dance." Could Arno hear her runaway heartbeat?

"I bought her dinner, not the entire evening. Trust me, it wasn't worth a fraction. She'd slapped together liverwurst sandwiches, salty potato salad, and pickled beets, heavy on the pickling. Her only saving grace," Arno raised a finger, "a cherry strudel for dessert, no doubt prepared by her mother."

Hattie laughed at his chosen details, particularly about the strudel.

"She's found an agreeable dancing partner." He nodded toward the curvaceous heartbreaker and Hattie's fresh-off-the-farm brother clenched in a substantial embrace.

Was Jeb falling in love with Priscilla? "It's impossible to miss. Tell me she's not going to break my brother's heart."

"He's a big boy."

"They still feel pain sometimes."

"How'd your date go with the pastor? Is there a third man vying for your affection?"

Her stomach lurched. Was Arno truly vying for her heart or merely amusing himself until a better prospect came along?

"Let me put it this way—Is the man of the cloth the answer to your dreams?"

"He haunts my nightmares, the type to scare a person for weeks." She winced at the memory. The evening had started at a local restaurant where the pastor complained about his lukewarm soup, sending it back to the kitchen not once or twice, but three times. Next, he ate off her plate. The night concluded on her porch with a sermon on promiscuity. Despite the subject matter, he'd stood too close and repeatedly tried to hold her hand.

Ever since, their interactions at church had grown stiff, clumsy, and borderline unbearable. Still, she'd continued to follow Daddy's rules by the book, one excruciating date a month.

"He longs for the type of wife who loves to clean, cook, and pray without ceasing," she said, determined to recite the man's exact words without laughing.

"Holy smokes. That's the man's criteria?"

"Basically, but then he explained how he'd settle for two out of the three."

Arno's belly laugh spurred her own. Then he sobered. "What are your three qualifications for a spouse?"

Hattie gulped and fumbled for the right words. "Someone who is always kind, trustworthy, and even-tempered. Do you think I'm asking for too much?" To soften the conversation's serious tone, she added an easy chuckle.

Arno stumbled before tightening his hold, drawing her closer against his chest. "Your standards are high. What if you never find anyone who measures up?" His whispered words barely reached her.

"What if I do?"

"Does Jordane fall in line with your qualifications?"

A frown threatened, but she fought the urge. "I'm unsure."

"What about me? Do you think I'll ever measure up to your lofty standards?"

She listened to the steady thump of his heart, matching her wild beat. Amidst the swirling dancers, stray popcorn scattered across the floor, and musical notes so haunting they tickled Hattie's skin, she stopped moving. The man before her, grown up and confident, had once held a prime portion of her heart. Could she ever again trust him with the same gift?

"I hope so."

Arno licked his lips, drawing her eyes to the moisture. "Are you saying you care about me and only me?"

Was she ready to toss Barrett aside, not to mention Daddy's concerns and her own questions about whether or not Arno had truly reformed? "Perhaps."

With his fingertip, he raised her chin. "You know what I heard?"

"Not likely."

"If you kiss in the middle of a crowded dancehall, it's a forever kind of kiss." His finger trailed down her nose, mouth, and chin.

Tingle after tingle shimmied over her spine. Eyes closed, she stretched onto her tiptoes to meet his lips.

Then a woman screamed.

"No!" Arno yelled and sprinted across the room.

Hattie nearly lost her balance. Arno raced toward a stranger holding a chair over Wilhelm's back. Lena dashed toward the violence. Then Hattie followed.

The band stopped, and the chair-touting fellow yelled, "You a German, boy?"

Wilhelm turned to face his accuser.

Arno skidded to a stop beside his pal. Hattie reached Lena's side. Jeb and Karl, along with others from Split Falls, came to stand in unity with one of their own.

The fool out-of-towner said, "I asked you a question, or are you deaf too?"

Wilhelm maintained composure. Arno did not. With fury in his eyes, he charged the stranger and bashed him broadside, knocking the man off his feet.

From that moment forward, everything snowballed. Arno and the stranger grappled across the floor, slammed into the refreshment table, sloshing the punch bowl and rattling the glass cups. A woman screamed.

A fist swung close to Lena, but she ducked. The blow smashed against Hattie's eye, spinning her like a top. She banged against a chair before a bone-jarring crash to the ground, smacking her head against the hard floor. A black nothingness swallowed her whole.

CHAPTER SIXTEEN

"Wake up, sweetheart."

Hattie blinked and then blinked again before closing her eyes tight. Why was she sprawled on her back in the middle of the dancehall, the same place she'd once retched on stage? Little by little, her memory returned.

"Are you okay?"

She cracked open one eye. With her head on Arno's rock-solid thigh, he brushed a strand of hair from her cheek, his fingertips soothing the chaos spinning her head.

Lena knelt close, concern pooling in her eyes. "Tell me you're fine, there's no permanent damage."

The pain wasn't unbearable, more an ache, but the electric lights complicated matters. Gawkers hung nearby, their faces hazy. Barrett, frowning as if he'd single-handedly lost the war, gripped her sweater in both hands.

Disheveled and panting, Jeb dripped blood from his lip to the floor inches from her right hand. A red scratch ran from his temple to his jaw, and perspiration beaded on his face.

"You don't look so good," Hattie told him.

He leaned forward, holding a handkerchief against his mouth and muffling his words. "Oh, the hypocrisy. You may want to glance at a mirror before hurling more insults. Good luck explaining your shiner to Pa."

The pain in Hattie's head sharpened. Daddy had lectured many times on the sins of fisticuffs, no matter the provocation. But in this instance, Hattie disagreed. Someone had intended to hurt Will because of his heritage, something no man could change.

"Goodness, but your face is bright red, Hattie—a geranium red, I believe." Priscilla, over-enunciating her flimsy words, swooped low to expose a neckline designed to showcase her ample figure.

Rolling her eyes would require too much effort. "Where are the men who started the fight? Outside?"

Wilhelm kneeled beside her. Blood seeped from a gash below his eye. He swiped it with his sleeve. A red welt blistered his chin, and several buttons on his white shirt had disappeared, exposing a patch of chest hair. "Some might argue Arno started the tussle. Guess it depends where you stood. Either way, we packed up the troublemakers and kicked their sorry backsides out the door. I'm sorry you landed in the crosshairs." He squeezed her wrist.

"Nobody comes into our dancehall and picks a fight," a voice said from behind Hattie, but her head thudded too much to look. "You tangle with one of us, and you tangle with us all. That's a given." A stirring cheer followed the bold claim.

Hattie's head boomed like a kettledrum.

A rail-thin man approached, dressed in all black and carrying a broom and dustpan. "I step outside for one minute, and mayhem breaks out. What's the matter with the lot of you? Who's gonna clean this mess? And who's gonna pay for the damages? My punchbowl needs replacing plus who knows what else."

Priscilla tiptoed around the shattered glass and then dropped a hand on the man's sleeve, drawing him away from the destruction. "It was completely the other party's fault, and ..."

A moan slipped from Hattie. She rose onto her elbow, eager to leave behind the blaring brightness and scrutiny. "I'm ready for home."

Barrett, clean and tidy—not a hair or button out of place—stepped closer, separating himself from the other onlookers. "Are you fine, Hattie? Do you want your sweater? Shall I fetch a doctor?"

Instead of answering, she glanced at Arno. Blood smeared his starched collar, and the first hint of a bruise discolored his cheek. Still, he smiled.

With care, she touched a massive welt on the back of her head then grimaced and wished for a cold compress or a handful of snow to press against it.

"If you don't want me to fetch the physician, let me take you to him." Barrett bent closer and extended his hand.

"You're not carting her anywhere." With each word, Arno's embrace tightened but not to an uncomfortable degree. "I'll take her home."

"But she's my date and my responsibility." Barrett straightened his shoulders.

"I'm nobody's responsibility."

After Barrett draped her sweater over her arms, he patted her hand and then squeezed, letting his hold linger. "Without a sleigh, I can't escort you to your farm, so I'll permit it."

"It's not your place to permit anything," Lena said, speaking Hattie's thoughts.

Barrett ignored the comment, his expression unchanged. "May I call on you tomorrow, Hattie?"

"Not too early, but yes." Although she hated inflicting pain on anyone, she probably would tomorrow when she told him farewell for keeps. In addition to a successful fundraiser, her goal for the night was to decide which man was right for her—Barrett or Arno. She'd accomplished her mission.

Still, Arno had started another fight. Perhaps he wasn't the ideal suitor either. Hattie sighed, worrying she'd never learn the dating ropes. But maybe Arno deserved a smidge of grace. Didn't it count for something that he'd raised his fists for a legitimate reason? She sure hoped so.

But what would Daddy think?

After a curt nod, Barrett wove through the bystanders and disappeared.

Rounds of goodbyes followed, and then Lena helped Hattie into her warm overcoat. "Now don't go getting any romantic ideas, but Will intends to drive me home. There's a nasty gash on his face that requires tending."

"You do that." Arno stared into Hattie's eyes. Faster than a hiccup, he hefted her off her feet, hugging her against his chest. "You don't weigh much more than a brown sugar sandwich."

She rested her cheek against his firm torso, deciding pillows were overrated.

The fresh air and light snowflakes eased Arno's throbbing jaw. A pesky wind nudged the sleigh south out of town, where drifts rivaled the height of the wooden fence posts lining the road. At each passing farm, a singular outdoor electric light stationed atop a high pole illuminated pungent chimney smoke.

With a loose grip on the reins, Arno glanced toward Hattie. Buried beneath a mound of blankets and a thick buffalo robe, she barely peeked out from the bundle. "How do you feel?"

"Considering the circumstances, not so awful. What about you?"

"Like a million dollars. Nah, two million." He flashed a grin, and she giggled, snuggling closer to his side.

"Your jaw doesn't hurt, not even a smidge?"

"Not while you're next to me."

She laughed. "If that's all it takes, perhaps I'll become a nurse."

"I suspect your healing powers only work on me." The last thing he needed was a hospital room crammed full of wounded soldiers vying for Hattie's attention. Too many extra men already competed for her heart.

"What do you suppose your pa will say when you arrive home with a shiner?" Arno didn't regret the night's tussle, an opportunity to help a friend, but he doubted Chester Waltz would feel likewise.

"With any luck, he's fast asleep. The last thing I want, or need, is a told-you-so lecture from Daddy."

"What's the first thing you want?" He held a hopeful breath, waiting to hear his name or, maybe, a little four-letter word—*kiss*.

"I can't give away all my secrets."

"I'll settle for one, a little one."

"All this anti-German-American nonsense scares me more and more each day. Believe it or not, the matter keeps me awake some nights."

Why did she have to bring that up now? He'd much rather she'd hinted about a kiss. Only the muffled clomp of horse hooves, the jingle of bells, and the rattle of the sleigh interrupted the wintery air. Arno worked on a reply, choosing his words with care. "You mustn't worry."

"That's next to impossible. The newspaper ran a headline on the front page last month stating, 'Your Neighbor May Be a German Spy.' Sure enough, the article riled the townspeople, and the next couple of editions featured editorials about disloyalty and a generous dose of anti–German-American hoopla."

"Heard about that. It's a shame."

"It's worse than a shame, it's downright ugly. The second I finished reading the article, I hurled the newspaper into the hearth." She grimaced. "That was a mistake. Daddy hadn't yet read the thing."

Arno chuckled as snowflakes skittered.

"If you ask me, tonight was a prime example that the dangers are spreading. Do you face problems at camp for … for your ancestry?"

Arno shrugged and watched the steady horse pull the sleigh. The less Hattie knew about his past harassment, the less she'd fret. "It's minimal down there, but Iowa has its fair share of German communities. I reckon more than Arkansas."

"The same article said someone threw yellow paint on a grocer's business somewhere across the Minnesota state line. Those same troublemakers then nailed an American flag over the front door."

Far worse tales had circled the barracks, but he'd not tell her those horror stories. Someone had tarred and feathered a suspect in a southern Iowa county, and another family's barn had burned to the ground, all based on suspicions and fears.

Everyone had heard of public bonfires to rid the world of books written in German. These days, nobody chowed on frankfurters and sauerkraut, instead choosing to devour *liberty sausages* and *liberty cabbages*. One family even renamed their dachshund a *liberty dog*. *Cute!*

"It's probably a silly question, but do you ever wish you weren't German-American?"

No, but with a last name like O'Malley or Dubois, he may have sidestepped the harassment at camp. Raised on polka music, schnitzel, and teatime every afternoon at three o'clock sharp, he'd not trade his German-American upbringing with anyone.

"Not exactly," he touched his bruised cheek, "but I've lain awake wondering about shooting at some distant kin over in Europe."

Hattie blinked her eye that wasn't swollen shut.

"A person could easily kill a second cousin or a great uncle and never be the wiser. I suppose it's not the best time for German-Americans."

"That's as disappointing as the meal Priscilla prepared for the box social." When she rubbed her hands together, he tucked the coverings tighter.

"They say General Pershing has German ancestors, so we're in good company." Arno steered the sleigh up Hattie's long, twisty lane. The porchlight glimmered at the top of the hill. A cow bellowed from the barn as if welcoming her home.

"Whoa, girl," he called to the horse, drawing to a stop a few feet from the Waltz's porch before turning to face his girl. *His girl*.

Snowflakes laced her fuzzy woolen hat. He swept the bits of moisture aside, letting his hand linger. Sparkly flakes laced her eyelashes. She blinked them away before nuzzling deeper under the blanket and against him. Her pink cheeks glistened.

"I'll miss you when I leave," he whispered. Unlike his canceled December five-day furlough, this stint ended in two. Far too short. Hypnotized by her rosy cheeks and open lips, he stared. If he wasn't mistaken, a kiss-me look sparked in her eyes.

"Me too. It hurts to breathe when I think about it. But, what if …"

He hushed her fears with a long-overdue kiss, softly at first and then with a firm persistence. Her lips were warm, sweet, and unforgettable. She trembled. Her nearness had the opposite effect on him, driving a river of heat through his veins.

She broke away far too soon. A crystal snowflake dotted her nose, and he rubbed it aside with his own before dropping a peck on the same spot.

"Thank you. Are you shocked to learn it's my first kiss?"

He caught and copied her warm, teasing tone. "Did it meet your expectations?" He probably shouldn't chase a compliment, but he needed to know he wasn't the only one tumbling head over heels.

"Exceeded." She caressed his unbruised cheek.

"Are you ready for kiss number two? Experts claim practice makes perfect."

Although her smile stretched, she declined his suggestion. "Two might spin my head. Next thing you know, I'm falling from your sleigh and into a snowbank. It sounds dangerous, not to mention cold."

"What happens after three kisses?" He whispered, clutching her mitten.

"Heart palpitations followed by the vapors."

"I'm willing to risk it." He laughed and settled for a kiss to her forehead.

"Goodnight, Arno. Thank you for the dance and the ride home, plus a dozen other things I'm probably forgetting."

"Did that bump to your head rattle your memory?"

"Partly, but you also make my head swoon … or is it my heart?"

What he wouldn't give for ten more minutes of her time, but he'd settle for five. "Are you sure you can't stay? I promise to keep you warm."

"I don't question your capabilities."

Inches apart, their breaths mingled in the bitter cold. His hands lingered on her waist. "Your eyes are the most amazing thing I've ever seen." Although he thought it impossible, they grew even wider. "They sparkle."

She initiated their second kiss.

The porchlight flashed, and he all but leaped back to his side of the sleigh.

Her pa filled the doorway. "Time to come inside, Hattie." His deep voice echoed over the winter landscape. "It's late and stone cold."

"Why don't I help you explain what happened?" Arno whispered.

"Thank you, but if I'm ready to court, I'm ready to face my father alone."

He hopped to the ground to help her out of the sleigh. A newfound protectiveness swarmed, but Arno dismissed his first instinct—to whisk her back into the sleigh and gallop down the lane to a safe place far from meddling fathers. Instead, he waited while she navigated the steps.

"Hattie," Arno called.

She turned back around, grinning. "What?"

"Nothing." He needed to see her smile one more time. Who knew when he'd view it again?

Her priceless grin pumped his pulse. Then she pivoted and reached her father.

Chester Waltz spoke to his daughter, but not loudly enough for Arno to hear.

Twice before, he'd butted heads with Hattie's pa. Once after Jeb's accidental shooting and then at a barn dance. Both times, Mr. Waltz had demanded Arno steer clear of his young'uns or else. Although a vague threat, the man's icy tone rang clear.

The Waltz's door slammed shut behind Hattie. Mr. Waltz came down the steps. "I have one question for you, Kreger."

Here it comes. "What's that, sir?"

"Are you good enough for my daughter?"

He wanted to shout yes loud enough for Chester, Butler County, and the whole world to hear. But it would be a lie. "Probably not, sir."

Hattie's pa grunted. "You return her home with a bruised face. Want to tell me about that?"

Should he explain that he'd defended Wilhelm, and he'd do so again in a heartbeat? His only regret was Hattie's involvement, a definite mistake. "I'm sorry about that."

"My daughter said you didn't hit her and begged me to give you the benefit of the doubt, Kreger. However, you failed to protect her. Her face will heal, but what about her heart? If you care about my daughter, leave her be."

Before Arno could respond, Mr. Waltz turned his back and went into the house. The porch light fizzled.

Alone in the dark, snowflakes piled onto Arno's head and shoulders. Mr. Waltz was right. Arno ought to hop into the sleigh, glide home, and forget about the girl. But it was too late.

He loved her.

CHAPTER SEVENTEEN

January 16, 1918

Dear Arno,

I hope all is well in your part of the country. It's still cold and snowy here.

After the dancehall brawl, Daddy actually listened to Jeb explain what happened with Wilhelm and the out-of-towners. He promises not to burn your letters if they arrive in the mailbox. That's a small victory. However, I'm still obligated to continue my once-a-month dates with locals. According to Daddy, you're not marriage material. He jumped to that hasty conclusion on his own accord. I haven't mentioned that scenario to him.

I've not heard from Barrett since he stormed off our property when I told him goodbye. The way his temper flared makes me happy I saw that side of the man now, not later.

Did you enjoy the train ride to Arkansas? Was it snowy? Did you pass the time thinking of me? Oops, I did it again, steered the letter back toward good old Hattie.

Since I'm a lost cause this afternoon, here are three little things I wager you don't know.

Your kiss caressed my lips like a slip of silk, smooth and feathery. To top it off, you tasted like tingly peppermint candy. If you can't tell, I think about the smooch far more often than a good girl should. Even now, I'm blushing.

When you carried me from the dancehall to the sleigh, I felt safe and secure tucked in your arms. We both know I'm capable of standing on my own two feet, but for the first time in years, it wasn't necessary.

I carved our initials into the bark of my favorite apple tree. Although it's a silly gesture, it makes me grin like the dickens whenever I pass it.

Hawk is pestering me for a game of marbles, so I'll close for now. Then there's knitting until the wee hours. I've fallen behind on my pledge for the Brigade to knit four items before our next meeting. I'm making fingerless mitts.

Before I sign off, here's one more confession—I miss you most at nighttime when there's nothing to do but sleep and ponder. By the way, I've had enough pondering to last a lifetime.

Interesting way to sign

As always and always,

Hattie

His heart had sped up halfway through her letter. She still dwelled on their kiss. That didn't surprise him. Mentioning the intimacy in a letter shocked him in a warm and agreeable way. But Mr. Waltz's question—*Are you good enough for my daughter?* —never let Arno alone.

Arno stuffed Hattie's letter into his trunk, grabbed his gear for the afternoon drill, and then hustled outside. Orders followed to *fall in* for their marching formation. Heads and backpacks bobbed before him.

The January thaw, resembling a warm spring day back home, popped sweat between his shoulder blades. Slush splashed beneath boots, staining trousers from ankle to knee. The soldiers' uniform steps pounded out a silent ditty.

"Over hill, over dale,
As we hit the dusty trail,
And our caissons go rolling along.
In and out, hear them shout,
Counter march and right about,
And the caissons go rolling along …"

The company marched three miles along a straight auto road then swerved left toward the same timber where Arno had captured the two bumbling foes in December. At the trees' fringe, Lieutenant Langley—a new officer—shouted, "Parade rest. Listen up, men."

Langley toted a brass whistle on a string and paced. "When I dismiss you, I want y'all to run into them woods," he pointed at the trees, "and catch yourselves a rabbit. Company dismissed!" A thick twang stuck to his words.

Soldiers raced right and left yelping like banshees. Arno hurtled a fern patch, blazing through overgrown brush. Unlike winter back home, not much snow littered the ground. "This way," he yelled to Karl.

"Right behind you."

Arno spared a glance over his shoulder and then bolted into the shadowy forest. His foot snagged on a root, and he stumbled.

Karl zipped past, swishing the bushes. "Nice move, clumsy!"

Forced to play catch-up, Arno passed sugar maples, burr oaks, shortleaf pines, and hickories. They navigated a steep slope before crossing a stumpy knoll. Faint hollers and a muffled gunshot trailed them as they followed a dried riverbed deeper into the timber. Sunlight flickered through branches overhead as the temperature plunged.

Karl skidded to a stop, raised one rigid foot behind him, and stiffly pointed his nose and a hand like an Irish setter. Dead ahead stood a gigantic hickory covered in gnarly bark. "Nuts." Karl dangled his tongue.

"Good dog." Arno patted his buddy's head, hoping they'd ditched the rest of the soldiers. "Let's go have a look-see. I'd eat a nut, or two, or three, or four." Arno set his backpack and rifle against a tree trunk. He counted each nut he collected.

Karl flopped beside his belongings. "I miss my dang dog. Shoot, he could track a titmouse in a briar patch. According to Ma, Romeo still waits on me every single day at the end of the lane. He can snare a rabbit faster than a wildfire."

"Rabbits … I've yet to see the likes of one around these parts."

"Ain't this the limit, pretending jackrabbits are Huns?"

Arno copped a seat on a patch of grass and loosened his boots. "Mm-hmm. If you close your eyes, it feels a bit like home." The scent of pine and smoke from a not too distant fire blended. A nearby crow cawed. Arno opened his eyes.

Karl cracked a nutshell with his teeth and then picked out the meat with his pocketknife. "Hyland showed some of the boys a picture of his sister last night. I caught a glimpse."

"And?" Although Arno was pretty sure he knew the answer.

"Close your eyes and picture CW in a dress."

"Not a handsome woman, I take it."

"I'll put it this way—she has facial hair." Karl's forefinger rested between his upper lip and nostrils.

"And here I thought you loved all women."

"That's debatable, but I do adore Sadie, and I may have finally ruined my chances with the gal." Karl shook his head. "I know full well she's out of my league, but you can't smite a man for trying to better himself."

"You and Sadie breakup and then makeup every couple of months. What makes you think that won't happen again?"

Of all the women in Butler County, would Arno pick Sadie for Karl? Nope, never. Back in grammar school, she'd shake her pigtails in Karl's direction, and a second later, he'd trot to her side. During their teenage years, she flirted with Karl one minute and then flipped her attention elsewhere the next. Her blondish-white hair and a noteworthy figure appealed, but not her scheming personality. Still, the woman held a corner of his buddy's heart, at least for the time being.

"I had a tiny mix-up with my letters. It seems I wrote Sadie a lovey-dovey note but somehow slipped her sheet of stationery inside another woman's envelope, which means Sadie opened her mail and read *Dear Sweetest Rose*."

Sadie wasn't the type to abide a two-timer, especially if she received the short end of the stick. "I feel for you, buddy. I do."

"She never wants to speak to me again, and if'n I never return from France," Karl's eyes met his, "she swears she won't shed too many tears. That's mean, don't you think?"

"Brutal." Karl juggled more hearts in one hand than a dozen other fellows. Although Arno tried to empathize, he also figured letters from a string of girls probably cluttered the post office back at camp—all addressed to Private Karl Ludwig.

"Shoot, I only strung Rose along for amusement. I meant no harm. Sadie is my one and only." Karl rolled onto his side, propping his head with a hand.

"She'll come around. Doesn't she always?"

"You don't know beans about girls, Kreger." Karl bombarded Arno with a barrage of nuts and twigs, shooting his weapons in rapid-fire succession.

Arno returned the assault before ducking an incoming nut. "Then how is it I got a girl, and you don't?"

"Shoot." Karl sagged against his backpack, crossing his ankles.

They listened to the wind until Arno threw a twig high in the air and caught it one-handed. "Hattie's pa still expects her to date other men. Have you ever heard of such a thing when two people court?"

"She should refuse. She's nineteen now, isn't that right?"

Arno grunted. "She lives under his roof. He has something stuck in his craw where I'm concerned. Although it's hard to fathom, he doesn't care for the cut of my jib."

"Nobody does." Although Karl pitched another stick, it bounced off Arno's boot. "I thought you intended to die a bachelor." Karl never forgot anything.

"I may have mentioned that once or twice."

"Or twenty times."

"It's not so much I don't wish to marry, it's that I can't wrap my head around ever becoming a father."

Karl nodded. "Because of Oliver."

"Exactly."

"Have you told Hattie?"

Arno sighed. "Months back, I mentioned my leaning in a letter, and she's not commented one way or another. Perhaps it's not a deal breaker, but I'm not ready to walk down the aisle yet. If her pa has anything to say about it, it'll never happen."

"Mr. Waltz is a tough old bird."

Every time he and Hattie inched forward in their relationship, something dragged them backward again, and that something was usually her pa.

Karl snapped his fingers close to Arno's face. "You disappeared there for a minute."

"Sorry, but I can't get something out of my head, no matter how hard I try."

"What's that?"

"Once we're in France, furloughs back home probably end. Tell me this—how long does it take for a man in flesh and blood to look better than a stack of moldy letters?" How long would Hattie wait?

"I have a confession, but you can't tell." Karl caught Arno's eye. "If you do, I'll flat out deny it."

"I'm intrigued."

"I'm no expert when it comes to women."

Wide-eyed, Arno dropped his jaw to feign horror. "Say it ain't so."

"That said, I honestly don't believe you need to worry about Hattie and other men. At some point, you'll have to trust her."

"Says the expert."

"I likely ruined things with Sadie. Don't start questioning Hattie."

Arno settled his back against a tree, stretched his legs, and then closed his eyes while his buddy's words circled. If he and Hattie splintered over a few dates with local men, fellas she had no intention to see more than once, how would they ever forge a lasting footing?

"Kreger."

"Hmm?" If Karl stopped yapping, Arno might steal a nap.

"Promise me something."

"Name it."

"If I don't make it home from France, write Ma and tell her."

Arno cracked open his eyes. "What are you yapping about?"

"I'll do the same for you."

A squirrel rustled a branch, and a tiny twig drifted onto Arno's lap. "Of course, I will." He wasn't ready to think about battlefield deaths, Karl's or anyone else's. He pressed the twig between his thumb and forefinger, bending it like a rainbow. It snapped into two equal parts.

"From the sounds of it, we'll leave Pike soon. I don't know why, but dying weighs on my mind. The army's notice would be cut-and-dried, but you, you'd do it right. It'd be easier on Ma if it came from you. While you're at it, you can list all the wonderful things you admire about me."

Arno rolled onto his belly. "It'll be a challenge, but if I ponder long enough, I'll think of something positive to say ... like that part in your hair is plenty straight."

Karl laughed and stood with his rifle. "Good, I'm glad we've settled on a strategy, though you best start improving your compliments, or Hattie might complain."

"Don't you worry none about my gal." Arno swiped at his stained uniform, tied his laces, and then gathered his gear. A gunshot echoed off to their left. "Sounds like someone got lucky."

"Or not."

They tromped through the dense timber on a mossy carpet toward the gunfire. A second shot cracked, closer than the first. When the pair broke through the trees in a clearing, garbled voices rose from a ring of men.

"That's a load of soldiers to catch one little critter." Karl pointed at the gathering.

"Maybe it's not a rabbit. Maybe someone shot a razorback. I wonder how that animal tastes." Ever since coming to Pike, their regular chow never measured up.

Voices boiled as they drew closer, men arguing over who'd shot the rabbit. A bloody animal sprawled on the earth near their feet. Hyland and Jordane comprised one side of the disagreement and three opposed. Jordane never pointed his firearm. Instead, he punched Arno with a lethal glare.

Uninterested in the argument's outcome or Barrett's bitter stare, he turned his back when a fuzzy rabbit scurried from the brush a few yards away and ducked under a heap of foliage. He elbowed Karl's ribs and then nodded toward the prey, mouthing the word *bunny*. The others caught on, and seven men rushed toward the brush.

"I told you there were two rabbits," someone yelled loud enough to scare lurking wildlife within a one-mile radius.

"This one has my name on it." Hyland kicked at a thorny shrub.

Men grumbled.

Arno veered right and circled back toward the spot where the animal dove moments ago. With the tip of his rifle, he brushed away a stack of soggy leaves. Out darted a rabbit. Like a trained sniper, he drew his weapon to his shoulder, cocked the trigger, and BANG.

A piercing burn, isolated and excruciating, shot through Arno's thigh. He crumpled to the ground. The word *German* resonated in his ears and his soul. With teeth gritted, he rolled over. A scarlet stain spread across his upper leg and pooled in the dead grass. To ward off the pain, he closed his eyes and missed the shooter's escape. Why had this happened now? At camp? Among his fellow soldiers?

Karl dropped beside him, ripping off his service coat and pressing the wadded cloth against the oozing wound. "What happened?"

"I'm shot." Another sharp stab stole Arno's breath. Warmth, then a chill crawled over him.

"I can see that." Karl smiled, nervous and half-hearted, but his eyes never strayed from his task.

Three more men arrived, and Karl ordered someone to fetch a medic. "They're down on the road where we climbed into the woods." He pointed with a bloodstained hand.

"Did someone aim at the rabbit and miss?" Was that Frankie who asked?

"If that's the case," Karl said, "they're a lousy shot."

Arno's head swam, and Karl's voice grew faint. Perhaps if he let himself sleep, he'd feel better, block out the pain. A catnap would cure what ailed him. That's all he needed.

"Stay awake, Kreger." Karl slapped his face, probably harder than necessary.

Arno cracked an eye open, but the cool ground was as soft as his bed back home. The shooting felt like a dream. Or a nightmare. Perhaps a foreshadowing of his future in Europe on the battlefield.

"We're wasting time," Frankie shouted, jerking Arno awake. "Let's carry him back. I got his ankles."

"Wait." Arno raised his hand. "If anyone bumps my leg, he won't see tomorrow."

"You heard the man." Karl gripped Arno's armpits. Two others positioned hands underneath his sides. "Nice and easy. On three, lift. One, two—"

"I'm here." The medic elbowed soldiers aside. "The stretcher bearers are minutes behind me." He flung Karl's blood-drenched coat aside and then sliced through Arno's trousers with scissors. After a hasty examination, he leaned back on his haunches. "It went in one side and out the other. Skimmed you, but there's a mess of blood."

Sweat soaked Arno from head to toe.

"Anybody know what happened here?" The medic's eyes swept the gathering of soldiers.

The stretcher arrived before anyone spoke. The crew transferred Arno onto the mobile bed as if they'd performed the maneuver a hundred times before.

"We all tracked the same rabbit," Frankie's words came in rapid succession. "Next thing you know there's gunfire, and Kreger here goes down. I reckon it's an accident."

"Someone got a beef with you, Kreger?" The medic tugged a towel from his bag and wiped his hands.

Arno sucked in his breath. Had someone whispered the word *German* before the bullet carved a hole in his leg, or had he imagined the ugly gibe? Two men rose to the top of a slim list, both with ample opportunity and motivation for revenge.

"They'll take you to the base hospital, stitch you up, soldier." The medic patted Arno's shoulder, leaning close to say, "You'll be as good as new."

SAD! Thoughts flung like arrows. Did someone hate him enough to shoot him? And where were Jordane and Hyland?

One obvious answer screamed—gone.

CHAPTER EIGHTEEN

Hattie loosened the scratchy scarf wrapped twice around her neck and waited.

Split Falls was the type of community where neighbors helped plant and harvest each other's crops, and a crock of chicken noodle soup landed on porch stoops when someone sneezed. Nobody locked doors because one man's home offered another man a haven. It was butchering day at Wilhelm Mueller's farm, but only a piddly few workers loitered in the yard, waiting for the entire shooting match to commence.

Wilhelm, an only child, nursed his ailing father seven days a week. The old man resided full-time in a bed propped against the front room window to watch cardinals, the changing seasons, and arriving guests. Mr. Mueller, Daddy's closest friend, only spoke German and hadn't ventured outside in years. Mrs. Mueller passed last summer from a bee sting. Naturally, father and son still mourned their loss.

Butchering ranked low on Hattie's list of favorite chores, right alongside corn picking and window washing. But her two hands helped lighten the load, especially when the load equaled a 900-pound steer.

Before the animal knew what clubbed him, Wilhelm dazed the critter with a hammer. Daddy slit his thick neck. Hattie gagged, a cupped hand pressed against her mouth. The January sunshine had melted snow to mush, and she zigzagged around clumps of slush to reach the porch where Meridee, the only other female in attendance, shook her head.

"For the life of me, I don't know why you and your queasy

stomach watched that nasty bloodshed." Meridee huffed up the half-dozen porch steps.

The pair entered the messy kitchen before shedding their winter garments and stacking the items on a cluttered bench designed to hold such things. The home smelled musty, masculine, and leathery, partly due to a saddle sandwiched beneath the kitchen table and the floor. Hattie dragged it across the room to an open space beneath a window stamped with lacy frost.

Meridee tugged a colorful apron from a satchel, wrapped it around her ample waist, and crossed her arms. "Death isn't a pretty sight."

"In my opinion, it's unfair to the steer."

"Says a farmer's daughter."

Although Hattie shrugged, she understood her opinions differed from Daddy's and ninety-nine percent of anyone else whose livelihood centered on livestock.

"And I'm the city girl who doesn't know the first thing about butchering, which means you'll need to show me the ropes today."

The time for a lesson on proper attire had passed. Meridee's swishy gingham dress, trimmed with shimmering embroidery, flared at the hem. Add a frilly bonnet and an umbrella, and she'd blend right in at an ice cream social. Hattie wore Jeb's castaway trousers from childhood and an old shirtwaist embellished with multiple stains.

"First, let's greet our host." After chit-chatting with Mr. Mueller, who pointed out a dozen feathered friends beyond his window, the ladies rolled up their sleeves and the instructions commenced. Meridee repeated aloud every direction Hattie uttered.

Hattie knew the entire steer-to-beef-roast process by heart. Daddy was the area's go-to butcher, and she and Jeb had learned from him. Twice a year, they helped the Mueller's butcher hogs and cattle, which meant she knew her way around the family's formerly tidy kitchen.

She and Meridee worked in tandem, transferring the sharp

knife collection from a cluttered sideboard to the kitchen table. They spread an oilcloth across the floor, piling old newspapers on top of the worn fabric. On their knees, they scrutinized their work.

"Now what?" Meridee asked, smoothing a bunched wrinkle on the newsprint with her forefinger.

"We wait on the menfolk."

Hattie helped Meridee to her feet and crossed to the cook stove, still hot from breakfast. She stoked the fire, catching a whiff of wood, coal, and corncobs. "What do you say we fire up the teakettle?"

"Sounds perfect."

After settling into a pair of high-backed chairs, they hashed over Brigade matters, the new millinery in town, and the latest local draftees destined for boot camp.

Meridee leaned forward and squinted. "I suppose those pearls once belonged to your mother.

"A gift from Daddy on their wedding day."

"I wish I'd known her."

The teakettle whistled, and Hattie jumped to answer its bidding. "It sounds funny to hear you say that since you're sweet on my pa."

"I suppose, but Chester loved your mother with every ounce of his being, and I care for him enough to wish he'd never faced the heartache of losing her."

A lump filled Hattie's throat. She scooped a handful of Mama's necklace into her fist. "Thank you. If you're not careful, you'll make me teary."

"Can I ask you something?"

"Of course." Hattie returned to her seat before the two sipped tea and measured one another over dainty cups. Seconds piled into a minute.

"If, and this is a humongous if, Chester and I decide to wed, would we have your blessing?" Meridee hiked her brassiere straps with her thumbs, first on the right, then the left.

A framed picture of a plow horse hung on the wall across the table from Hattie. She studied the stocky steed, mulling over her friend's question.

Emma Waltz and Meridee Moss differed like moonshine and communion wine. The first three adjectives Hattie pinned to Meridee—loud, brassy, and overbearing. While Mama's noticeable traits included a gentle spirit, poise, and a resemblance to precious jewels, at least that's what Daddy claimed.

But both women loved with all their hearts and fought tooth and nail for something—or someone—they cherished. Wasn't Daddy happier these last few months since the widow had entered his life? More and more, whenever Hattie yearned to talk to Mama, she sought out Meridee, who scattered wisdom and hugs. What more could a girl want in a potential stepmother?

"You don't need my blessing. It's your decision and Daddy's."

"Hogwash. You're the apple of your father's eye." Meridee tilted her head. "Do you honestly believe he'd ever get within an inch of a wedding band without your approval? Of course, I need Hawk on board with this potential plan too. Jeb is his own man, but I'm pretty sure he's fond of me."

"He bought your auction basket."

Meridee tossed her head back to laugh. "That's an excellent point."

"If you and Daddy find happiness alongside one another, I'd be in your debt. Heaven knows we could use another female in the house."

Hattie wrapped her arms around Meridee, sinking into the woman's plushness. When the drawn-out embrace ended, she stood before folding her apron over the back of a chair. "I'm stepping outside a moment."

"Take your time, dear. I'll fetch the meat grinder."

"It's in the shanty."

"Then we're good to go on this end, correct?"

"Yes, ma'am." Hattie retrieved her overcoat and then picked her way around dwindling snowdrifts to reach the backyard. A pair of leafless oaks flanked the farmhouse, where melting snow dripped from the roof, plopping into puddles.

Since the mail had arrived late yesterday, they'd not fetched it until this morning on the way over. In short order, Hattie tore open her sweetheart's envelope and found two sheets of ivory stationery and a hand-drawn portrait of Arno in his military uniform.

Karl's pencil etching not only captured Arno's physical likeness, but it also highlighted the glow in his eyes and on his lips. Forever grateful, Hattie refolded the treasure, careful not to add additional creases. She tucked the drawing inside the envelope to exchange it for the letter.

> *January 22, 1918*
> *Hello Gorgeous,*
> *This is Karl, not your soldier boy. He had a mishap this afternoon. He's on the mend at the base hospital. A bullet grazed his leg. They'll keep him here no more than a few days, maybe three or four.*

Although Lena had already shared the news of Arno's injury, it still fluttered Hattie's heart when she read Karl's words. What if the bullet had pierced an artery?

> *They've pumped medicine into him, and he's asleep now. The nurses like to fuss over him but not too much if you catch my meaning.*
> *He received a promotion to private first-class. Yep, the son-of-a-gun outranks me. Cripes!*
> *It's hard to judge the war. My guess is we'll win eventually. Ma sent a letter and asked me to tell the Kaiser to surrender. Doesn't that beat all? I'd jot the fella a note tonight if it'd work.*
> *Arno, who snores, by the way, asked me to pen you a quick letter with his three little things. Here you go:*

He wants you to promise not to worry.

He rereads every letter you send him at least a half-dozen times, probably more.

He loves the color of your eyes. They remind him of a steamy mug of hot chocolate, which we both know is his favorite.

Stay strong, Hattie, and write me if you have the time and notion. If Arno closed this letter, he'd probably end with sweet words like "I'm devoted to you forever and ever." Since he's currently dead to the world, I'll close with my version of farewell—hope to receive a letter from you soon.

Sincerely,
Arno and Karl

With a newspaper tucked under his arm, Jeb rounded the two-story farmhouse in route to the privy. Plowing right through the mud holes as he went. "Why you back here by your lonesome?"

Hattie ended her lazy lean against the wall. "Do they need me in the kitchen?"

"Not for ten, fifteen minutes, I wager. I'm surprised Priscilla hasn't shown yet."

If Jeb believed Priscilla might roll up her sleeves to help grind meat, he was more naïve than Hattie suspected. "Don't hold your breath. Miss Snodgrass isn't the butchering type."

"What's that supposed to mean?"

Priscilla carried herself with an air of sophistication as if she'd never slopped a pig a day in her life, yet everyone knew that wasn't true. Her pa raised more sows than anyone else in the county, but Hattie doubted the woman had ever wielded a knife on butchering day.

"It means you ought to watch your step where she's concerned."

"Aren't you the pot calling the kettle obsidian."

Hattie jutted a hip and then tilted her head. "Why do you dislike Arno? Do you blame him for your accident?"

"Nah, I can't pin my injury on the man. But I once told him

I favored Priscilla, and he courted her anyway. He kiboshed my plans to woo the woman."

Hattie rolled her eyes.

"It's a word. When you get home, go find the dictionary."

Did Arno and Priscilla's version mirror Jeb's, or was there more to the dating story? Sometimes, her big brother held tight to outdated grudges, the type where someone forgets what fueled his anger in the first place.

"I'll make a deal with you, Hattie. You stay out of my romantic business, and I'll keep my nose clear of yours." Jeb's outstretched hand waited for hers to seal their deal.

The smart move was to agree to the terms. But Priscilla had a penchant for jerking hearts into downward spirals. Someday, hopefully soon, all the eligible servicemen would flock back to Split Falls. Then what? Would she still favor Jeb, or flop her attention and heart to her former prospects and suitors?

"Hattie!" Daddy's voice bellowed.

She turned and fled. In her haste, she stumbled, tripping over a snow pile in her path. Jeb's laughter, deep and irritating, shadowed her until she reached the porch.

Wilhelm and Daddy, and eventually Jeb, sliced meat slabs into meal-sized portions to a silent rhythm, while Hattie and Meridee trimmed and lobbed off hefty chunks of fat. Hawk, relegated to the front room, built wooden block towers under Mr. Mueller's watchful eye. At dusk, Jeb left for home to do the milking.

"Why don't I rustle us up some supper," Wilhelm offered, sopping meat juices off the kitchen floor with a towel.

"None for me. I'm nearly asleep on my feet." Meridee raised a tin dipper to her lips from the water pail in the kitchen corner.

"I'll cart you home." Daddy hauled his navy suspenders over his shoulders. "Hattie, I'll swing back to fetch you and the boy. In the meantime, help clean up this mess."

"That's not necessary." Wilhelm transferred a handful of knives to the washbasin, dropping a couple in route. "But don't rush out the door, Meridee. I have something."

Hattie collected soiled newspapers from the floor, bunching the soggy journals into a ball before tossing the wad onto the porch. Thank yous and goodbyes followed, along with hunks of beef wrapped in newspaper and given to Meridee.

Interesting

"*Danke*. I'm much obliged for your help today." Wilhelm slapped Daddy's shoulder. "Couldn't have done the butchering without you."

"*Gute Nacht*." Daddy ambled out the door with Meridee as close as a back pocket.

At first, Hattie and Wilhelm worked in silence, returning the room to its original order. "We have all this beef at our fingertips," Wilhelm said, "but what if I fix flapjacks and bacon for supper?"

"I'm not about to turn down my favorite meal."

"I figured as much." A pair of work gloves dangled from his trouser pocket. The growth of a new beard and longer hair in dire need of clipping made him appear more rugged than usual, like a lumberjack.

Wilhelm knew his way around a kitchen. He sang a familiar ditty, collecting plates, cups, silverware, and napkins, stacking his collection onto a pile. Jeb, on the other hand, probably didn't know the difference between a frying pan and a butter churn.

While Hattie gathered ingredients for the batter, Wilhelm readied the cast iron skillet. "You're not one of those who likes her bacon crispy, are you?"

"I won't dignify your question with an answer." She and Will had shared dozens of breakfasts over the years. He knew her food preferences, especially regarding salty slab bacon. Hattie transferred a screwdriver, a stack of magazines, and an empty tin can to the table, clearing space for her mixing bowl.

Him at the stove and her at the sideboard—no more than two feet apart. They concentrated on their respective supper tasks. "We're like an old married couple, aren't we?" Will asked, followed by a lengthy chuckle. "All we need is a houseful of young'uns."

Hattie froze. They'd always shared an easy, companionable friendship, not a wedded bliss-type relationship. "You want children one day?"

"Of course. Doesn't everyone?"

Maybe everyone but Arno. "I don't believe so."

"I want a dozen, perhaps more."

Hattie laughed, picturing Wilhelm with a child on each knee and a couple hanging over his shoulders. No doubt he'd make a first-rate father. Hawk often clung to Will's side for one excellent reason—he treated the boy with equal portions of respect and love.

"I feel like I missed out on all the brother-sister shenanigans."

Hattie resumed her stirring, smashing lumps against the side of the bowl. She needed to pack away all thoughts of Wilhelm's fatherhood potential. "What's the latest between you and Lena? I know where she stands, but how do you feel about it all?"

"I'll tell you after you tell me this." Wilhelm leaned an elbow against the sideboard to view her face. "What lucky man did you date this month?"

"Sid Delaney."

"The fella who runs the opera house?" Bacon sizzled, and Wilhelm resumed his task at the stove.

"A while back he asked me to audition for his vaudeville show, and it took me months to finally tell him no." The thought sent a fresh wave of chills down her back. "Next thing you know, he asks me on a date to go dancing."

The businessman—with his oiled hair combed straight back—arrived late, barely spoke a word, and fell asleep in a chair at the dancehall. Plus, he'd smelled like an oilcan.

"I haven't met him."

It was high time to swap the focus from her romantic life to Wilhelm's. "Let's talk about Lena. Is she bluffing, or does she truly plan to fly the coop?" Hattie retired to a kitchen chair to wait for her turn at the cook stove.

"I don't know." He drained bacon grease into a crock. "Can I tell you something funny?"

"You know how I appreciate a good laugh. Go ahead."

"Perhaps it's more thoughtful than humorous." Wilhelm shrugged. "Either way, I always assumed you and I would wind up together one day, not you and Arno or Lena and me. Answer me this—do you truly see yourself as Mrs. Arno Kreger down the road?"

Hattie's spoon hit the ground, and then she scrambled to fetch it. "Why?"

"Just curious." Wilhelm hummed "Let Me Call You Sweetheart," carrying a plate of bacon toward the table, toward her.

She gulped. Whatever game the man played, he neglected to share the instructions. Hattie hopped to her feet and then scurried toward the parlor. "I'm gonna check on Hawk."

In full voice, Will sang,

"Let me call you 'Sweetheart,' I'm in love with you."

CHAPTER NINETEEN

On his back in a base hospital bed, Arno tossed a baseball in the air, catching it over and over again. "Sixty-seven, sixty-eight, sixty—"

Charlene, a nurse with hair the same color as his chestnut horse, snagged the ball from midair. "It's time for your vital signs." Instead of returning his only form of entertainment, she placed the ball on her jam-packed cart.

"I thought you planned to kick me out of here today."

"We're still waiting on doctor's orders."

Arno's wound had festered, turning red and oozy, spiking his temperature, and delaying his release. The infection had lessened, yet nobody appeared eager to sign the necessary papers to free him from the sickbay prison.

When Charlene finished her ministrations, she leaned over Arno to tuck a scratchy blanket around the curve of his shoulder.

"I'm not cold."

"You have the most striking eye color. It's the oddest combination—a cross between a robin's egg and something sparkly."

"A sapphire," a passing nurse said.

Charlene laughed, smelling like apple blossoms and sunshine, yet her chortle resembled a swashbuckling pirate. "Your eyes are memorable. I'll give you that."

"Hold on." Karl walked up to Arno's bed. "Who ordered compliments for this soldier? The doctor?" He handed him a book and the nurse a wink. "How's your day, beautiful Charlene?"

The flirting drew a giggle from the nurse. "It's been a long day, and I'm nearly off duty."

"Who comes on after you?" Arno asked, not that it mattered overly much, but a pleasant nurse trumped an ornery one every day of the week.

"Nurse Grey."

Karl visibly shuddered.

"Happy birthday to us." Arno smiled at his buddy.

"Excuse me?" Charlene straightened. "You expect me to believe it's both your birthdays?" She paused in handing Arno his ball. "I may look naïve, but I didn't fall off the turnip truck an hour ago."

"It's the God-honest truth." Karl folded his hands beneath his chin as if in prayer. "Kreger and I arrived on earth the same day, same year, same town. He's a hair older, but that makes us brothers in a sense."

"It makes you something, anyway." With a shake of her curly head, Charlene steered her cart away, tossing the ball over her shoulder.

Karl caught it, returned the ball to Arno, and eyed Charlene's backside before scraping a chair closer to Arno's bed. Then he leaned backward on its hind legs. "She's a looker."

"You think they're all gorgeous."

"Even I have standards, and Nurse Grey doesn't measure up."

Unattractive inside and out, if Nurse Grey could get him out of the hospital, he'd gladly deliver her a thank-you note and a kiss on the cheek.

"We pitched our tents this forenoon, fixed everything in front of 'em, just like they taught us." Karl lowered his voice. "If you ask me, it's a bunch of malarkey. They surprised us again yesterday with bayonet practice, which I hate like the devil. So, you see, you've missed nothing, at least nothing good."

Arno yawned. "It sounds better than this monkey business." He gestured at his surroundings, all white, silver, and sterile. Unlike some patients, he'd not stepped outdoors since arriving. Several had received passes to visit the Y. or stroll the grounds, but not him or anyone else with what the physicians labeled *serious infections*.

Trapped and isolated, he had too much time to think. "What are people saying about the shooting?"

"There's buzz, that's for sure. Most consider it accidental. Anybody official talk to you?"

"An officer asked a few questions and took notes. Said someone else will be in touch. But when?" He stretched, exhausted from lazing in bed all day. "Seems like everything moves mighty slow around here."

"Not necessarily."

"Oh?"

"I received surprising news today."

"Good or bad?" After what Arno had been through, it'd better be good. It was only fair.

"I'm moving out soon."

Arno flinched. Relocations typically took weeks from start to finish. "When?"

"Two days."

The ache in Arno's leg moved to his chest. "Back up, that doesn't sound right. The entire company is moving out or only you?"

"Captain McKenzie showed my doodles to his superiors. It's not clear what happened next. But they're sending me to France as a mapmaker of some sort."

"A mapmaker? There's a need for that sort of thing?"

"Who do you think draws all the trenches and the enemy line and whatnot?"

Karl's artistic skills were good, but why not use someone already serving in France? Why pluck the one soldier Arno'd miss the most?

Neither spoke for a spell, until Arno finally said, "Could be dangerous."

"Or exciting."

"That's a nicer word." They were supposed to leave for France together, fight side-by-side. "So, you'll go without me then?"

Seconds passed while Karl fiddled with a cord on his laced boot. "I always thought we'd leave for France together. You watching out for me, and me keeping track of your backside like always. Foolish, huh?"

"Perhaps we'll hitch up again down the road."

"Maybe." They locked eyes until Charlene returned.

"Howdy again, Nurse Charlene." Karl flashed a smile. The woman strongly resembled his type, a female void of facial hair.

"Howdy yourself."

"Aren't you off duty?" Arno passed the baseball from hand to hand.

"Nurse Grey is assisting with an emergency in the operating area, so you're stuck with me a tad longer. I brought you both a birthday surprise."

"I told you she'd fall for it." When Karl winked, Charlene's face dropped.

"You were funning with me. It's not your birthdays."

"No, no. We both turn twenty-two today. Ignore Karl. He's the only one who thinks he's funny."

His buddy nodded, somber for a change. "With God as my witness, today is my birthday, same with Arno."

With a skeptical look, she yanked a towel aside, revealing two pieces of vanilla cake on her cart. "I smuggled these out for you, but now I'm second-guessing my decision."

"Please don't." Arno reached for the treat, his mouth watering. "Your gift is the highlight of my day."

"I forgot forks. I'll be right back." Off she dashed.

Karl winked. "I'm about to catch a spunky nurse."

"Good, I'll eat your cake."

The next night, Karl sauntered toward Arno bearing a bag of corn candy, a pile of stationery, a *National Geographic* magazine, and the Little Rock newspaper. Arno probed about the windfall. His buddy patted his trouser pocket, explaining that four aces had treated him kindly.

They ribbed each other about their younger days. Karl yakked about the times to come in Butler County, not France. When visiting hours ended, Karl ducked between the beds, hiding until Nurse Grey caught him on the floor and threatened a court-martial if he tarried five minutes longer.

Arno offered Karl his hand. His pal shook it twice. They hemmed and hawed but uttered nothing of consequence. Karl, sporting damp eyes, saluted his oldest friend. "PFC Kreger."

With stomach muscles clenched, he nodded. "You're dismissed, Private."

Karl about-faced and marched away like a model soldier.

His buddy's bootsteps faded. Around camp, plenty called their best friends brothers. Perhaps their statements rang true. Arno wasn't sure, but he believed he'd die for Karl and vice versa.

The next day limped along like a lame horse in a soupy pasture. Arno read the newspaper, Karl's magazine, labels on medicine bottles, letters that belonged to others—anything with words. He even penned notes for other soldiers, men who'd never learned to read or write.

Around dinnertime, a nurse arrived with his mail. The generous stack included a letter from Hattie.

January 30, 1918

Dear Arno,

My prayer is you're healthy, happy, and back in the barracks. Perhaps letters from home brighten your days.

You told me you're fine, but Lena says you've developed a troubling infection. Please listen to the doctors' and nurses' instructions. Sorry to sound bossy, but I'm serious. We both know infections are nothing to trifle with.

I'm trying not to think about the nature of your accident. It's rather fuzzy. Like Jeb, did you accidentally shoot yourself in the leg? Did someone else shoot you by accident? Or did something entirely different transpire? Your sister doesn't appear to know much about it either.

No need to read the newspaper for the latest bulletin—Meridee asked for my blessing to marry Daddy even though he's not yet proposed. Granted, the groom typically asks the father of the bride such a formal request, but everything remains upside-down when it comes to those two.

The longer I consider the possibility, the more I'm warming to their marriage plan. Meridee is a special lady. For some reason, Hawk frowns on the idea. In other courtship news, Jeb continues to chase Priscilla. Wait, he's caught her, I think. Ugh!

I've decided Lena and Wilhelm are destined for a long and happy life together. Therefore, I intend to take matters into my own hands. How? I'm unsure but will keep you informed.

There are two dozen things to complete before the Brigade's knit-a-thon. With Lena's assistance, everything should fall into place. She's such a help to me, same as Meridee.

Here's a grand idea—the army ought to send you home for rest and relaxation. I hear it's the best medicine.

The following three little things center on our next face-to-face visit.

I can't wait for the day we hold a picnic at Catfish Creek. Priscilla and Barrett stole our last opportunity to dine together, meaning we're due. After we polish off every crumb, we'll hold an old-fashioned stone-skipping contest, same as when we were kids.

I also want to sing with you—no audience, only you and me.

Will you kiss me twice the next time we meet? I'd never ask such a question in your presence, but I'm far more forward on paper. It's not that I've forgotten your last kiss. It's that I remember your lips too well.

It's time to add a stamp to your envelope and post this mail. I miss you beyond belief and counting the days until we see each other again.

As always,
Hattie

His wide grin probably labeled him a fool in the middle of the hospital ward, but he couldn't stop himself. Nothing healed a man faster than a kissing compliment and the desire for a return trip home to see his gal.

He reread Hattie's letter to memorize her two most intimate sentences. He'd reply tonight and tell her he'd never forget the kiss either.

An orderly pushed a squeaky wheelchair into the room, paused beside the empty bed across the aisle, and transferred an injured soldier to the cot. Arno focused on his reading, not the newcomer.

"Gonna say *howdy*?"

Arno gawked at the man whose bristly voice sounded like he'd either swallowed a splintered board or a rusty saw.

"It's your old pal. Miss me?" Gauze bandages covered one eye and half of CW's head.

He continued to stare at the man who'd likely pulled the trigger. Of all the possible soldiers to claim a bed across from him at the hospital, why this one? "What happened to you?"

"Got into a little tussle. How's the leg?"

Arno laughed, but it wasn't a happy-go-lucky chuckle. "That's a funny question coming from the man who shot me from behind."

"Don't know what you're yammering about."

"Liar." Arno returned to Hattie's letter. Not a word registered.

"How's your little German girl? What's her name? Hannah?"

Determined to appear calm even though blood crashed through his veins, his heartbeat surged, and his mind twisted like barbed wire—he bided his time, refusing to snap at CW's bait.

"If memory serves, her last name is Waltz." CW tapped his

chin with his finger. "Say, is she a little Kraut too, a fellow German lover?"

Arno blasted off the bed before anything else fell from CW's ugly mouth. "If you know what's good for you, you'll shut up." His forehead nearly brushed CW's bandages.

Laughter erupted, out of place in the quiet infirmary.

Charlene, cluttered cart in tow, arrived to dispense meals, reeking of yesterday's beef stew and more cabbage. "What's so funny?" she asked, pausing between Arno's bed and CW's.

"Kreger just threatened me."

"Then I suppose you had it coming."

With one focused breath and then another, Arno returned to his bed, lugging his throbbing leg onto the cot. Once settled, he dipped his head toward CW. "He's a brand of trouble you don't want to tangle with."

"Thanks for the advice." Charlene served Arno his meal on a tray. "I've got just the thing for ornery patients."

"You don't say." CW groaned his lack of concern. "I'm pretty sure I can handle you with one hand behind my back, my eyes closed, and a monkey on my shoulder."

Charlene squatted beside the cart's bottom shelf and withdrew a syringe, featuring a needle thicker and longer than a fountain pen.

"Aren't you a hoot?" With a huff, CW rolled onto his side, his back to the nurse's weapon of choice.

"Thank you, Private Hyland. You're in the proper position for your injection." Charlene, with mischief on her lips, winked at Arno.

CHAPTER TWENTY

Hattie folded her hands in her lap and fought the urge to daydream.

The modest wood-framed church drew almost everyone within five miles, even those who didn't favor Pastor Neymeyer's sermons. The parishioners stuck together through thick, thin, and tedious preaching. They had no right to judge the one who filled their pulpit, a man who failed to measure up to his predecessor. Still, everyone did.

The pastor's eyes strayed to Hattie while he preached, same as every other Sunday since their shared supper at the restaurant. "Please, God," she whispered in silence, "make him stop."

The pastor prattled his last "amen," and Hattie charged for the sunshine to wait for Lena in the churchyard. Her fellow parishioners didn't lag far behind. Wilhelm, followed by Meridee, breezed out the door, steering straight toward Hattie. Warm from the unseasonable temperatures, she unbuttoned her overcoat.

"What a lovely blue frock." Meridee shielded her eyes with her pocketbook. "You match the sky today. Doesn't she look pretty, Wilhelm?"

Heat pricked Hattie's neck and scaled her face. She waved a hand to fan the damage.

"Beautiful." His warm gaze exacerbated her temperature problem.

"Are we set for the knit-a-thon on Friday?" Meridee waved to Priscilla's mother, crossing the churchyard. "You've arranged everything with the schoolmarm, correct?"

"Miss Bakker is thrilled we intend to include the school children.

The older students agreed to compete on two different teams. Here's another update—the mayor wishes to say a few words."

"Let's hope it's only a few." Meridee chuckled. "I shouldn't imply he's a windbag, but ... the title fits."

Hattie refrained from smiling at the jab. "I still need to find a third judge."

"What qualifies a person to judge?" Wilhelm crossed arms over his broad chest.

Something about the way he stared at her made Hattie second-guess her appearance. Did crumbs blemish her face? Food in her teeth? She swiped a hand across her mouth. "Impartiality. Why?"

"I reckon I'm as fair-minded as the next fellow."

If Wilhelm filled the vacancy, it eliminated one more item on her lengthy to-do list. "You're hired, Mr. Mueller." They shook hands to make it official.

"Is everything else in order?" Meridee asked.

"Thankfully, all the big tasks are completed. Lena is helping with a hundred little ones."

"Excellent, dear." Meridee patted Hattie's arm. "I can't chitchat any longer, or your charming father will depart without me. Are you sure you and your brothers can't join us for dinner?"

"Not today, but thank you." With a stack of new library books on her nightstand, Hattie intended to rush through the noon meal and then whittle away the afternoon with a novel tucked in her lap.

"Wilhelm, can you come?" Meridee shifted her attention. "I'm serving meatloaf."

"Thank you, but I best scoot. Father is under the weather but insisted I not miss services. Next time, I promise."

"I'm gonna hold you to your word, sir. Don't think I won't."

He raised a hand, then ambled toward his Ford. The bone-dry weather had opened the auto roads earlier than most years. No doubt they'd close again with another round of snow in a week or two.

"Don't tell your pa, but if I were twenty years younger."

Meridee delivered an exaggerated nod toward Will. "My, my, my." Then she strode back toward the church steps to draw Daddy from a conversation with the pastor. The couple strolled to the row of parked vehicles and climbed into her auto.

Perhaps if Meridee were thirty years younger, Will might ask her on a date. But even then, it felt like a longshot.

Hattie glanced at the church. Where was Lena? The five-year-old Dittmer twins sat side-by-side on the steps, singing, forcing folks to step around the little girl barricade.

If Wilhelm judged the knitting contest, and Lena's responsibilities included interacting with the judges, they'd cross paths frequently over the two-day event. Hattie grinned at the possibilities, proud of her ingenious scheme.

"What are you staring at?" Lena's voice almost shot Hattie out of her Sunday shoes. After a settling breath, she wheeled around, a smile pinned in place. "Wilhelm offered to judge the knitting contest."

"He doesn't know a knitting needle from a garden spade."

"It's not a predictable choice but a good one nonetheless."

Hattie glanced toward her brothers, faithful as hounds, waiting by their Buick. Hawk's slumped back leaned against the auto's hood. Jeb and Priscilla mingled near the vehicle's rear end in a not-so-churchy manner. The woman, wearing a buttery gold dress with a wide satin sash, had shed her overcoat. Jeb's one hand rested on her shiny bow and his other on her shoulder. Their foreheads appeared pasted together.

Hattie longed to march over to the lovebirds, wrench the pair apart, and suffer the consequences. But she refrained, saving Jeb's lecture on meddling and Priscilla's holier-than-thou grin for another day. She turned her back on them.

"Let's stroll." Lena threaded her arm through Hattie's, steering her toward the south side of the church. "How much time do you have?"

With one last peek over her shoulder she said, "Perhaps ten

minutes, give or take a few."

Behind the church, a tidy cemetery fanned across a hill. Slanted tombstones and wooden crosses dotted the well-groomed grounds. The gals maneuvered around the markers to Mama's grave. Hattie knelt.

After her burial, Hattie'd failed to understand how others continued their everyday, mundane lives while hers unspooled. Nobody'd seemed to realize the most important person in the world had died without a suitable goodbye or a final *I love you*. If Mama hadn't passed, would Jeb be less peculiar? Hawk less fearful? Daddy less wary? What about herself? A better version?

"You're too quiet." Lena's gentle words tugged Hattie from her memories. "Are you fine?"

"This place stirs up thoughts." A dull arrow pinged at Hattie's heart. Would the ache of missing her parent ever completely fade?

"Of course. Take your time."

She drew her eyes from the marker to her friend, who'd telephoned last night, hinting about a major announcement. "What's on your mind?"

Lena paced a narrow strip amongst the graves, gnawing a fingernail. "Remember the day after Wilhelm and I ended our courtship, and I told you I desired a change?"

A soft alarm bell clamored in Hattie's temples. "I'd hoped you'd changed your mind."

Lena spat a piece of fingernail and then drew a hearty breath. "I'm moving to Philadelphia to live with Aunt Charity."

Hattie blinked while Lena's unsettling words gummed together. "You're jesting."

"I leave on Saturday."

The second day of the fundraiser? Hattie dropped her chin to her chest. Fear of shouldering the event without Lena's assistance suffocated. If she glanced at Lena's face, she'd crumble like five-day-old cake.

"I realize the timing isn't ideal, but I fully intend to help you before the knit-a-thon and volunteer three-fourths of the day on Friday. For the most part, you're ready. Plus, I've completed my knitting commitments. You ought to see my stack of socks."

Last September when Lena had sprung the I-nominate-Hattie-to-chair-the-Brigade news, she'd promised to cover her friend's back. Tears loomed, but crying wasn't an option. If Lena aimed to leave Split Falls … why weep for someone who didn't care?

"Aren't you going to say anything?" Lena knelt and touched Hattie's sleeve.

"You've made your choice." Sadness knifed at her chest, the type she'd not felt since Mama's death. With a yank, she freed her arm and stood.

"Don't act like this."

"Like what?"

"Hurt." Lena pleaded with her eyes.

"When someone hurts someone else, pain is inevitable." The constant drumbeat of *I'm moving* dinged inside Hattie's head.

Lena stood. "I can't bear to leave if you're upset with me."

A new type of distance separated them. "We'll mend."

"I'll miss you so much."

Hattie chose silence as her weapon to deal with the predicament. Practically since birth, Lena had done whatever she jolly well pleased. Why stop now?

"I feel bad." With a sniffle, Lena stretched an arm toward her friend.

"Hattie, Jeb's waiting," Hawk hollered from the side of the church. He appeared smaller than usual next to the sturdy structure. A feisty breeze played with his bangs.

"I have to go." Hattie raced toward her brother, skirt flailing around her legs. She recognized her selfish slant, similar to Lena's, but it failed to turn her around to make amends. She reached the Buick and slid into the backseat.

"Surprise!" Priscilla grinned. "Close your mouth, Hattie. Jeb invited me to dinner. Isn't he the sweetest?"

"Sickeningly so."

She stared at her lap, fighting down the bubbling fear. What if Lena forgot about her and collected new fancy friends in the city? What if the knit-a-thon failed without Lena's handholding and what-will-be-will-be attitude? Hattie couldn't persuade the rational portion of her brain to relay a positive message to her irrational heart.

The scenery rolled past like pages in a picture book. Clusters of black-and-white cows milled in pastures giving passersby no never mind. An appaloosa frolicked, racing nothing but a stiff wind. None of the distractions beyond the Buick sidetracked her stormy thoughts.

Priscilla rambled on about a bunch of nothing the entire jaunt home. She flirted with Jeb, teased Hawk, bragged on this and that, name-dropped—which surely impressed no one—and ignored Hattie. Otherwise, she examined her cuticles.

Once or twice, Hattie chimed in with an "mm-hmm" or "you don't say," but for the most part, she focused on the landscape. Then Hattie's disinterest in the conversation screeched to a stop.

"Hattie, dear, are you nervous about the upcoming fundraiser?"

Petrified summed up the accurate response. "I'm fine."

"But there are a million and one preparations. Unfortunately, I'm too busy myself to lend you a hand." Priscilla spoke in the same bland voice she'd request apple butter for a biscuit.

"Of course, you are." She glanced at the woman's face, heart-shaped and satisfied.

"I assume you know that if you fumble this, the entire town will never forgive you."

"That's a lie." Hawk twisted in the front seat to face the girls.

Mama's advice—to hold one's tongue even when others unkindly wagged theirs—echoed inside her, but Hattie ignored the sage advice.

"Priscilla, sweetie, do you ever wish you possessed an ounce of empathy for others? And what are your intentions toward Jeb?"

"Careful, little sister." From behind the steering wheel, he shot her a glare.

Priscilla's laughter, gentle at first, exploded in volume.

Hot tears stung, and Hattie blinked them away, reaching for her necklace.

"First, those pearls are fake and second—"

"So are you, Priscilla." Genuine or phony, it didn't much matter. The pearls once belonged to Mama. They were priceless.

Priscilla presented an artificial smile, the type she rationed as needed. "As I was saying, you're not Jeb's mother."

"I'm well aware."

"You do know that Arno doesn't plan to marry, don't you, Hattie? That's why he and I called off our courtship."

Hattie flinched. According to Lena, Arno and Priscilla had ended their relationship due to the woman's flirtatious nature. "That's not true."

"Don't believe me if you like, but that's what he told me once upon a time."

Silence stretched until Jeb parked alongside the barn. Hattie burst out the door and up the lane, tears dripping. In her bedroom, she tugged off her Sunday dress and exchanged it for a sensible frock. A half-dozen garments littered her floor, and she kicked aside a pair of trousers in route to her bed.

Arno's last letter rested on her pillow, but the spuds wouldn't cook themselves, and she'd catch the dickens from all angles if she lingered. Hattie tugged the epistle from its envelope, fluffed her pillow, and leaned against her headboard for another read. If Priscilla spoke the truth about Arno, why court? Why string her along for amusement?

February 19, 1918

Dearest Hattie,

I'm getting plenty of mail. A postcard arrived yesterday from Karl. He's on the East Coast but ships out soon. He sounds happy enough. I hate that he and I might never fight together. Perhaps I'll look into a transfer to try and join him. I'm mulling over my options.

I'm much improved since the hospital. The army ruled the shooting an accident. I disagree, but I don't intend to dwell on it.

I'm to leave Camp Pike in a few weeks for Camp Dix in New Jersey. Nothing is definite. There's a fair chance I'll land on a different list. We'll likely train a stint there before shipping overseas. Is it possible to receive a furlough home from there? Let's hope so because I'd sure love to see your smile one more time before Europe.

My thoughts often jump back to our growing-up days. Is it homesickness? I suspect. Here are three little things I recall.

You won a watermelon-spitting contest. Remember? Before the competition I thought I had it won, but then this little pipsqueak showed me up.

Your mama once found me by the sandbar shedding a tear or two. I must have been six. I fell from my pony, skinning my knees and elbows. She swiped at my wounds, held me tight, and sang to me. Even before she died, I called her an angel.

I bet you don't remember when I picked you first for Red Rover. It surprised everyone on the playground, even you and me because you were puny. We held hands, and not a single person broke our bond. Can we make the same thing happen again—the unbreakable hold?

It's a shame you're not here this evening, but I feel that way every night.

As always,
Arno

That he'd chosen to share those specific memories lifted Hattie's troubled heart. That unforgettable day in the schoolyard when he—someone older and favored by their classmates and teacher—

cherry-picked her above all others was the precise moment she handed Arno a sample portion of her heart.

"Hattie?" Jeb's voice carried an edge. "You up there?"

"Coming."

"If I thought you'd lollygag over making dinner, I'd have gone to Meridee's for burnt meatloaf. She can't cook worth a fig."

She tromped down the stairs two at a time. "I said I'm coming."

"It's pert near time to start supper. Besides, you have a guest."

Elizabeth Parker, Sadie's younger and sweeter sister, wore a pink-checkered dress and matching hair ribbon, complimenting her ivory complexion.

"What a nice surprise."

"You invited me over."

"That's right." They'd bumped into each other at the millinery last week, both intrigued by the same fetching hat. When Elizabeth inquired after Jeb, Hattie's plot to separate her brother and Priscilla had crystallized.

They padded into the kitchen, with Hattie talking over her shoulder. "I'm running a tad behind schedule. Had to stay late after church, but your timing is perfect. Why don't you join us for dinner?"

"I ate an hour ago." Elizabeth lowered her voice. "Are you positive Jeb wants me here? Isn't he courting Priscilla Snodgrass?"

"A mere infatuation. As youngsters, you tailed Jeb everywhere."

"I was six, and he carried butterscotch candies in his pocket."

After collecting potatoes from the bin, Hattie peeled them, her back to her friend. "It seems like yesterday to me. Answer me this, if given half a chance, would you court Jeb?"

"Hattie!" Jeb shouted.

She swirled around. Her brother filled in the doorway. His eyes flashed dangerously. "What do you think you're doing?"

"Fixing dinner."

"Elizabeth, will you please excuse us a moment? I need to talk to my sister in private."

Where was Priscilla? Tucked in the parlor with her ear against the pocket door?

Elizabeth speared Hattie with a deadly glare and then fled. The front door slammed.

"I've asked you a dozen times to keep out of my business with Priscilla. I don't know how to say it any other way. When it comes to who I court and who I don't, it's my decision, mine and Priscilla's, not yours or anybody else's."

"Put the boot on the other foot. What if I courted a man you detested? What then?"

"You do, and I live with that fact every single day."

Not that long ago, Jeb had defended Hattie no matter the circumstance, no matter the opponent. "How can you watch Priscilla torment me time after time?" Hattie rubbed her stockinged toe against a raised nail on the floorboard. "You heard how she spoke to me in the automobile. It was ugly."

Jeb massaged his forehead. "Priscilla was trying to engage you in a conversation, but you ignored her. Once or twice you responded with a mumble. She doesn't understand why you dislike her so much. She isn't always in the wrong. You're at fault too."

She missed the old tried-and-true Jeb. The new Jeb split time between an unhealthy preoccupation with his admirer and an exasperating know-it-all attitude and vocabulary.

"Starting today," Jeb wagged a finger, "I expect you to treat Priscilla with more respect."

"And if I can't?"

"Then you're even more infantile than I suspected."

Hattie fired a potato at his head.

He caught it one-handed and then slammed it on the kitchen table. "Thank you for proving my point."

cute,

CHAPTER TWENTY-ONE

On a Sunday afternoon, in a spacious clearing on the north end of camp, Arno and Frankie joined a double row of soldiers from Company E for a round of catch. The day's warmth invited men to roll up their shirtsleeves for nine innings of baseball.

In between throws, Arno searched the crowd. Where was the captain? According to the nurses at the base hospital, McKenzie had visited him twice. He'd slept through both. If given a chance, he'd have gladly traded a good night's sleep for a crack at a one-on-one talk with the captain. He wasn't a brownnoser, but who wouldn't want an opportunity to rub shoulders with McKenzie?

"Kreger." Frankie flung a fireball, smacking against Arno's glove. "Is there somewhere else you'd rather be?"

"Play ball," the umpire shouted, saving Arno from fumbling for an answer.

He jogged to the sidelines—his leg healed for the most part. Shoulder to shoulder with the other bench players, Arno watched the first pitch. The rowdy cheering section included a few high-ranking officers to swell their numbers. The game stretched on, and the bulk of the second and third string players copped seats in the spikey grass to lob jeers and encouragement in equal measure.

At the bottom of the ninth, the score six to five, Company E led by one run. Zeke Blashka whipped a pitch. WHACK! The pitcher jerked sideways, but the blinding line drive smashed his *OUCH* Adam's apple. He dropped to the ground. A half-dozen men raced forward, but Zeke waved them away before staggering off the diamond to the spectators' applause.

Lieutenant Langley, the team's self-appointed coach, sprinted from the outfield toward the reserves. "We need a pitcher. Any volunteers?"

Arno raised his hand while CW yelled, "I'll do it." A gauzy bandage still covered his left cheek.

"I only need one of you," Langley said. Hyland sprinted toward the pitcher's mound, pounding his glove with his fist, before the coach spoke another word.

"Put Kreger in," a deep voice bellowed. "I've seen him pitch. He's not half bad."

Langley, a long-limbed man with a red birthmark halfway up his neck, scratched his pointy chin. "You've pitched before, Kreger?"

"Back home." He'd thrown his share of shutouts on the schoolyard. Granted, they usually played with a cracked bat. "You could call me a hefty fish in a slight stream."

"That's good enough for me." Langley nodded, cupping his hands around his mouth. "Hyland, you're out. Kreger's in."

"Time's ticking," Frankie, the team's starting catcher, yelled from behind home plate when neither man budged. A few teammates applauded, but Company F's sideline hollered with enthusiasm. Everyone knew nobody could pitch like Zeke or even come close.

Hyland's shoulder jarred Arno's when the two met halfway between the sidelines and pitcher's mound. "I wager five dollars you'll choke, you yellow-livered German."

Twice CW had called him a choker. A loser. "I'll take that bet, Clyde Walter."

After a string of cuss words, CW stormed off the field.

Arno eyeballed the distance to home plate. Although his leg had fully healed, if he bumped the wound, it still hurt plenty. He'd best not catch a line drive there.

"Fire one in here," Jesberger slammed his fist against his catcher's mitt, pounding it twice. "Show me your best pitch."

Arno bulleted a ball, soaring it high and wide. Like the first, his second throw swerved cockeyed. Arno squinted, scanning the troops from left to right. Captain McKenzie had joined Company

F's side of the ball field, his towering form impossible to miss.

"Play ball," shouted the umpire, squatting behind home plate.

Arno walked the first two batters. The third hitter smacked a ball high to center field, which the lieutenant snagged with ease. On a full count, the fourth batter popped a fly above the catcher's head. Frankie dove. On his belly, he raised the prize high in the air.

The roar of appreciation resembled a cannon blast, especially from the men to Arno's right. Only one out from a victory, Arno paused, sweat beading his back before gathering at his waistband. He stole a second glance at the captain, who stood rock solid with his legs apart and arms folded across his chest.

Arno's pulse quickened when Frankie flashed a series of fast, jerky hand movements, which Arno promptly ignored. He launched the first pitch low and inside, but the batter swung and missed. On the second pitch, the opponent slugged the ball a hair shy of the right foul line. Pitch number three dribbled across home plate. The umpire labeled pitches four and five balls, yet Frankie questioned both calls. Each stood.

With a full count, the silence grew fat, except for CW's distinct voice soaked in bitterness and malice. "Hey, Kreger, it all rests on your shoulders. I bet you choke."

"He won't choke," someone hollered. "He's the next Cy Young." Laughter rolled.

Arno hurled the ball toward Frankie's eager hands. The batter swung early, spun in a full circle, and almost toppled over.

"Strike three, and you're out!" screamed the umpire, jumping from his squatting position.

Teammates swarmed the mound, pounding Arno's back and exaggerating his skill. The crowd dispersed except for three—Arno, Captain McKenzie, and Frankie, gathering equipment behind home plate.

"Can you spare me a minute, Private First Class?" McKenzie asked, turning on his heel.

"Yes, sir." He trailed the captain to the pitcher's mound, attempting to stand tall before the man's looming six-foot-five or so frame.

"Congratulations."

"Thank you, sir." The praise widened Arno's smile, a ridiculous span.

"However, that last wild pitch of yours was a ball, nowhere close to a strike."

"I agree."

"But the batter swung, and the rest is history." A breeze teased the captain's cap, and he tugged it tighter to his head. "When they pegged you to pitch, you didn't flinch. You stepped into a pair of mighty big shoes."

"Clodhoppers."

The captain laughed, loud and throaty. "I haven't forgotten how you single-handedly captured the two prisoners months back." McKenzie's stare intensified. "We're moving out soon and knowing there are soldiers like you—good, hardworking men—helps me sleep better at night."

The unexpected praise settled onto Arno's skin, seeped into his pores. Not many had found him worthy. Words skipped beyond his reach. Later, he'd find the perfect retort, something wise to convey appreciation without sounding like a simpering fool. In the meantime, he merely grinned.

"Keep up the good work."

"I will, sir. I'm much obliged for your faith in me."

When McKenzie's stubborn stare deepened, Arno maintained eye contact. After a prolonged stretch, the captain nodded and then exited the diamond at a clipped pace.

Arno rerolled his shirt sleeves to his elbows. Had the captain wanted to say more? Even a numskull knew not to quiz his superiors, yet Arno almost had.

Frankie slapped his friend between the shoulder blades. "You gonna make me guess or tell me what McKenzie said?"

"Not much." Adrenaline whipped through Arno, pushing his steps into a jog. "He enjoyed the game."

"That's it?"

Arno shrugged, not knowing how much to share. "He called my last pitch a ball."

"Even a lunatic knows your last pitch wasn't a dilly. Slow down. Why are you off to the races?"

Unable to remain still, Arno jogged in place until Frankie reached his side and handed him two bats to tote back to camp. "He congratulated me, that's the short of it."

"Nothing else?"

"Here's the thing, it felt like he wanted to."

"Wanted to what?"

"Say more."

Frankie stopped in his tracks—one eyebrow arched. "Name one thing that would stop the man from speaking his mind."

Arno walked backward, facing his friend. "It's a gut feeling, but he stared a hole straight through me and wore this odd expression." Arno shook his head. "I'm probably wrong."

"That I believe."

The two agreed to meet later at the Y., while Arno passed his buddy the equipment he'd hauled from the diamond. Arno swerved toward the main road, threading through the camp's core. Usually, military vehicles paraded across Pike's infrastructure, but not on Sundays.

A few soldiers strolled in groups of twos and threes. One man yelled, "Good game, Kreger." Another shouted, "Nice pitching." Arno's already springy steps grew jauntier with each praise.

He mounted a small hill across camp to a leafy maple's shade. The knoll offered expansive views of the entire camp, an ideal location to reread Hattie's recent letter. He flopped onto the grass, hunched on an elbow. The wind fluttered the notepaper, and Arno tightened his grip.

March 12, 1918

Dear Arno,

Your letter arrived today. Happy to hear you're back to health. Next time you write, slap a stamp on yourself along with your letter. I wager the U.S. Post Office delivers you home faster than the army!

Days ago, a blizzard buried the mailbox and doghouse, canceling the knit-a-thon. To be honest, my heart wasn't in it, especially since Lena left town. But it's a shame we didn't raise any money for the soldiers.

Although Lena's departure stung, I'm past the disappointment stage. Of course, I miss her beyond belief, but if she hadn't taken this big step, she'd always wonder if there was more to life beyond Split Falls. No doubt she's busy with a million and one things in Pennsylvania.

Here's another troubling development—Jeb is head over heels for Priscilla. His unwillingness to even consider a more suitable match boggles my mind. Last night he claimed the heart wants what it wants. Ugh! Now he's quoting Emily Dickinson!

We read in the Split Falls Gazette that one of the Triplett boys landed on the latest casualty list. Talk is he died from a German airplane attack. What a heartbreak for his family.

According to Jeb, one of the troublemakers involved in the dance tussle landed in jail. The crime—arson. The victim— Hans Schmitt's hog house. In case you're wondering, no pigs perished. The attack stems from Mr. Schmitt being part German, same as us.

I miss 2,084 things about you. Maybe 2,085. Unfortunately, there's not enough stationery at my fingertips to record all your positive qualities. Plus, you might turn proud after reading them, how awful for your fellow soldiers. That said, I'll mention three little things.

I miss how your smile seeps into your voice when you speak words I've only dreamed about hearing, especially from you.

I miss dancing together. Every night I close my eyes and remember the box social. To be clear, I fixate on the part when your arms held me tight, not the fight that followed. In my opinion, we moved in concert to our own music, not the notes performed by the band.

I miss your hand holding mine, especially when you rub your thumb across the inside of my wrist.

Write back soon. I'll wait by the mailbox, not literally, of course. It's cold outside.

As always,
Hattie

P.S. There's an important matter I wish to discuss but only when we're face to face. Will a furlough occur in a couple of weeks or months? Let's hope the answer isn't years!

If she missed him 2,084 different ways, he missed her 2,085. But what was the mysterious topic up for discussion?

Arno stretched and spied CW barreling along like a bulldozer—shoulders back and nary a sidestep when another man approached. Jordane trailed behind, taking two steps to Hyland's one. Even high on a hill with yards between them Arno felt Hyland's hot, ugly steam. Good thing he wasn't heading Arno's way. Without a doubt, the man still seethed over the game—not the victory, just the pitcher.

Arno stood and brushed off his clothes before swinging toward the barracks. He passed the mess hall where an unidentifiable supper smelled encouraging. He'd pay five dollars for Mother's pork roast and ten to find chicken pot pie—with a buttery crust and thick, steamy filling—featured on the evening menu.

In the half-empty sleeping quarters, most of the men sagged across their beds. Four soldiers dealt cards in a far corner with gawkers lurking around them. Arno passed Frankie's cot, and that soldier scrambled to his feet.

"I've thought about your conversation with the captain, and I've figured it out."

"Go on."

"Some might say Company E has you to thank for today's win."

"Right." The opposing team's batter had unwittingly decided who won and lost the game, not Arno.

"No, I'm serious. The captain wanted your autograph but stopped himself short from asking."

Arno laughed. "Because he's bashful."

"Precisely. Aren't all army captains shy and reserved?"

"Not any I've encountered." Frankie's humor had helped fill the void left by Karl.

"It's just a hunch." Frankie peered over Arno's shoulder and frowned. "Here comes Jordane and Hyland. One of the two looks like he's fit to be tied."

"Talking about me?"

Arno turned, CW's sweaty face inches from his own. "Don't you think highly of yourself?"

"And you don't?" Jordane spit the words as if distasteful. The soldier reminded Arno of a weasel—shifty black eyes, lurking in shadows, waiting to attack. They'd not spoken since the day someone shot Arno from behind.

Grady Iverson peered from a nearby cot. "Nice job today, Kreger."

"Thanks. I had plenty of help."

CW propped a clammy meat hook onto Arno's shoulder, which Arno brushed away. "You were lucky today. That's all it was—stupid luck, you dumb wisenheimer."

"Thanks for your two cents, but it's not worth half."

"You wanna talk fractions?" A tic flashed in CW's cheek. "You ain't half as special as you think you is, Kreger. I saw you sweet talking the captain. You thought nobody watched, but I saw you." CW poked a finger against Arno's chest. "And I'm not paying you a dime."

"Welcher, keep your lousy money." Without much thought, Arno whacked Hyland's finger aside before thrusting the heels of his palms against the man's shoulders.

The soldier stumbled over his own feet, crashed onto the cot behind him, and smashed onto the floor with an explosive thud.

Iverson, the only soldier in the vicinity bigger and brawnier, braced both of his hands against CW's shoulders and held him down. "Don't move."

A second nearby beefy soldier parked himself between Arno and CW, his feet braced.

"You think you're the tough man around here, don't you?" Arno shouted in CW's face.

"Leave it alone." Frankie yanked on Arno's arm, dragging him toward the barrack's exit.

CW grunted, rising to his feet. "Tougher than some."

Arno wrenched free, storming back toward trouble. "I'm not afraid of you."

"Then you're an idiot." CW's shoulders rose and fell with each pant. "You know what they say."

"I reckon you're gonna tell me."

"You ought to be afraid." The room trapped CW's laughter, coarse and loud. Jordane joined in with more of a cackle than a chuckle.

"Or what?" Arno clenched and unclenched his fists, reminding himself to breathe, not let the taunts spark his temper. "You'll shoot me again?"

"What a tempting invitation."

Before Arno's swing connected with CW's jaw, Iverson intervened, shoving Arno aside.

"Either take it outside or stop your bickering here and now." Iverson directed stern eyes at Arno and then swiveled toward CW. "If you two know what's good for you, you'll go your separate ways."

Arno rarely chose the good-for-you route, but after a deadly glare at CW, he turned his back and plowed toward his cot, wishing for the hundredth time that he was home again.

CHAPTER TWENTY-TWO

On a warm April afternoon, Hattie stepped off the train in Philadelphia.

The whirlwind had started when Lena mailed her a train ticket, compliments of her wealthy aunt. Initially, Hattie'd refused to consider the adventure, especially traveling alone. Daddy agreed, calling it *ludicrous*, while Meridee explained how once-in-a-lifetime opportunities worked. A person jumped toward something amazing one minute and then blossomed in new and exciting directions the next.

The flower reference ranked as over-the-top, but Hattie caught the woman's point. And she missed her friend. If seeing Lena again meant traipsing east, why refuse an all-expenses-paid jaunt? That didn't mean the upcoming adventure hadn't starred in her nightmares once or twice.

The word *buzzing* best described Philadelphia. With a firm hand on her pocketbook and the other on Meridee's borrowed suitcase, she hunted for an open park bench to wait for Lena.

Fancy automobiles zipped past, one right after the next. Pedestrians garbed in the latest fashions scurried as if late for supper. A fire bell clamored. The hint of smoke tainted the air, but no flames in sight. The sun tumbled low toward the horizon.

Hattie settled onto a wrought iron bench with her belongings on her lap. A man hawked fresh-roasted nuts nearby, wrenching an audible growl from her stomach. A teetering woman in high heels almost wheeled a baby carriage over Hattie's old-fashioned shoes. When two sailors strode past, she swung her knees to the side to avoid a bump.

Why? Did she look like an imposter, a farmgirl hoping to blend into the scenery? Or was she simply invisible?

"Hattie!"

She jumped to her feet as Lena enveloped her in an embrace. The pair almost tumbled into the street before releasing one another. "I've missed you."

"Me too. I want to hear all about the Brigade, the doings back home, everything."

Hattie gawked at Lena. The woman she thought she knew better than anyone else in the entire world sported hair cropped to her chin and breeches. BREECHES! "You look, I don't know, older and—and—mercy. Look at you."

With a laugh bordering on a howl, Lena pirouetted. "Tell me the truth. Do you love it?"

The dramatic changes highlighted Lena's big eyes and accentuated the length of her neck. "I think I do. No, I definitely do."

What if Hattie were to step off the train in Split Falls outfitted like Lena? Would people laugh? Stare? See her in a fashionable new light? Hattie shook her head. She'd never gather the nerve to pull off such a stunt.

"I want to show you and tell you a thousand different things but first meet Aunt Charity."

From the grey-streaked hair bundled atop her head to a pair of sharp blue eyes, the widow matched her sister back in Iowa. Mrs. Merriweather opened her arms wide for a quick embrace. "I feel as though I already know you."

It was a warmer welcome than Hattie had expected, not that she'd feared the woman wouldn't be kind, but she wasn't accustomed to hugs from strangers. "Thank you for the train ticket and your hospitality. My deepest condolences for the loss of your husband."

"You're welcome, and thank you." Mrs. Merriweather's face held sadness, yet she smiled. "You're as lovely as Arno exclaimed."

"What?" Hattie's heart hammered. Was Arno here? Her heart almost stopped entirely.

"I received his letter yesterday." Two dimples formed in Mrs. Merriweather's cheeks.

"And we'll see him tomorrow in person." Lena's smug smile followed the shocking announcement.

"What?" Hattie gripped Lena's arm.

"Did you stop reading geography books? Camp Dix is in New Jersey, which is awfully close to Philadelphia. Arno's three-day leave starts tomorrow and guess where he's overnighting?"

Hattie clutched her pearls but wanted to pinch herself. "Oh, my stars."

With a dollar fifty jingling in his pocket, Arno studied every postcard in a crowded Philadelphia novelty shop. Why had his sister insisted they meet here rather than Aunt Charity's house?

"My gal kicked me to the curb," Frankie said out of the blue.

Arno dropped a fistful of postcards to the shop's dusty floor. Last week Frankie had outlined his plan to propose the next time he received a furlough home. Instead, he nursed a broken heart.

"I thought we'd wed one day, but the minute I turn my back, some jerk sweeps Belinda off her feet."

"I'm sorry." Arno picked up his mess and then looked at his friend. "What happened?"

"She's a nurse at a hospital in Des Moines. She fell for a doctor, a surgeon. I can't compete with that."

"Who can?" What Arno longed to purchase wasn't for sale—a fool-proof guarantee that Hattie would never mail him that type of letter. He deposited the soiled postcards, a heart-shaped bookmark, and a king-sized box of saltwater taffy onto the counter beside a brass cash register.

"Things are good between you and Hattie, right?"

"They're fine. I'd like to see her once more before shipping to

France."

Two weeks ago, Arno's company had marched into Camp Dix. Since nobody greeted the out-of-towners, the road-weary soldiers had marched behind their own regimental band while searching for their assigned barracks.

For days, they'd drilled with full packs, an exercise that sapped everyone's strength. When a three-day pass had landed in Arno's lap, his spirits soared. Although it wasn't to Split Falls to see Hattie, a visit to Aunt Charity's ranked a close second.

They walked outside and leaned against the novelty shop's cool brick wall. Sophisticated-looking women strolled past, one more beautiful than the next. Frankie pointed out his favorites, Arno tended to agree. Men in either blue or khaki uniforms cluttered the street.

"I hear Barrett Jordane has a new girl from Louisiana." Frankie shrugged. "Courting—what a deal."

"Yep." Arno kicked a cigarette butt to the curb. Jordane now bunked in the officer's quarters. Arno rarely saw him, which suited him fine.

Frankie elbowed Arno again, a direct jab to his ribs. "Maybe I am ready to move on with someone new. Take a gander at these two gals, why don't ya?"

Arno cranked his neck.

"Can anybody lean against this wall or only soldiers?"

He recognized Hattie's face and voice, but shock rooted him to the sidewalk for a moment before he wrapped her in an embrace. He lifted her to the tips of her toes. "Are you real?"

"I think so." Her laughter loosened the tight hold on his stomach muscles.

He held her out at arm's length, studying her face. Then his lips jumped before his brain, and he kissed her right there. In front of everyone.

They pulled apart. She was really here.

"I take it Lena failed to mention my train trip east." Hattie stepped back but reached for his hand.

Frankie lit a cigarette. "I'm hoping you're the infamous Hattie."

Introductions followed with Lena giggling through the greetings. Lena invited Frankie to join them and overnight at Aunt Charity's, explaining the woman boasted more bedrooms than a hotel.

They visited the major tourist attractions that afternoon—Independence Hall and the Liberty Bell. Lena pointed out historical details and droned over each description. Then they meandered the populous streets, sampled food vendors' wares, and ducked inside shops.

When they passed a stretch of gardens that pleased Hattie, her reactions to everything fascinated him. He held her hand, occasionally lifting her palm for a quick peck to her wrist.

How long until she asked him her mysterious question, the one she'd written about in her last letter? Was she about to press the marriage question? Was he ready for that? He nudged her arm. "Is now a good time for what you wanted to talk about?"

Her shoulders drooped. "I think I'd rather wait until there's less of a chance we'll be interrupted."

"Uh-oh. How ominous."

Her chuckle was half-hearted at best. "I wouldn't say ominous, but it's definitely serious."

"Then let's arrange for a little alone time," he whispered, several steps behind the others.

"Isn't that rude?"

He winked. "Lena, I'm gonna drop off my carryall at Aunt Charity's. Why don't Hattie and I meet you two later, say suppertime?"

Lena backtracked her steps. "Let's all go. This sunshine is stifling, and I can't wait to show you Aunt Charity's stunning home. It's nearly the size of the opera house in Split Falls. It's like a gigantic mausoleum."

"Have you ever seen a mausoleum?" Frankie's eyebrows slanted into a vee.

"I have a vivid imagination."

Arno buried a groan. How long until he'd have Hattie all to himself?

CHAPTER TWENTY-THREE

Although not mausoleum-worthy, Hattie ranked Mrs. Merriweather's twenty-room house a mansion. Parked on an impressive hill, it included thirty acres overlooking a bendy stream and an incomparable view. Every room smelled like cherry blossoms.

The differences between home and Philadelphia almost staggered Hattie. She caught herself gawking far too often. Mrs. Merriweather's wealth sprang from her deceased husband's inheritance and occupation—an art dealer. Framed masterpieces lined the walls upstairs and down. Hattie strolled the corridors after the most delicious supper of her life. Highlights of the seven-course meal prepared and served by uniformed staff, included quail eggs, chocolate mousse, a platter of merriment … and Arno.

"Look at this one." She pointed at a winter scene of snow-dusted streetlights and pedestrians. Blues and grays dominated the canvas, adding a frosty touch.

"I'd rather look at you." Arno's soft and alluring words tickled her insides. He tugged on her sleeve.

"And this one is gorgeous." The watercolor featured a red rowboat on a brilliant sea of vibrant colors. She tilted her head right, then left, noting how the artist had captured the waves' movements.

"Not as gorgeous as you."

She loved how he looked at her as if he wanted to paint her portrait by memory. She'd never felt more beautiful, more cherished, more blessed. "You're a smooth talker, aren't you?"

"I'm trying."

With her hands clasped behind her back, she strolled to the next painting. Generous beyond measure, Mrs. Merriweather had offered to donate one of five pieces to auction off at the upcoming Brigade fundraiser, instructing Hattie to choose which one—an impossible decision.

"I can't fathom the value of your aunt's collection." She studied a portrait of a curly-haired toddler clutching a ragdoll by the foot. The child appeared lifelike. Hattie raised her finger, but Mrs. Merriweather's warning had been—*Never touch the art. It lowers the value.* "We'll be lucky to raise a fraction of the painting's worth."

"Which one will you take?"

"I'm unsure. One minute I favor the child, and then I lean toward the rowboat. What do you suggest?"

"That we sneak outside." Arno winked.

"That's your recommendation?"

"It'll give you more time to consider. The fresh air will clear your head."

She glanced at the window. "But it's dark outside."

"I'll protect you."

"Who will save me from you?"

Her mischievous grin increased his. His smile hadn't changed over the years—still as readable and sunny as ever. It squeezed Hattie's heart. "What will your aunt think if we disappear?"

Mrs. Merriweather, Frankie, and Lena played whist in the billiard room. Why an entire area for the sake of a gaming table? Laughter traveled the corridor.

Arno wrapped his arms around her waist from behind. "My guess is she thinks we're young, courting, and rarely see one another, not to mention I'm soon leaving for Europe." His warm breath nuzzled her neck, flipping her stomach in circles.

"You probably know this already, but ..." Her eyes drifted shut.

"What do I know?" His curled whisper caressed, tingling the tiny hairs on her arms.

She wrestled for the strength to open her eyes and face Arno, stepping beyond his grasp. "I'm a good girl."

"Everybody knows that."

Although she longed to trace his lips with her finger, she folded her hands together and drew them against her chest. A ready reply failed somewhere between her brain and her tongue.

Arno scratched his jaw. "I'm well aware. All I want is to step outside with you, that's it."

Despite her best efforts, heat torched her face.

"Come here." He crooked a finger.

Hattie sucked in a deep breath, wishing she'd never started this conversation. But it was too late to stop now. "You courted Priscilla a long spell."

"I never pictured her as my wife."

"Then why did you two court for nearly a year?"

He shrugged as if brushing it aside and stepped to the next painting, a single pink rose in a matching vase.

She joined him to stare at the simple but stunning beauty while she gathered her courage. "Before we go outside, I'd like to hear your answer."

"I was young. Priscilla is pretty and quick-witted, which is always appreciated, and ..."

Weary of her rival's list of attributes, Hattie closed her eyes. Even though Priscilla lingered in Split Falls, her presence wedged a roadblock between them. Someone had once labeled Priscilla bigger than life. Now Hattie understood.

"Please look at me."

She cracked open one eye, still keeping her distance. It was the perfect moment to ask Arno whether or not he intended to marry one day, but his nearness tilted her heart, her thoughts, and her judgment.

"I never cared for Priscilla as much as I care for you."

"You didn't?" Hattie gulped. Something—probably, happiness—warmed her skin all over again.

"No, ma'am."

She longed to toss her arms around his neck, lean into him, and forget everything else but his lips on hers. Instead, she extended her hand. "I'd love to accompany you outside."

Arno matched his steps to Hattie's shorter strides. Arm in arm, they meandered the grounds. A row of hedges cast long shadows. They crossed to the edge of the yard by a tall iron fence which separated the lawn from a deep crevice. A dog barked in the distance.

He cupped her shoulder and nudged her against his side. If he could stop time, he would. This moment was perfect, except one question nagged. "What's the latest with your hometown dates?"

"I may run out of eligible prospects if the war lasts much longer, and I'm not about to date the pastor twice."

"What about Wilhelm?" That was one suitor who wouldn't worry him. "He's a friend, and you'd get your father off your back."

Hattie fiddled with her necklace. "Maybe. Wilhelm is awfully busy these days."

"It's a thought. Odd, huh—me pushing you toward another man?"

She chuckled, but it sounded forced.

"A regular riot."

"You won't leave me for someone else while I'm gone, will you?" Although he asked the question in jest, it carried weight. Still, if he wasn't going to offer Hattie a future, he had no right to string her along. One day he'd probably cut the cord, let her find someone who shared her dream of a family. But not yet, not before he shipped out to France. He liked knowing someone from home, especially Hattie, pined for him. Even though it wasn't fair to her, he couldn't let her go.

"The way I see it, you'll need to trust me, and I'll need to trust you. For all we know, a beautiful French lady might steal your heart."

"That's not gonna happen."

"To me, either." Hattie crossed her heart.

That eased most of Arno's worries. Why plan too far into the future? Why not advance one day at a time? They strolled the lawn to a glider parked under a pear tree and stargazed, pointing out the various constellations.

"What if I told you your eyes are like liquid pools of gold?" Arno asked.

"I'd wonder if you'd guzzled spirits of some sort."

He chuckled, resting his cheek on the top of her head. "What if I claimed you smell sweeter than a million wildflowers."

"Hmm … I'd search through the bushes for Cyrano de Bergerac."

"Who? Is he from Split Rock?"

Hattie's giggle sounded more like a snort. "A character in a novel."

"What if I asked for a kiss?" He swiveled to face her.

"I'd say yes."

He brushed his lips against her warm mouth and then trailed a second kiss to her soft cheek. What if he blurted his feelings? An internal tug of war battled—his heart versus his head.

With a sigh, she snuggled closer. "What's the latest news from Karl? He's mailed me one postcard, a brief one at that."

Several moments passed as Arno forced his focus from the little indentation between Hattie's collarbones to his buddy overseas. "He can't say much, but from what I gather, he's happy enough. He's a lot like Lena. Never wants dust to settle on his boots."

"Am I boring?"

He laughed until the glider rocked sideways. "As boring as a tornado."

"Honestly?"

"There's a big difference between not living for thrills and being dreary, which, my dear, you are not."

Side-by-side the couple rocked, Hattie's head tucked under his chin.

She pulled back and looked at him. "Here's another question."

"Ask away."

"How will I survive, knowing you'll soon land in harm's way?" Did her voice shake?

"I guess you'll need a little faith."

"Or a lot of faith because I'm still scared." She pressed her hand against his chest and sat upright.

Arno leaned his forehead against hers and recited the proverb she'd tucked into his farewell socks last September. "If thou faint in the day of adversity, thy strength is small."

A teardrop gathered on her eyelashes and spilled over.

"Why are you crying?"

"Because you memorized something important to me."

"Pack away your tears and worries, Hattie. You don't need them anymore. You have me."

Their next kiss—long and perfect— nearly tested his restraint, but then Hattie ended the smooch.

"Arno?"

"Yes?" Eyes closed—he savored the memory of her lips against his.

"True or false—Priscilla says you never intend to marry?"

Tested again—this time to lie—he opened his eyes. "True."

Little by little, her face crumbled. She broke for the house. After a few steps, she whipped around to face him. "You haven't changed a bit, have you?"

Before he latched onto a reply, she was gone.

Alone in the dark, he cradled the back of his head with his hands and searched the stars for answers. Why couldn't he be the man Hattie needed, the one who shared her dreams? Why couldn't he ever be enough for someone he … loved.

CHAPTER TWENTY-FOUR

April 21, 1918—New York City, New York

Two weeks later, Arno filed onto a pier with a trainload of other Europe-bound soldiers. Seagulls circled and squawked overhead, swooping for handouts amidst the raindrops. A patriotic band boomed "Over There."

Garbed in his newly issued cotton uniform—an olive drab O.D. shirt and trousers, puttees, socks, hobnailed trench shoes, and a blouse coat—Arno waited for refreshments. When he reached for a coffee and sandwich from a Red Cross worker, the volunteer splashed both treats onto Arno's shiny boots.

"I'm sorry. It's my first day." The petite blonde knelt and wiped his boots clean. There was nothing for his damp sock and trouser leg.

"It's fine." He helped her stand while she continued to fuss.

"I'm all thumbs today." When she rose, her tears filled her eyes.

"Listen, don't worry. No harm done."

She gave a shy smile, two grape jelly sandwiches, and a full-to-the-brim beverage. "An extra for your troubles. Please don't tell on me."

"My lips are sealed."

"I don't know why I'm jittery. You're the one headed toward danger."

Unable to argue, Arno nodded and inched forward, one minor cog in an endless wave of soldiers marching up a gangway.

A naval officer inside the vessel dispersed instruction cards with sleeping quarter, mess hall, washroom, and abandon-ship assignments. Rows of hammocks dangled side-by-side in his new dormitory. The men stowed their rifles and haversacks in the assigned compartments and then waited.

Finally released to explore the upper deck, Arno stationed himself at an open slot alongside the railing as the ship steamed out of a New York City harbor.

"Goodbye," he whispered to the Statue of Liberty, tightening his grip on the railing. A soldier sniffled. Seagulls flapped and fluttered, calling out farewells.

Tucked in an orderly convoy, Arno's ship traveled beside merchant vessels, other troop transports, a half-dozen destroyers, and a torpedo boat. The floating parade cut through the water and picked up speed.

"Hey, fellas, can one of you lend me a hand?"

Arno and the soldiers alongside him all turned to face a man who grinned back.

"I'm documenting the voyage. Need someone to pose for a photograph. I've set up my equipment over yonder." He nodded toward the starboard side of the ship. "How about you?" The photographer pointed at Arno.

He stifled a groan. "I suppose I can help you out."

"I'd be much obliged."

Arno followed the man until someone called out, "Sure, pick the one German in the group." Laughter erupted back at the rail.

Arno's stomach muscles tensed. Then he turned to face his accuser. A half-dozen men stood clumped together. He recognized one mug but not the fella's name. Was he the rat? It didn't matter. "I'm as American as you." Arno assumed his best fist-fighting stance. "Who wants to call me something different to my face?"

Lights remained sparingly lit, and men were not allowed to smoke on deck after dark due to German U-boats rumored to swirl nearby. Soldiers devoured meals, no matter how disgusting, during daylight.

Scads combated seasickness. Arno grew sea legs from the get-go, settling into the ship's rhythm—almost against his will. One day tripped into the next, and every night he dreamed of home.

Ten days later and after a stint of calisthenics, Arno relaxed on the top deck, sucking in the briny air while wrenching Hattie's lone letter from his pocket. He'd shipped the remainder home for safekeeping.

April 18, 1918

Dearest Arno,

Sorry, but I don't care to beat around the bush.

Does the reason you don't plan to marry stem from Oliver's death? Do you intend to forgo marriage to avoid fatherhood? If that's the case, I won't argue with you, but I don't agree with you either. You see things your way, and I view them in a different light.

Since I can't imagine not being a mother, it appears we've reached an impasse. However, I'm open to the possibility that either you or I may change our mind down the road. I realize it's a slim possibility, but as they say, I'm not ready to throw out the baby with the bathwater.

If you feel similarly, please let me know. I care about you too much to say goodbye.

I wonder if you'll receive this note before you set sail. If not, I'm sorry for the stale news. Let's hope the rocking ship doesn't turn you queasy or knock you overboard. Word around here is some boys remain seasick for the entire two-to-three-week voyage.

Is this whole war business getting out of hand, or is it my imagination? Every direction I turn, I learn more bad news—someone gassed by the enemy, another lost a limb, or worse, a life. This morning I heard Jeb's good chum, Patrick Wallerstein, died from heart trouble in France. His kin call it plain-old homesickness. By the sounds of it, he stopped eating, drinking, and eventually living.

Night after night, I sit on the porch and look at the stars, wondering what you're experiencing. It's almost too much to imagine. Ever since visiting Philadelphia, I feel less isolated. I always knew life existed beyond Split Falls, but the entire opportunity opened my eyes to a newness. That said, I still believe my hometown is the best place on earth. The only thing missing is you.

While in Philadelphia, I learned three new little things about you and me.

We have the makings of a lifelong relationship. No, I'm not proposing, I'm only saying I glimpsed our potential. Of course, parenthood is a stumbling block.

For three days, we spent nearly every waking hour together, and I gleaned plenty. You prefer poached eggs over fried and pepper, not salt, on filet of beef. You catered to your aunt's needs and never once complained or objected. You don't cheat at cards or chess, and you swing a croquet mallet like an expert. And last but not least, you care for me more than I ever hoped.

Farewells aren't so simple anymore, are they? The war has changed everything.

I'm trying not to fret about your safety and to trust you'll soon return home unscathed. Although difficult to package, I tucked a handful of hugs and kisses inside this envelope. Let's hope they don't scatter between here and there.

As always,
Hattie

Arno slipped the letter into the frayed envelope and glanced skyward. Would he ever measure up to Hattie's expectations? Would he ever change his mind about marriage and fatherhood? Would he ever not feel stuck in a canoe without a paddle?

A wave of sadness surfaced. He reached for the railing, a suitable anchor. Oliver died. Opa died. His relationship with Father had shriveled and died too. Others like Hattie had lost close relatives, but their worlds didn't fall apart. Why had his? A salty spray peppered his cheeks. There was nothing like an ocean to make a man feel small on the inside and out.

A commotion interrupted his thoughts. Several soldiers hunted for German U-boats—a pastime favored by many. Dozens had claimed to spy periscopes, yet no official had confirmed any bona fide sightings. Arno had heard it all over the last ten days—tales of onboard fires, threats of mutinies, and soldiers forced to teeter down the plank for insubordination. He'd not witnessed anything firsthand and doubted they'd happened at all. The rumor mill claimed the highest-ranking officers relaxed in luxurious staterooms on upper decks and ate delicious meals. That, Arno believed.

Captain McKenzie bumped into him, minus an apology, before staggering a few steps to heave his lunch over the rail. White as a cloud, the officer yanked a handkerchief from his trouser pocket.

Arno saluted.

Although the army frowned on overt fraternization amongst the ranks, it happened daily. He and McKenzie had formed a friendship of sorts over the last few months. Arno counted it a blessing.

"As you were." The captain grasped the rail with one hand and stuffed his dirty handkerchief into his pocket with the other. "I aim to swim home when this war ends."

Arno pictured the captain, sunburnt and floating on his back with nothing but waves for company. "Good luck to you."

"You don't believe me."

"You sound dead serious."

One side of the captain's mouth tilted upward. "Let's hope *dead* isn't the key word. I suppose you feel fine."

"Fit as my daddy's fiddle."

"I thought I'd whipped this nasty business. Sometimes I have six meals a day—three down and three up." McKenzie ran a hand over his long face. "Care to change the subject?"

Arno paused to ponder the possibilities. "Got a girl back home?"

"I do. You?"

"Miss Hattie Waltz." Saying her name out loud made her seem more real. Brought her closer.

"Do you ever worry someone might snatch her while you're away?"

"Every skinny minute." If he loved Hattie the way she deserved, wouldn't he let her go, let her build a future with a man who wanted the same things?

McKenzie chuckled a raspy sound. "Whenever I count the reasons my gal might throw me over for another, I'm miserable. However, no more negative thinking. Those days are over and done."

Arno sighed. "How's that working out for you?"

"Good most days. We're engaged."

"Congratulations." A big step. Would he ever hear the clang of wedding bells?

Side-by-side, they studied the horizon in silence. Mild weather had blessed their journey until today. Gloom blanketed the sky.

A strong fishy scent spoiled the fresh air. Supper, or a pitiful excuse for the evening meal, stood a good hour away. Maybe they'd find better food once they landed.

"The men are saying we'll report to a rest camp in England before France. Is there any truth to that?" Arno gripped the sides of his life preserver, a cumbersome requirement for soldiers roaming the top deck.

"That's the latest plan." The captain's unwavering stare grew familiar, resembling the pensive gaze on the baseball diamond several weeks ago. "I apologize for gawking, but it's the strangest thing. You're a dead ringer for my kid brother—same height, the same blue eyes, fair complexion, that cleft in your chin. You're stockier, though." The captain shook his head. "I've nearly called you James a half-dozen times. I know … it sounds idiotic."

"I've heard everyone has a twin somewhere."

Arno sized up the captain who looked more like him than Oliver had. Arno and Lena had inherited Mother's fair skin and pale eyes while Oliver matched Father—skin that tanned easily, hair as dark as black bullheads, and a bundle of freckles.

"You're his spitting image. I'd show you a photograph, but it's not on me."

A half-dozen soldiers jogged past, jostling one another with elbows and shoulders. Shouts and laughter straggled behind. A second pack followed, all racing toward the ship's bow. "What's the fuss?" Arno stretched for a better view.

"Let's go have a look-see." McKenzie motioned toward the other end of the ship. "What's on your agenda this evening?"

"Oh, the usual—a five-course dinner, maybe some dancing with my gal."

"Don't you wish?" Their steps matched.

He'd probably reread Hattie's letter for the millionth time and then shoot the breeze with some of the fellows. "Nothing special."

"Care for a diversion?"

"Keep talking." On most days, a diversion meant a random white cloud, interrupting an unblemished blue sky.

"Meet me back here after supper. I'll show you James' photograph, By any chance, do you have a brother who looks like me?"

"Only a sister, and she's ten times prettier."

McKenzie chuckled.

Arno never talked about Oliver, but since the captain had a kid brother himself, maybe he'd understand.

It felt like yesterday when Oliver had died in that blizzard. It'd snowed so hard they couldn't see the barn from the house. Arno had fastened a rope between the two buildings. He'd whipped through chores and then hurried to the barn's doorway. The rope had disappeared.

The electric light in a kitchen window was barely visible as he trudged through mounting snowdrifts and blinding flakes. Mother asked about Oliver as he sat down to eat. The boy had followed Arno to the barn. They found him hours later smothered beneath the snow next to a stubby cherry tree in the orchard. He died the next day.

If only Arno had secured a better knot, Oliver would be home, the place where he belonged.

Another dozen soldiers zipped past, drawing Arno's thoughts back to the ship. Hyland lagged behind the others.

"Hey!" Arno hollered, "Where's the fire?"

CW retraced his steps, adding a swagger. He saluted McKenzie. "They spotted land, sir. We're finally getting off this floating bucket of bolts. No disrespect."

"As you were." The captain offered a dismissive nod, then looked to the east. "Nobody wants off this ship more than me."

After a pointed sneer at Arno, CW jogged away.

"I wish he spoke the truth." With his elbow on the rail, the captain twisted to face Arno.

"Maybe, he is."

"It's a false alarm. We're not scheduled to reach shore for two or three more days." Another unfounded rumor.

"Isn't Hyland one of the two men you captured during a sharpshooter drill?"

Arno nodded, suspecting the captain already knew the answer.

"And didn't he accidentally shoot you from behind months later?"

"I'm not convinced about the accidental part." He rarely thought about the incident, but that didn't mean he'd forgiven Hyland. Initially, he'd pinned the blame on Barrett, but that man lacked the guts to shoot a fellow soldier—or had too much integrity. Hyland had proven himself ruthless, cunning, and more than capable.

McKenzie arched his fair brow. "What evidence do you have?"

"My gut." Arno jammed both hands deep into his pockets and then stroked the edge of Hattie's photograph.

"If I wore your shoes, I might hold the same opinion," the

captain said after a lengthy pause.

"A sharpshooter missing a rabbit by a yard?"

Cheers escalated up front while soldiers strained to snatch a hopeful peek at a not too distant shore that wasn't there.

"Believe it or not, we share a few things in common, Kreger."

An officer and an enlisted man? Not much. The army made sure of that. "Is that so?"

"You're from Iowa."

"Born and reared."

Ocean spray spattered them, and they stepped away from the handrail. The darkened sky whipped wind at the waves. "I grew up on a farm in southwestern Wisconsin, not far from Prairie du Chien. I have relatives in your neck of the woods. My aunt, Minna Winterberg, lives in—"

"Split Falls." That meant German-American blood surged through the captain's veins too. "I know her well, but then I know nearly everyone there. Sorry about your uncle."

McKenzie nodded. "I haven't been back since his memorial service, but I ought to visit her. Maybe I'll call on you if I ever do."

"You'll have to join us for supper." The thought of a home-cooked meal twisted Arno's stomach. "My ma's a blue-ribbon cook. She's won prizes for jams and pies."

"Speaking of amazing suppers, are you planning to meet after we finish ours tonight?"

"Are you positive we're not landing any time soon?"

"Have you heard the man in the crow's nest with the telescope holler 'land?'" The captain pointed skyward.

Arno glanced up and laughed.

"Mark my words, we won't abandon this liner tonight. Let's join up here in, say," McKenzie consulted his wristwatch, "an hour. Who knows, maybe I'll bring you some leftovers."

"I'll be here." Even a small sample of the captain's meal sounded better than his usual fare—a stale slice of bread, a wiener, and half a peach.

McKenzie nodded and then strolled toward the ship's stern. Arno turned back around to watch the waves.

"Sounds like you two got a rendezvous planned for later." CW leaned against the railing.

Arno's fists tightened, then he released his tension one finger at a time. "What about you? You got a date for a court-martial anytime soon?" He copied CW's stance.

"Looks to me like you're doing a little old-fashioned boot-licking. Am I right?"

Arno spared a quick over-the-shoulder glance at the captain. He stood beyond earshot, talking with a lieutenant. "I ought to pop you one right now."

Last night he'd thrown one leg over his hammock and froze. Karl's pencil drawing of Hattie lay scattered across his bed in a dozen pieces. He'd interrogated the men bunking nearby. Each claimed innocence, swearing he knew nothing. Either they spoke the truth or refused to squeal. A confession mattered little. Arno knew who did it.

CW chuckled. "I think the sea air has turned your mind to mush, Kreger. I don't know what you're yammering about."

"Don't touch my stuff." Thunder rumbled in the distance.

"Or what? Sweet revenge?"

"You mean bitter." Arno told himself to walk away, to put the ship's length between them.

"No, sir. It's as sweet as a lump of sugar."

"Not to me."

The drowning drill whistle blared. "Now there's an idea. German overboard. By the time someone realizes you're missing, you'll be on a one-way sink to the bottom of the sea."

The threat hung like a barnacle on the ship—irritating, clingy, and real.

CHAPTER TWENTY-FIVE

Bareback on top her palomino mare, Hattie led the way out of the corral. Ian Moss, Meridee's youngest of three sons, trailed behind on a chestnut quarter horse. After twenty yards or so, she tugged on the reins and waited for her companion. "I know you've ridden before, but Arrow is a tad temperamental."

Ian paused before responding. "I like to take chances."

That probably meant parting his thinning hair on the right instead of the left.

Even on his day off, the man dressed like a banker. At least he'd shucked his suit jacket before climbing into the saddle. He'd canceled a half-dozen business appointments to tend his mother who suffered in bed from rheumatism. Tuckered from the extra fussing, Meridee had recruited Hattie's help, which led to today's outing—or date, as far as Daddy was concerned.

"Giddyap!" Ian screamed and jabbed his heels into Arrow's flanks. The twitchy horse whinnied and bucked, flinging her rider onto his back in the well-trodden cow pasture. "Ouch!"

Adrenaline flung Hattie from Gypsy's back. "Are you all right? Is anything broken?"

Ian moaned, lurched to his feet, and wiped down his clothing. "I can't believe your horse bucked me off."

Warm air whizzed from between Hattie's clenched teeth. Ian wasn't hurt. "I'm sorry."

Arrow circled back and galloped to the corral, where Jeb ushered her inside then closed the gate. He soothed the animal before marching to the fence. "I told him to pick a different horse!"

"Everything's fine," Hattie hollered to her brother before

206

offering the man at her side a sympathetic smile.

Pale as the sheet flapping on the clothesline, Ian's Adam's apple bobbed. "If it's all the same to you, I'd rather not go back quite yet."

"How about a stroll?" She collected Gypsy's reins.

"That trumps the alternative." Ian plucked a trio of fragrant daisies from a prosperous patch. "I know about your arrangement."

Hattie's breath caught. "Which one?"

"The one where you court a soldier in France, but your father insists you continue dating other men."

"Oh, that arrangement." Hattie raised her chin, admiring the afternoon sky, cloudless and a brilliant blue. Wildflowers dotted the pasture, stirring an aromatic fragrance she longed to roll in for a long spell.

"I have no designs on you, Miss Waltz." Ian nodded, emphasizing his hard-to-miss message.

"Thanks for the bulletin."

"I'm not interested, not in the least. Have I made myself clear?"

Hattie tilted her head to the side. Although Ian's words bordered on offensive, he spoke with honesty. "Let's enjoy the day for what it is—a carefree afternoon." With a doozy of a two-day fundraiser looming, she hadn't ridden her mare or relaxed much in weeks. The thought of a lazy day, even with Ian, appealed.

"Is that a stream over yonder?" He pointed toward the creek.

"It is."

"You don't happen to have a fishing pole or two stashed somewhere?"

"You never know, you might find one hidden in the brush on the bank."

He rubbed his hands together in anticipation. "Let's go take a gander."

The pair chatted nonstop, stepping around ripe cow pies until they reached the stream's embankment. Although a stuffier version, he reminded Hattie of his mother, a born conversationalist.

"Do you mind if I wade?" Without waiting for permission—not that he needed her approval—Ian tugged off his shoes and socks, chucking the items into a stand of foxtails before rolling his trouser cuffs halfway up his white calves.

"I haven't indulged since childhood." With an *ahh*, he dipped his big toe into the clear water fed by a natural spring.

Hattie dropped Gypsy's reins, knowing she wouldn't wander far. June sunshine glinted off the creek. Dense woods lay on the opposite side, belonging to Arno's family. The view held the same beauty as the artwork on Mrs. Merriweather's distinguished corridor in Pennsylvania. A frog croaked close enough to catch.

Ian wandered downstream, and Hattie lost sight of him around a bend.

She found a not-too-bumpy seat near the water. Damp hair stuck to her neck, and she swiped at the spot with her skirt hem. She pulled Arno's most recent letter from her pocket and settled in for a reread.

Carrying Arno's words around with her was like having a piece of him close.

May 11, 1918

Dear Hattie,

I'm not ready to give up on us either, but we both know it could lead to heartbreak. I'm sorry, but it's the truth.

Greetings from overseas. I'm safe, sound, and far, far from Iowa. On the boat ride over, I found my sea legs in no time. The scenery never changed. We slept in hammocks, and once I grew accustomed to the rollicking, it rocked me to sleep in a snap.

We've yet to reach France. I wonder how soon we'll receive mail. Some say letters move quicker than you'd expect, but the next person claims it takes forever and a week. I suppose I'll have my answer soon enough and, hopefully, also a mountain of mail.

According to Captain McKenzie, his brother is my long-lost twin. He showed me a photograph. He's not my spitting image, but we could pass as brothers. If I've not said it before, the captain is a heck of a guy. I'm lucky to have met him.

I've decided to recite three things I'm most looking forward to when I return home.

Mother's cinnamon coffee cake slathered in gooey vanilla frosting.

Riding Smokey through the timber. Who knew a man could miss a horse so much?

And you. I could go on and on about why, but there's not enough time or stationery to do you justice. You'll have to wait until we see each other again. In case you're wondering, you rank above baked goods and Smokey.

Taps will soon sound, so I'll sign off for now. Even though we're miles apart, you hold my heart in your hands. Please be careful.

As always,
Arno

Ian splashed toward the bank and then paused to lob rocks at floating targets from the sandbar. The buttoned-up man she'd met two days ago had disappeared, replaced by a fun-loving version.

His enthusiasm drove Hattie to shed her shoes and stockings behind a prickly bush. She gathered her full skirt to keep it dry as mushy sand oozed between her toes. She waded onto the sandbar and looked for the perfect flat-sided rock.

"Mother told me she intends to wed your father," Ian shouted upstream, scattering blackbirds. "I don't know how to say this delicately, but is he after her money?"

"What?" Of all the mad ideas.

"I had to ask. My mother is the richest woman in Split Falls. My guess is a lot of men would like to get their hands on her money." He approached, sweat beads dotting his upper lip.

She swiped at her damp forehead with her arm. Ian had a lot of nerve. "She chased him. He doesn't want her money, and for the longest time, he didn't want her."

Hawk and Wilhelm broke through the brush.

"Uh-oh, buddy." Wilhelm fanned his face with his hat. "There's trespassers at our fishing hole."

"Don't worry." Hawk carried a cane pole in one hand and an old fruit jar brimming with dirt and night crawlers in the other. "Hattie's not very good. She won't steal our fish."

"Say, young man." Ian splashed through the water toward her brother and Wilhelm, scaring away every fish within a mile. "I don't suppose you'd let me join your fishing expedition? I haven't indulged in the pleasure in … in … I don't know how long."

"Sure. I know the best spot. It's right below the dam. There's bass and northern this long." Hawk stretched his hands apart. "Can we, Hattie? Can I go there with Mr. Moss?"

What if Ian offended Hawk? She gave a mental shrug. She couldn't shield the boy forever. "As long as neither of you tumbles in."

"Aww, thanks."

Her brother's grin tugged at her heartstrings. He rarely asked for much, which meant she tended to overindulge when he did.

"Want to come, Wilhelm?" Hawk asked, hope in his voice.

"Not quite yet. You run along but save me a fish or two."

Hawk scurried away with Ian tiptoeing behind, obviously not used to running barefooted.

"You know what I think?" Wilhelm shoved aside his bangs before putting on his hat.

"Not usually."

For a split second, he smiled. "You'll make an excellent mother one day. Actually, you already are one to Hawk."

Hattie savored Will's compliment. If only she'd fallen in love with the man before her and not a complicated soldier she rarely saw. Daddy and Jeb respected Will, and Hawk called the man his best friend. To top it off, he wanted a family of his own. By most people's standards, Wilhelm was perfect. Hattie agreed except for two key points—he wasn't Arno, and he once belonged to her best friend.

She plucked free a smooth white stone embedded halfway into the soggy sand before striding to the stream's edge, her toes in the water. "I'm about to break the Catfish Creek stone skipping record."

Settled amongst the weeds and spikey grass near the creek's bank, Will leaned back on his elbows and crossed his ankles. "Bold statement. Shoot, I can't remember the last time I skipped rocks. Must have been when we were youngsters."

"That's the difference between you and me." Although nineteen, she still took pleasure in tossing rocks, skipping rope, and catching lightning bugs. She told herself it was merely to amuse Hawk, but she knew better.

She gripped the palm-sized rock just so, flicked her wrist back and forth, and tilted her head, zeroing in on her mark. "Ready?"

"Since yesterday."

She let the stone fly. Its flat bottom soared parallel to the calm surface before dipping enough to send soft ripples in its wake. "One … two … three … four, five, six, seven, eight, nine, ten, eleven, twelve, thirteen, fourteen!" She threw her hands in the air, jumping up and down. "It's a new record! I'm the king of the stone skippers!"

"I only counted twelve." Wilhelm sent her a lazy smile.

"Were your eyes closed? There were easily fourteen, maybe even fifteen." With a hand on her hip, she waited for a rebuttal.

"Are you on a date with Ian Moss?"

Hattie concentrated on the fishy water bathing her ankles. It wasn't the response she'd expected. "In a manner of speaking."

"Does he make your heart pitter-patter?"

Bent at the waist to find a second flat stone, she glanced at Wilhelm. "He told me flat out I don't interest him and then asked if Daddy sniffed after his mother's money. In other words, no. I'm not attracted to Mr. Moss."

Will laughed, rolling onto his side.

"What's so funny? I'm happy he told me the truth. It makes," she fluttered her hands, "everything easier."

He sobered. "Is that what you want, something easy?"

Water dripped from her skirt hem as she weighed a handful of potential replies. "It certainly beats something hard."

"What if I took you on a date? You know, when your next allotment is due."

Arno had suggested the same. Halfway across the creek, a fish surfaced, rippling the still water.

"I don't know. It sounds risky."

"How so?"

"What if it ruined our friendship?" For Arno's sake, Lena's sake, and her own, she'd never go on a sham date with Wilhelm. She cared about him too much to open that tin of worms.

"Again, how so?"

The first tingles of a blush threatened but failed to bloom. She plopped onto the bank near Wilhelm. "This probably sounds foolhardy, but what if one of us developed lopsided feelings for the other? Then what?"

The silence stretched until Will shoved her shoulder. "Do you have a crush on me?"

"Heavens to Betsy, no." She stood and turned to leave. "I'm gonna check on Hawk."

"I'll join you."

She whipped around, wet skirt flapping against her legs. "Wilhelm, what do you want from me?"

With nothing more than a few weeds stuck between them, he peered at her with a mixture of sadness and longing. "I don't rightly know the answer to your question, but I do know this much—my pa's sick, and the doctor wants me to stay away until suppertime. He's under observation until then." With a weary sigh, Will hung his head. "When I return, I'll learn whether or not I'm to cart him to the hospital."

"Oh, my goodness. I'm so sorry." Out of habit, she reached for her friend's hand. "How can I help?"

Before either uttered a word, a faint scream reached them.

"It's Hawk!" Hattie took off at a run.

Wilhelm zipped past. "I'll fetch him."

She raced at full speed. Who required saving—Hawk or Ian?

CHAPTER TWENTY-SIX

May 30, 1918—Le Havre, France

Arno's boat bobbed like a chunk of driftwood in the choppy English Channel. His thoughts remained divided between the impending frontline and Hattie. Each topic was packed with risks.

The stormy weather eased when the ship neared the French coastal city of Le Havre. The midday sun shone on a lush green countryside resembling Iowa. But the cottages dotting the landscape were foreign.

A smattering of folks, mostly women and youngsters, witnessed their arrival. Soldiers stood shoulder to shoulder against the rails, anxious to step on solid ground. Once the boat touched the dock, Arno tossed a couple shiny coins toward scruffy French children, palms raised to the soldiers. "Catch." Most folks scattered once the gangplank was lowered.

Red Cross workers plied hungry troops with *hello*s, sponge cake, and weak coffee. The soldiers, stiff from their cramped trip, finally marched onward, crowding the streets. A few broke ranks to gawk at shop windows and townsfolk. Occasionally an elderly Frenchman applauded them parading past.

They were wrangled into side-door Pullmans and departed the port city within twenty-four hours. They slept in short shifts on the crowded floor. Arno snoozed scrunched in a ball with his haversack as a pillow and someone's hobnails rammed against his hip.

The train carried them south and west toward Pons near France's western shore with occasional stops to drill, march, and fill their bellies with more than bully beef and biscuits. Assigned to the Service of Supply—far from the battlefields—Arno's regiment continued training in preparation for their eventual turn at the front.

Rain flipped from drizzle to downpour. Arno lugged his one-hundredth bag of provisions from a half-empty train car via his weary shoulder. Stuck with the backbreaking chore for the past week, he hit his bunk with aching wrists and ankles each night.

He dumped his load into the back of a massive military truck and then swiped a soggy sleeve across his forehead. Water dribbled off his elbows and chin. Water sloshed inside his boots.

"Kreger," Frankie hollered from inside the truck, "Captain McKenzie wants you. He left here three, four minutes ago."

"Now?" Arno shouted over the downpour.

"I'm almost done. Give me a minute, and I'll help you find him. I want to tell you something I heard this morning." Frankie jumped from the truck and motioned toward a nearby tree that offered some shelter. They huddled beside its sturdy trunk. "Word is CW landed in a bucket of hot water again, this time with a local gal."

Arno wrung his cap while staring at Frankie. "Are you yanking my leg?"

"Supposedly, he had a run-in with a peasant girl. According to the story, CW walked to one of the villages where some woman made cow eyes at him. Here's the interesting part, she told a translator CW shoved her to the ground and then kissed and grabbed at her."

"I'll be jiggered." So now Hyland had attacked an innocent woman. "I wouldn't put it past him. It sounds like something he'd do."

Frankie yanked out a soaked pack of cigarettes, grimaced, and stuffed them back in his pocket. "I still wager it's not enough to ship the man home."

Someone gripped Arno's shoulder. "Who's shipping whom out

of where?"

Captain McKenzie.

Caught gossiping, Arno suppressed a grimace, then he and Frankie snapped to attention.

"As you were."

"Jesberger was filling me in on Hyland's trouble."

"Why don't you fill me in too?"

Frankie shifted his feet. "The story is CW got overly friendly with a gal from the area, someone not eager for his company."

A firm line replaced the captain's smile. "Walk with me, Kreger." After a few steps, McKenzie paused. "How's your workload?"

"Same as most, I reckon."

"Any chance you can drive a motorcycle with a sidecar?"

Was Arno imagining it, or was the thrill of a lifetime within grasp? "I reckon so."

With a laugh, Mac steered him along a rain-soaked path and toward the barracks, a series of old stone dwellings and barns.

"I suspected as much. We'll head out after tomorrow morning's mess, and you can chauffeur me to Bordeaux for my meeting. They say the scenery takes a man's breath away. I wager that's an exaggeration, but I'd like to see for myself."

"I'm more obliged than you know." Anything was better than unloading boxcars. "I've always wanted to drive one of those beauties."

McKenzie veered right, and Arno continued to the makeshift barracks. A bugler sounded mail call, the first since setting foot on French soil. Arno jogged to the noisy waiting line. After a lengthy delay, he collected three letters for his patience, one from Hattie.

The sky broke as he sped toward his billet.

May 18, 1918

Dear Arno,

Are your feet on dry land? Although I've tried countless times, it's impossible to picture all the new sights you witness each day. It must feel overwhelming at times, even a tad scary. I know, I know—big, brawny soldiers like you aren't afraid.

When I'm not busy with chores, the Brigade steals my time. I'm in shock because the governor agreed to attend our August fundraiser. Don't you think he'll pull in an impressive crowd? I do.

Let me know if I should stop mentioning my hometown dates, but you'll appreciate the last one. Arrow bucked off Ian, Meridee's youngest, in the pasture. He told me not to expect advances from him, which, thank heavens, eased my mind. Then he had the nerve to ask if Daddy is a gold-digger. To top it off, he tumbled headfirst into Catfish Creek while fishing with Hawk. Will was there, too, and jumped in to drag Ian back to the bank. What an odd day!

For today's true confessions, here are three things that scare me.

Squirrels. I know they're relatively harmless, but they spy on me whenever I'm outdoors. Whether gardening or hanging clothes, I turn, and there's a beady-eyed animal watching me, ready to pounce. My guess is they watch the back door, spot me on the porch, spread the word, and then track my steps.

Public speaking, but it's getting better little by little. When I sing before folks, lyrics and accompaniment push me along from start to finish. When I'm called to address a crowd of strangers, my heart races like a jackrabbit.

You. Sometimes, I worry I still like you more than you like me. I drag that thought around like a ratty baby's blanket.

It's time to set the table, and if I say so myself, the ham smells heavenly. I'm sorry if images of pork make you even more homesick. On second thought, the meat is probably tough and dry, so you're not missing anything special.

Stay safe and never forget someone back home misses you with her entire heart. In case you're wondering, it's me. Sweet dreams tonight!

As always,
Hattie

Arno pressed the paper against his chest. All his dreams were sweet since he dreamt of home most nights. Home and Hattie. Those two went together.

For the first time since leaving the New York harbor, joy lurked nearby.

After a bouncy solo test run with the showy motorcycle, Arno looped a wide circle across a bumpy acre of grass to greet the captain. A combination of oil and gas fumes followed him. The motor sputtered in rapid succession.

"What do you think?" McKenzie ran a hand across the sleek machine before folding his legs inside the sidecar.

"If you ever itched to fly, today is the day."

"Do you suppose the sidecar helps with balance?"

"Let's hope so." A corporal at the motorcycle depot had forked over a hand-drawn map that pinpointed landmarks and intersecting roads between Pons and Bordeaux. "I'm ready when you are."

"Let's roll, Corporal Kreger."

Corporal Kreger. Those words went together like meat and potatoes. He'd written Father about the promotion. No reply yet.

The wind rippled their clothing and the skin on their faces. The sun warmed fertile vineyards lining both sides of the auto road for miles. In a few months, a heady grape scent would sweeten the air like in Arno's small patch of vines back home. A string of hills rolled before them. Flying down the road on the motorcycle sure beat puttering on a tractor.

Had Karl ever sketched similar landscapes or only bloody trenches and shell-torn roads? Arno hadn't heard from his friend in weeks. Worry ricocheted for a moment, but he squelched it. No sense in borrowing trouble.

More like a vacationing tourist than a soldier on assignment, Arno sucked in the experience. It was hard to imagine occupying a trench when seated on a glossy motorcycle.

Bordeaux, nestled in a bend on the Garonne River, bristled with military vehicles. The motorcycle sliced through traffic, making excellent time. He deposited the captain at a nondescript military building with time to spare.

McKenzie worked himself from the sidecar and then stretched. "What do you say I drive back, and you can stuff yourself into that box?" He chuckled.

"Sounds fair to me."

The captain handed Arno his motorcycle goggles before adjusting his cap. "Do you have your paperwork? We don't want anyone thinking you're a defector."

With a pat to his trouser pocket, Arno grinned. "I'll be at your beck and call again in three hours."

McKenzie raised an arm in farewell and then disappeared inside.

Arno roared off and parked on the top of a picturesque hill overlooking cobblestone streets, lush vegetation, and the ocean in the distance. He did his best to memorize it. A soldier squatted in the grass, absorbed in a book. It couldn't be. Arno dismounted the motorcycle and walked closer.

"Karl?"

The soldier raised his head. Neither of them moved until Karl flung his book aside. Laughter filled the air between them. "Not two minutes ago, I thought about you. Now, you're standing here beside me."

"But," Arno shook his head, trying to clear the confusion, "why are you in Bordeaux? Aren't we miles from the war zone? Are you well?" Like a slingshot, a dozen more questions peppered his thoughts.

"Hold your horses. Which question should I answer first? Don't I look well?"

Sturdy and familiar, nothing about him had changed. "I always hoped we'd find one another in France but never expected to track you down here."

Their handshake lingered. "I'm in town for a map meeting and free the rest of the day. What about you?"

"Chauffeur business." Arno pointed toward the motorcycle.

"*Ooh-la-la*. That's French for impressive." Karl let loose an appreciative whistle.

"Aren't you the linguist?"

"Gonna give me a ride in that fancy contraption or keep yapping all day?"

They explored the city at leisure, steering the motorcycle up one winding street and down the next, past Gothic architecture and ancient churches sprouting spires. Arno parked on the street beside a corner café with vinery climbing the building's stone wall. A string of wrought-iron chairs and matching round tables spilled onto a sidewalk. They claimed the nearest vacant seats.

A young waitress with black eyes and blacker hair approached. "*Je m'appelle Gisèle*." She placed a hand against her chest and nodded. "*Oui?*"

Was Gisèle the female's name?

"Ka-rl." He over-enunciated, speaking far too loud for a quiet café.

"*Vous etês* German?"

"No, no." Karl plucked at his uniform sleeve. "A-mer-i-can soldier."

Arno almost introduced himself, but then the woman's smirk indicated she fully understood. They were two paying customers serving in the United States Army, not for the enemy. Of course, she knew that tidbit.

She pointed at the menu. "*Vous avez choisi?*"

Arno swept the French words. Should he take his chances and randomly point to an option? What were the odds he'd select something delicious or at least passable?

She tapped her foot, painted lips in a pout. A second waitress delivered a neighboring patron's meal. It smelled heavenly.

Arno pointed at the items and nodded.

"Me too," Karl practically shouted. The woman didn't speak English, she wasn't deaf. Shouting wouldn't help.

"*Croissant* and *chocolat chaud*? *Oui*?" Gisèle squeezed Arno's forearm.

He'd almost forgotten the soft touch and fragrant scent of a woman. He absorbed it, but only for a moment. "*Oui*. Definitely. I'll take that." He wagged his finger between himself and Karl and then flashed two fingers. "Make it two."

Gisèle dipped her head before scooting into the brick café.

"In my opinion, a certain French gal likes the cut of your jib."

Arno laughed. The French girl didn't tempt him. Only Hattie could do that.

"They say the women around these parts are mighty friendly." Karl plunked one elbow at a time on the tabletop and folded his hands.

"I reckon it's the same as back home. Some are, others not so much."

"That's true. What's the latest with Hattie? I don't suppose her letters still arrive like clockwork anymore."

The waitress delivered the two cups of sweet-smelling hot chocolate and the flaky pastries. They offered their thanks.

"Mail is spotty, that's for certain," Arno said, his mouth half full. "But I got one from her yesterday."

"She still dating all those extra men?"

Arno grunted.

"I'll take that as a yes. Hyland still a loose cannon?"

"I reckon he's the same as always. Whenever I get within a foot of him, he either calls me *German boy* or *German lover*. A few others have picked it up too." The taunts had grown old and crusty.

"If you ask me, Hyland is a sorry excuse for a soldier."

A seagull dove between them. They jumped to their feet while the greedy bird snatched errant crumbs. Arno dug into his pocket before flipping a franc, leaving a tip on the charming café's tabletop.

They returned to the motorcycle and glided around town. Rows of Allied heavy artillery parked in the ordnance yard. A crane unloaded military trucks from a hefty ship at the port. Intrigued by the maneuver, Arno switched off the motorcycle. They watched until an army tank lugging a railroad car nearly ran over their boots. Then it was back on the motorcycle, away from the seaside, and a return trip to the city's heart.

McKenzie barged out the door and into the afternoon sunshine. Arno waved from across the street, the same place he'd left the captain. McKenzie smiled. "Are my eyes tricking me?"

Karl scrambled from the sidecar to salute. "Corporal Ludwig at your service, sir."

"Well, I'll be." McKenzie shook his head as if in disbelief. "Aren't you a sight for sore eyes? How's the map business?"

"Excellent. I'm in town for a meeting, but it ended this forenoon."

"Which is when, I assume, you ran into your old friend." The captain slapped Karl's shoulder.

"Exactly." Arno couldn't have outlined a better day for himself. *yea*

"I've saved my best news for last." Karl gave Arno a playful jab. "The map business is slowing down. The French have done most of the work. I mainly update small sections of the trenches these days, which is why I'm rejoining my old company come Friday."

Unbelievable. Arno resisted the urge to whoop and holler. "The army figure out you're not half the artist they thought you were?"

"Nah, I shamed the others. Gotta give them more time to practice."

Everybody laughed, especially the captain. "You're quite the jokester, aren't you?" McKenzie reached for his motorcycle goggles.

"Yes, sir."

"Then I suppose we'll see you on Friday." The captain adjusted the eyewear.

"Bright and early, sir." Karl clicked his heels and saluted. McKenzie dismissed him with a nod before Karl's boots pounded the cobblestone.

"Good day, I take it." The captain climbed onto the machine.

"Absolutely." Arno squeezed himself inside the sidecar. "Good meeting?"

"More informative than good. I can't offer any specifics, but I'll tell you this much—our peaceful life back at camp is about to change drastically."

That didn't need specifics. Arno got the picture. "Sounds like we're about to prove we're capable of something more."

"Those are your words, not mine. I'll tell you one more thing. CW Hyland didn't pillage a peasant girl. CJ Hyrum, a fella from Alabama, is the accused." McKenzie revved the motor.

"Huh." So, the man was innocent this time. He hated admitting it, but CW excelled around camp, hefting cargo two men typically toted. Even Arno had to admire the man's strength.

By the time they reached the city's outskirts, the sunshine faded. Arno refueled the motorcycle as he stowed away the day's memories—the shock of finding Karl, the windswept shoreline, the melt-in-your-mouth pastry, and his conversations with McKenzie.

With a tight fist, he clutched each one, because changes were coming and most likely not for the better. At least he'd fight beside Karl—the world's best possible sidekick.

CHAPTER TWENTY-SEVEN

Hattie and Priscilla strolled down the lane toward the corral following an afternoon Brigade meeting in the Waltz's parlor. The other committee members had scattered, possessing the decency not to overstay their welcome.

"Samantha Shamrock." Priscilla fanned her face with her hand. "What about Samantha Shamrock?"

Drooping irises and peonies begged for a downpour. Hattie's hopes to throw a successful fundraiser had also drooped. The governor and his wife had canceled their promised appearances. To make matters worse, the governor backed the Babel Proclamation banning the German language. How long until the next restriction targeting German-Americans?

That wasn't the only chink in Hattie's well-planned agenda. The man who'd agreed to construct the outdoor stage had broken his collarbone shoeing a horse. Meridee remained sick in bed, and no other Brigade member had volunteered to help shoulder the load other than Priscilla—on a sporadic basis.

"Let's invite Miss Shamrock to the fundraiser." Priscilla clapped three times in front of her sunburned nose. "She'll surely draw a crowd."

"The starlet?" Of all the harebrained ideas, this one ranked alongside the invitation to President Wilson.

"Do you know another Samantha Shamrock?"

"Of course not, and you don't know this one." Hattie mopped a hand across her forehead before stuffing stray-hairs into her hefty braid. The heavy air, combined with the lengthy Brigade meeting, had depleted her energy. She wished for nothing more than a square of shade, a promising novel, and a glass of lemonade, preferably in the path of a substantial breeze.

Instead, she debated an impossibility. "Why in tarnation would a famous person travel all the way to Split Falls for a simple fundraiser?"

"Does she or does she not hail from Iowa?"

"I suppose, but don't you think someone like her is busy with, I don't know, starlet obligations?"

"Typical." Priscilla crossed her arms with a huff.

"What is?"

"You pish-posh my idea and don't suggest a better one. Chairing the Brigade has inflated your head."

Hattie stopped. Was that true? Over the last few months, she'd found her leadership footing but still struggled in one way or another with the responsibility. To avoid loopholes and potential pitfalls, she ruled their meetings with a firm grip, but was it too tight? Did the other committee members hold the same opinion? She'd ask Meridee.

Priscilla was right about one thing. Hattie lacked a better prospect than Samantha Shamrock. "Fine, if you can persuade the woman to perform, I'll buy the first ticket. But it's your task, your responsibility."

Priscilla clapped again.

They continued on their path around the barn to the corral. Jeb trotted a white-faced sorrel around the ring, parading the beauty before Wilhelm. The men's shirts clung to their muscular forms.

Hawk darted out of the barn door, scattering cats and hurrying to Hattie. Pieces of hay stuck to his shirt, breeches, and unruly hair until he shook like a dog. He smelled like a walking, talking bale of hay. "I'm supposed to tell you, Daddy and I are leaving for the hospital now. We're stopping for ice cream after."

A strand of hay dangled from her brother's chin, and she brushed it aside. "Tell Tobias, hello, and please bring me back a scoop of chocolate."

"Me too." Priscilla raised two fingers.

Hawk's dirt-streaked face scrunched. "It'll be soupy, but I'll try, and Daddy says to keep one eye on the weather." He trotted toward the Buick. The sky's eerie copper tinge matched Hattie's mood.

Despite the heat, Priscilla climbed onto the sunny top fence rail. Hattie plopped into the shady grass, leaning against the barn to reread Arno's latest letter.

> *May 31, 1918*
>
> *Dear Hattie,*
>
> *I'm in sunny France, as the locals like to say, but it makes no sense. It rains every day.*
>
> *I bumped into Karl, and he'll soon return to our company. I'd hoped we'd meet up over here, but it still surprised me. He's well, by the way.*
>
> *Some of the men I knew at Camp Pike were on the casualty list yesterday. Fighting continues at the front. It makes a man wonder why God spares some fellas and not others. It's a head-scratcher.*

"Thank you," Hattie whispered, thrilled Karl and Arno had found each other again. She mopped her face with dirty hands. She wasn't so naïve to think that friends, or friends of friends wouldn't die in combat. News of someone's death inched the war closer to home.

> *The last thing I want is for you to worry about me. I'll probably only glimpse the battle, duck into a dark hole, and pretend I'm a woodchuck when it's my turn.*
>
> *They're saying Uncle Sam wants more and more men in France by year's end. You won't need to worry about hometown dates much longer, that'll leave only the elderly in Split Falls.*
>
> *Here are my three little hopes for someday.*
>
> *We win the war and everyone I care about returns home*

unscathed.

You and I sort out our futures. Although I don't believe either of us has changed our opinions.

I find peace over Oliver's death, at least a measure.

Know what I miss? Pot roast. And you.

If you don't hear from me for a while, know I'm unable to write but please don't worry.

As always,
Arno

P.S. All my letters now get inspected. I can only say so much. But no matter what, don't stop writing. Your letters are my everything.

The urge to blubber like a baby nearly overwhelmed her.

"A nickel for your thoughts." Wilhelm dropped to the shade beside her. "Did you notice how the price shot up?"

"You're very generous."

He tilted his head closer to Hattie's, brushing his hair against hers. "I don't want Jeb to hear this, but your brother is an excellent judge of horseflesh. And it just so happens, I'm on the lookout for a new filly."

Hattie ran a finger over her pearls. Was Wilhelm referencing a horse or, for goodness sakes, a woman? She stuffed Arno's letter into its envelope and fanned her face. "She's an impressive animal."

"Gumdrop," he nodded toward the mare, "is the perfect name for a sweet horse. If Jeb drops the price, I may purchase her. You have a smudge on your cheek. Let me help you." Wilhelm wetted his fingertip with his tongue, while his eyes asked a question she had no idea how to answer.

Her heart skittered and she drew back, bumping her head against the barn wall before scrambling to her feet. It was past time to nip Wilhelm's unnecessary flirting in the bud. The sun dipped behind a blackening cloud, but its harsh rays continued to stalk.

From the corral fence, Priscilla stared as Hattie approached.

What would it take to saddle the complicated woman on the charming Will, killing two birds with one mighty stone—separate Jeb and Priscilla and find somebody else for Wilhelm?

Hattie reached Priscilla. "Why not stay on for supper tonight?"

The woman hopped from her roost, fluttering her dove gray skirt to expose trim ankles. "What's on your menu?"

Really? Did the main course make one speck of difference? Hattie racked her brain for a worthy retort. "Chicken?" It wasn't her shiniest reply.

Jeb slid from the sweaty horse's back and then scaled the fence. Perspiration and dirt mingled on her brother's chin. "You definitely ought to stay on for supper." He scooped a measure of oats from a bucket hooked to the fence, letting the grain sift through his splayed fingers. "My sister isn't a half-bad cook."

"I'll think about it."

Thunder clapped in the distance. Jeb stretched like a satisfied feline, peering over Hattie's head. "Take a look at the sky."

"I think we're in for an old-fashioned gully-washer." Wilhelm joined them by the fence.

Hattie undid the top button on her clingy cotton dress. Lightning zigzagged overhead followed too closely by another rumble of thunder.

"Hattie, fetch the clothes from the line." Jeb barked orders like a drill sergeant. "Priscilla, give her a hand, will ya? Wilhelm, shoo them chickens into the henhouse."

Flying dirt prickled the girls' skin as they scaled the hill. Each time Hattie raised her hands to free a garment from the wobbly clothesline, a hefty gust rocked her balance. Like a bully, the storm yanked a towel from her grip, dancing away toward the storm. Toward the storm?

"Root cellar," Jeb bellowed, running toward the girls, Will at his side.

A freshly laundered skirt escaped Hattie, but Wilhelm plucked it from midair. Steps from their hideaway, Hattie stumbled over a fallen tree branch, scraping both knees and spilling the laundry. Wilhelm helped her stand, as Jeb braced a foot and yanked with both hands to pry open the cellar door.

Hattie pointed at a well-defined funnel cloud and screamed. Crabapple-sized hail pelted their heads and shoulders. One by one, they scrambled to safety.

A musty odor flooded the space draped in cobwebs. Numerous times Mama had explained nothing lurked in the cellar Hattie couldn't swat away, but the eerie air still circled and loomed. They huddled in the dark pit.

"I'm scared." Priscilla shrieked the words Hattie held inside. Without much thought, she offered the frightened woman a reassuring hand pat.

"That's my thigh." Wilhelm chuckled.

Hattie yanked her hand away, striking something hard which thumped to the ground. The tang of prune sauce permeated the cramped space. Did the seal break? Mason jars, filled to their brims with fruits and vegetables, lined the cellar's one side. A potato bin, bushel baskets, and numerous stone crocks occupied another.

"Don't move." Would the others follow her advice, not her example? "If we flail about, we'll spill my jars."

"I'm trying not to budge, but my knees keep shaking." Priscilla punctuated her sentence with a moan.

"It's a cacophony outside," Jeb said. "That means …"

"We know what it means." Hattie squatted, tired of her brother's inflated vocabulary. She rested her hands on the ground to steady her trembles.

When the wind shrieked, she shuddered. Were Daddy and Hawk safe? What if the storm whisked away Arno's letters and photographs? Warm fingers grasped hers in the pitch blackness.

"Hush, Hattie," Jeb said in a soothing tone he normally reserved for children or sick animals.

"I didn't say anything."

"Yeah, but it was only a matter of time."

"Ewww!" Priscilla screamed. "A spider crawled up my skirt. Or maybe it's something even worse!"

"Want me to fetch it for you?" Jeb asked.

At least Priscilla laughed, an improvement over her caterwauling.

An uninterrupted silence followed, with only the wind raising its eerie voice. Hattie stood. After an extra loud thump against the cellar door she collapsed, and wrapped her arms around her chest.

The manic storm's tempo slowed, and Jeb hoisted the cellar door a sliver, casting a slice of light into their hideaway. Hattie and Wilhelm squatted in a corner, a smidge too close for comfort. She lurched sideways and bumped her brother, rattling the door shut.

Jeb murmured under his breath and raised the rickety cellar door again. He poked his head through the opening and then went outside. "It's over." He peeked into the cellar. "Come out but be careful. Everything's a mess."

Hattie climbed out and blinked before turning in a full circle. Lingering raindrops fell from the gray sky. The bruising storm had spared the house and barn, but tree limbs and branches, the busted trellis, and the shanty's roof littered the lawn. A rosebush had snared Daddy's Sunday shirt. A tangled white towel hung from a pussy willow tree. The field corn was broken and beaten flat.

"I'm gonna check on the animals." Jeb jogged toward the barn, disappearing down the slope of the hill.

"I'll come with." Wilhelm started to leave but then turned back to face the women. "You two okay?"

"As well as can be expected." Priscilla shoved debris from the porch step before collapsing to sob into her hands.

Songbirds riffed overhead, ignoring the storm's aftermath. Fresh rain dripped from the trees like tears. With each tentative step, new damage appeared. Hattie rounded the bend in the lane and gasped. Her apple tree—the one she'd carved with her and Arno's initials—lay uprooted on its massive side. Her foot caught on her skirt, and she stumbled forward to hug a battered branch.

"Why?" Things couldn't get worse.

Wilhelm crouched next to her and gathered her into his arms. "Shh … you're safe," he whispered, his palm flat against the middle of her back. "Everything is going to be fine."

It was a bald-faced lie, but Hattie longed to believe it. She uttered none of the fears swamping her. Cradled against his chest, she closed her eyes and pretended he was Arno. Just for a moment.

"Hattie."

"Yes?" Wrapped in his arms, her heart slowed to a steadier beat.

"I've fallen for you." With his callused fingertip, he raised her chin for a kiss.

The soft pressure soothed, dulling her raw emotions. Then the enormity of what she was doing smacked against her already pained head. She flung herself backward, rubbing her lips as if to wipe away the evidence. What had she done? When she turned her back, he placed his hand on her shoulder. She jumped.

"I think I love you." His voice was husky, and right in front of her, Priscilla watched from the lane.

Queasiness crashed in waves, and Hattie feared she'd lose her lunch. Had Priscilla heard Wilhelm? Read his lips? The kiss was bad enough, but the *I love you* was like getting hit by another natural disaster.

Priscilla marched down the lane. Hattie raced after her on shaky limbs. "Please, wait."

Near the barn, Priscilla whirled around, a fine crease between her eyebrows. "Is there something you'd like to say to me?"

Hattie snuck a quick peek at Wilhelm, who'd parked one foot on the apple tree's fallen trunk. "Please don't tell anyone about this little incident."

"Little? An *I love you* is little?" The meddlesome woman's high-pitched laughter grated.

"Don't write Arno about this. I'll tell him." A hammer banged against Hattie's heart, threatening to break it.

"What exactly do you plan to tell him?"

"I—I don't know yet."

"Will you beg for forgiveness or tell him you've fallen in love with another man?"

Hattie gasped. "I haven't."

"I see how Wilhelm looks at you."

The day's events spun, the bits failing to fit together. By the time she could speak again, Priscilla had turned away calling Jeb's name.

"I love Arno," Hattie shouted at the top of her lungs. It wasn't fair. The first time she'd spoken the special words aloud, she yelled them at a barn.

She limped toward the house, skirting obstacles in the yard—especially Wilhelm—but not the self-loathing. Bandit whimpered beneath the porch steps until she lured him into her arms for a snuggle and reassurance. "Don't worry, everything will turn out fine." The dog shivered, not believing her any more than she did.

In her bedroom, she yanked writing materials from a bureau drawer and then slid to the floor. With a tight grip on the pencil, words refused to flow. Her chest heaved and twisted like the storm. A deep sob burst free, shaking loose a passel of tears. She cried until dread replaced her self-pity.

She crawled across the room to collect two picture frames from her nightstand. The images stared back at her. Who would hate her more—Arno or Lena?

CHAPTER TWENTY-EIGHT

New orders arrived in July.

The Eighty-Seventh Division marched onto an eastbound road. Arno and his fellow soldiers, primed for combat, cut through picturesque villages, tree-hedged pastures, and luscious vineyards. He often counted his steps to beat the monotony, losing track around the two thousand and twenty mark. Each footstep shaved away more distance between him and the front lines.

Rain spit as the men hiked through a hamlet. Injured soldiers waited in the streets and alleyways for mercy at a congested Red Cross hospital. Someone shouted, "Go back. The poison gasses are gonna kill you!"

The regiment remained in formation, funneling through the town. The haunting plea echoed in Arno's head. Roads pock-marked from shellfire replaced the well-maintained routes. Burned-out farms and cratered fields flanked the troops.

Last night, Arno had slept in a roofless barn. Intermittent flares of light, mixed with July Fourth–sounding fireworks, had provided a mesmerizing show. The scent of death hung in the air from a mass of unburied bodies nearby. He'd tied a handkerchief over his nose and mouth before drifting off to sleep.

Since daybreak, they'd drilled with full packs, first across dew-drenched grass and then through sucking mud. It was another day of scattered downpours followed by brief bursts of sunshine. Every forty-five minutes, the bugle blew, and the regiment relaxed. The soldiers now teetered on safety's brim, where every combatant parked in a filthy trench longed to be.

"Fall out!" shouted the lieutenant, a mild fellow with a matching voice.

The soldiers spilled across a muddy hillside. Arno slumped to the cushiony grass, savoring the earthy scent and hoping this break lingered longer than the last. His pack slid to the uneven ground covered with rocks and ruts. He rested his back against its bulk.

"I'm bushed." Karl dropped, adding a heavy sigh to his statement.

Hyland, the last person Arno expected—or wanted beside him—lowered his gear near Arno and sat but remained closed-mouthed.

"Ditto." Blisters lined Arno's feet like wool socks, and he longed to shed his boots. Instead, he parked his Springfield rifle between his knees.

A cemetery nearby featured small white crosses. Some stood bare, others held helmets and military tags. Cedar and pine trees hemmed the meager graveyard on two sides, shielding the below-ground occupants from further pain and suffering. Did he know anybody buried there?

CW lay on his belly, his pack a pillow. "How much farther, you reckon?"

Focused on sparrows scolding one another, Arno said, "Dunno."

"I'd sure like to jump in that river and drown these lousy cooties." Karl scratched his scalp. "Who'd a thought we'd catch 'em back here behind the lines?"

"Why does one itch lead to a thousand more?" Tempted to scratch one little patch of scalp, Arno sat on his hands.

CW sneezed.

"*Gesundheit*," Arno said.

"What?" Hyland shot upright.

"*Gesundheit*. It's what you say when someone sneezes. It means 'good health.'"

CW's smile exposed two rows of decayed teeth.

For a long moment, Arno's eyes dueled his opponent's. Then

he checked for eavesdroppers. A pebble toss from the enemy, he'd uttered German. How could he have been such an idiot?

"You always act so high and mighty, Kreger." A hearty laugh followed the insult. "I reckon I ought to report you to the captain. I hear he don't cotton to traitors."

"At least Kreger never shot anyone from behind." Karl moved closer to Arno.

"You're still harping on that?" CW rolled onto his side, propping his head with his hand. "On another note, guess what I heard last night?"

It had to be something nasty by the look of CW's face. Arno plucked blades of grass.

Karl crossed his arms and stared at the sky.

"The army suspected two Americans on the front line of being German sympathizers. They were forced to kiss the flag and then dig their graves. Then," CW positioned his thumb and forefinger like a gun, "in they fell."

"You know what I heard?" Karl tapped Arno's boot with his own.

With a grunt, CW rolled onto his back. "I reckon you're gonna tell me whether I want to hear it or not."

 "They've reopened the investigation into when you shot my buddy."

Arno quirked a brow at the falsehood but kept his mouth shut. If Karl wanted to pursue a fact-finding mission, why interfere?

"How many times do I have to tell you it wasn't me?" A cuss word crossed CW's lips before he folded his hands to pillow his head.

"Then, who?" Arno tossed aside his grassy collection. Did CW even understand the difference between a truth and a lie? He'd wager a paycheck the answer was no.

"What if I told you his first name is Barrett and last name Jordane?"

Arno flinched before meeting Karl's eyes. "I'd say you're passing the buck."

"You stole his girl."

"Nope." Arno shook his head. "Hattie wasn't ever Jordane's girl."

"That's not how he saw it." CW sneezed again. "It's no skin off my nose, or back, or rear end if you don't believe me. But I swear on my sweet mother's grave, Barrett shot you, not me."

Churning traveled from Arno's belly to tighten in his chest. He'd ruled out Jordane. He didn't trust the Louisianan, but was the man capable of shooting someone from behind?

"Why a new version of the story now?" Karl hunched onto an elbow.

"I've told everyone it weren't me. Jordane and I were pals. These days, he's too good to chew the fat with anyone who doesn't have four stripes on his shoulder."

"If CW is ready to pin the blame where it belongs, the army may listen." Karl raised a valid point.

"I'm no snitch." CW swatted at a swarm of insects. "It's one thing to set the record straight with you two, but why travel that bumpy road?"

"I think you're yanking my chain, Clyde Walter," Arno said. "Next time I set eyes on Jordane, I'll ask for his version of the story."

"You go right ahead, but I'll bet good money he's not about to confess. Now leave me be. It's time for a nap."

When CW slung his forearm over his eyes, Karl mouthed the word *maybe* before rolling onto his side, his back to Arno.

A far-off boom rattled the earth. How many lives had it claimed? Arno studied the sparrows' reaction and pondered CW's words. Would he ever know the truth? According to rumor, they'd soon stand knee-deep in a filthy trench.

He shut his eyes, allowing memories to parade past like a moving picture on a screen, untouchable and distant. Oliver sledding down Bisbee's Hill. Mama in the kitchen with flour in her hair. Lena dancing in the parlor with an imaginary suitor. Father perched on a tractor. Hattie plucking wildflowers long ago.

While CW snored, Arno watched the man he'd butted heads with for far too long. They were as different as mud and milk. Was CW innocent of the bullet-in-the-leg crime?

Shackled by hate for too many miserable months, Arno hung his head. The weight on his shoulders felt like hail on a corn crop. Maybe they'd both die on the front lines within the week. If ever there was a time to start praying, this was it.

"Take cover!" someone yelled.

Arno dove for the trees next to the graveyard. An airplane shell whistled past. With a WOO-KA-BOOM, it smacked the ground. On his gut amongst pine needles and mud, Arno's cheek rested against the sludgy earth. His arms shielded his head, and his stomach muscles worked double-time.

The gunfire broke again, more distant—or was it? An acrid odor stained the air. He took his hands away from his head. An airplane dipped in and out of thick clouds. CW lay nearby, also uncovering his head. Some distance away, a fallen soldier lay exposed.

The airplane droned, but the buzz grew fainter. Arno scrambled to the edge of the brush while scanning the sky. He inched forward, elbows sinking into the mud. Halfway to the wounded soldier, he recognized Karl.

"No!" The word snarled in his throat. Arno sprinted forward, dropping to his knees beside Karl and feeling for a pulse—weak but there. Blood oozed from a deep gash across his forehead. He gripped his buddy's armpits, dragging him toward safety.

"Is he dead?" CW asked, gathering Karl's feet.

"His chest moves."

"How'd a plane slip from Hun land undetected? Why didn't the bonehead guards shoot back?"

Arno's heart continued to clunk while they barged through the scraggly brush, shoving Karl under a tree for shelter. "*Shh*, listen." He raised a shaky finger to his lips. Silence. The enemy hid out of sight and hearing … but for how long?

Karl moaned. Smeared blood and mud plastered his pale face, his cheek ice-cold against Arno's palm.

A yell tightened Arno's throat, but he tamped it down and pressed his hand against Karl's oozing wound to stop the bleeding.

"I'll fetch a medic," CW said about the same time an officer issued the all-clear signal.

Soldiers emerged from hiding places to retrieve abandoned gear.

Frankie stood over Arno's shoulder. "We were easy pickings. That's what we were—sitting ducks!" His voice increased in volume with each word until he knelt beside Arno. "Karl was hit?"

"Something bashed his head. He's gonna pull through though."

A slender pine tree caught Arno's eye. One side stood erect, the other limp on the ground. A sparrow's nest rested in the upright portion, snug in a branch's crook, unmarred. So, this was the senselessness of war.

A few miles from the bombing run, Arno's company set up their camp of two-person pup tents. They were tucked behind the front lines, afforded a measure of comfort and an opportunity to move about with comparative ease. Yet Arno couldn't forget what lay ahead.

The afternoon's attack had resulted in abrasions, broken bones, and a few concussions but no loss of life. Medical staff treated the wounded at a church in a nearby valley. An update on Karl's condition hadn't reached Arno yet.

They'd hammered their last tent stake into the ground when the mail arrived. Would he receive letters today? He hadn't heard from home in weeks.

A corporal hand-delivered six pieces of mail addressed to Arno. A half-dozen. The bent and battered envelopes were priceless.

Three bore Hattie's return address, one Lena's, one Mother's, and the final one Priscilla's. Bit by bit, he ripped Priscilla's letter and then showered the ground with scraps, which the wind whisked away. Her prior letters had carried more poison than news from home, the last thing he needed or wanted. On the troopship, he'd had plenty of time to reflect and compare the two women. Hattie was the girl for him.

Arno headed toward the canteen to read his mail and check for word on Karl. Halfway there he tore into Hattie's envelope with the oldest postmark.

June 14, 1918

My Arno,

How I wonder where you are and if you've received at least a measly portion of my letters. One dated May 31 arrived back today. If possible, please send word of your safety. By the sounds of it, the mail system remains awry over there. I'll continue to write and pray my words somehow find you.

Uncle Sam decided to teach us to appreciate our sweethearts, and it's working. I miss everything about you— your smile, your laugh, your hands on my shoulders when we kiss. In case you've forgotten, we've kissed four times. How long until number five?

I'm swamped with Brigade duties, but that's not overly surprising. Although nervous about accomplishing my tasks in time, I'm also excited to prove I'm capable. Jeb now calls me Madame Chairlady, adding a French accent to the title. I've never heard anyone speak French, yet I'm fairly certain he falls short.

Daddy finally talked to Hawk and me about his intentions to marry Meridee before the year is out, although she's ill as of late. One of us embraced the news. The other ran from the room, crying. I've asked Hawk why he objects, but he refuses to confide in me. I believe he'll come around.

If only possible, I'd love to hand you the following three little things:

Frosted cinnamon coffee cake, one for every day you're away. You'd turn tubby, but I'd pay that no mind.

A guarantee I'll wait for your return, not let some local boy sweep me off my feet.

A downpour of peace regarding your brother's tragic death.

Hurry home, sweetheart.

As always,
Hattie

P.S. I hope the following official (or maybe unofficial) contract prompts a smile.

Being of sound mind (sound enough, anyway), I, Hattie Waltz, hereby promise Arno Kreger I'll wait until the end of time for his return.
However, should he tarry, I'll never lose faith or patience.

Arno's heart lurched, and he reread Hattie's letter with added care. He wasn't surprised she failed to mention their impasse—their differing opinions on a future family. With him in France and her in the States, that was a discussion for the future.

Absorbed in Hattie's letter, he reached the canteen quicker than he'd expected. Captain McKenzie strolled out the door.

Arno dug into his pocket to wave a fistful of envelopes. "Finally, the mail arrived. Can you believe it?"

The captain ran a hand over his somber face and then paused. "I have something to tell you."

"I wager it's not as good as my news."

"No, no. You're right about that." McKenzie dropped both hands onto Arno's shoulders, anchoring him to the ground. "I'm just back from the hospital, wanted to check on the men."

"Did you see Karl?"

"I didn't."

Karl must have lingered in surgery. The nasty wound probably required extra sutures. By the time the stretcher bearers had hauled him off to the hospital, his pulse had stabilized, and the bleeding lessened. All good signs.

"He didn't make it." McKenzie tightened his grip. "Karl died on the way to the hospital."

So Sad!

In a haze, Arno stumbled forward, ramming the captain's chest. A flash of light exploded. With a scream, both men crashed to the ground.

CHAPTER TWENTY-NINE

Armed with a satchel brimming with library books, Hattie toted the awkward load down the sterile hospital corridor. The August heat popped perspiration down her spine. At the entrance door to the veterans' wing, she parked her weighty bag onto a vacant wheelchair to catch her breath and peek into a well-lit oblong room.

Fresh white drapes adorned the plentiful windows. An oil painting of a distinguished benefactor hung between two. A frizzy-haired nurse scurried here and there, a white blanket in one hand and a red water bottle in the other. Hattie recognized three of the wounded soldiers.

How long until Arno joined the ranks to convalesce from multiple fractures and injuries tucked deep inside? Today? Or not for another week? Despite mounting Brigade duties and chores at home, Hattie had found excuses to visit the hospital every day for the past week. She hoped to welcome Arno home or at least catch a glimpse of him soon.

No letters had arrived since his accident, not that she'd expected it. Had the army delivered hers to his bedside or piled the stack sky-high somewhere?

Worries nagged her nonstop, about Arno's physical wounds and his grief over Karl. When someone you loved passed, unrelenting rain poured on the inside—gloomy, cold, and soggy—with no hope of a rainbow. If she could, she'd hand Arno a special umbrella to protect him from internal storms. Her other concern caused even more unrest—whether or not he'd read her letter, the one where she broke his heart.

She and Wilhelm remained civil in each other's presence, tiptoeing with polite steps since the kiss. Every time he suggested speaking in private, she offered an excuse—too busy, too tired, too hungry, too mortified. She'd not voiced the fourth, but the emotion had dogged her every day.

She'd abandoned her plan to write Lena about the kiss, deciding her best friend deserved a face-to-face explanation. Although the plan bought Hattie time, how long until Lena paid her wounded brother a visit?

Wherever he was.

Hattie retrieved her bag, captured a fortifying breath, and plunged forward into the quiet ward. She caught a whiff of either antiseptic or cleaning supplies, perhaps a mixture. Nerves almost tossed her stomach. What if she failed to find the proper words to comfort the hurting soldiers? What if the men rejected the library books? What if she turned around and went home?

Junior Brandt slouched in a wheelchair near a sun-drenched window. At the age of ten, he'd trudged a mile through waist-high snowdrifts to deliver a valentine to her doorstep. "Hello, Junior. Are you up for company?"

A pale-yellow blanket covered his lap, hiding the fact his legs never made it home. "Why not? Days drag around here."

"I suppose so." She lowered her bag and then scooted a chair closer to his side.

He'd married his neighbor Mary Kate a week before boot camp. That labeled the couple newlyweds since they'd not spent ample time together—due to the war and Junior's injury.

"It's a shame about Karl Ludwig." Junior sighed.

She gulped. Like three-fourths of the town, she'd attended Karl's memorial service. On the tail end of it, his dog padded up the aisle and halted next to his master's pinewood box and then curled into a furry ball. Even the pastor had choked back a sniffle and refused to shoo the beast from the weepy house of worship. In the graveyard, the mongrel moaned. Hattie had wanted to join him. "He was a good man."

"Yep." Junior drew his finger across a blanket crease. "Karl and I swapped letters a few times. He mentioned how he and Arno were snubbed a bit at camp, all because of their German blood. I never faced none of that."

Hattie's stomach muscles tightened, and she leaned forward. "Arno never mentioned a word of that business to me."

"Hmm ..." Junior nodded. "I reckon he didn't want you to worry none. I hear he's coming home soon. It's good he's returning to Split Falls. Not everyone gets the chance."

She nodded, battling tears. "I wish I knew when."

Junior's face lit, and then he pointed over Hattie's shoulder. "I think someone who knows just arrived."

When Hattie twisted in her chair, she met Mrs. Kreger's gaze. One word described Genevieve Kreger—*regal*. With a ramrod posture, high cheekbones, a perfect jawline, and eyes that missed nothing, Hattie always sat straighter and minded her manners in the woman's presence. But they rarely spoke.

A deep breath slowed Hattie's thoughts before she turned to face Junior. "She's talking to Dudley, and I shouldn't interrupt. You don't suppose she's here because Arno is back?"

"Hard to say. Mrs. Kreger comes around most days to play a song or two on the piano. Then she talks to each one of us. In my opinion, she's a lot like Arno—real decent." He tugged the top novel from the satchel, turning it over in his hands. "Why all the books?"

"They're from the library. I wondered if you and the others might enjoy a book or two. There's a mystery, a biography, and a—"

"I can't read."

"Oh." She'd forgotten and longed to crawl into a hole, or a well, or something else several feet deep.

"Pa needed me on the farm and didn't see no reason to send me to school." SAD

"If you like, I can read to you." She dug into the book pile, spreading the collection across the floor.

With a flick of his wrist, Junior tossed the novel in his hands back into the open bag, shifted his body away from Hattie, and then looked away. "I'm not interested."

She twisted pearls around her finger, wishing she'd never come, and then stuffed the books into her carrier. "What time do you expect Mary Kate today? I need to speak with her."

Although Junior laughed, it wasn't a happy sound. "On a good week, I see my wife once or twice but never for more than fifteen, twenty minutes." He dropped his eyes to where his legs belonged. From his disappointed frown to his soft voice clogged with sadness, pain radiated from him and spilled onto Hattie.

"I see."

"Aren't you part of that Brigade, the one Mary Kate busies herself with?"

"Yes, she's a key part of our committee. Our big event is this weekend."

With a list of duties longer than the floor-to-ceiling window behind Junior, Hattie itched to practice her speech and finish tying dozens of red, white, and blue ribbons into festive bows, not dilly-dally at the hospital. But she'd not miss Arno's arrival for all the Brigade work on earth.

"Your goal is to help the soldiers, right?"

Hattie raised her chin and smiled, delighted to serve her country in a small way. "That's our objective."

"Then why is this the first time I've ever seen you here?"

PING. That pierced her heart, trickling guilt from the wound.

"Mary Kate stops by on occasion, she's obligated, but none of you other Brigade ladies ever do. Why is that?"

A king-sized lump lodged in her throat, and she struggled to swallow.

"I don't mean to offend, Hattie, you're a good egg, but a man starts to wonder why everyone pats him on the back when he leaves for battle but ignores him when he returns home. To be frank, it makes a person feel like half a man."

Blinded by a teary haze, Hattie blinked against Junior's gut-wrenching truth. How had she dared to forget these hometown heroes who'd fought and suffered and continued to face pain day after day? Shame lit her cheeks, and a mirror wasn't necessary to confirm the redness.

She scanned the room again, but this time, she truly noticed the veterans.

Bent at the shoulders, Slim Klinkenberg drooped on a stiff-looking sofa, swaying and murmuring. Before the war, they called him the shiny-penny man as he handed out coins to youngsters following church services.

Raymond Zimmerman, Arno's old friend and schoolmate, wore matching casts from wrists to shoulders and a red, jagged scar across the length of his face. Gauze and bandages covered his left ear. He nodded when Hattie's eyes brushed his hooded pair.

Blinded by mustard gas, Daniel Hook tapped a finger on an ivory piano key. A shapeless hospital gown covered his back. He'd once accompanied Hattie during a patriotic performance in the city park. Back then, she'd envied his musical talent.

"It's nice to see you." Mrs. Kreger lowered a hand onto Junior's shoulder but devoted her generous smile to Hattie.

"Thank you. I brought library books, but maybe it wasn't such a good idea."

"Library books? That's brilliant. Show me what you brought."

Hattie collected the book bag and then followed Mrs. Kreger to a nearby table. They spread the books out. Hattie longed to ask about Arno, but was it the right time and place?

"When," Hattie said as Mrs. Kreger started with, "If." They chuckled, tripping over each other's words.

"Please, you go first." She smiled, hoping Arno's mother was full of details about her son and willing to share.

"If you're wondering if I know Arno's precise arrival date and time, unfortunately, I don't. However, I'm confident it's soon."

Hattie released a deep breath. "Thank you. Not knowing is killing me a wee bit." She measured the distance with her thumb and forefinger but probably should have used her outstretched arms.

"You may ring our place day or night."

Unexpected tears threatened. "I don't care to bother you."

"Don't be silly. Both my children adore you, as do I. Are you reluctant because of your father?"

Torn between defending her parent and throwing both arms around Mrs. Kreger, Hattie clasped her hands behind her back. "His opinions aren't necessarily my own."

Mirth twinkled Mrs. Kreger's eyes, and she suppressed a chuckle with her hand. "Arno will be glad to hear that."

When Mrs. Kreger laughed, she resembled her daughter. Hattie missed Lena so much that it twisted at her insides. If her best friend still lived in Split Falls, Will probably wouldn't have snuck a kiss, Hattie would fret less over the fundraiser—life, in general, would shine brighter.

Mrs. Kreger picked up a copy of *Life on the Mississippi* and leafed through the pages before pressing the book against her chest. "Has your father ever told you about the two of us?"

With one hand on the tabletop, Hattie braced herself as her heart ratcheted its pace. "There's a you and him?"

"I lived with your grandparents for a spell, while my parents traveled west to stake a homestead."

Hattie blinked. "I had no idea."

"My folks planned to fetch me after establishing themselves, but my mother perished on the trail. When my father's dream ended, he eventually returned to Iowa. During my time with your father's family, he and I became friends, traipsing all over the countryside together. Although only half-grown, I met Arno's pa and fell hard for him."

"My goodness." Hattie lowered the book in her hand to the table.

"Max left to work with the railroad for a stint, and I fell into my old pattern, spending more and more time with your father. I adored him, but I loved Max, who was older and confident, not to mention a tad mysterious."

Why in nineteen years had nobody ever shared this tale? Speechless, Hattie stared at the woman who'd divulged more family secrets than Hattie knew how to stack.

"My guess is if Max hadn't returned, I'd have married your father and lived happily ever after, growing my adoration into love. But once I told him I intended to marry Max—he never spoke to me again."

Hattie's heart missed a beat. Had Daddy carried a torch for Mrs. Kreger, even while married to Mama? "But my parents were happy together, well matched."

"Oh, they were." Arno's mother placed a hand on Hattie's arm. "Please don't question that. Your mama moved to town one day, and your daddy tumbled for her the next. I believe with all my heart that he never loved me half as much as her."

Warm wetness dribbled down Hattie's cheeks. Mrs. Kreger drew her into a warm, rocking embrace. The sheltering arms filled a need buried deep inside Hattie's soul. Mrs. Kreger had loved a man, told him goodbye, and waited for his return despite gaining favor from another.

After finding a hankie in her pocketbook, Hattie dried her face and gained control of her sniffles. "I'm sorry for blubbering, but I still don't see why Daddy all of a sudden despised the lot of you after Mama passed."

"Grief is tricky and difficult to define. I suppose it helps him cope in some strange fashion, yet he's always favored Lena."

"That's true." What if Daddy had forbidden their friendship? Hattie shivered despite the stifling room.

"Before we distribute these books, I want you to know how happy I am that you're a big part of Arno's life. He struggled so after Oliver's death, and I know the loss of Karl adds to his pain. I count it a blessing that you'll help him recover. And in my heart of hearts, I hope you'll stay around for the long haul."

Hattie reached for her pearls. In so many words, had Mrs. Kreger implied she wanted her for a daughter-in-law? It couldn't be, could it? Despite differing opinions on parenthood, did Arno want the same thing, or had he chucked the notion and deepened his bachelorhood dreams?

"But he doesn't want children." Hattie slapped a hand against her forehead. Ugh! She had no business blurting Arno's secret. "By any chance, can you forget my last sentence?"

Emotions flitted across Mrs. Kreger's face, mostly sadness. She dabbed at her eyes. "Is it because he blames himself for Oliver's death?"

"Forgive me. I shouldn't have blabbed Arno's private thoughts. It wasn't my place, but it's a definite roadblock to our happily ever after."

"Don't worry, dear. I won't tell my son what you shared. But I'm glad you spoke up. He's going to need understanding from all of us."

Hattie nodded but cringed on the inside, knowing if Arno hadn't yet read her letter, she'd soon inflict more pain on his weary shoulders. If he'd already digested her Will-kissed-me news, he might choose to wave goodbye. Either option cut like a sickle in a hayfield.

"What do you say we distribute these wonderful books you brought?"

Hattie pushed aside her worries and woes. "I'd like that. I'm afraid I've been more focused on fundraising than assisting the soldiers back from the war."

After a nod, Mrs. Kreger raised her voice. "Pardon me, everyone, may I have your attention? Hattie Waltz has brought library books to share. You may come and select something, or we'll deliver to you. There are plenty of excellent titles."

One man joined them, then another. Before long, half the

books found new, temporary homes.

"Unfortunately, not everyone can read," Mrs. Kreger whispered. "Sometimes, I sit in a corner and read aloud. Any chance you'd like the honor today? Feel free to select any book you like. I wager you'd draw a crowd."

Hattie rummaged through the assortment and chose one she hoped offered widespread appeal.

"You're in for a treat, gentlemen." Mrs. Kreger leaned closer to Hattie, glancing at the book's title. "Today's selection is *Life on the Mississippi*. Hope you're ready for Mark Twain. Let's gather over there." She pointed to a cozy grouping of chairs.

Fresh tears threatened, not prompted by sadness but by something else, something peaceful. Had she finally found her place in the world? Unashamed, she wiped her eyes with the back of her hand, settled onto a chair, and then stared at a dozen somber faces.

"I've chosen this book because the Mississippi River borders our state. Who has stood alongside it?"

Most every hand flew high, at least those unencumbered by casts or slings.

"Chapter one. *The River and Its History*. The Mississippi is well worth reading about. It is not a commonplace river, but on the contrary is in all ways remarkable ..."

Hattie closed the book in her lap after half an hour, but the men urged her to continue. She did and another half hour slipped by. Only one patient dozed, snoring in moderation. When her voice turned hoarse, she stopped reading. The first twitches of twilight darkened the windows.

"We're much obliged you took the time to sit with us today." A veteran wearing thick gauze wrapped around the top of his head extended a hand to shake hers.

"Thank you." She wrapped both of her hands around his clammy one.

"Not many young ladies come by here, and if they do, it's only to drop off this or that."

"They don't linger," another soldier said, scratching his jaw. He wore civilian clothes, not a hospital gown like everyone else.

Hattie failed to spot his injury, but that didn't mean the man didn't suffer. "It was my pleasure, and I'll see you all next week."

She gathered the leftover books and searched for Arno's mother to tell her goodbye. Hattie caught Junior's eye and moved toward him. "I may have overstayed my welcome."

"I'm certain you didn't."

When she smiled, Junior returned it. "Goodbye then."

"I like Mark Twain, I guess."

"Me too."

At the doorway, Mrs. Kreger, her face pink and animated, almost barreled into Hattie. "Arno's back." She danced up and down on her tiptoes, wringing her hands.

Although Hattie wasn't the fainting type, the room spun like a raging tornado.

CHAPTER THIRTY

Arno hadn't remembered Karl's death. It took three long days at a Red Cross Hospital in France before someone let it slip. That blindside ignited a constant throbbing in his temples, more painful than his fractured left leg and foot, broken ribs, and internal bleeding combined.

According to the physicians, his concussion from the shellfire hadn't caused true memory loss. It only jumbled certain things, turning them as slippery as suds.

Except for the constant headache, the return boat ride across the Atlantic was peaceful. He'd faced enough excitement in France to last a lifetime. All he wanted was the quiet company of family and friends. Of Hattie.

He'd dreamt about his homecoming almost since he'd left. Mother welcoming him at the train station and smelling like a hedge of lilacs. Father pumping his hand and bragging over his son's heroic war efforts. Lena chattering nonstop about big-city adventures and squeezing his hand as if she'd never let go.

Karl by his side.

Then he'd spot Hattie in the background, not wanting to intrude. After exchanging smiles, they'd step toward one another, cautious at first, and then run to close the gap. They'd whisper sweet endearments until he hushed her lips with a lingering kiss. That story's classification—fiction.

In the nonfiction version, he dawdled in a hot room reeking of something pungent mixed with a hint of urine and wore bandages and a scratchy hospital gown while waiting for visitors.

The last thing Arno wanted was to fall asleep. But his heavy eyelids failed to cooperate.

Arno and Hattie played a game of Red Rover. No matter how tightly he held her hand, the opposing team broke through their barrier time and time again. He despaired over another rush toward them. Whispers rustled nearby as he came out of that dream.

"I think he's waking up." His mother's soft voice.

"How can you tell?" Father's tone carried a rasp. Out of concern for his son, or from stringing four words together?

Arno opened his eyes. His parents stood on each side of his bed. They both grinned—even Father. When was the last time he'd seen the man smile? Hot tears stung, but Arno blinked the nuisance away.

"You're home." Dark circles dipped below Mother's eyes. "May I hug you, or will it hurt?"

He opened his arms, savoring her familiar touch and the scent of lilacs.

"Your return to us is answered prayer." She breathed the words more than whispered them.

Father hauled a nearby chair closer. "You worried your mother."

"That wasn't my intent."

After a pat to his shoulder, Mother released him and stepped back. "Don't let him fool you. He was a bundle of nerves too. After that first telegram, we didn't know what to expect or how badly you were hurt. It's a blessing they sent you home to heal."

Arno couldn't count the times he'd thought the same thing. If not for the head wound, he'd probably still linger in a French hospital, a definite second choice.

"How do you feel, son?"

Arno's breath caught. When was the last time Father had called him anything other than *boy* or an occasional *Arno*? Years. Not since Oliver …

"I'm sorry I worried you."

With a sigh, Father sagged against the back of his chair. "When a man's son goes to war, he regrets the times he's failed h-him." Father hung his head. "I'm the one who needs to apologize, not you."

Shock that rivaled the explosion in France doused Arno. He gaped at his father.

"I've done a heap of soul-searching since you left. I shouldn't have blamed you for anything. You were a kid. A boy who'd tied his best knot. O-oliver's passing was an accident." Father drew a hand over his craggy face, stopping to cup his mouth and chin.

"If I'd made the knot tighter, then maybe ..." Relief filled Arno at finally saying those words out loud.

"What if I'd joined you in the barn that afternoon instead of tinkering on that clock?" Father whispered.

"What if I'd kept Oliver inside as I'd intended? He had a cold. What if a blizzard hadn't blown across our land?" Mother squeezed Arno's wrist. "We had your brother for twelve years. That was a gift."

In his bones, Arno knew she spoke the truth. But could he ever fully forgive himself?

Mother slid her arm around Father's ample waist. "Lena is coming home, returning for good. There's a dangerous influenza up in Philadelphia, and we want our daughter clear of its path. Plus, she's eager to see you."

"When?" Tears slipped down his throat, and he coughed. What was wrong with him? He never cried.

"Perhaps as soon as tomorrow. Like usual, she neglected to mention the finer details such as train times."

How long until they'd all be together again like a true family? How long until the hospital set him free?

"However, there is a different pretty girl in the corridor waiting to greet you." Mother smiled, leaning her head against Father's shoulder. "No doubt she's wondering why it's taking so long to fetch her."

Soldiers never cried, but Arno wasn't a soldier any longer. A couple of tears dropped, which he quickly rubbed aside.

"Max, these kids need time to reacquaint without a couple of fuddy-duddies gawking." She looped her arm through Father's and urged him toward the door. Fading footsteps and the *tap, tap, tap*ping of Father's cane soon disappeared.

Time held still until Hattie stepped into view, knocking the breath from his chest. Clad in a blue dress with white dots, she clutched her pearls with both hands. Loose strands of hair framed her face. Four months had passed since they'd met in Philadelphia. She appeared older, more adult-like today. He probably shouldn't mention that.

He took her small hand, drawing it to his chest. Could she feel it beating like he'd run a mile? "Are you going to kiss me or w-what?"

With a tender smile, she lowered her soft lips to his.

He savored the moment. So right. So sweet. So … Hattie. Far too soon, she leaned back. A grin lit her face, and his breath caught on the brightness.

"Hello." She caressed his cheek. He held her wrist so she couldn't pull away. "I think I forgot to say that."

"I prefer kisses."

Her laugh sounded like piano music. "I wager you do, but let's hope only from me. I can't believe you're here."

"You told me to hurry home."

Her brown eyes clouded. "How can I help? Are you … are you in pain?"

"Now that you're here, everything else is tolerable."

"Not Karl's passing." She frowned and grasped both his hands. Sadness and concern creased her forehead.

No. That blow had left a crater-sized hole in his … everything.

Hattie detailed Karl's memorial service, and he shared stories about the day in Bordeaux when Karl surprised him in that French port city. They never dropped hands, and he drew strength from her touch.

"Goodness, you're pretty." He'd never seen anything more breathtaking than the woman before him, not even the sunrise over the vineyards in France.

Not releasing his hands, she rubbed at her tear-stained face against her shoulders before sitting in the chair Father had pulled close. "I look pretty frightful, I wager."

"Nope, just pretty." Her eyes bore into his, drilling to the center of his heart. He sighed. The best medicine for his ailment held his hands. "I can't believe I'm truly—"

"Home."

"Able to kiss you, but home sounds good too."

She scooted to the edge of her seat, her knee bouncing. "I need to ask you a serious question."

"Okay."

"What was the last letter you received from me? Do you recall a postmark date or something noteworthy?"

"I'm not sure." He closed his eyes to reconnect the missing dots in his memory. Right after the accident, concentrating had ignited sharp lights and piercing pain in his temples, but that was gone now.

"I think your last note arrived the same day that enemy pilot hit us." Memories flooded back. "We'd just received our first mail in weeks including three letters from you. I'd only read one and—*kaboom*."

"Was it a-a friendly letter?" She let go of his hands to toy with her pearls.

"I think so. My recollection is every one of your letters was top-notch. I don't believe I've shown my appreciation. Come here." He curved a finger, urging her forward.

Instead of drawing her lips to his, she leaned back in her chair and sighed. "In that case, there's something I need to tell you."

"That sounds serious." Her face carried a doom-and-gloom type of frown. What now? He'd had enough bad news to last two lifetimes.

"It is a serious matter. First, I want you to know how much I care about you."

"Your kiss convinced me."

She smiled. "And second—"

"I'm sorry to interrupt, but it's …" Sadie Parker, Karl's old girlfriend, stopped her speech to glance back and forth between him and Hattie.

"How's the new job?" Hattie asked.

"Hectic."

"You're a nurse?" Of course, Arno knew the answer. She wore a smart uniform and held a bedpan.

"Yep, and I need a urine specimen."

"Now?" With Hattie here?

"Yes, and visiting hours have ended for today."

"Can't you bend the rules this one time?"

"Afraid not," Sadie said in a matter-of-fact tone.

"Hattie, what did you want to tell me?" Arno extended his arm, beckoning her close.

She squeezed his fingers and then picked up her pocketbook from the floor, slipping the short strap over her wrist. "It can keep. We'll both get a good night's sleep and tackle the issue in the morning."

"It requires tackling?" His mind raced in a dozen directions. Why did he have a bad feeling about this?

Instead of explaining, Hattie grinned, waved, and left. Sadie slapped the bedpan on top of his covers.

After a never-ending cycle of interruptions throughout the night, Arno stretched and yawned the next morning.

Hattie had dropped by earlier to inquire after his health and enumerated her long task list of Brigade duties. When he encouraged her to finish last night's conversation, she told him *later*. Before long, she zipped toward the door, with a final backward glance and a familiar grin, the one he'd missed for far too many months.

Mother arrived and fawned—puffing his pillow, tucking a scratchy blanket under his chin, and combing his hair with her fingers. She asked after his aches and pains and then left to interrogate the doctors and nurses.

By the time she returned, he'd devoured four cookies. He sniffed a fifth. "These are even better than I remembered."

"You've never met a cookie you didn't polish off in less than a minute. Shall I push you in the wheelchair?" Mother pointed at the contraption.

Stuck in the center of the ward, he couldn't see out the window. Even a brick wall next door would look better than bedpans and stethoscopes. "That might work, but you'd best fetch a nurse to get me situated."

Mother complied, and the nurse assisted with the transfer. Then Mother wheeled him toward the floor-to-ceiling bay of windows. The August sun highlighted the town square across the street, decorated with frills and patriotic ribbons. Despite the full foliage, nothing obstructed his view of the makeshift wooden stage at the center. Where was Hattie? Hadn't she mentioned working in the park all morning?

"I'd like to scoot over to Lottie's to collect a few staples. Is this a good time to run my errands?"

"Sure."

After a quick peck to his brow, she walked away, stopping halfway across the room to speak with a nurse.

Automobiles rolled up and down the street and then a calico cat captured his attention, sneaking up on an unsuspecting wren. The sunlight glared, so he turned his head.

Arms crossed, Sadie stood a few steps away and stared at him. She approached and wiped her hands on her white apron. Without asking, she angled the wheelchair away from the brightness. "By the looks of things, the Brigade is planning quite the shindig across the street tomorrow."

"Are you part of it?"

"Goodness gracious, no. I have better things to do with my time." After transferring two medicine bottles from her left fist to her right, Sadie stepped closer to the windowpane.

"Hattie's been working her tail off."

"Her tail, huh?" Sadie's attention stayed on whatever was outside.

"She's the chairlady. The responsibilities fall onto her shoulders, not that she complains."

"Oh, no. Hattie would never grumble. She's a perfect little angel, isn't she?"

That was why he'd never warmed to Sadie Parker. The girl tore people down. "I'd say she's better than most."

"Hattie is as sweet as a ripe plum, isn't she?" Sadie tapped a long finger against her puckered lips and arched a brow.

He'd known Sadie all his life. She was the moody, prickly sort, and the best way to get to the bottom of her tedious innuendos was with a direct frontal attack. "If you have something to say, spit it out."

"Hattie wasn't faithful to you while you served in France."

Did she mean Hattie's father-mandated dates? Which were none of Sadie's business. "What's your point?"

"My point is that Hattie kissed Wilhelm Mueller, and then he told her he loved her."

Pain resembling the ache when Oliver died stole his breath. The poisonous words swirled. "That's not true."

"Priscilla witnessed the incident firsthand the day a tornado blew through town. She told me not to tell anyone, but you deserve the truth, especially since you were Karl's best friend."

A little hammer banged away at Arno's skull as a sledgehammer badgered his heart. It took a moment for him to find his words. "I don't believe you."

But a strand of doubt wormed into his core. What if Sadie's tale and whatever Hattie hadn't yet shared were the same?

Without a word, Sadie swiveled Arno's wheelchair until he faced the windowpane. He squinted through the sunshine. A couple on the middle of the stage were locked in an embrace. Arno drew a sobering breath, leaned forward, and placed both hands on the glass. "It's Hattie."

"And Wilhelm."

Ever since the day he'd fallen in love with the girl, he'd feared one thing—she'd find a better man. But why his little sister's old beau? He drew his arms against his chest to protect his heart. It didn't work.

CHAPTER THIRTY-ONE

"When did he pass?" Hattie drew back from Wilhelm's snug embrace, offering a final tight squeeze before dropping her arms to her sides.

"During the night. The nurse woke me."

She ached for those closest to Mr. Mueller, especially Wilhelm and Daddy. Over the last two years, his health had steadily declined. Although suffering, Mr. Mueller had remained positive, an inspiration to those around him.

The fundraiser's importance dimmed in light of his death. Between the man's passing and meeting the veterans at the hospital yesterday, Hattie had started to reorder her priorities.

"How can I help?" She meant the question to ease Wilhelm's woes, whatever that entailed. Heaven knew she wasn't the only Brigade member in town capable of preparing the park for the fundraiser.

He dragged a hand across his scruffy chin. "Thanks, but there's nothing you can do. At least Pa was ready to go, and that gives me peace."

"I always respected your father." Hattie kept one wary eye on a squirrel in the maple tree above them.

Wilhelm smiled, his first she'd seen in days.

"Why don't you go home and rest?"

"Nah, I still need to firm up those steps on the other side of the stage, string that light, and—"

Hattie raised both of her hands to halt his lengthy chore list. "It doesn't matter. Even if we have wobbly stairs, it won't ruin the fundraiser. We'll manage fine." She started to usher him off the stage. "Please forget all about this Brigade business. I'll send Jeb over with your supper tonight. How does that sound?"

Wilhelm shoved his hands into his trouser pockets. "Hattie, wait a minute."

"What's wrong?"

"I know this isn't the best time or place for this discussion, but you like me, right?"

Surprised by the conversation she'd avoided for weeks, Hattie flinched. "Of course, we're friends."

"Or are we more than friends?"

Of all days, why this confrontation now? After a deep breath, she barged forward. "I'm still with Arno."

Red-eyed and hurting, he reached for her hand. She clutched them behind her back.

"I heard he's in town."

"Recuperating across the street." Hattie nodded toward the hospital. Would Wilhelm visit his old friend? "He and I talked last night and again this morning."

"I know you like me, at least a little."

Should she tell him to open his eyes, not to mistake kindness for romantic love? But driving her point home felt heartless, cruel. "I'm sorry."

"You're saying there's a chance for us, right?" His crooked smile signaled a joke, but sadness turned his eyes darker.

"I'm saying I love Arno, and I should have been clearer about that from the start. I'll never change my mind, even if he does. I'm afraid it's a permanent condition."

Wilhelm searched her face, but did he hear her words?

"I hate causing you pain, particularly today. I truly care about you the way I adore Jeb and Hawk. My feelings for Arno are different." When he brushed his bangs from his eyes, he resembled the little boy she'd always known.

"I'll go finish those steps then." He shuffled away, tugging free a hammer from his belt loop.

Hattie crossed to the front of the stage, sat, and dangled her feet toward the grassy earth. A fragrant patch of wild roses hummed with honeybees, and she swatted at a bold insect that landed on her sleeve.

Wilhelm's hammer thumped nails into a board, jolting the stage with small tremors. Was it wrong to speak the truth after he'd lost a loved one hours before? Wasn't it better to gently tell him to stop pining than to offer false hope? She leaned back onto her elbows, allowing the sun to graze her face and neck.

At least she was ready for tomorrow. Her list of duties was twenty-four and counting—everything from preparing the refreshment table to placing programs on empty chairs and hanging the more delicate decorations.

She still couldn't believe that Priscilla had, somehow, persuaded Samantha Shamrock to perform. Priscilla hadn't stopped yapping about it since the telegram arrived. Once word hit the street of the starlet's upcoming attendance, sales soared, and they'd needed to issue additional tickets. A newspaper reporter from Des Moines had rented a room at the local hotel to cover the event.

All in all, Hattie was ready for anything. They'd printed "rain or shine" on the tickets and encouraged everyone to pack an umbrella. They had cold lemonade ready if it turned out hot and sunny. They even had decent local talent lined up in case the starlet was a no-show. And Meridee had offered to match any donations dollar for dollar. But Hattie didn't want to mention that bonus unless necessary.

She peered at the hospital. Would Arno watch the event from an upstairs window tomorrow? When she'd first spied him yesterday, it felt as if she'd swallowed a hummingbird. She'd seen his outer injuries but not the ones buried inside. He still resembled an Iowa farm boy—big and brawny—but he'd changed, lost at least twenty pounds. Cheekbones interrupted the planes of his face, and redness dimmed his eyes. Despite a blanket of stubby whiskers, fine lines stamped a pattern near his mouth and eyes. His bandages blared the message *I hurt*.

But he remained the same Arno—sweet and wonderful.

Even though she worried how he'd respond to the Wilhelm news, the time had arrived to blurt her darkest secret. Would Arno remain rational or kick her out the door? Would today end their courtship or strengthen their relationship after scaling the stumbling block?

After mustering her courage, she braced her head and heart for the upcoming challenge and crossed the street. A squirrel scampered in her path, and she offered the animal a wide berth.

Sadie leaned against the hospital's brick wall near the entrance. Her blonde hair was tucked up under her nurse's hat, and she fiddled with a heart-shaped locket around her neck.

"Time for a break?" Hattie smiled.

"Actually, I'm off duty and waiting for you."

Panic swooped. "Has something happened to Arno?"

Sadie threw her head back and laughed, a deep-pitched cackle. "Now, you're finally worried about his well-being?"

"What's that supposed to mean?"

"He knows about you and Wilhelm."

Hattie's knees buckled, but she caught herself. "What are you talking about?"

"Priscilla told me about the little tornado incident, the kiss you shared with Wilhelm, and how he's in love with you. My guess is you love him too."

From ankle to brow, a cold sweat scrunched up Hattie's body. "That's not true."

"Which part?"

Unable to deny all of the accusations, her eyes dropped to the ground. Why was she still standing with Sadie? She turned toward the hospital's steps, clutching the rail.

"By the way, you're banned from the premises. It's what's best for Arno's health."

Hattie froze. "But I need to talk to him, to explain the truth."

Sadie swiped her hands as if brushing away crumbs. "But that pitches a problem—he doesn't want to talk to you ever again. If you try to sneak upstairs, they'll boot you out the door."

The world tilted, and she tightened her grip. Was it true? Did Arno never want to see her again?

"Look at it this way—Wilhelm is a mighty fine red ribbon if you can't win the blue."

This was Hattie's life, not the Butler County Fair.

Two options crossed her mind: stand there and let Sadie spit more venom or call the woman's bluff. She whipped around, darted down the sidewalk, and turned at the intersection. Nobody stopped her at the back door, on the staircase, nor in the corridor outside of Arno's ward. Her heart slammed against her chest. Perhaps Sadie had fabricated the entire tale.

After a deep breath, she approached Arno's bed, his eyes drilling into hers.

Ten more steps, nine, eight ...

"Stop." Arno raised his hand. "If you ever cared for me, even a little, leave. I don't want you here."

"But ..."

"Get out!" He rolled onto his side, away from her.

His cruel words soaked into her bones, searching for a way to enter her heart. A few patients stared from their beds, but she wasn't embarrassed. She was too numb. Mesmerized, Hattie stood there, while the ward continued to function.

"Miss, are you okay?" An unfamiliar nurse stepped between her and Arno.

"I don't think so."

Somehow, she found the strength to leave the hospital and find Daddy's Buick parked along the street. Why hadn't she told Arno about the kiss herself? She steered the auto home, replaying her exchange with Sadie over and over in her mind. Accusations had ruled the conversation without Hattie ever giving her side of the story. Arno's angry face had ripped at her insides.

Once home, she told no one about the heartbreak. She barely told herself. A groan escaped. She'd probably love Arno forever, but her affection was once again one-sided. Eyes closed—she reran the day's events through her mind one more time.

"Will you play with me in the tree house?"

Hattie jumped. Hawk stood close by, picking at a scab on his elbow. His shirt gapped at the neckline, exposing half a skinny shoulder.

She crossed the room and sank into the sewing chair and then fanned through the pages of a seed catalog. "I'm sorry, buddy, but I'm too busy."

"I want to show you my treasure map. Nobody's seen it yet. You'll be the first, and you'll be impressed. It would take a million years to figure out where I buried my treasure without it, and ..."

Hattie's mind wandered to Arno, particularly the kisses she'd never taste, the teasing words she'd never hear. How could they live in the same area and never again hold hands or dream about a shared future? Perhaps she'd move away from Split Falls after all.

"Hattie!" Hawk shouted, arms akimbo. "You're not busy, you're daydreaming."

She stared at her brother. If only she had someone to talk to about her current dilemma, someone other than an eight-year-old. Someone like Lena. But that wouldn't work. How soon until her best friend caught wind of the kissing fiasco? How long until Lena hated her too?

"Say something."

"Go run and play." For a moment, she leaned her head against the back of the rocker and closed her eyes. "You can show me your treasure map tomorrow."

"But you have that fancy thing in town tomorrow and the next day."

"Okay, Sunday."

Hawk crossed his arms to pout. "Daddy's always with the widow, Jeb's with Priscilla, and you never have time for me anymore."

"That's not true, honey."

"It is too." The outside door banged behind him.

Hattie winced. After Saturday, she'd find loads of time to entertain Hawk. They'd visit the creek and skip a few rocks. She watched him from the window as he scaled the rickety stairs to his hideaway with jerky movements. Torn between chasing after him, starting dinner, or continuing to mope, she watched Bandit chase his tail in the yard.

The first weeks after Mama passed, sadness had trumped everything else in Hattie's life until the day she spotted a naked two-year-old Hawk wandering in the yard. After a hearty round of self-scolding, she'd vowed never again to feel sorry for herself, especially if it hurt others. But she'd backtracked.

Once upon a time, she'd believed in fairy tales, those featuring wand-waving godmothers, pots brimming with rainbow gold, and magic beans. If still the case, she'd beg for Arno—her hero—to blast through the door, promise to love her forever, and shelter her in his familiar arms.

But that wasn't going to happen.

CHAPTER THIRTY-TWO

B y the time Friday morning dawned, the aches and pains in Arno's head had subsided. Too bad his heart still smarted.

Sadie pushed a cluttered cart next to his bed. "How do you feel today?" She handed him a napkin and a set of silverware.

"Fine." The scent of blueberries swirled, but his belly burned. He raised a hand to refuse the meal.

"Don't be silly. Everyone loves hotcakes." She ignored his request and settled the tray onto his lap. "You prefer coffee over tea, correct?"

Why argue? She handed him a full cup, which he balanced on his tray, the aroma strong enough to clear a man's sinuses.

Before he could take a sip, Mother blasted into the ward almost jogging to his bedside. "I just heard the most disturbing news." She fought to catch her breath. Although neat as a pin, her eyes flashed with alarm. "Hawk Waltz has been missing ever since last night."

Arno tipped his tray, spilling lukewarm coffee more on the bed than himself. His heart punched against his achy ribs while he righted his breakfast. "H-how?"

Chaos broke loose with Sadie and Mother scrambling to mop up the mess.

Arno grabbed his mother's wrist. "Tell me what you know."

She took a deep breath. "Hawk never came home last night. Hattie spoke to him around three o'clock yesterday. They'd argued."

With the pain of losing a brother all too fresh, Arno closed his eyes a moment. Hattie was probably past the worrying stage and knee-deep in a vat of panic by now. She'd raised the boy.

"Half the town is out looking for him. I'm about to join the search party, but I thought you'd want to know."

There was nothing he could do from his bed. He'd never felt more … useless.

"He's a sweet little boy." Sadie collected Arno's spilled meal. "I'll be back in a flash with a fresh breakfast and a dry sheet."

"Don't bother," Arno said to her back as she whisked away.

"Here's another piece of sad news." Mother fussed with the damp sheet, hauling the wet fabric aside to expose his legs. "Tobias Mueller passed on."

"When?" A bullet lodged in Arno's chest. He pictured Mr. Mueller, a warm and jovial man, an ideal parent to Wilhelm. He'd always envied their relationship.

"Night before last." Mother bent close, wrapping her hand around his cheek. "Try not to worry overly much, and I'll be back with an update." She all but bolted from the room.

Arno's heart continued to crumble. Why must Hattie face this ordeal without him by her side? Why did life repeat itself? His brother. Her brother. He remembered the proverb tucked into his farewell gift last September. Back then, he'd told himself he wasn't afraid of anything. Eleven months later, trapped in the middle of a lonely hospital ward, he stared face first at fear.

Rung after rung, Hattie lugged herself up the uneven stairs to Hawk's tree house. Long ago Daddy had pounded a ladder into the side of the massive tree. Steps had gone missing over the years but not enough to make climbing impossible, even for Hawk. Near the top, her necklace caught on a raised nail. The fine string holding her pearls broke free. The round gems scattered in every possible direction.

"No!" she hollered, having passed the point of caring who witnessed her outburst.

Too exhausted to descend the steps and collect her keepsake, she flung herself through the narrow doorway. She'd searched it twice before, finding cake crumbs covered in ants, the missing Sears, Roebuck and Company catalog, a half-dozen dominoes, and a mewing barn cat. No brother. Why did she think she'd succeed this time?

Like Daddy and Jeb, she'd assumed her kid brother intended to parade his anger for a spell when he didn't show up for supper. But by the time fireflies dotted the dusky evening, a full-scale panic filled the Waltz household. They'd searched the corncribs and haystacks in the thick of night.

Although eight years old, Hawk still hated the dark and never slept without his favorite pillow, a threadbare piece of fluff. Where had he laid his head last night?

She'd never reached her bed. Questions had kept her awake. What if Hawk had slipped on a rock in the creek? What if he'd turned himself around in the cornfield? What if a railroad tramp had helped him run away?

When dawn broke, so did she. An hour ago, she stopped crying. The well deep inside her soul, the one cradling her water supply, had cracked. Friends and neighbors still combed the property, hollering Hawk's name.

A pesky horsefly circled Hattie's head. The rustic boards of the tree house biting into her knees, she shivered despite the sweltering temperature. With eyes squeezed shut, she tried to focus. "Where is he?"

The tree house vibrated as someone climbed the stairs. Was it Hawk? She scrambled toward the entrance.

"Why are you lollygagging?" Lena rested her elbows on the tree house floor. "We've got a boy to find."

With a shriek, Hattie tugged her friend into the shelter. They hugged, both sobbing.

"We've searched everywhere." Hattie tightened her embrace. "It's like he's disappeared off the face of the earth."

"He's somewhere, and we'll find him. This time, I won't let you down."

"What do you mean?"

"You know—I promised to help you with the Brigade, no matter what, but then I moved to Philadelphia. I'm sorry. This time, I'm staying by your side until Hawk is safe and sound."

Hattie drew back and patted the floor beside her. Lena sat, their bent knees touching.

Lena tilted to the side to avoid scraping her head on the ceiling. "Next time you build a tree house, can you make it a smidge taller?"

Under different circumstances, she'd have laughed. But not today. "I need to tell you something important." Hattie rolled her skirt hem between her fingers, drawing it above her knees.

"Now? Can't it wait until we find your brother?"

"No."

Lena draped an arm over her friend's shoulders. "Why?"

After a hiccup, Hattie ran her opening sentence through her mind for practice. "Weeks ago, a twister passed through while Priscilla, Jeb, Wilhelm, and I cowered in the fruit cellar. It left a mess behind. Once upon a time, I carved Arno's and my initials into the bark of an apple tree. You probably think that's trite."

"I think it's sweet."

She captured a deep breath worthy of a confession. "The storm uprooted it, and I dropped to my knees and cried beside a broken branch. Next thing I know, Wilhelm kneels beside me, with kind words and a hug. Then he surprised me with a peck on the lips."

"I'll be doggone." With a sigh, Lena rested her chin on her knees. "The man does favor kissing."

"There's more. Will said he loved me."

Lena reared back with a thump, smacking her head against the ceiling. "Goodness."

"I agree." Hattie reached for her pearls, but they were gone—same as Hawk. "To top it off, Priscilla witnessed it."

"Holy smokes."

"Will caught me off-guard. I've always been kind to him but

never, ever encouraged him, not intentionally anyway. What I think happened is you left, and I was the next best thing. Plus, he knows I'll never leave Split Falls."

Silence brewed inside the cramped space. Shouts of "Hawk" and "Can you hear me?" reached them.

"There's no way he loves me as much as you. It's a fact." Hattie believed every word. She was pretty sure Wilhelm did too.

"Why didn't you write to me about this"—Lena waved her hands as if washing a windowpane—"predicament?" A fair question but not an easy one.

"I'm sorry. I had planned to tell you in person. I did write Arno, except he sustained the injury and never read my message."

"Wait a minute." Lena crossed her arms. "Does he know about this incident with Wilhelm?"

"Sadie told him yesterday."

"Priscilla's best friend."

Hattie nodded, remembering the way Sadie had flung that fistful of accusations at her. "She's now a nurse at the hospital."

"Poor Arno."

"I know. Sadie banned me from seeing your brother, but I snuck in the back way."

"Good for you."

"Not really. He refused to speak to me."

"Huh." Beyond the tree house, birds chirped cheery greetings despite the dismal day.

"Are you mad at me?" Too much hinged on her friend's response. Hattie held her breath.

"Furious." Lena rested her head on Hattie's shoulder. "You warned me Wilhelm would find someone new the minute I left town. Who knew it would be you?"

"There's something else you need to know. I'm head over heels in love with your brother. I'm afraid it's a permanent condition."

"I know. Let's go find Hawk." Lena scrambled to her hands and knees. "Too bad this unfolded the day of the Brigade's fundraiser, not that there's ever a good day for a brother to go missing."

"I rang Priscilla first thing this morning and asked her to assume my duties."

"I'm sure she readily agreed."

Hattie paused, recalling the conversation, almost word for word. "But she also telephoned folks, broke the news about Hawk, and asked everyone to help with the search."

"She's not all bad. I understand she ended things with your brother."

"Thank goodness."

"By the way, are those your pearls scattered at the base of the ladder?"

Hattie reached for her absent necklace. "They're not as important as finding Hawk."

The tree house shook again. But this time with more force. She and Lena popped their heads out of the doorway, one above the other. Jeb climbed the stairs.

"Hello, Lena." He tossed his bangs back to peer upward.

"Hello, yourself."

"Ladies," Jeb filled his lungs with gulps of air, "I'm here … to tell you … there's been an epiphany."

"Spit it out," Hattie yelled.

"Wilhelm figured out how to find Hawk. He's safe, but we think his arm is busted."

"Where is he?" Lena squeezed Hattie's arm.

"Get down, and we'll talk, no more of this up and down business. I need to fetch a saw. Hawk tumbled into a beaver dam."

"What?" Hattie scooted down the ladder before jumping the last few rungs, landing near her brother.

Lena copied Hattie's leap.

On the way to the creek, Jeb explained the epiphany. Wilhelm remembered Hawk's fascination with the dam after Ian Moss tumbled into the stream weeks ago. Hawk had discovered a secret hiding place amidst the sticks to bury his treasure. For weeks he'd stashed a host of special items in the hideaway, a surprisingly brave move.

After his disagreement with Hattie, he'd returned to his hidey-hole to retrieve a bag of marbles. Instead, he toppled into the den, sinking deep into the muck and spilling sticks and sludge on top of him. The lower half of his body dangled in the water—his upper half wedged in the mire. Nobody had heard his cries until Wilhelm got there.

"Hawk was a chatterbox, telling his full story while we tried to free him," Jeb said.

They jogged toward Catfish Creek until Hattie sprinted ahead through the wildflowers. She reached the embankment as Wilhelm lowered Hawk, mud-encrusted but smiling, onto a patch of grass.

Townsfolk who'd set aside everything to help in the search gathered near. Daddy knelt next to his son. "I think you're the bravest boy I know."

"I am?"

"You might be the bravest person I've ever met." Hattie sat in the grass beside her little brother and cupped his muddy cheek with her hand. His arm rested in an unnatural angle at the elbow. "Guess what Wilhelm said?"

"I haven't the foggiest."

"Once my arm mends, we're holding a fishing contest."

"Can anyone enter this competition or only you and Will?" Lena dropped onto her knees beside Hattie and ruffled the child's matted hair.

He scrunched his face. "Are you talking about yourself?"

"I am."

"Wilhelm, are girls allowed?" Hawk looked at his rescuer.

"Only if they behave themselves."

"Then I'll need to think about it," Lena said with a chuckle.

"Hey, Hattie, I'm going to the hospital. Ain't that something?" Hawk said.

"It sure is." After a kiss to his palm, Hattie cradled Hawk's dirty hand against her heart.

Two hours had passed since Mother'd left and still no word on Hawk's whereabouts. The entire town had hightailed it to the farm to join the search party, everyone but a few helpless fools tarrying in hospital beds.

"You have a visitor," Sadie said as she approached, her hands wrapped around the arm of Captain McKenzie. He looked odd in civilian clothes.

Arno blinked and stumbled to find his voice. On the troopship in route to France, McKenzie had mentioned a possible future visit to Split Falls, but today? Arno had assumed in a couple of months or years—if ever—not the day after returning home.

"C-captain." He saluted, a catch in his voice.

"These days, I'm Mac. Thank you, Miss Sadie."

"My pleasure." The nurse winked at Arno before slipping away, humming as she left.

The captain scratched his whiskered cheek, a major change from their clean-shaven military days. "How are you?"

"On the mend. You?"

"Lost my sight during surgery."

Arno gaped and scrutinized his friend. The captain's blue eyes appeared the same as before. "Is it permanent?"

"A dozen physicians can't say for certain, but I'm adjusting." His friend stared straight ahead.

"I'm plenty glad to hear it."

"When I was young, my father told me to either light a candle or curse the darkness when troubles come. I'd love to see a candle's flame, but I won't turn bitter." Positioned in the sunlight, Mac smiled, radiating more warmth into an already-toasty ward. "I'm blessed beyond measure."

The words rolled over Arno. For a moment, he questioned their genuineness. Then he remembered who sat beside him. McKenzie's positivity had shined during their best and worst days at camp and in France. After the shellfire, they'd landed in different Red Cross hospitals, hadn't seen each other since.

"My mother and I are in town to visit her sister. She mentioned a big celebration. When do the festivities start?"

"I don't know." The Brigade fundraiser should have been Hattie's day to shine. Instead, she was probably dim from sadness and worry.

The two men swapped stories, filling each other in on what had happened since France. The captain said that Barrett Jordane was arrested for desertion, and CW Hyland promoted for a series of heroic acts. Frankie Jesberger had caught a bullet in the abdomen and was scheduled to recuperate in Des Moines.

In many ways, Arno felt detached from his military service as if he'd read the details in a novel and not experienced the eleven months firsthand, but he continued to fight a private war, one that scarred on the inside.

"How's your gal? Tickled pink to have you home again?"

"Not exactly. We had a falling out yesterday." A small tremor of pain nicked Arno's brain, and he focused on his breaths until the ache receded.

Mac's smile took a lopsided curve. "What happened?"

Arno explained the fiasco with Wilhelm.

"I'm not your captain any longer, but how about a piece of advice?"

From anyone else, he'd say no, but the captain hadn't ever steered him wrong. "Why not?"

"Listen to her side. Just because someone says Hattie cares for another man doesn't make it so. There are many kinds of love."

His pulse sped, surging heat through his veins. Was the embrace he'd witnessed from the second-floor window nothing more than condolence? But that possibility didn't negate the post-tornado kiss and love declaration. "Wilhelm's pa died yesterday. Perhaps I caught Hattie offering sympathies, yet there's still the whole issue after the twister."

"I try not to judge others too harshly." The captain raised his chin a notch. "Especially when I haven't heard their side."

Arno silently berated himself. Why hadn't he let Hattie speak her piece? His answer arrived as soon as he asked the question—*Because I'm a fool.* "There's more. Hattie's kid brother went missing last night."

"And you're confined to a bed and can't help in the search."

"It's not the first time." Oliver, Karl, and Hawk's faces filed before him.

"I don't catch your meaning."

"I'm no help. I can't save anyone."

The silence expanded but never grew uncomfortable. "Are you sure that's your job?"

The captain's words settled on the bedsheets, the floor, and the soldier eavesdropping from a nearby bed. Arno heaved a sigh. Was that his problem, trying to save the world single-handedly? If so, he had a lot of nerve and a rotten record.

CHAPTER THIRTY-THREE

Daddy, Jeb, and Hattie drew straws to determine who'd remain by the boy's side at the hospital overnight. Hattie followed her hunch, choosing the middle toothpick in Daddy's outstretched fist. Jeb argued for two tries out of three, but nobody fell for his scheme. She'd won fair and square and stood her ground.

Only a few snores, whispered voices, and soft footsteps disturbed the ward while Hattie's thoughts screamed for hours. One long corridor separated her from Arno. Did he know she was here? Perhaps a better question was, *did he care*? Curled in a blanket, she finally slept until a cheery nurse arrived to check Hawk's vitals.

After a favorable update from the attending physician, a kiss to her little brother's brow, and a promise to return with Hawk's favorite pillow, Hattie drove the Buick home. Daylight emerged pink, pretty, and perfect as the sun cut into the sky, prodding her to crush the throttle to the floor. She bounced over ruts at speeds between harrowing and a smidge faster than usual. With each jolt, her belly dipped while the vehicle's wheels spewed up road dust.

She spied Daddy's note when she walked into the house, a half sheet of ripped stationery. He'd plunked a spoon on top, anchoring it to the kitchen table.

Button,
*   Awoke early. Jeb and I are doing chores. Will get to the*
hospital soon. Enjoy your celebration in town. Kiss Samantha
Shamrock for Jeb and me. I'm jesting—just me.
*   Daddy*

She scribbled a reply.

Daddy,

In case Hawk isn't released today, please take him the pillow from his bed. He claims the one at the hospital rivals a bag of boulders. I still have the Buick and hope that's fine. If you want to kiss the starlet, you're on your own. I'm not getting between you, Meridee, and Samantha Shamrock.

Hattie (a.k.a. Button)

With no time for a full-scale bath, she rushed through her toiletry, swapped her stale dress for a fresh one and then tugged a hairbrush through her tangled locks. She rummaged through her bureau for her favorite hat, tossing garments onto the floor. No luck. On her way out, she nabbed an apple from the fruit bowl and a handful of oatmeal raisin cookies. She slammed the door, scattering chickens, and jogged to the vehicle for the return trip to town.

yummie

After devouring her first breakfast cookie, she reached for a second. Last night, Priscilla had stopped by the hospital with a new slingshot for Hawk and a couple of tears, plus a lengthy update on Brigade doings for Hattie. Although first-day attendance at the fundraiser had lacked numbers, donations surged. The only issue occurred when a stray mutt howled during a musical performance. Priscilla empathized with the dog, ranking the yodeler as subpar.

They'd also discussed Saturday's agenda, splitting duties down the middle, each serving as backup for the other. Priscilla deserved to feel the sun at today's grand finale. She'd rescued Hattie yesterday, stepping up to spearhead the fundraiser and encouraging the community to help find Hawk. If not for her, Samantha Shamrock—the event's big draw—wouldn't arrive on the eleven o'clock train to dazzle the audience until they emptied their pockets.

It made sense for Priscilla to introduce and escort the starlet throughout the day. Hattie intended to claim a backseat, watch the well-known singer from afar. She'd never met a famous person and would probably stumble over her tongue to squeak *hello*.

She wasn't mad at Priscilla for spilling the after-the-tornado-kiss news to Sadie. If she'd worn Priscilla's shoes, she'd have blabbed the juicy details to Lena in a heartbeat. A part of her had expected the rumor to spread like butter on a baked potato long before now. There was only one person to blame for not telling Arno the disastrous details sooner, and her initials were H.W.

Once in town, she parked on an off street and then jogged toward the stage, leaving the closer spots for guests. At the city square, the hospital across the street cast a looming shadow onto her pathway, yet she refused to let the darkness stain her mood.

Arno may not believe in her any longer, but she believed in herself. With shoulders back, she stepped into the sunlight.

The buzzing in Arno's head had disappeared. He savored the peace with his eyes closed, listening to others bustle around the ward. Someone stopped near his bed. When he opened his eyes, Chester Waltz towered over him, arms crossed, toothpick in his mouth, and a whiskered face alarmingly close.

"Good morning, sunshine," Hattie's dad spoke in a voice far too chipper for either the crack of dawn or a man of his demeanor.

A minor thump against Arno's skull returned. Perhaps if he ignored the intruder, he'd leave. Wasn't that the proper behavior when visiting the infirmed—let the patient snooze? Last night, he'd dreamt of Hattie floating on her back in a sea of wildflowers. If he squeezed his eyes shut and tried hard enough, would she return?

"Rise and shine." Mr. Waltz's cavernous tone hadn't changed over time, bouncing off the room's walls. Arno halfway expected an echo. "I spoke with Genevieve."

Those four words pushed Arno upright or as erect as his broken ribs would allow. "How is my mother?" He glanced around the room, wishing she'd show up. Now.

"Feisty." Mr. Waltz claimed a nearby chair with an *oomph*.

"Early on a Saturday morning? That doesn't sound like her."

"She called me a classic nincompoop and chicken-livered. She may have recited other unbecoming names, but I lost track after chicken-livered."

Arno would have loved to hear that string of insults and could have thrown in a few of his own. But he pursed his lips, unwilling to ruin an opportunity to make nice with Hattie's dad.

"She claims I haven't given you a fair shake, and now you're doing the same thing to my daughter."

How much did the old man know? "Does Hattie know you're here?"

"She knows I'm at the hospital tending Hawk. I s'pect you've heard about that."

"I'm glad he's safe. Must've scared the daylights out of you."

Mr. Waltz sighed. His red-rimmed eyes, weathered face, uncombed hair, and stubby whiskers proved it true. Manure clung to the man's boots. He must have hurried to his son's bedside without changing them. But why was he here, with Arno?

"Hawk only busted his arm. Young bones heal fast. Should come home tomorrow. When are they springing you?"

"Yesterday would be good."

Mr. Waltz's eyes cut to Arno's. "You always did like to run wild and free."

"Only after Oliver died."

The toothpick wedged between Chester's lips bobbed. "I know about that. Once Hattie's mama died, I squatted in a swamp of nothingness for weeks, maybe months. I wasn't me anymore, as your mother boldly pointed out earlier. Criminy, she read me the riot act."

He'd never seen Mother and Hattie's dad in conversation, but today she must have given him the business. That made no sense. Zip. Zero.

"Why do you care what my mother thinks?"

Without a breath of hesitation, Mr. Waltz spilled the story about how he'd once loved Arno's Mom. Arno sat mute until Chester ended his shocking tale with a slap of his palm against his thigh.

It circled Arno's head until a new realization dawned. If Hattie's pa and his mother had married, he'd not exist, nor the woman he loved. That cracked open his heart. He still loved her. No matter what had happened between Hattie and Wilhelm, he loved her.

"What's this?" Mr. Waltz picked up a clear drinking glass from the floor and raised it toward the light. It held Hattie's pearls.

Lena had collected them from the base of the tree house yesterday, at least as many as possible. She'd also given him Hattie's account of the kiss with Wilhelm and the man's profession of love.

"Hattie's necklace broke yesterday. Lena found those," he nodded toward the beads, "and instructed me to first fix the necklace and then repair things with your daughter."

Mr. Waltz withdrew a fresh toothpick from his pocket and chewed the end. "She sure does love her mama's pearls. I sure do love my daughter."

Silence stretched between the two men until Arno whispered, "Me too."

Mr. Waltz handed Arno the glass. "I know. I might be a foolish old man, but I can still recognize love."

Arno accepted the clear container with one hand and extended the other for a handshake.

Mr. Waltz's grip belied his age. "If you intend to patch things up with my daughter, repairing this necklace would be a good start." With a nod and a hint of a smile, Hattie's father lumbered away.

Was it true? Had Mr. Waltz's extended his blessing? Arno struggled to wrap his mind around the possibility. But did he still have Hattie's blessing? He poured the pearls onto his lap and then fished inside the glass for the worn string. Fixing her necklace was one thing but repairing the damage between them …

Mother arrived with a platter of frosted coffeecake. Sweet

cinnamon replaced the lingering odor from Mr. Waltz's boots.

"I suppose I should say *you shouldn't have.*" Arno grinned. "I'm going to say *thank you* instead."

She handed him a thick hunk, still warm from the oven. "It's your favorite."

"I appreciate this, and," with a bite almost to his mouth, he caught his mother's eye, "for speaking to Mr. Waltz."

"Somebody needed to knock sense into that old coot."

His chest tightened. "I think I need some of your sense-knocking too."

After brushing crumbs from his hospital gown, Mother claimed the same chair Mr. Waltz had, the platter poised on her lap. "Lena told me everything."

"I jumped to conclusions about her and Wilhelm."

"Then apologize." Mother's blue eyes delivered a blaring message—make things right.

"Perhaps, she won't accept."

"Perhaps, she will."

Arno wiped sweat from his brow with his sleeve. What if he wrote Hattie a letter, told her three little things? But what if she needed more? What if she needed a man who shared her future dreams?

CHAPTER THIRTY-FOUR

The entire area buzzed. Hattie didn't recognize half of the growing crowd. Although Priscilla'd called yesterday's attendance slim, today's guests scavenged for a patch of grass to call their own in the packed town square.

A thin veil of clouds screened the sun but didn't dim the heat. Moisture gathered at the back of Hattie's neck. The scent of shrub roses, stacked in two untidy rows in front of the stage, perfumed the August air.

The program unspooled without a hitch. Ian Moss purchased Charity's donated art, paying an eye-battingly high price for the privilege, and helping the Brigade raise more money than their original goal. To top it off, Meridee promised to double the proceeds of the final tally, no matter how high. Samantha Shamrock not only showed but sang her stockings off.

Hattie filled the next to the last spot on the jam-packed agenda. She rushed toward the stage stairs but with one foot on the bottom step, she paused. After a hurried consultation with the accompanist, she beelined for center stage. Her heartbeat rampant, driven by adrenaline.

A hush captured the audience. Not a single baby cried, bluebird tweeted, or breeze swooshed the overhead leaves in the canopied trees. With her eyes trained on the crowd, she drew a greedy lungful of air, appreciating the beauty of the day after yesterday's storm with Hawk.

"I'd like to take a minute to talk about the wounded veterans convalescing across the street." Hattie added a smile to her words.

The audience applauded, many nodding in agreement. Pastor

Neymeyer added his two cents with an "Amen."

When a hush returned, she continued, "Let's never forget these brave men still need our time and attention. Along with mailing letters overseas, we can now visit our soldiers face to face. Whether they fight in France or now recuperate in Split Falls, let's keep them close in our thoughts and prayers."

Two of the hospitalized veterans sat side-by-side on a wrought-iron park bench a stone's throw from the stage. Mrs. Kreger stood behind them, smiling. Hattie dipped her head in their direction and grinned.

"I'd like everyone to turn and wave to the soldiers in the hospital. Many have gathered at the windows to watch our program." Jubilant cheers, whistles, and clapping followed. Hattie saluted the men. Did Arno witness the tribute?

When the fanfare finished, she continued. "I also want to thank everyone who helped search for my brother yesterday. I'm happy to report he's on the mend."

"Again, amen," Pastor Neymeyer shouted. Several folks echoed the sentiment.

"Up until a few minutes ago, I fully intended to sing you two patriotic songs. I hope you don't mind the switch."

Instead of worrying she'd not meet the onlookers' expectations, Hattie sang with all her heart.

> *"Amazing grace, how sweet the sound*
> *That saved a wretch like me.*
> *I once was lost, but now am found*
> *Was blind but now I see ..."*

When the hymn and applause ended, she raised her hands. "Please join in on this next tune, I know it's a favorite for many."

> *"... From the mountains, to the prairies,*
> *To the oceans white with foam,*

> *God bless America,*
> *My home, sweet home.*
> *God bless America,*
> *My home, sweet home ..."*

Young and old, locals and out-of-towners, united voices and spread music across Split Falls. One by one audience members clutched hands, like a game of Red Rover. They stood stronger together than apart. German-Americans clung to Norwegians, and strangers found friends.

Hattie glanced toward the hospital. Did Arno hear the message? She'd love him with her last breath, but if he no longer felt likewise, she'd survive. More than anything, she longed for his happiness. He deserved joy with someone he cherished by his side. She sounded like a martyr, but that didn't negate her sincerity.

The crescendo boomed, prickling the hairs on Hattie's arms. She waved to the audience, acknowledging their hearty applause as she walked to the edge of the stage.

Priscilla grabbed her arm and whispered, "A certain starlet better watch her back. Here comes Hattie Waltz."

With a laugh, Hattie descended the steps. Never before had Priscilla complimented her. An even bigger miracle—she hadn't felt an ounce of stage fright all day. Was the secret to overcoming her fear as simple as taking the focus off of herself? She'd have to ponder that.

Priscilla lowered an empty bushel basket, lined with fabric and decorated in curlicue ribbons, to the front of the platform. "Ladies and gentlemen," her sultry voice carried, "there are only a few minutes left to our Brigade fundraiser, and if you've enjoyed yourselves this afternoon, why not help us stuff this basket with cash?" She perched a foot on the edge of the wooden hamper. "We all owe a debt of gratitude to our soldiers. That includes you, Mayor Carmichael. I see you sneaking away."

On that brassy note, Hattie ducked around a corner to peruse her task list one last time. She bent to retrieve her pocketbook from underneath the stage when someone tapped her shoulder.

"For a pint-sized lady, you have a powerful set of pipes."

Heat scorching her face, Hattie realized her rear end faced the legendary songstress. The woman's silvery voice, clear and light, spun Hattie around. "Thank you."

Garbed in all white, Samantha nursed a cigarette. Her off-the-shoulder dress molded the top half of her body and flared at the waist with layers of netting. Matching ballerina slippers, stockings, and a flat hat rimmed with pearls completed her big-city ensemble.

"Ever consider the vaudeville circuit?"

Hattie cleared her throat, sounding less than ladylike. "Not seriously."

"You should. It's a decent way to line your coffers. But perhaps your coffers don't need lining."

"Oh, they do. Yes, ma'am." Ugh! Should she have called her miss? Should she correct the mistake? Should she keep her mouth shut until the end of time?

With the lit cigarette wedged between her lips, Miss Shamrock opened her purse and withdrew a calling card, handing it to Hattie.

"What's this?" Hattie took it and read the name _Kip Carter._

"My agent and his telephone number." Samantha's tapered finger tapped the stiff card.

Any hope of a coherent reply or even a grunt vanished.

Thankfully, Lena arrived. "You were amazing today, Miss Shamrock."

"My friends call me Sammie."

Lena's mouth gaped, probably for the first time in twenty years. Once she regained composure, a half-truth slipped past her lips. "By the way, I'm also an artist."

"Singer?"

"Performer."

"Good for you." Sammie looked back at Hattie. "I need to scoot but don't lose that number." She pointed at the card Hattie pressed against her chest. "Who knows, perhaps you and I can sing a duet next time." After adjusting her neckline, the starlet left, whistling as she waltzed away.

"Thank you," Hattie hollered at her back, rising onto her toes with a wave.

Without turning, the singer stretched her arm into the air and then swatted it back and forth to acknowledge the farewell. The girls watched the guest-of-honor disappear between rows of parked automobiles.

Hattie tucked the treasure into her pocketbook before grabbing Lena's forearms and vice versa. Together, they hopped, suppressing their screams while the program onstage rolled toward the finish line.

"Geeza Louisa May Alcott." Hattie squatted to catch her breath, a touch wooly-headed. "Did that truly happen?"

"Maybe." Lena crouched and faced Hattie. "Are you ready for a second surprise?"

"Nope."

Lena stood and brushed down the hem of her apricot skirt. "Yes, you are."

"You always know best, don't you?" Hattie rose and grinned. She'd missed her friend, bossiness and all.

"When are you done with your official duties?"

"For the most part, now. Priscilla will thank our guests in a minute or two. I'm on the cleanup crew, but we won't start until everyone leaves. It's rude to begin beforehand, I think."

"Me too." Lena entwined her arm with her friend's. "Arno wants to talk to you."

Hattie's stomach tightened. "Button your lip. He did not ask to see me."

"If you don't believe me, let's go ask him."

Thrilled by the prospect, yet jittery as a cornhusk in a windstorm, she stewed. "I'm not ready. Besides, why his sudden change of heart?"

"Last night, I told him about our conversation in the treehouse."

The new development sprinkled into her soul. Nothing appealed more than throwing her arms around Arno. Still, she wasn't about to jump heart-first into anything. Not before talking to an expert. "Honestly, I need time to collect my thoughts."

Lena nodded, backing away. "All right, but you're wasting precious moments …" Her voice trailed off, leaving Hattie alone.

But not for long.

By the time she reached the side of the stage, Priscilla had wrapped up her final speech. A wave of applause splashed, even a few cheers crested. Hattie clapped along, weaving through the throng on a mission. She rose onto her tiptoes. *Where is she?*

A neighbor asked how long Hawk might tarry in the hospital. A handful of Brigade members offered congratulations. Hattie smiled, nodded, and halfway listened.

She excused herself from a ring of friends and backtracked her steps. Maybe if she climbed onstage, she'd find the one person equipped to …

Someone called her name, and Hattie whirled around. "Thank goodness. I need to talk to you. Sometime soon. Somewhere private"

"Follow me." With a nod, Meridee led the way out of the city square. They limited their chitchat on the half-block walk to Meridee's shady wraparound porch, a reprieve from the heat. The house sat back from the busy street.

Hattie claimed a seat on a grass-green bench and Meridee a rocking chair angled to face her guest. Six potted ferns graced the wooden porch rail. "When you're ready to talk, I'm ready to listen."

Where to start? Hattie's knee bounced to a silent rhythm. "Maybe this can wait a couple of hours. Let's go back and help with the cleanup."

"Fiddlesticks. You've done more than your fair share already. Me, too, for that matter. Let the others pick up the slack. Sit back, relax, and tell me what's wrong." Meridee stretched her legs, crossed her ankles, and settled in for a stay.

"Would you believe me if I said everything?"

"No."

"Alright. Short version or long?"

"You choose."

Armed with a deep breath, Hattie confessed. "Will kissed me on the day of the tornado."

"*Uff da.*" The Norwegian expression floated in the air with the mosquitos. "How do you feel about that?"

"Mortified. I wrote Arno immediately, but he never read my letter due to his injury. Before I had a chance to tell him in person, Sadie Parker broke the news. When I tried to explain what happened, he booted me from the hospital."

"That darn Parker girl." Perspiration beaded on Meridee's brow, and she dabbed at it with a hankie.

"Yesterday, I explained the kiss to Lena, especially how I wasn't an active participant."

"Uh-huh."

What was that supposed to mean? "Anyway, Lena relayed the information to Arno. Now, he wants to talk to me."

"Wouldn't you say that's a giant step toward patching up your differences?"

When Hattie reached for her necklace, she touched nothing but her stiff dress collar. "This morning, I convinced myself to let him go. But this," Hattie swatted her hands about, "changes everything. Two days ago, he didn't care enough to listen to my side of the story."

Meridee leaned forward and folded her hands. "That must have hurt. But let's place ourselves in Arno's boots. Hadn't Sadie just given him an earful? Wasn't his heart freshly bruised too."

A pesky bumblebee buzzed and circled. Hattie kept one eye on the enemy until a different concern niggled. "Arno doesn't want kids. Ever."

"And you, I assume, dream about a lapful."

She nodded.

A hush settled onto the porch until the rocking chair creaked. "Here's my twenty-five-cent advice—you need to ask yourself two questions."

"Go on."

"Can you forgive Arno for rejecting you at the hospital?"

A bitter grudge never helps, always hinders. She could almost hear Mama saying that. "Yes. I think so."

Meridee rose from her chair and wedged herself beside Hattie. "If you can't have both, what do you want more—Arno or babies?"

Dusk fell, muting every hue. With a sigh, she lowered her head against Meridee's soft shoulder and pondered her new middle name—Torn.

CHAPTER THIRTY-FIVE

"She'll be here soon." Lena patted her brother's hospital-gowned shoulder that evening. "I bought Hawk a new fishing lure. Once he's well, we're holding a friendly competition. You don't mind if I take him his gift, do you?"

"Of course not. Tell him I said hello."

"I will. Now don't blow it with Hattie."

He barely nodded as she left. Was Hattie down the hall with her brother? Or busy with something else? Someone else?

Footsteps sent his heart rate into overdrive. He glanced toward the promising sound. His cousin Molly and her mother approached, sending his heart rate into a downward spiral. Each carried a wrapped gift and a grin.

It took all of Arno's strength to smile back, not because he wasn't happy to see his relatives. But because they weren't Hattie.

Greetings and small talk followed. He opened his presents—three mystery novels from Colleen and a hand-drawn picture from the child. "I made it myself." Pride coated her boast. She'd grown over the last year, perhaps up toward a foot. Was that possible? Was she six now?

"Thank you kindly. This must be you." When he pointed at the stick figure in a skirt, she nodded and squealed. Confident, he continued. "And the taller one is, without question, me."

Molly giggled, collapsing against her mother's side. "That's not you and me, silly. That's my friend Isaiah. I'm gonna marry him one day."

"So, I'm out of the running then?" Arno drew a loose fist to his breastbone.

"Mother says you can't marry your cousin. You can only kiss them."

"Heavens to Betsy. I did not say that." Colleen heaved an exasperated sigh. "I said there's something called kissing cousins, cousins you know real well."

When Molly bobbed her head, her hair ribbon bounced into her eyes. She shoved the thing aside. "You have to marry someone old, Arno, someone like Hattie."

"Oh, child." Colleen shook her head in an I-can't-believe-she-said-that manner. She opened her pocketbook, withdrew a wadded handkerchief, and handed the cloth to her daughter.

"Thank you for trusting me to keep this safe while you were gone." With a loud "ta-da," his cousin unveiled his gold-cased compass, the one he'd given her almost a year ago. "It's from your opa. It belongs with you." She twisted to face her mother. "Did I say that right?"

"You said it perfectly."

"I'm much obliged." Arno accepted the keepsake and traced his finger over the inscription on the back of the case—*To Arno, from Opa, December 25, 1909.* The compass felt at home in his hand. He tightened his grip.

An hour had passed. Moonlight streamed through the hospital's open window, and still no Hattie. Well past visiting hours, his head thumped to the beat of the timepiece around his wrist.

Where was she? Gone for now or gone for good?

Her poignant song had drifted through the hospital windows. Even the physicians and nurses had paused to listen, gathering in clumps. Soldiers in nearby beds had listened. A couple who were able had stood to attention.

Had she thought of him while she'd sang? With Hattie's necklace cupped in his fist, he released a heavy sigh.

Footsteps clicked in the hallway. He sat up straight and held his breath. A smart man wouldn't let his hopes balloon. But intelligence wasn't his long suit these days.

Hattie arrived confident and gorgeous alongside his bed. She stole his breath. Her pink cheeks, loose hair, and a smile—as if she knew something he didn't—kicked his pulse into a staccato beat.

Time escaped while he searched for words. He'd rehearsed a few lines in his head, but they were gone. "I'm sorry, Hattie. I should never have doubted you."

She clutched her purse. "And I'm sorry I didn't tell you about the incident with Wilhelm when you first arrived back in town. That must have been hard, hearing it from Sadie." A little wobble accompanied her words.

Arno opened his arms, and she shot forward, resting her soft cheek against his. When she didn't pull away, he held her tighter.

"I guess we've both made mistakes," she whispered. "Do you forgive me?"

"Always." He nuzzled her until their lips met. The gentle kiss took its time. When she stood, her warm smile broke like the crack of dawn, growing in intensity. Hattie melted his heart.

Something, maybe contentment, settled on him. For so long, he'd dreamt about a happy ending to their story, yet the last couple of days had been anything but a fairy tale. "I have something for you."

"Trust me, I don't need gifts. I only need you to heal and to know you still care for me."

"I see. But what if I told you I want to give you three little things?"

"Three, huh?" She wiggled the same number of fingers. "I guess that changes everything."

"The first one is under my bed. Can you fetch it for me?"

Her forehead crinkled before she bent, retrieved a bouquet of wildflowers and buried her nose in them for a deep sniff. "Did you pick these yourself?"

He laughed, recalling the last time she'd asked that question. "I had a little help from Mother."

"They're beautiful. Thank you." She snapped the stem of a perfect daisy and tucked the blossom behind her ear.

"Are you ready for gift number two?"

"I think so." After one last sniff, she lowered the bouquet to the floor.

He patted his bed for her necklace near his hip. With a grin, he handed her the repaired string of pearls.

"How ..." She blinked, clutching the necklace to her chest. "How did you ... they broke yesterday in the yard while I searched for Hawk." Her eyes misted.

"Lena found them by the tree house, collected every gem she could find and brought them to me."

"I appreciate this more than you know." Her grateful words were almost a physical touch. Instead of looping the pearls around her neck, she opened her pocketbook and dropped them inside.

"And I have this." Arno scavenged under his pillow for the third promised present—a woolen sock. "Although I didn't knit the garment myself, it's from me to you."

Her head tipped to the side. "You're giving me men's footwear?"

"I decided," he waved the sock above his head before passing her the present, since we've confessed our deepest secrets in letters, I ought to continue the trend."

With a raised brow, she dug for his note and then read his sentence aloud.

I love you,

Eyes closed, Hattie appeared frozen, like those marble statues in France. Time paused before she opened her eyes. Then, her smile exploded, overflowing onto him. "I love you too. More than likely, I always have. I came here to tell you those same three little words, but you beat me to it."

Although a part of him still didn't believe he deserved the girl before him, he tamped down those thoughts.

She leaned forward for a kiss, but it wasn't an ordinary peck. Warm and hopeful, it lingered beyond what was proper for a hospital ward. Arno didn't care. She tasted sweet, like their best-shared memories and the promise of brighter tomorrows bundled together.

Finally, she drew back and trailed her hand down the side of his face. "Do you want to know why I arrived late this evening?"

"Only if you want to tell me." A dozen reasons had tormented him. Most had centered on her thinking he wasn't worth the effort.

"I wanted to talk to Meridee first." Hattie licked her lips. "She's probably the wisest person I know."

"Did she offer sage advice?"

"I'll let you be the judge." She sat on the edge of his bed, dipping the mattress. "According to her, I should peek into my heart and then decide what I can't live without."

Arno gulped. "And?"

Emotions skipped across Hattie's face. He looked away, letting her pick through each one at her own pace. When she touched his cheek, she drew his eyes back to hers.

"I've decided I can live without experiencing motherhood, but I can't live without you."

Her sacrifice stunned, leaving him tongue-tied. Nobody had ever given him such a selfless gift. He took her hand and ran his thumb across the inside of her wrist, searching for the right reply.

"First, Meridee is brilliant. Second, I've decided I'm open to the idea of fatherhood. Third, will you marry me?"

Hattie gasped, then pressed her closed fist against her lips.

"This isn't how I pictured proposing ... in a hospital ... in public. But more than anything, I hope you'll marry me one day. Whenever you're ready."

"Truly?"

With his fingertip, Arno crossed his heart.

She copied his action across her own heart then pressed her

nose against his.

"I—" Like the brush of a feather, her lips teased his.

"Will—" This time her lips pressed sweet and warm.

"Marry—" Her lips lingered, their breaths mingling for several moments after that word.

"You." The next kiss … *mercy*. His girl sure knew how to accept a proposal.

AUTHOR'S NOTES

About the same time my mom and aunts uncovered love letters their parents had exchanged, I needed a new project for a college creative writing class. Inspiration struck, and I persuaded my relatives to loan me their keepsakes. It wasn't easy. Nobody wanted me to smudge the letters or memories of Arno and Hattie. Neither did I.

Doubt rode my shoulder for the entire semester and joined me on the next one too. What I knew about WWI filled one side of a postcard. Even the war's timeframe blurred in my memory. Part of the required coursework included reading 25 books on the topic. I studied WWI fiction and nonfiction, the Iowa home front, the Spanish flu, anti-German-American prejudices, and epistolary writing—especially wartime letters.

After reading hundreds of wartime letters, I discovered one dominant theme running through every generation of correspondence: the desire for mail from home. Much of what I learned about Iowa's home front stemmed from Hattie's letters. For the most part, her life remained unchanged after America joined the war. Household and farm chores dominated her days, and neighborhood get-togethers and dances filled her nights. Her biggest change was Arno's absence.

My grandmother passed away two months before my birth. But I met her through her letters. Her wartime courtship with Grandpa played out nicely on the yellowed stationery, but an incomplete picture unfolded. My imagination filled in the gaps.

When I was a young adult, Grandpa passed away. I wasn't interested in his military days. But I was intrigued with the ham radio in his basement, where he talked to war buddies for hours each night. As a child, if we promised not to speak, he allowed my sister and me to sit near his boots and listen. One of us usually abandoned her post early. Yep, that was me.

In his war journal, Grandpa recorded the names of the people to whom he sent letters, the dates he received mail, supply lists, addresses of fellow soldiers, the dates he moved from camp to camp and sailed to France via Southampton, England. And finally, the dates and locations of his return trip home.

From *Letters from the Homefront*, Linda George writes, "People who lived through the First World War did not come to be known as the Greatest Generation, as journalist Tom Brokaw has termed those who lived through World War II. Instead, they were called the Lost Generation, people who came out of a senseless, brutal war disillusioned and broken." How sad. In the final chapters of *Three Little Things*, Hattie faces that troubling reality.

In two semesters I finished my novel and then packed it away for 11 years. After a move back to Iowa, I reread the manuscript. Although it needed work, it still carried a little shine, luring me to deepen my research and tackle several rewrites.

Initially, I'd handled my grandparents with kid gloves. That's a no-no for a hero and heroine, which is why I then kissed the real Arno and Hattie goodbye. Although my grandparents inspired the novel, it's not their story any longer.

A few of the events are true. Arno kicked off his military career at Camp Dodge, relocated to Camp Pike, then transferred to Camp Dix. His trip across the Atlantic, his stay at a rest camp in England, and the move across the English Channel stick to the facts. But, for the story's sake, I sped up a few dates.

In one of Grandpa's letters, he talks about lounging under a tree in Arkansas, eating nuts while the rest of the Company scurried to hunt rabbits. Unlike in the novel, nobody shot him. Thank goodness! On leave from Camp Dix, he visited Philadelphia and wrote home about the eye-opening experience.

Like the fictional Hattie, Grandma dropped out of school when her mother passed, and her family broke colts and butchered hogs during the long winter months.

To keep my book historically accurate, I met or emailed several experts. Michel W. Vogt, Curator at the Iowa Gold Star Military Museum, sharpened my understanding of Camp Dodge in 1917. For the price of a cup of coffee, Tom Clegg, living historian and WWI re-enactor, answered my top ten military questions. Raymond Screws, Director of the National Guard Museum in North Little Rock, checked if the barracks at Camp Pike did, indeed, sport a tin roof. We think so.

The staff at the Des Moines Public Library assisted with my research, delivering a stack of books to my table as I explored the era's fashion, speech, and farm life. At the Garnavillo Historical Museum, I teared up at the sight of Grandpa's khaki army uniform, old ham radio, and other family heirlooms. I visited the WWI Museum in Kansas City to rifle through old military files. To my dismay, I discovered many WWI records had burned in a fire. Through email, I corresponded with staff at the National Museums Liverpool to investigate Grandpa's Europe-bound adventures. If any facts in *Three Little Things* are inaccurate, I apologize. At least it's fiction.

Although the book no longer features my maternal grandparents, the make-believe Arno and Hattie couldn't feel more real to me. I hope you love them too.